INTO THE GRAY ZONE

Into the Gray Zone

A PIKE LOGAN NOVEL

Brad Taylor

WM

WILLIAM MORROW

An Imprint of HarperCollins*Publishers*

INTO THE GRAY ZONE. Copyright © 2025 by Brad Taylor. All rights reserved. Printed in the United States of America. No part of this book may be used or reproduced in any manner whatsoever without written permission except in the case of brief quotations embodied in critical articles and reviews. For information, address HarperCollins Publishers, 195 Broadway, New York, NY 10007.

HarperCollins books may be purchased for educational, business, or sales promotional use. For information, please email the Special Markets Department at SPsales@harpercollins.com.

FIRST EDITION

Designed by Michele Cameron

Library of Congress Cataloging-in-Publication Data has been applied for.

ISBN 978-0-06-322208-3

25 26 27 28 29 LBC 5 4 3 2 1

The "gray zone" describes a set of activities that occur between peace (or cooperation) and war (or armed conflict). A multitude of activities fall into this murky in-between—from nefarious economic activities, influence operations, and cyberattacks to mercenary operations, assassinations, and disinformation campaigns. While the United States has spent more than two decades focused on its conventional power, Russia and China have occupied the gray zone where they can pressure, coerce, destabilize, and attack the United States and its allies without risking conventional escalation.

—Clementine G. Starling, deputy director of
the Forward Defense practice and a resident
fellow in the Transatlantic Security Initiative

One can argue that activities in the gray zone have always been a feature of great-power competition. Proxy wars, destabilizing insurgencies, legal warfare (lawfare), and information warfare—by adversaries and allies alike—have been a feature of conflict for millennia. But the cost of conventional conflict in the nuclear era has grown too steep, and the risk of escalation too profound. As a result, nations seek to promote their national objectives through aggression conducted covertly, or with obfuscated attribution or justification, in order to achieve their goals.

—Robert J. Giesler, nonresident senior
fellow in Forward Defense who served
in a number of senior roles within the
Office of the Secretary of Defense

INTO THE GRAY ZONE

A full moon created a kaleidoscope of reflections on the Arabian Sea, but Kamal could smell the rain coming. It was the tail-end of the monsoon season, and they would get wet tonight, he was sure. In more ways than one.

He watched a rubber Zodiac skiff lowered over the side of the larger boat, waited until it was stable, then scampered down a cargo net into it. He turned, took a duffel bag from the man above him, set it on the deck, then began helping the others. The last of the four slipped coming down, bouncing off the rubber side and falling backwards toward the hull of the mother ship. He let out a scream, the sound cut short when his body went beneath the water.

Kamal scrambled to the stern, holding the skiff away from the larger boat to prevent his man from being smashed between the two in the light chop of waves.

He shouted, "Agam! Randeep! Grab him." The two others in the boat leaned over and snatched the man by his arm and clothes, hoisting him over the gunwale. The man sat up and Kamal saw it was Manjit, his second-in-command and the one who was to guide the skiff to their target.

With a sheepish smile, Manjit shook his head, throwing water like a dog coming out of a lake. He said, "That's not a good beginning."

Kamal looked up at the larger boat and saw the man they only knew as Mr. Chin staring back at him. Mr. Chin raised his fist with a thumbs-up, the gesture a question. Kamal said, "Manjit, start the outboard."

Manjit scrambled to the back, pulled a cord, and the little motor sputtered to life. Satisfied, Kamal returned the thumbs-up. Mr. Chin shouted, "See you in an hour. Remember, he either comes out alive, or you kill him yourself. Leave no one to talk if the mission fails."

Kamal nodded, a little disgusted. He didn't fully understand who Mr. Chin represented, but he knew the reason behind the order: China could not be implicated in interfering in India's affairs.

Kamal turned to Manjit and said, "Let's go."

Within seconds they were bouncing across the soft waves, the lights of the shore growing larger, the mother ship lost in the darkness. He felt the wind tussling his hair and realized it was the first time he'd had that sensation since he was a little boy.

Like the men in the boat with him, Kamal was a Sikh, and as such, was required by his religious duty to wear a dastaar covering his head whenever he was outdoors, only unwrapping the cloth when inside his home. Like him, none of his men wore one on this night, and neither did the man they hoped to rescue. In fact, the very reason they were conducting this nighttime operation was precisely to prevent the authorities from learning the man they held was not a potential Muslim terrorist but a Sikh.

Kamal Singh and his men were all from a small village in the Punjab state of India, and all of them had spent time in jail as agitators for a separate Sikh state—regardless of whether that was true or not. Called Khalistan, the aspirational goals of a Sikh state within the borders of

India were something the Indian government was incredibly sensitive about.

In today's world, it's usually Muslim terrorists that make the news. Al Qaida, the Islamic state, and, for India, Pakistani groups like Lashkar-e-Taiba. But in the not-so-distant past, it was members of the Khalistan Commando Force—Sikh separatists looking for a state they could call their own.

In the 1980s, the KCF caused most of the Indian national terrorist deaths, to include aircraft bombings in Canada and murderous attacks all over the Indian state, so much so that Indira Gandhi, then the prime minister of India, decided to stop it once and for all. In 1984 she ordered the storming of the holiest of Sikh religious sites looking for the leaders of the movement, ultimately killing upwards of four hundred innocent Sikhs in the process.

The action directly led to her own demise, as she was assassinated shortly thereafter in retribution—by her own Sikh bodyguards. That killing ultimately led to the destruction of the Khalistan Commando Force, as the Indian population erupted, slaughtering Sikhs in an orgy of violence while the state itself made a concerted effort to snuff out the irredentist tendencies.

To a great extent, they succeeded, at least on the surface, but the fear of the Khalistan myth within the Indian government persisted like an abused housewife fearing the return of the husband, with Sikhs who professed any discontent being arrested and charged with wholesale offenses against the state. Which is how Kamal had been arrested.

He'd never been particularly in tune with the underbelly of Sikh separatism and had little knowledge of Khalistan aspirations. His father had been infatuated with the cause, but his mother less so. Kamal was only ten when his father had died in a car accident. After that, his mother steered clear of anything resembling Sikh independence, forcing

4 / BRAD TAYLOR

him to try to blend his Sikh faith into a multicultural world. Which is to say, he'd heard about Khalistan, but it wasn't something he put any thought into. He'd gone to school, learning computer network operations, and had a solid job working remotely for a U.S. company, doing customer support for computer systems. That all changed once he was incarcerated.

Arrested for some inflammatory social media posts and connections to friends who were being tracked as separatists—something that everyone in his Sikh-majority town fell prey to—his life had been upended. Prison had caused his anger to fester, and also introduced him to others who'd been unjustly arrested. They began to talk, fantasizing about revenge, long-lost memories of his father talking about the cause resurfacing. Ultimately, grand visions of Sikh independence had taken a back seat to survival, although it had lingered in the back of Kamal's brain. What Kamal had actually learned in prison was how to be a criminal.

Released from prison but now tainted by his arrest, he'd been unable to find a job using his computer networking skills, with every one of his former corporate contacts afraid of being associated with him. The fester in the back of his brain slowly started moving to the forefront, and he began to explore the cause his mother had jettisoned but his father had embraced. Just to survive, he'd worked in the seedy underbelly of Indian society, utilizing the black market for everything from crypto scams to call centers fleecing Americans.

And that was how he'd met Mr. Chin.

Manjit slowed the motor of the rubber skiff, bringing Kamal out of his thoughts. He turned, seeing him looking at a GPS. Manjit said, "The dock should be right in front of us."

Kamal said, "And? Keep going."

"We need to work this slowly, in case Mr. Chin's information is wrong."

"If his information is wrong, it won't matter. The RAW will be behind us right now, waiting to scoop us up. But he hasn't been wrong yet."

Manjit kept the engine low, saying, "Then why is Sidak in jail? There weren't supposed to be any RAW personnel at the target site."

The RAW was the vaunted Research and Analysis Wing of the government of India—the Indian version of the CIA or MI6, but unlike those organizations, the RAW answered only to the prime minister. Different from intelligence services in other democracies, the RAW was a force unto its own, with little oversight. It was the RAW that had arrested Kamal originally, and had also detained Sidak.

Kamal couldn't argue with Manjit's logic. The RAW *had* been there and rolled up Sidak, when Mr. Chin said it would be safe.

Kamal considered, then said, "Continue at this pace." He hissed to the front, saying, "Agam, get out the night scope. Scan the dock."

CHAPTER 2

Exasperated, I threw the handful of receipts on the desk and said, "You told me this would take ten minutes! It's been two hours. I'll never find all the paper you want from that long ago."

Jennifer gave me her disapproving teacher look and said, "It would have taken only ten minutes if you had some sort of filing system. How come all my receipts are filed neatly, but when I ask you for *your* receipts, you're digging through duffel bags and rucksacks?"

Wearing a ballcap with a blond ponytail coming out the back, she looked like she was about to go surfing instead of analyzing our accounts. Seated behind a computer with a spreadsheet displayed, she was trying to match up our claimed deductible expenditures with the proof they were actually true.

It was time for our quarterly update to our accountant for corporate taxes, and I hated this paperwork bullshit. Which is why Jennifer did it all. She was now asking for rental car receipts, clothing purchases, ferry tickets, and other items to match up to the spreadsheet. Receipts that I'd supposedly saved but now had no idea where I'd stored them. It was ridiculous. Why wouldn't the U.S. government just assume I was telling the truth?

I said, "Look, this is all I have. This is it. If we're missing a taxi receipt, then we're just missing a taxi receipt. Nobody's going to check."

She said, "Until they do. We can't risk that."

Which, as much as I hated to admit it, was absolutely true. Our company was called Grolier Recover Services, and as far as the overt U.S. government knew, it was an above-board business that specialized in facilitating archeological work around the world. Unfortunately, that wasn't exactly accurate.

I waved my arm at a rifle case holding a custom AR 10 chambered in 6.5 Creedmoor, saying, "If I don't get on the road, I'll lose the shooting lane to some prima donna with an eight-thousand-dollar bolt gun trying to figure out if the brass casing he's using affects the flight of the bullet. Let me go. Please."

She said, "Speaking of that, I'm not sure we should claim the range membership as a deduction. I mean, that's going to cause questions."

"Questions? For what? That's literally how we make money. You do the egghead stuff, and I do the Neanderthal stuff. People hire us because we keep them alive, and shooting this gun is what does that."

Our company was a little unique in that we didn't do the digging for the artifacts, we basically sold the shovels. In the world of archeological relics, it turns out that the majority of the digs around the earth were in areas that were less than hospitable, with most being in regions wracked by strife. So if you wanted to go dig up some bones somewhere, you needed someone to facilitate it, which is where we came in.

Jennifer used her degree in anthropology to convince them we understood what they wanted to do, and I used my degree in killing bad guys to keep them safe. We facilitated such things as government permits in the country in question, logistics for the dig, and then provided security on site. Which is where my guns came into play.

Jennifer said, "Yeah, I get that, and you get that, but I'm not sure the IRS will understand. If they start to question, we're in trouble."

She had a point. The truth of the matter was our business was all a sham. We actually did real archeological facilitation, to a certain extent, but only to give us cover for what we really did—putting some national security threat's head on a spike.

Since much of the unrecovered archeological stuff around the world was in what could charitably be called ungoverned space, meaning that it held a lot of bad guys, we leveraged my company to eliminate national security threats. Grolier allowed us to penetrate as eggheads instead of commandos wearing camo swooping in on helicopters, giving the United States plausible deniability for any fallout.

All of my "employees" were apex predators, drawn from the most elite units of the Department of Defense and the CIA, and most of our real work was directed by the National Command Authority of the United States. Which is to say, most of my business was paid by good ol' Uncle Sam, under the rubric of something called Project Prometheus.

Our unit was so classified we never even utter the assigned code name, instead simply calling the umbrella organization the Taskforce, but being that deep in the black had its own problems—namely, paying our taxes like a real company, which is what Jennifer was trying to do. It sounds insane, but if some guy in the IRS started digging, he might find something we didn't want him to. You'd think we could just tell him to back off and swagger back to the bar, but that wasn't how it worked. We needed to be legit—even to our own government—and I'd given that task to Jennifer.

Jennifer said, "Yeah, I can plausibly claim the range time, but I can't claim the guns. You buy them like candy. How am I going to sell that? The IRS is going to ask why you need so many—especially since we never take them with us. We always use Taskforce stuff."

"They don't know that. I mean, we need guns to do the job. That's why I buy them."

She squinted at me and said, "We might have more guns than the Taskforce itself. If I didn't know better, I'd believe you thought they wore out after a single use. I mean, what's up with the gun you're going to shoot today? We have three long-range precision rifles, and you bought a fourth? How am I going to sell that?"

A little miffed, I said, "Technology marches forward. This is a precise tool. I need to see if it stands up to what they say it does. I'm not driving a Model T today either."

"Right. You need to see if it works. Which is why you paid a bunch of money to some guy from your old unit to build it."

"Hey, if he builds them better, and it works, he'll be building the ones we use on operations. The Taskforce will buy them. I can't help it if he knows what he's doing."

She scoffed and said, "I'll claim the range fees, but I'm not claiming that new gun."

Honestly, I didn't care. We were making a pretty good living, as we had to do at least three honest trips for every one we did for the government, and I wasn't looking to own a Porsche. I was happy where we were, the satisfaction of the job meaning more than the money. Well, that and I'd rather have a new precision rifle than a Porsche.

I said, "Okay, keep it off, but if you do, we're leaving money on the table."

Exasperated, Jennifer waved her hand and said, "Go shooting. It'll be easier for me without you here."

I smiled, hearing exactly what I wanted to. All I had to do was be obstinate for a little bit, and then she'd let me go. I leaned in and kissed her on the lips, saying, "You're doing God's work."

She smacked me on the top of the head and said, "Yeah, yeah, right.

Don't think I don't understand what just happened. If the IRS cracks us open, you'll be the one asking Wolffe for help. Not me."

George Wolffe was the commander of the Taskforce, and a good man. A paramilitary officer in the CIA, he'd been running and gunning his entire life, and he was one of the men who'd designed Project Prometheus when it was formed. Now he was in charge of the entire shooting match. If I needed to call in a chit because of some IRS audit, I'd do so, and he'd help, but I didn't think that was going to happen.

I grabbed my rifle case, wanting to get out of our office as quickly as possible before Jennifer changed her mind. I was six feet from the door when the computer dinged, sending a tone out that meant only one thing: the Taskforce was calling on our encrypted VPN.

Jennifer glanced at me, then clicked the protocols for encryption, saying, "What's this about?"

I set the rifle on the floor and went behind her in the chair, saying, "I have no idea. Nothing was on the horizon at the last update."

The screen went through its protocols and then cleared, George Wolffe's head staring back at me. I said, "Hey, sir, what's up with the call?"

He smiled and said, "Where's Amena right now?"

Amena was our adopted daughter, and the question told me he was going to hand us a mission. I said, "She's in Europe on a school trip. Italy. Why?"

"Because I need your little company right now. As in yesterday."

CHAPTER 3

Kamal waited while Agam put the night-vision scope into use, the small rubber boat rising up and down in the gentle swell. Kamal didn't think Mr. Chin was setting them up to fail, but he'd been drastically wrong once before, and Kamal wasn't going to use his word alone.

He trusted Mr. Chin, as far as it went, but he had been an enigma from the moment Kamal had met him. Originally contracted for various small-time cell phone scams, he was now sure the earlier taskings had been nothing but vetting.

Eventually, Mr. Chin had paid him for more audacious actions, involving hacking Indian corporations for information, focusing on those that dealt with mining operations. The taskings had narrowed to one mining conglomerate in particular, with Kamal simply passing the information requested to Mr. Chin. Then had come the big ask: Would he be willing to follow an Indian billionaire? Set him up for a kidnapping? For money?

At that point, Kamal had balked, the invitation clearly ludicrous. He wanted to know who Mr. Chin really was.

What Mr. Chin told him didn't clear things up. He claimed to work for a Chinese conglomerate that wanted to stop the billionaire from creating a mine in India, and that was all. It was nothing more than corporate competition at its roughest edge, and according to Mr. Chin, that's how the game was played at his level.

But why use Kamal? Yeah, he had skills in computers, but nothing that transferred to a kidnapping. Surely, if this was how the "game was played," Mr. Chin had others who could do the job. People he'd used before. People more qualified. Why recruit Kamal? And then Kamal learned why: two of his childhood friends were now on the personal security detail of the billionaire—and they were already on Mr. Chin's payroll.

Mr. Chin had provided the contact numbers for his friends to prove his sincerity, and he'd called them, trying to find out who Mr. Chin really worked for. He'd learned nothing more than he already knew about his identity, but also that he paid very well. His friends had served close to a decade in the Army before going to private security, and now they were telling him that the Chinese man meant what he said.

Kamal had agreed, on the surface, but he also had an ulterior motive. Something Mr. Chin would learn the hard way. The mining billionaire they were targeting worked hand in glove with the state of India, and if Mr. Chin wanted to take it to the assholes who'd destroyed Kamal's life, he had no compunction about helping. They deserved everything they got, but it would be more than Mr. Chin envisioned.

Agam said, "The dock looks clear. It's all dark. I see maybe one or two lights on in the prison."

Kamal said, "The gate wall? What about the front gate?"

"It's well lit, and I can see some guards, but they're sleeping in their chairs."

Kamal said, "Good." And thought, *Shouldn't have picked a tourist site to hide your detention.*

Mr. Chin had given them the original target set, an expansive Grand Hyatt property in the state of Goa, right on the water. The beach area of

India, Goa was known for both its expensive resorts as well as its hippy bare-bones enclaves.

The billionaire was apparently going to stay there in a few weeks, and Sidak had been sent in to apply for a job, acting as a Muslim resident. His entire reason for employment was to conduct pre-assault reconnaissance of the grounds, but for some reason, he was detained within a week of reporting for work.

He was nothing more than a groundskeeper and should have been below any suspicion, as he was literally doing nothing suspicious. Just using his job to report back weaknesses in the hotel security. Six days in, he was approached by his boss, then taken to a room with two strange men. Then he'd disappeared.

The last contact Sidak had made was a frantic call saying he was under detention and being taken away, then nothing. Mr. Chin had come back with his location, one that was surprising, which had started this entire operation. Kamal had questions about how Mr. Chin knew where Sidak was being held, down to the room, but he kept them to himself. At this stage, the key thing was getting Sidak out.

Kamal said, "Bring the boat to the dock. Keep your eyes out. Someone might be hiding."

The little rubber craft edged into the spit of concrete snaking out into the harbor, the rock walls dim in the darkness.

Agam said, "Careful, careful. We need no noise, no light. Make no mistake, someone is filming right now."

He pointed up the coast to a mansion hanging over the cliff, one with a raucous party, the tinkling of laughter and music filtering down to their location. Agam was right: someone would be taking videos and pictures from their cell phones. They had no idea what they would catch in the recording, but later, after the assault, the RAW would be looking.

Kamal pulled a scarf around his neck, covering his face, even as he knew the resolution of whatever device the house held wouldn't be good enough to identify anyone on the boat. He felt the hull hit the concrete and said, "Hold it here."

Agam grabbed a bit of rock, stabilizing the rubber boat. Kamal opened the duffel bag and began pulling out pistols. Old Makarov service weapons, known as the PB in KGB/Soviet parlance, they were 9mm semi-automatics with an integral suppressor. Provided by Mr. Chin, they were another question of his true organization, as the pistols had never been sold to anyone outside of the old Soviet system. Used solely for assassinations back in the Cold War, it was an open question as to how Chin had procured them.

They each took a pistol, Kamal saying, "Remember the training. Because of the cold bore, the first round will be louder. Don't let that scare you. Once the suppressor gets hot, the rest will be quieter. Fire two at first contact."

His men nodded, and he said, "This is it. We're attacking the very prison with our name. Freedom Fighter prison."

The dock was servicing a place called the Fort Aguada Jail Museum, a prison established when the Portuguese ruled Goa. It was an infamous location where thousands of Indians were incarcerated and tortured in their fight to overthrow Portuguese rule. Liberated in 1961, it was now a tourist attraction highlighting the quest for independence from the Portuguese.

They began clambering out of the hull of the small rubber craft, climbing up the rock wall, and Kamal turned to Manjit, saying, "Be prepared to move on a moment's notice. We'll probably be coming back on the run."

Manjit nodded, saying, "Good luck."

His other men were already waiting on the dock, crouched down and facing out, toward the prison. He took a knee, saying, "Let's hope Mr. Chin's intelligence on Sidak's location is better than the intel was before his arrest."

The prison sprawled along the rocky coastline behind a seawall festooned with old cannons from the days of Portuguese rule, with only one section open to the public. The other sections had yet to renovated for display, and this was where Mr. Chin said Sidak was being held.

Kamal stood up, the tallest of the men, his broad shoulders giving him an air of authority. He went to Agam, a wispy man wearing eyeglasses that had fogged over in the humid air. He tapped Agam on the shoulder, saying, "Let's go."

Agam stood in a crouch, Randeep to his left, and they began shuffling down the concrete dock, reaching a single chain that was designed to prevent entrance. They crossed it and Kamal took a knee, saying, "He's to the left. Down the pathway past the group cells. He's on the second floor, in a funnel room."

Mr. Chin had told them that Sadik was being held in one of the infamous torture rooms, with hooks in the ceiling and a sloping hole in the floor to wash away the bodily fluids of someone unlucky enough to be incarcerated.

Kamal pointed to the building to their front, the façade illuminated in the dim glow of a single incandescent bulb, saying, "One at a time. Get into the shadows."

Agam sprinted across the courtyard, highlighted by the light for a split second before he was lost from view. Randeep followed. Kamal glanced at the main gate to the prison, seeing no reaction, and scuttled across himself. He reached his men and said, "Stay in the shadows."

No sooner were the words out of his mouth than a guard came around the corner, ambling along without paying attention. He stumbled into Kamal's group and sprang back, grabbing at a pistol in the holster on his hip. Kamal leapt up and hammered him in the head with his Makarov, knocking him to the ground. He stood over the body and the man shouted, the sound cut short by a double tap from Kamal's pistol.

Time stood still, the man's scream louder than the bullets that ended it. Kamal looked at his team, the smoke wafting from the end of his barrel, their eyes wide at the destruction he'd caused, the reality of the mission settling in for the first time.

Kamal snapped, "We need to move, now. This guy was on a circuit. If they didn't hear him shout there will be an alert when he doesn't show up where he's supposed to. The clock is ticking."

Agam said, "What about the body? Should we hide it?"

"No time. He's a hired security guard, not RAW. We need to exploit the gap in time right now. Follow me."

He began to sidle down the wall, keeping to the shadows. They crossed an open area, then began crawling again, backs pressed against the stone, until they reached a winding staircase. Kamal halted, took a moment to get his bearings, then said, "Sidak's up there."

CHAPTER 4

It didn't take us long to get to DC, mainly because we had our own jet to fly us there. Wolffe had sent down what I called the Rock Star bird. A Gulfstream 650 that was just like the one rock stars used to fly around, only this bird was a little different.

It was leased to my company through a myriad of commercial cut-outs and was really nothing more than a high-speed infiltration platform. Instead of a king-sized bed with rubber sheets, it held all manner of weapons and surveillance gear within its walls, with the compartments hidden from a casual look-through by nosy customs officials. In this case, though, it was just a ride to Washington.

We taxied to the private FBO area at Reagan National and were met by Bartholomew Creedwater, our resident computer network engineer—which is a polite way of saying he was a hacker.

We bundled into an SUV, and I said, "You're turning into the Taskforce Uber driver."

The last time my team was unceremoniously called to DC we'd been picked up by Creed. Hopefully this trip wouldn't be as big a mess as that one.

He laughed and said, "It *is* getting to be a habit. Wolffe didn't want to wait for you to get an Uber. Apparently, this is pretty time sensitive."

"What's this all about? Give me some skinny before I walk into the lion's den."

Creed glanced at me in the passenger seat and said, "I don't know. I was pulling an all-night shift and got tasked to pick you up. I'm out of here and going to bed. All I know is it has something to do with India."

India? That was the last thing I expected. I said, "So why couldn't we do this over a VPN? Why did we have to fly up here?"

"Pike, I honestly don't know. I'm just the taxi driver."

I went silent, thinking about the implications. We drove down the George Washington Parkway to Clarendon, passing Arlington Cemetery along the way. Jennifer saw me looking at the gravestones and clasped my hand, giving it a squeeze. I knew more people underneath that ground than anyone had a right to, but no words were necessary. I squeezed back.

We left the GW and wound around the Iwo Jima memorial, eventually pulling into a parking garage for a building owned by Blaisdell Consulting. It was four stories tall and looked like every other lobbyist building in DC, but this was the headquarters for the Taskforce. Like Grolier Recovery Services, Blaisdell Consulting was a cover.

Creed pulled up to the entrance door inside the garage and said, "Here you go. Wolffe's inside the conference room waiting on you."

I sighed and said, "What about the team? Knuckles, Brett, and Veep? Are they called in as well?"

My "employees" at GRS lived all over the United States, but I wasn't going to do anything without them. Creed said, "Yeah, Knuckles and Brett are here. Veep is still on the way."

Which made some sense, because Knuckles and Brett lived in DC. Veep was a vagabond who couldn't decide where he wanted to end up. He used to live in Charleston, like me, but then moved to Montana for some reason.

I muttered under my breath, then said to Creed, "Well, get us in, then."

Technically, GRS had nothing to do with Blaisdell Consulting, so we didn't have the proper credentials to walk right in. With its DC connections, the last thing we needed was something like an overzealous congressman or journalist digging into who was allowed access and why, as the Taskforce itself was most definitely operating outside the bounds of the U.S. Constitution.

Creed, on the other hand, was a card-carrying employee of Blaisdell and reported here daily, so he had the badge and RFID pass to get us through the security protocols.

Creed said, "I told you: I'm headed home. Wolffe is waiting for you in the SCIF, and you know the non-badge procedures."

Jennifer and I exited the vehicle and watched it drive away. I said, "This is a lot of work that could have been done over an encrypted Zoom call."

She said, "Yeah, makes you wonder why they told us to pack for four days."

I said, "At least it has nothing to do with Russia. You know this month's code, right?"

We had a method to protect both the cover of Blaisdell Consulting as well as the members inside. Each month two different phrases were promulgated to all the various cover organizations, which was your bona fides to get through the door. One phrase just proved that you belonged, were fine, and needed to come in. The other phrase would relay that you were under duress and trying to enter against your will.

Jennifer said, "Uhhh . . . no, I don't."

As Creed's vehicle exited into the sunlight I snapped back to her and said, "You don't know the code? You *always* know the code."

As for me, I thought the whole thing was a little overboard and never paid attention to the pass phrases. The camera would show us both standing alone, and we were a known quantity. I mean, if I *really* wanted to enter, I'd kidnap Creed and force him to use his physical badge. That would negate the whole stupid dance, but nobody listened to me.

Jennifer said, "Don't blame this on me. You don't know it either."

Which was true. I said, "Marge will never open the inner door without it."

While the outside of the door to the building looked like any other, in fact, it was a trap to keep any nefarious actors from conducting a strike. Comprised of bulletproof glass, it had two doors—an outer one where you'd talk into a camera, and an inner one, which let you into the building proper. Once inside, you were trapped if you couldn't prove why you were there, the outer one locking you into a glass cage.

Jennifer said, "Call Wolffe or Knuckles. Tell them to come down."

"Creed said he was in the SCIF, and if he is, he won't have his phone on him. Neither will Knuckles."

SCIF stood for Sensitive Compartmented Information Facility and was basically a room designed to prevent any eavesdropping from malicious actors. As such, nobody using it was allowed to bring in a cell phone.

Jennifer said, "Use the old code. Marge will open it when she sees me behind you."

Marge was Blaisdell Consulting's office receptionist, and she took her job seriously. She'd worked here since the Taskforce had been created, and I wasn't so sure she hadn't developed dementia. Sometimes it was hard to tell whether she was crazy or just cranky.

I said, "If we don't know the code, she might believe we're here under duress and lock us in."

"The old one and the camera should work. I mailed her cookies last Christmas. She'll let us in."

I shook my head, opened the door, and said, "So the magic entrance to this top-secret clandestine counterterrorism force is a bunch of chocolate crinkles?"

She entered behind me and said, "If it works, it works."

She let the door close. I heard it click and turned to the camera, saying, "If not, this is going to be embarrassing."

I pressed the button and stared into the camera. I heard, "Yes? May I help you?"

I said, "Hey, Marge, It's Pike Logan, here to see George Wolffe."

"I'm sorry. There's nobody here by that name. I'm going to unlock the outer door. Please be on your way."

Just great. I threw out the only phrase I still remembered, from months ago, "Hey, we're here about your team-building services. We were told about it from Xavier Barclay."

We heard nothing for a moment, Marge's cranky brain knowing the old phrase meant we knew something, but it wasn't the correct something. Finally, she said, "Xavier no longer works here. Do you have another name?"

Exasperated, I said, "Marge, Wolffe called us up here. Come on. Just call him on the phone."

"Sir, there is nobody here by that name. If you wish, I'll call security and have you escorted out."

Jennifer bumped me out of the way, leaned into the camera, and said, "Marge, it's Jennifer here. Sorry our data is old. Before we go, did you get my cookies?"

There was silence for a moment, then, "Why yes, I did. They were delicious." Another pause, then, "Okay, I really shouldn't be doing this, but hang on. I'll see if I can get George on the line."

I muttered under my breath, "So the security protocols can be breached by Christmas cookies? I'll let ISIS know."

Jennifer elbowed me and said, "Thanks, Marge."

I heard the inner door click open and snatched it before Marge could change her mind. She said, "Third-floor conference room. He's expecting you."

We went to the elevator and exited on the third floor, walking down to the conference room—the SCIF—and entered without preamble, seeing the Taskforce version of the White House Situation Room.

The space was dominated by a long wooden table, the grain polished to a luster, plugs and ports in front of each seat. The walls were adorned with various trophies from different operations—flags, weapons, and the like—with the far wall holding nothing but a giant flat-screen monitor.

Two high-backed leather chairs swung around at our entrance and I saw a tall Caucasian guy, hippy looking with shaggy black hair, and a black man built like a fireplug, short and nothing but muscle. Knuckles and Brett, both grinning at me.

Brett said, "So you had some issues getting past Marge?"

Damn tattletale. I fist bumped both of them and said, "Not really. I'm here, aren't I? I've penetrated security tougher than Marge before."

They stood for a hug from Jennifer, who said, "My cookies got us in."

Damn tattletale. I changed the subject, saying, "Where's Veep?"

Knuckles said, "Still on the way. We'll get this briefing without him."

I'd rather have everyone here for the brief, as everyone on my team was an Operator and they knew to ask any questions I would miss. With this call-up, I figured George Wolffe would have waited for the whole package.

My team was a little eclectic—as the makeup could attest—and the longest-serving commercial cover organization within the Taskforce. Most of the Operators in the Taskforce fell into a cover for an operation but didn't really live it. They just used it for that specific mission, then fell into another one for the next mission, usually burning the first to the ground. The covers were all plug-and-play, run by bureaucrats and bean counters with just enough of a veneer of respectability to allow the Operators to penetrate a hostile area.

GRS was different in that we lived it daily. It was a legitimate company, with legitimate business contracts. As such, we were the only cover organization that was run by Operators, and my team makeup showed it.

Knuckles was a Navy SEAL, and my second-in-command. Brett was a former Force Recon Marine who now worked within the paramilitary branch of the CIA. Veep—aka Nicholas Seacrest—was an Air Force combat controller, who also happened to be the son of the current president of the United States. I'd given him the callsign when his father was still the vice president.

I said, "So what's the rush? What's this all about? Where's Wolffe?"

The door to the SCIF opened, and Wolffe said, "I'm right here, and sorry for pulling you up to DC, but you need to get on the road."

"Where?"

"Goa, India."

CHAPTER 5

Kamal poked his head around the stone wall, taking a quick glance. At the top of the stairwell sat a single man in a chair dressed in civilian clothes, the lightbulb above his head creating shadows around his body. Kamal whispered, "That man is RAW. He won't be like the security guard. We need to take him out immediately."

Agam said, "I'll handle him. Be prepared to follow me up the stairs on the run."

Kamal nodded and Agam said, "Wait here." Kamal watched him retrace his previous steps, going back to the body of the guard they'd killed. When he returned, he was wearing the top blouse of the guard, the patches on the shoulders making him look official.

Kamal smiled and said, "Good thinking."

Agam said, "It's still risky. Don't leave me in the wind. We don't know how many are beyond the door."

Without waiting for an answer, he stepped out into the light and began walking up the stairs. The man in the chair leapt to his feet, saying something Kamal couldn't hear. Agam said something back, then jogged the rest of the way up the stairs. He reached the top, and without another word, Agam raised his pistol, stuck it in the man's face, and pulled the trigger.

The sound of the weapon was barely louder than a cough, but the damage was catastrophic. The man's face split open, and he toppled sideways as if all the control of his muscles quit at once, sliding four feet down the stairwell.

Kamal leapt up, hissing, "Let's go!" He and Randeep broke from the darkness, sprinting up the stairs into the light, reaching Agam, who was frantically working the old door. He heard them arriving and said, "It's locked!"

Kamal said, "Move back."

Agam did, and Kamal raised his pistol, aiming for the ancient bolt going into the wall. He fired once, twice, three times, and the bolt finally gave, bending inward. Kamal leaned back and slammed the door with the ball of his foot, splintering the lock, the door swinging in.

They were immediately met with a fusillade of fire, the unsuppressed weapon inside splitting the night with explosive noise. Kamal dove to the left, Agam and Randeep to the right, the gun inside still firing blindly out of the open doorway. Kamal saw the location of the muzzle flash, rolled up to the edge, and returned fire, silencing the weapon. He sprang to his feet, running into the room in time to see another man fleeing to a hallway deeper in. He sprinted to catch up, the man racing to a cell midway down, with a guard in a chair looking bewildered.

Kamal started firing, chipping the wall around them both, the ricochets louder than the sound coming out of his pistol. One dove into the cell, the other against the opposite wall, firing his pistol blindly back at him. Kamal ducked instinctively and kept pulling the trigger, his magazine locking the chamber open, empty.

The guard stood up from the ground, smiled, and took aim. Kamal charged him, throwing the pistol at his head. The man flinched, shocked that Kamal wasn't retreating; the weapon hurled at his head caused him to fire into the ceiling, and Kamal dove into his chest, slamming him to the floor.

He grabbed the hair of the man's head and began bashing his skull into the stone, hearing Agam and Randeep rush past him into the cell. He heard shots from inside the cell, felt the crunch of his target's skull, snatched the guard's pistol, and turned into the cell doorway. He saw a shadow hanging and raced inside, the weapon at the ready.

He swung the pistol around, saw two dead guards slumped on the floor, then Agam and Randeep standing still, arms at their sides, staring into the corner of the room. Naked but for his underwear, hanging on a hook from the shackles on his wrists, was Sidak. Kamal said, "Cut him down . . ." and then paused, seeing the destruction to Sidak's head. Someone had put a barrel to his skull and pulled the trigger. Sidak was gone.

Agam said, "When we came in, a man was working on him, another was shooting at us. We killed the one shooting, and the man next to Sidak shot him in the head."

He shuffled, then said, "We killed him too."

Randeep said, "What now?"

The seriousness of their situation slammed into him. They had failed to save Sidak, but that didn't alter their fate. The gunfire would have alerted anyone who was on station at the prison. He stuffed the death of his friend into the dark recesses of his mind, something to deal with at another time, and said, "We need to move, right now, back to the boat."

Agam said, "What about Sidak? His body?"

Kamal took one more look at his friend and said, "It stays."

Randeep said, "No. No way. He comes with us."

Kamal snatched Randeep's shirt, bored into his eyes, letting the anger of the loss of his friend permeate the room, and said, "If you want to succeed in what we have planned, he *stays*. Let it go."

Randeep nodded, and Kamal released him, saying, "They'll be coming, and we can't fight them all. We need to find another way out. Deeper in."

They returned to the hallway, hearing men shouting about the man they'd killed guarding the stairwell door. Kamal turned away from the entrance they'd used and began running, Agam and Randeep right behind him. They reached the end just as men began bursting in. Kamal snatched open a door and they were through, Kamal shutting it slowly, then listening.

The men on the other side were shouting orders and screaming obscenities, but nobody was following down the hallway, apparently all focused on the cell. He nodded, holding a finger to his lips, and they began shuffling in the darkened room, looking for an exit. Kamal found one, and they entered a circular staircase, a single bulb illuminating the ground floor below. Kamal peeked over the edge, saw nothing, and began descending the stairs two at a time, his men behind him. They reached the bottom, moved to a door, and Kamal cracked it open, seeing the rain had finally arrived.

The outside promenade was streaked with the torrent of falling water, the wind blowing it sideways, Kamal barely able to see the old cannons along the seawall across from the door. He slid out from the door, feeling the rain strike his face, and glanced up the promenade to the entrance of the fort. He saw a milieu of men at the base of the stairwell they'd used to reach Sidak's cell, dancing in and out of the shadows of the bare illumination, waving their arms and shouting. Beyond them, he could make out the entrance to the dock.

He said, "We can't get back to the boat the way we came. They're in between us and the dock."

Behind him, becoming agitated, Randeep said, "What are we going to do? We can't hide here. They'll find us eventually."

Agam said, "The seawall. We go over the seawall and swim to the boat."

Kamal considered it a moment, thinking that the jetty with the boat jutted out into the water for at least seventy-five meters. That might work. He said, "Yes. That's the best bet."

Randeep said, "We'll get crushed on the rocks. We can't do that in the dark, especially in this weather."

Agam said, "I'd rather get crushed on the rocks than be killed by these assholes."

With that, he sprinted through the rain to the far wall abutting the sea. Kamal hesitated a moment, then turned to Randeep and said, "Come on. It's the only way."

They ran across, the rain slapping against their faces like pebbles. They reached the rock wall next to an ancient Portuguese cannon overlooking the ocean. Kamal looked down and could make out the swirling foam in the darkness, the waves crashing into the rocks in a rhythm. Seeing the maelstrom, he had second thoughts.

He looked at Agam and said, "Maybe Randeep is right."

Agam said nothing, his actions showing his answer. He leapt over the wall, holding on to the barrel of the cannon, his feet now perpendicular to the stone. He looked at Kamal, then at the surf below him, timing his fall. He waited until the moment the waves crashed and then let go, falling the thirty feet to the water.

Shocked, Kamal leaned over the stone wall, seeing Agam in the surf, swimming away from the danger of the waves. He looked at Randeep and said, "He goes, we all go."

Randeep said nothing, simply staring into the blackness of the ocean. Kamal slapped the back of his head and said, "Get over. Go."

Snapped out of his fear, Randeep repeated Agam's maneuver, dropping to the water below. Kamal followed him, holding on to the barrel of the cannon and taking great gulps of air, feeling the sting of the rain on his face. He watched below, saw the waves strike the rock wall, and willed himself to let go.

He windmilled his arms, the fall much longer than he anticipated, the drop through the rain seeming to take forever. He hit the water sideways, the impact punching the air out of his lungs. He sank for a moment, then began to fight to the surface, knowing he had to get away from the wall before the next crash of waves. He broke the surface, took a gasp of air, and saw the waves coming. He ducked underneath the water, just like he'd done as a child, and began swimming away from the rocks. When he ran out of air, he surfaced, finding himself twenty feet away from the wall.

He glanced around but didn't find either Agam or Randeep. He saw the tip of the jetty in the dim light and continued swimming, the powerful need for survival driving him forward.

Seven minutes later, he reached the end of the dock, clinging to the rocks like a barnacle. He used them to work his way to the northern side of the jetty, seeing the rubber Zodiac. Climbing over the gunwale was Agam, Randeep's head bobbing in the water next to him.

He smiled and scuttled to the boat. In minutes, they were all aboard, Manjit powering the outboard into the sea, the rain still pelting them. Kamal took one last look back and saw nothing to indicate they'd been seen escaping.

Nobody talked. Not even Manjit. He knew what it meant when they'd arrived. No words were necessary. Sidak was dead, and no amount of discussion was going to bring him back.

Kamal knew Sidak's death was his responsibility, and that knowledge weighed heavily on him. The others had agreed to the mission because they felt the pull of their Sikh heritage, and had agreed solely because the money offered would help them further the cause of Sikh nationalism.

Sidak had been different. Barely out of his teens, Kamal had hired him to work with Mr. Chin on the computer side of things, using his technical skill. He had wanted no part of hunting the billionaire and, unlike Kamal and the others, held no burning desire for Sikh independence. A skinny kid with an analytical mind, Sidak wouldn't draw any attention, and having never been incarcerated, Kamal knew he would be perfect for the reconnaissance mission. Kamal had played on their friendship, telling him it would be nothing more than a two-week stint at a hotel. Sidak had trusted Kamal, and he'd finally agreed. And now he was dead just as surely as if Kamal had pulled the trigger.

They reached the mother ship, the rain now a light mist. Mr. Chin helped them anchor the small boat to the side of the hull and they clambered up the netting to the larger boat, collapsing on the deck.

Mr. Chin said, "Where's Sidak?"

Kamal said, "He's dead. They killed him. He was hanging like a slab of meat in the cell, posing no threat, and they killed him when we came. Shot him in the head."

The speed of his speech increased the more he spoke, the words tumbling out as if he were trying to absolve himself of the blame, his mind now grasping what had happened to his friend. He finished, feeling the tears roll down his cheeks and hoping they were camouflaged by the rain.

Mr. Chin said, "Did he talk?"

Kamal couldn't believe the callousness of the question. He said, "How the fuck would I know? He was hanging from a hook. They put a bullet in his head."

"They? Did you kill them?"

His eyes now slits, Kamal said, "Yes, we killed them."

Mr. Chin went to the console of the boat and turned on the twin outboards, saying, "Good. So we're still a go for the billionaire."

Kamal stood up at the words, saying, "You killed my friend. *You* did it. You said he'd be fine going into that resort, and he wasn't."

Mr. Chin turned from the wheel of the boat and said, "Sometimes my intelligence isn't perfect, but he was paid well. He knew the risks, as do you now."

Kamal was sickened by the discussion, the thought of Sidak dying for nothing more than a paycheck disgusting him. He decided that Sidak's death would be about more than money. His sacrifice would mean something to the Sikh brethren.

And Mr. Chin was going to help him do that.

CHAPTER 6

Wolffe walked to the head of the table and took a seat. I pulled out the nearest chair, saying, "Goa? What's in India? Nuclear weapons on the loose? A sighting of Big Foot?"

Wolffe said, "Nothing that sexy. You won't be doing any kinetic operations. It's a simple favor for Kerry Bostwick. Just a site survey."

He saw my expression and knew I was less than enthused. I said, "Site survey for the CIA? Seriously? If I wanted to be a clown I would have joined the circus. Tell them to do it themselves."

Kerry Bostwick was the director of the CIA and a friend of the Taskforce, but that didn't mean I wanted to start working for him. I had a job, and it was a hell of a lot more important than hauling his spit buckets around the gym while he was in the ring. In fact, by the Taskforce charter, I wasn't *allowed* to do it.

Created as a scalpel, we specifically attacked problem sets that other parts of the government couldn't, or wouldn't handle. Because of that, we were specifically designed not to duplicate other agencies. They had their roles and we had ours.

We didn't do traditional intelligence collection—that was CIA. If there was a target that could be handled by one of the DOD's special mission units, then they did so. We only dealt with national security threats that stymied other overt agencies because of bureaucracy, geo-politics, misbegotten United States code, or simply logistics. We were unlike anything else in the United States arsenal, and I was being asked to basically be the CIA's JV team for something they could handle on their own.

Wolffe held up his hands and said, "Hang on, hang on. It's a little more important than that. Bostwick himself is meeting the head of the Research and Analysis Wing, but he's doing it clandestinely. Nobody outside of RAW knows he's coming, and he can't use anyone stationed there because they're known to the host nation."

"So bring in some pipe-hitters from DC. Bostwick's got them. Why are we being tasked?"

Wolffe clicked on the giant TV and said, "Let him tell you. Just don't cuss him out."

Which was dirty pool. Wolffe knew how I felt, and he also knew I couldn't very well tear into the D/CIA without looking like a loose cannon. The screen cleared and I saw Kerry Bostwick larger than life, staring back at us. He said, "Can you hear me?"

Wolffe said, "We got you Kerry. I've got most of the team here, and they're raring to go."

Bostwick laughed and said, "I'll bet. First off, I appreciate this. I know it's unorthodox, but Wolffe said you guys were available, and your cover is perfect."

I scowled at Wolffe, then went back to the screen, saying, "Whoa there, I haven't agreed to anything yet. Just tell me what's going on and why my team is needed when you own the entire CIA."

Taken aback, Bostwick said, "Oh, sorry. I was under the impression you'd packed and were ready to fly. Rock Star bird and all that."

"We *are* packed, but I still don't know why."

"Okay, look, here it is: I'm meeting secretly with the head of RAW and an Indian billionaire. All I need is four days of security while I'm on-site. The location is the Grand Hyatt resort near the capital, Panaji."

"You didn't answer the question: Why don't you use CIA assets? Why us?"

Bostwick sighed and said, "Believe me, if I could use my own assets, I would, but I don't have them and I'm out of time. You were the last resort."

That sounded worse than what I'd originally thought. Now we weren't *good enough* to be the first team?

He saw my face and said, "I don't mean in skill, I mean because of the Taskforce charter. Look, all of my personnel at the India station are either declared at worst or suspected of being agency at best. The RAW chief has forbidden me from using them, as he wants to keep this meeting completely off the books from his folks."

I said, "So bring in someone from here. Paramilitary guys from Ground Branch."

"I would, but I'm not dictating the timeline. The meeting is going to happen within the next few days and I simply don't have anyone to pull. Every single asset I have with the skill set I need is currently either stacked against the mess in the Middle East or over in Ukraine. It's vacuumed up every available asset. Tel Aviv is bursting at the seams with my guys, Beirut is on fire, Iraq is about to implode, and Iran is trying to play puppet master throughout. All of that has left the National Command Authority demanding answers, wanting me to predict the future. Houthis, Hamas, Hezbollah, and every other crack-pot group that starts with an 'H' has sucked me dry, and that's not even mentioning Russia and their nuclear threats. Every paramilitary officer I have is in the fight right now."

I couldn't argue with that. Ever since those assholes in Hamas had slaughtered Israelis, the world had been on fire. Well, actually since Putin had invaded Ukraine before that. I didn't envy Bostwick's job and felt a little bit selfish at my earlier reticence. After all, it was supposed to be one team, one fight. Still, I asked, "Won't the RAW have security on-site? I mean, how dangerous could this meeting be if it's at a resort?"

"Yes, they will have security on-site, and in fact I was willing to forgo any of my own security because of that, but two days ago they detained a worker at the resort. Turns out he has ties to Lashkar-e-Taiba. He'd just started working there a week before."

Lashkar-e-Taiba was an Islamic terrorist organization from Pakistan. Their stated goal was to "reunite" the Kashmir area of India with Pakistan, and their most famous action was the 2008 Mumbai terrorist attack, where they hit various iconic hotels, restaurants, and stores in a downtown Mumbai shopping district, slaughtering close to two hundred civilians over a four-day rampage.

I said, "Well, sounds like the RAW is on their game. Stopped a threat before it could execute."

"Yeah, but there are indicators that the man had contact with the ISI, which means this was planned at a much higher level than just some lone wolf from a substate terrorist affiliate. It's why I'm caught short for security and asking for you at the last minute. I was going to trust RAW, but now, with this information, I don't want to put my faith in RAW being 'on their game' during the meeting time."

The ISI was Pakistan's Interservice Intelligence Agency—their version of the CIA. They'd played a double game with us in Afghanistan for years, taking our money with one hand while helping the Taliban with the other. I had no doubt they were instrumental in hiding Osama bin Laden in their country when we found him. How else would he have a mansion a couple of miles away from the Pakistani version of West Point?

I nodded and said, "Okay, sir, you've got me. What's this meeting about?"

"Well, the Middle East and Russia aren't the only things I have to worry about. China is still an eight-hundred-pound gorilla. This meeting is about them."

He paused, then said, "You guys know anything about rare earth elements?"

CHAPTER 7

I glanced around at my team, and Jennifer said, "Yeah, you mean like the metals used in magnets and batteries for cell phones?"

"Exactly. Rare earth elements aren't really rare, like diamonds. They're found everywhere, but not in great enough quantities to be worth mining. Getting them out of the ground is painstaking and creates a huge environmental mess—which basically means the tree-huggers here in the United States have shut down most of our mines.

"Today, China has a monopoly on the mining, accounting for about eighty percent of the world's production. Thirty years ago it wouldn't have mattered. Now everything we use relies on rare earth elements, from cell phones to electric cars to home computers to just about anything that requires a microprocessor or a screen."

I saw where this was going, saying, "Including all of our defense systems."

Bostwick nodded. "Exactly. There would be no night-vision goggles or F-35 fighters without them. Any time you hear someone saying 'next generation,' what they're really saying is 'rare earth elements,' and China's monopoly on them is an enormous vulnerability. If they decided to stop exporting them to us, we'd be in trouble—and they've shown a willingness to use that leverage. In 2010, China had a spat with Japan over some islands that both claimed. China's response was to stop exporting to Japanese industry, which was an eye-opener for us."

I nodded, having never given a lot of thought to the brass tacks of what our technology required. Knuckles said, "Let me get this straight—we're always talking about how China invading Taiwan would cause a major tech disruption because of Taiwan's monopoly on semiconductor production, but what you're really saying is that's small potatoes. China could stop that production without firing a shot?"

"Correct. China could stop *our* tech sector without firing a shot as well, which is where this meeting comes in. India has found a large deposit of rare earth elements in the north of their country. Enough to give China a run for its money, and we'd much rather deal with India—a democracy—than China. The problem is—like I said before—extracting the elements is labor-intensive and messy. It almost requires a state to support it because it's very hard for a private entity to make a profit—which is precisely why we don't mine our own. Our mining industry decided the profit margin wasn't worth the hassle. We have an Indian billionaire who's willing to give it a go, but he wants support from the Indian state. We *also* want the Indian state to support it."

"What's the quid pro quo here? Why is CIA and not the State Department doing this?"

"Well, honestly, because it's going to be done below the waterline. If China thinks we have an overt hand in helping India break their rare earth monopoly, there will be repercussions for both India and us. China might pull what it did with Japan right off the bat. We'd prefer this look like an amateur effort solely directed by India, with no fanfare from the State Department or the administration."

I laughed and said, "So the CIA is getting into the mining business, is that it? You're going to do this covertly?"

"Yes, but make no mistake, this is much bigger than a mine. It's also a lever to keep India out of China's sway and on our side. Don't worry, a presidential finding has already been presented to the Gang of Eight."

By U.S. Code, any covert action done by representatives of the United States government has to have a presidential finding detailing the scope of the operation and the intended outcome, which was then given to Congress. The Gang of Eight was a nickname for a small group of congressional members read on to highly compartmented intelligence matters, comprised of the leaders of both parties in the House and Senate and the ranking and minority leaders of both the House and Senate intelligence committees. Already having a finding presented to Congress told me that this thing had been brewing for months, if not years.

Presidential findings and briefings for covert actions didn't happen in a week, which meant the administration considered this high priority, but it *did* beg the question about using the Taskforce. We were an extralegal force that didn't operate under any U.S. law in existence.

I said, "That's great and all, but you know the Taskforce doesn't fall under any finding. What about the Oversight Council? What are you telling them? Have they approved the mission set?"

Bostwick said, "George, you want to handle that?"

Wolffe said, "Sure." He turned to us and said, "The principals of the Council have concurred that the operation is in the best interests for our national security."

Which, of *course* they did. While the Taskforce didn't fall under congressional oversight like the CIA or DOD, we did have oversight in the form of a thirteen-person panel that vetted and approved all operations. The "principals" were the most important members—sort of like a "gang of eight" for Taskforce operations—comprised of the president, the secretary of state, the secretary of defense, the director of the CIA, and the national security advisor. Out of the five, two—the president and the D/CIA—were already on board, so approval was a no-brainer.

I started to say something else but Wolffe beat me to the punch, saying, "I know what you're going to argue here. No, we aren't turning into the CIA. No, we aren't going to become a bureaucracy that's subject to congressional oversight. No, this isn't mission creep. You aren't going to do anything overt here. It's a simple Alpha mission. It will never get to Omega."

We called each phase of an operation a different Greek letter, with Alpha being the first phase: advanced force operations to collect intelligence on the art of the possible against a target. Each phase had to have separate approval from the Oversight Council, with Omega being the last one—meaning we were going to eliminate a target to remove it as a threat.

Wolffe was telling me this was going to be nothing but a walk in the park, just some sightseeing to protect the meeting. What he was forgetting was the same thing the U.S. government habitually did when it put its men and women in harm's way: the enemy gets a vote.

I said, "Sir, you're sending me to protect Kerry against a possible threat. This could go from Alpha to Omega in the span of seconds. Either I'm needed to protect the meeting—meaning there's a possibility I might have to engage—or I'm not, meaning I can fly back home to Charleston."

Bostwick spoke up, saying, "Just for argument's sake here, you have Omega approval. If it comes down to you using lethal force to protect this meeting, then you have it. That's from the president, by the way."

I nodded, satisfied that all the T's were crossed and the I's dotted. He said, "How soon can you fly? The meeting is in four days, but I'd like you on the ground before we get there to create a break from our arrival."

I said, "We can go as soon as Veep shows up and I get a package in the Rock Star bird."

Wolffe said, "Package is being loaded as we speak. Weapons and surveillance gear only, but you won't need anything else. Kerry's already seeded your cover. There's a UNESCO heritage site in Old Goa about ten miles away. Called the Church of Saint Augustine, it's a falling-down wreck they're still excavating. You're doing a site survey for a contingent from the University of Pennsylvania."

I saw Jennifer perk up, because she always loved looking at old shit as part of our job. I said, "Does that mean we have to meet a bunch of UN or government types, proving we're who we say we are? And if so, does Penn know we're going? Is that part real?"

"No, that part's fake, and you don't need to interface with anyone there. We've already done it at a higher level when we expedited your visas. They think you're going to check out lodging, logistics, and that sort of thing. The most you'll have to do is make at least one trip to the church for your cover. If you have to prove who you are, you'll use the cover package we give you. They'll end up calling us, not Penn."

Which was fine by me. I said, "And you've already got us rooms at the resort?"

"Yes. Paid by Grolier Recovery Services. They're expecting you."

I chuckled and said, "What if I'd have said no on this?"

He smiled back and said, "Wouldn't happen. Might as well throw a steak into a lion's den and ask, 'What if he doesn't eat it?' I knew your answer before you got on the plane."

CHAPTER 8

Kamal heard a knock on his door and said, "Come in."

The old brass knob rattled but didn't open. He shouted, "Pull up, then turn it." That worked. The door released and his men filed in, looking a little ragged.

Kamal smiled and said, "So Tito's Lane lived up to expectations?"

Agam let slip a sheepish smile, saying, "We're Sikhs. We don't imbibe alcohol."

Kamal said, "Sure. Right. As long as you didn't do anything stupid to draw attention, I don't care."

The men took their seats around a small wooden table with enough drink rings to make it look like an Olympic emblem, the wooden chairs creaking ominously with their weight.

Manjit stood back up, saying, "Nothing in this place is safe. Last night, I thought my bed was going to collapse to the floor."

Randeep pointed at a plaque on the wall, saying, "And what's up with all the Russian?"

Kamal looked where he was indicating and chuckled. On two red plaques were the twenty-five rules of the hotel, one in English, the other in Cyrillic/Russian. There was only one rule in bold type: "PLEASE

DO NOT BRING IN ANY DRUG DEALERS OR PROSTITUTES WHO ARE NOT ALREADY REGISTERED IN THE HOTEL."

He guessed it was okay to bring in both if they had a room.

He said, "Before they invaded Ukraine, this place was like the Riviera for Russians. They all came here for the beaches and night life. The same night life you saw last evening. They don't come here anymore."

Manjit said, "So if this place is not good enough for Russians, why are we here? I thought we were going home."

"We are, but I'm waiting on Mr. Chin before we go."

"It's been two days since Sidak died. What are we waiting for?"

"For payment. That bastard is going to give us our money. Once we're paid, we're out of here."

Agam leaned back and said, "I don't even want the money. I just want to go home. Forget all of this happened."

Incensed, Kamal said, "Forget about Sidak? Is that what you want? They killed him. We agreed we were doing this for a reason."

Agam said, "They killed him because they thought he was an Islamic terrorist. We sent him in with that blanket to wear. We can't blame them for killing what they fear when we dressed him up like a terrorist and sent him in."

"We didn't dress him up as anything! He was just a Muslim. They killed him for no reason, just like they kill us. Sikh, Muslim, it makes no difference. The RAW and the government is against everyone except Hindus. It's why we started on this path."

Manjit said, "We started on this path to protest against the oppression. We didn't start on this path to get killed as Muslim terrorists. Even I don't give a shit about them."

At that, Kamal stood up and said, "So you aren't willing to kill to get our own state? Did you think they'd just hand it to us? Make no mistake, we'll be called terrorists as well."

Manjit jerked upright, slammed his palm into a wall, and shouted, "That's *not* what I meant. We can't do anything for Khalistan by acting like Muslim terrorists. You talked a good game, and all it got us is one of our own killed. For *nothing*."

The words stung, because Kamal knew they were true. They faced off, the tension thick enough to fog the air. Agam stood up and said, "Stop it! Stop right now. Sidak wouldn't have wanted this. He would have wanted unity."

Kamal stared at Manjit, and Manjit broke the tension, turning to his chair and saying, "This whole thing was stupid anyway. We aren't the Khalistan Commando Force. We're a bunch of kids from the Punjab. Nothing more. We should have never begun this."

Kamal sat down, knowing this was a turning point. He said, "The government is killing Sikhs all over the world. They tried to kill two in the United States and assassinated one in Canada. We all saw that. It's time we took the war back to them."

He looked each man in the eye and said, "We aren't a bunch of kids from the Punjab. We were once, but we're more than that now. Slumdog millionaires. That's what we are."

The men chuckled at the reference to the movie, all of them having scoffed at its misappropriations of Indian society, but each believing the heart that beat within it.

Kamal continued, "We agreed in the prison that when we got out, we would make a difference. We would fight for the Sikh cause. It's why I called you to work with Chin when it was just internet scams. We were going to use the money to fund organizations that would help the Sikh. Now I think we do something more overt. We do the action ourselves."

Manjit said, "How? We aren't the KCF. We have no contacts with them. I'm not even sure they actually exist anymore. We're a lone wolf organization. We can't do what they did. We have no following."

Kamal said, "We create the following. *That's* what we do. We're the new Khalistan Commando Force."

Manjit said, "That's easy to say but harder to execute. Mr. Chin had a plan before, but it's gone now. With Sidak dead, so is his original plan. We can't do anything against the billionaire now."

Kamal said, "Maybe. Maybe not. Let's see what Mr. Chin says. At the very least, we can use his money. We can leave here and start on our journey as the new KCF. Are you with me? Or do you want the sum total of your life to consist of scamming old women in America?"

Agam flicked his eyes to the others, then said, "I'm with you. Let's cut ties with Mr. Chin and go our own way."

Randeep nodded and said, "I'm good with that."

Kamal said, "Manjit? How about you?"

Before he could answer they heard a knock on the door, causing them to jump, all of them jittery. Kamal went to the door and said, "What? I told you no maid service. I don't want it."

He heard: "Open the door. It's me, Mr. Chin."

Kamal looked back into the room, then swung the door. Mr. Chin stood outside, a short, bespectacled man whose slight stature belied his true nature. He was wearing a suit complete with a tie, looking completely out of place in the environs.

He said, "Can I come in?"

"Only if you're bringing a paycheck."

He chuckled and pushed past Kamal as if he owned the room. He said, "A paycheck for what, exactly? We aren't done yet."

Kamal grabbed his arm and said, "We did what you wanted, and it failed. There was no success part of the contract. You owe us for a service, not for success."

Mr. Chin pulled his arm away and said, "Yes, I paid you for a service, but there was no time limit on it. The service is still outstanding."

"What's that mean?"

"It means the mission is still a go. It means I want you to execute."

Manjit stood up and said, "How? Sidak is dead. They know we're coming. He probably won't even show up now."

Mr. Chin said, "Yes, Sidak is dead, and I regret that. I know you don't believe it, but I do. And the mission is happening. The billionaire, Thakkar, is still coming to the resort. Nothing we've done has altered that."

"How do you know?"

"Your friends. The ones providing security for him."

Kamal said, "Then why don't you just use them to kidnap him? Pay us now for what we did and get this over with."

"They are, shall we say, tainted. If they are involved, then my company will be compromised. They have a trail. It has to be a clean hit. Something with no connections. They can give us the intelligence, facilitate the capture, but they can't do it themselves."

Kamal took that in, but he didn't like it. He said, "Well, you're out of luck. We're done. I'll continue doing the computer stuff for you, but we're not doing this. Give us our money and we'll be gone."

Mr. Chin looked at him, then went from man to man, settling back on Kamal. He said, "It doesn't work that way. You'll do this, or you'll all be rounded up."

Kamal stood up and said, "What's that mean?"

"It means you work for me now. That's all. Nothing different from yesterday."

Kamal stood there, letting the words sink in, then said, "So you're now threatening us? Do what you say, or go to a RAW funnel room?"

"No, no. I didn't say that. You did. But that is the end state. Fail me here, and you'll never go home."

Kamal looked at his men, saw the trepidation, and said, "How about we just kill you right here? Leave you to be found by the maids?"

Kamal expected to see fear. Mr. Chin showed none. He said, "You can do that, but it won't end well for you. I have powerful friends."

"Friends from where? Who do you really work for?"

Mr. Chin simply said, "I work for a company that wants to make money. That's it."

Manjit said, "We can't continue the mission. All the intel we got was the outside perimeter. We know the guard stations along the grounds, but we have no idea which room he's in or anything else. They'll be looking for us now. This is just stupid."

Mr. Chin placed a briefcase on the table and said, "They aren't looking for us. Yes, Sidak was caught, but the pocket litter I made him take worked. They're chasing a number for ISI on his phone, and his employment address is tied to a Lashkar-e-Taiba man. They'll be hunting down the wrong thread."

Kamal snarled, "That *pocket litter* is what got him killed. If he'd have gone in as a Sikh, he'd still be alive. Still be working at the resort. Don't act like that was some strategic genius. It's what got him captured and killed. Yeah, it protects us now, but it's a protection we wouldn't have even needed."

Mr. Chin took in the words, nodded his head, and said, "Yes, I see the point, but mine still remains valid. They're looking for someone else. They aren't looking for you. We can still do the operation."

CHAPTER 9

The wheels of our aircraft touched down, jarring me awake. I rubbed my eyes, raised the shade of my window, and saw a lush, tropical landscape, the sun glaringly bright.

I turned away, saw the rest of the team rising out of slumber, and said, "What time is it?"

Next to me, with two different books on India splayed open on her lap, Jennifer said, "Ten A.M., Goa time."

"What day?"

She smiled and said, "Tomorrow, for you."

I hollered up to the cockpit, "What are we looking at here?"

I saw the copilot bend around and say, "Nothing much. Simple customs check. The tower said they were expecting us, so should be routine."

Which meant we could do everything on the plane without leaving our seats. Sometimes it paid to have powerful people pave your way.

Knuckles came up to me and said, "So, what's the play here?"

"Let the customs guys come through, get our hotel rooms, and find a rum and coke. Twenty-four hours of traveling has left me thirsty, and it's got to be five o'clock somewhere."

He laughed and said, "I meant weapons. We're going to take a surveillance package, but given that last update, do you want to take weapons, or come back to the plane if we think we need them after an initial assessment of the grounds?"

Originally, we'd planned on providing security with our eyes only, simply providing early warning should we see anything amiss, acting like tourists who just happened to find a threat and letting the RAW security take over. At our layover in Ireland, we'd been given an update on the terrorist that RAW had captured: an attempt had been made to rescue him, leaving multiple RAW officers dead.

It hadn't been successful, and the terrorist had been killed in the process, but the men who'd tried to do it had escaped and were in the wind. The only evidence that had turned up was a unique integrally suppressed Makarov pistol, something that your average Joe on the street couldn't have procured—especially in India. It showed they had training and the backing of a state—in this case, given the evidence, probably the Pakistani ISI.

I turned to Jennifer. "What's the distance between here and our hotel?"

She tapped on her tablet and said, "Looks like about thirty minutes, but it's easy travel. No traffic time to worry about."

"Yeah, well, that's more than I want. We'll take weapons. Concealed sidearms only."

Knuckles nodded and the door opened. Two perfunctory customs officials entered and asked for our passports. One went through the paperwork while the other moseyed about the cabin, peering behind chairs and checking the galley. We answered all of their questions, Jennifer provided our cover documentation, signed by the government of India, and we were done. They didn't even ask to see our luggage.

We watched them leave, and when they were clear, I said, "Okay, let's download the kit and get out of here."

I left them to it and went to talk to the pilots, who had the best job in the world. All they did was fly to some exotic place, then sit around a hotel waiting to fly somewhere else. The only thing that sucked was that they couldn't booze it up because they never knew when they'd be called for action. In this case, I could give them at least two nights of fun.

I said, "We're heading to the resort. You guys have a place near here?"

The captain said, "Yeah, right down the road. Hope it's not a shithole."

I laughed and said, "Well, the good news is we've got at least two days of advanced force work before anything happens, so you're off from General Order One for two nights. After that, stand by for a call."

The copilot blurt out, "Yeah! That's what I'm talking about!"

He held out his fist for a bump. I tapped it and said, "Don't go overboard here. I might need at least one pilot available and I don't want to be bailing you out of an Indian jail."

I turned back to the cabin, seeing Veep and Brett removing panels in the walls of the aircraft, exposing weapons and surveillance gear. I saw Veep pull out what looked like a 1911 pistol with an integral compensator and a red-dot sight. He said something and Brett countered with another 1911, this one more compact, with a threaded barrel. Neither were the striker-fired guns we had used in the past.

I said, "What are those? Where are the Glocks?"

Veep turned to me, looking embarrassed. Not for him, but for me. Knuckles said, "You shouldn't spend so much time laying on the beach in Charleston. They're Staccato 2011s. We've gone to them as our standard firearm."

That surprised me. "Forty-fives? We've gone back to old-school stuff?"

Honestly, I didn't mind, as I'd grown up in the special operations world with a 1911 forty-five caliber. It was like pulling teeth to get me to switch to the Glock in the first place.

He said, "No, they're nine-mil double stacks. But they're sweet shooting. Trigger like an icicle and a recoil impulse that is about perfect."

I took the compensated one, racked the slide, eyed the chamber to ensure it was empty, then let it ride home. I took aim at a screw in the wall and pulled the trigger. It *was* crisp. I said, "Leave this one. Take the compacts with the threaded barrel."

Brett smiled, looked at Veep, and said, "Told you."

Veep said, "But you won't believe how flat this one shoots, and with the SRO, you can't miss."

I said, "I hear you, but we're going for concealment over capability. And we might need to suppress."

That ended the argument. I turned to Knuckles and said, "You got a surveillance package we can take out of here without looking like we're setting up for a movie shoot?"

"Yeah. Already packed. One Pelican case with a little of everything. IP cameras, Growlers, GPS tags, and Wi-Fi penetration kits. Creed did a deep dive on the resort. It should all be plug-and-play on their own Wi-Fi system. All I need to do is log on, according to him."

"Perfect." I turned to Jennifer and said, "Transportation?"

She said, "Here now. Waiting on us."

"Even more perfect."

I got the attention of the group and said, "This should just be a walk in the park, but as usual, we won't treat it that way. First order of business is to get a layout of the grounds. We'll check in, then split up the property." I handed out a sheet of assignments with a map of the grounds, detailing who was checking out what. "Teams are Jennifer and me, Brett and Veep. Knuckles, you're on your own."

"Why am I alone?"

"Because you're so handsome. Work your magic on any female you see. Find out what you can."

That brought out a laugh, but I was only half kidding. Knuckles was a man-whore of the first order, with women flocking to him for some strange reason I could never understand. He might actually find something useful by himself.

He scowled but took the assignment list without any other protest. I said, "Keep your eyes and ears open and we might just get to enjoy this trip."

Brett rolled his eyes and said, "If they wanted a walk in the park, they wouldn't have asked for you."

CHAPTER 10

Inside the seedy hotel room Kamal was incredulous. He said, "Do the operation? You mean capture the billionaire? Are you mad? I'm sure they've locked down the resort, and that's if he's even going to show."

Mr. Chin said, "He'll show. He's looking at pre-wedding celebration venues for his daughter. This one and a place in Jaipur are the final two that made the cut. The RAW caught our man for terrorism, but they have nothing to do with his search for a wedding party site. He's going to rent the entire place, if he chooses it. He'll come."

"How does that even matter? Sidak was captured before he could learn any important information. We have the outside schematics and the guards along the seacoast, but we have nothing for the interior. We don't have the room number, the floor plans for the restaurants, the entry in and out of the kitchens, the parking structure, the security for the front doors, nothing. All we have is the back area by the ocean."

"That's all we need."

"What? That's the *least* of what we need. The original plan was to infiltrate while he was at dinner, utilizing the kitchen access as staff. We don't know anything about any of that. Ingress, egress, assault plan, it's all a vacuum."

Mr. Chin stood up and opened his briefcase, spreading out computer printouts of satellite pictures that were much more precise than any-thing seen from Google Earth. He said, "This is the resort. Yes, we don't know the interior of the buildings, but we know the grounds next to the ocean."

Manjit said, "Where did you get these? How does a Chinese com-pany have access to satellite technology?"

Mr. Chin said, "It's just commercial technology. We do mining all over the world. Of course we have access to such things. It's avail-able for purchase, if you have a subscription, which my company does. Enough with the questions. Let's get to the answers."

He pointed at the edge of the ocean on the printout and said, "As you can see, the drop down to the water is about seven feet for about a half mile both up and down from the resort. If you can get to the rocks out of the eyes of the guards, you can walk all the way into the resort without being seen."

He traced a finger along a cut that traversed the back of the hotel to the ocean, a scar that split through the greenery of the lawn. He said, "This is a water-drainage canal. There's a simple iron grate at the ocean, easy to defeat. Once you get inside here, you're on the grounds and behind the lackadaisical guard force. From here, you can snatch the target and retreat back to the ocean."

Kamal leaned over the printouts, seeing what he said was true but realizing he had glossed over a lot of tactical considerations. "What you say sounds easy, but it's much harder. For one, we'll have to hide the boat away from the resort, so it's either drag the target kicking and screaming to it, or bring it closer initially, where the guards will see it. For two, yeah, we can pop up behind the security and have the element of surprise, but once we conduct the assault, we'll have to deal with them. We'll have to kill them and fight our way out. Finally, this is all based on timing. He must be outside, near the pool, for us to even have a chance of succeeding. We can't penetrate the hotel, blazing our way in looking for him."

Mr. Chin nodded and said, "Yes, that's all true, but we also have assets on our side. We have your friends on the security detail. They can alert us to when the man is outside, within targeting range."

He pointed at the image and said, "This is a restaurant by the pool. From previous intelligence, I can say with confidence that he'll have lunch or dinner there during his stay. He enjoys the outdoors."

Manjit said, "So, what, we're supposed to sit on a boat out in the water for the next five days, waiting on a call? Then go barreling in because you say he's vulnerable?"

"No. You stay right here. In this hotel. You're two minutes from the beach. I'll have a Zodiac just like you used before. When the call comes, you can be within targeting range in under ten minutes."

Kamal considered the words, then said, "Even if all of that was true. Even if everything aligned, I'd need more men. I can't do this with four, and if the personal security men are only providing early warning, then this is not going to happen."

Mr. Chin said, "I have two more men. Not Sikhs, like you, but good men nonetheless. They can use a gun and are worth the money."

"If you can get them, then get four more and do this yourself. Pay us now and we'll be done and gone."

"It doesn't work that way. For one, they have no ties to the security detail. They have done none of the work you have on this. For another, they're just muscle. They obey orders, but don't make them. I need you for that. You and your men have proven adaptable and resilient."

Kamal showed no reaction, but deep inside, he was pleased by the compliment. He *did* matter in this world. He looked at his men, then said, "If—and it's a big *if*—we get him, what will you do with him?"

"Not your concern."

"Let me put it another way: if his life prohibits our ability to escape, do you want him dead? Or just let him go? Because my team comes first. If we get him and we're trying to escape but he's slowing us down, I'm not dying for the mission."

Mr. Chin tapped a finger to his chin, saying, "I see." He paused, then said, "Kill him."

Kamal said, "If that's the decision, then I'll just kill him on sight and escape."

"No. We want him alive. We need to know what he knows about the mine. Kill him only as a last resort."

Kamal nodded, looked around at his team, then said, "I need to discuss this with my men."

"What's to discuss? I told you the alternative."

Kamal stood up, the other three following his lead. Kamal said, "The alternative is being detained by RAW. I understand. What I don't understand is why RAW detained Sidak. He was just a groundskeeper. Why was RAW even there? What are you not telling us?"

Mr. Chin rose as well, and for the first time, Kamal saw a little fear. He said, "I'm not hiding anything. I have no idea why RAW zeroed in on him. It must have been something he said or did."

Kamal advanced on him and said, "Or something to do with the billionaire's visit. You say he's looking at wedding venues, but maybe he's doing something with the government, and they were waiting."

Mr. Chin said, "No, no, that's not it at all. I would know if that was the case. It was just bad luck."

"Why would you know? How *could* you know?"

Mr. Chin closed his briefcase, leaving the satellite imagery on the table. He said, "I'll give you a day to decide. Make the right decision."

He turned and left the room. Manjit exhaled and said, "We should just pack up and go. If they're going to roll us up, we shouldn't make it easy on them."

Kamal sat back down, tapping his finger on the satellite image, thinking. Agam said, "I agree with Manjit. We should go."

Kamal turned to Randeep and said, "What do you think?"

Randeep was a follower. Someone who wanted to please and didn't like being caught between his leader and the other men. He waffled, saying, "I guess it depends on what you're thinking."

Kamal said, "I'm thinking we can either get rolled up running like dogs, or we can take it to the enemy. This is our chance to really become the KCF. To do something with our lives instead of just donating money to the cause. The RAW might get us either way, but at least our death will be for something greater than a paycheck. *Sidak's* death will mean something."

Manjit said, "How? If we capture this guy it'll only help Mr. Chin. He'll take him, exploit him, and then blame us. You know that's what he'll do."

Kamal nodded and said, "Yes, that's exactly what he'll do if we follow his plan."

"Then why would we continue?"

"Because we're not going to follow his plan."

CHAPTER 11

I followed Jennifer into the Hyatt Club—a private area for high rollers and a little perk courtesy of Grolier Recovery Services reservation. Apparently Jennifer had been accumulating points. Either that, or the CIA was getting points off of us.

We checked in with our room number, proving we belonged, and then stepped down to the lounge area. They had a table set up with a bunch of fancy hors d'oeuvres, complete with little ceramic spoons holding individual sushi pieces, but that wasn't what I was looking for.

We wound through the area, Jennifer scanning for a section big enough for the team, and me scanning for the bar. I saw it in the corner, an oak cabinet set into the wall with self-service bottles. *Perfect.*

Jennifer found a couch opposite two chairs in the corner, right next to the plate glass windows overlooking the ocean, the sun starting to set on the horizon. The view was spectacular, with lush gardens, thick grass, and palm trees spreading out to the seawall, interrupted only by gravel paths threaded throughout. It looked like a photograph created by AI instead of the real world. I had to admit, after my initial complaining, this trip was turning out pretty good. I let her sit, then said, "Pirate drink?"

She smiled and said, "I guess it's after hours. Sure."

I left her, saw Brett and Veep come through the door, and pointed to her location. They nodded and went that way. I began to make a couple of rum and cokes but was stopped by one of the hostesses, a strikingly pretty Indian woman. She said, "Let me, please," with a charming accent.

Her beauty left me at a loss for words for a second. Ordinarily, I'd push such a request away, because I definitely knew what I liked and didn't need someone to do my own work, but in this case I backed off, saying, "Sure, I'd like—"

She said, "Two Bacardi and cokes, highball glasses, with a twist of lime?"

Now confused, because that's exactly what I wanted, I stuttered and she laughed, a little melody floating out. Knuckles appeared behind her, saying, "I'll have a bourbon if he can't talk."

She said, "Of course. He's just like you said: a stoic American."

I looked at Knuckles, and he smiled, saying, "I met her working the pool service today. Nadia, this is Pike. Pike, this is Nadia. Treat him well, because he's my boss."

She let out her tinkling laugh again and said, "Of course. Take your seats. I'll bring the drinks."

We walked away, and I said, "What the hell, man? I was only kidding about using some honeypot operation for information."

He said, "It's not like that. We struck up a conversation and sort of clicked. She's pretty cool, and she's also switched on to the entire flow around this place."

"So you gave her my name? What else did you give her?"

"That just came about because I told her my name was Knuckles. She didn't believe me, so I told her my boss was named Pike. It's not a big deal."

"She knew what I drink, for God's sake. How deep did this conversation go?"

"Just enough to solidify our cover. She knows why we're here by the cover. That's all."

We reached the table, and Brett said, "So you met Knuckles' latest conquest."

I sat down on the couch next to Jennifer, giving Knuckles one of the chairs, and said, "Yeah, I did. That didn't take long."

Jennifer said, "To meet her? I see she's very pretty."

I felt my face start to flush, and said, "What? No. Not that. It didn't take long for Knuckles to get to work. That's all I meant."

She let out a little smirk, showing me she still had the ability to penetrate my armor, and like clockwork, I got aggravated. I said, "Enough of this shit. What do we have?"

She squinted her eyes and pushed her knee into mine, letting me know that she was kidding and that I was being an ass. Which I was, but it was *her* fault.

Knuckles said, "Well, she's not a conquest yet—and probably won't ever be—but she's a wealth of information. Everyone on the staff here is on pins and needles because of the billionaire mining guy's visit. He's ostensibly here to check out a location for a pre-wedding party, but we know that's shit. The good news is there's no indication that Bostwick or the RAW are having a meeting. The staff all think the security upgrades are for the rich dude. The bad news is Nadia knows his visit here is fake."

"How?"

"Believe it or not, she's friends with the daughter who's getting married. They've already settled on party locations in the upstate. Jaipur and Agra. She knows he's not here for a recce."

"Does she know why he's here for real? That could be a compromise."

"We didn't get that far. I didn't want to push it."

I nodded and said, "How is a hostess at a resort in Goa friends with a billionaire's daughter from Mumbai? That doesn't make any sense."

He raised his hands and said, "How would I know? That's just what she said."

Which set a little tick in the back of my brain. Something to explore later. I said, "When's he getting here?"

"Tomorrow. Two days before Bostwick. I guess he's either really checking out the place for a party or just wanting to relax for a few days on the Indian government dime."

Nadia showed up with our drinks, setting ours on the table but handing Knuckles his bourbon straight to his hand, saying, "Are you enjoying the stay?"

I had to admit, she was definitely a damn hammer. She'd give Jennifer a run for her money any day. Not that I'd say that out loud.

Knuckles said, "Best ever. Sorry, everyone, this is Nadia. Nadia, this is everyone."

She smiled, a radiant shine that would captivate every single American male under the age of ninety, and said, "So, do any of you have names that don't resemble a fish or a part of the hand?"

Jennifer smiled and said, "Not specifically. In our line of work, everyone gets a nickname."

Nadia scrunched her eyes and said, "Archeological work makes you have nicknames?"

Jennifer glanced at me, clearly wondering if she'd said too much, then said, "It's more of a company thing than an archeological thing."

Nadia nodded, then said, "What's yours?"

Jennifer took a breath and said, "It's a company thing."

Nadia waited, and finally Jennifer relented. "It's Koko."

Jennifer absolutely hated her callsign, and having to say it out loud to a woman who was genuinely interested must have driven a spike into her self-esteem.

Nadia looked confused, turning to Knuckles. He said, "It's the talking gorilla. The one that died a couple of years ago."

If possible, she looked even more confused. She went back to Jennifer and said, "Your nickname is from a gorilla?"

Jennifer said, "It's complicated. I don't like it either."

That caused all of us to laugh, and it clearly made Nadia uncomfortable, thinking we were making fun of her because she was a woman. Which absolutely wasn't the case. She just didn't get it.

More sharply than was probably allowed by the Hyatt staff, she said, "If you want anything else, let me know," and then stalked off.

Knuckles said, "Was that necessary? Jesus. She now thinks I'm a Neanderthal."

Jennifer chuckled and said, "Sorry about that, but honestly, it's your fault. You gave me the damn callsign, and now you can live with the repercussions."

Knuckles said, "Touché, I guess."

I said, "Okay, down to business. What did we find?"

Brett said, "The front access is pretty secure. It's a long winding drive up to a circular turnaround, with a single entrance coupled with a metal detector and guards. Nobody's armed, but if you were coming in that way, you aren't guaranteed successful exfil. It wouldn't be my choice."

Veep said, "But there are plenty of infiltration areas on foot. The area is huge, with plenty of ways to get inside without going through the front. If the mission is kill instead of capture, it could be done."

Knuckles said, "Nothing on the restaurant side of the house. There are four, but only one of them is good for an assault because it has a patio leading to the outside, but the others are like Veep said—no good for exfil. If someone wants to use them to ambush, they could do so, but they aren't getting away without a running gunfight. The only one that's a true risk is the pool bungalow restaurant. It's open three hundred and sixty degrees."

I said, "Cameras?"

"Got two facing the ocean on the north and south side of the property, right on the ocean, and one at an entrance to a maintenance section at the north end. It's full of plants and sheds, but it's a channelized access, as the fence runs east and west beyond it."

"Could you get in, just as a tourist?"

"Yeah, I did. No issues."

I nodded and said, "Well, that's about what we found. The shore side is wide open, but you'd be hard pressed to infiltrate using that with the guard force on the water. We counted three separate posts, all inside the grounds, but looking out at the ocean. None of the guards are paying any attention, but they *are* there. The one area of concern is a drainage cut that winds straight into the grounds. It's deep enough that you could walk down it hunched over and get inside past the guards without being seen."

Knuckles said, "I saw that as well. Want another camera on it?"

"Can't hurt, if you have one to spare, but this is looking like an easy day."

Brett said, "So it *is* going to be a walk in the park. Perfect. Tomorrow, let's go get our jihad on at the crash site and come back here for some pool time."

By "crash site," he meant our cover stop at the archeological location we'd ostensibly come here to service, mainly because the old church looked like someone from heaven had crashed a huge bus into it in the past.

I said, "Yeah, this is panning out to be easy enough. Everyone get some sleep tonight and we'll head out to the church in the morning. The only thing that concerns me is that the enemy knows everything that we do, and they were here conducting a reconnaissance. If they're coming, they'll exploit any gap we've found, and probably ones we haven't."

CHAPTER 12

Using one hand to steady himself in the shallow wooden boat, his other holding an old set of binoculars, Kamal said, "Varsha, you want to look at anything else?"

In front of him at the bow, Varsha said, "No. I didn't need to come out here in the first place."

Kamal wasn't surprised by the answer. A large, hairy man with dark skin and a bulbous head, Varsha was one of two men Mr. Chin had provided, and true to Mr. Chin's word, both of them were more muscle than brains. They rarely talked and offered nothing to advance the planning, but both had a brooding aura of violence around them. Kamal suspected that they were into the drug trade, especially after seeing the ease with which they'd moved around the town of Baga after nightfall. As if they'd been there before and had no fear of any of the dark alleys outside the neon lights of Tito's Lane.

Kamal was convinced they could execute whatever linear task he gave them, but they couldn't act on their own or deal with any unforeseen complications. They were muscle, pure and simple, and Kamal would need to remember that.

Kamal turned to the rear of the boat, saying, "Manjit, you?"

Working the outboard motor, Manjit said, "I'd really like to see how close we can get to the resort dock before those guards react."

"Me too, but the risk is not worth the reward. No need to get them nervous before we attack. Tonight is probably going to be the night."

Last night Mr. Chin had brought over the two muscle heads and told them that the billionaire had eaten dinner on the outside patio restaurant near the pool. The good news was they'd cleared out everyone else from the restaurant, claiming it was reserved for a private party, so there was little worry about harming innocent bystanders, something Manjit was adamant about. The bad news was they didn't know if the billionaire would eat there again.

Manjit said, "I know, but what if I can't get in? What if they're alert enough to start shooting at me? What are you going to do?"

"Don't worry about that. For one, the guards aren't armed. For another, they'll be focused on the inside once we attack. They won't be looking for you because we're going to be the biggest diversion on the planet," Kamal said.

"You hope. I don't like a plan based on hope."

"Well, you're getting the easy part. I'm not sure we can get through the grate to the drainage cut. That'll be the end of it if we can't."

The Grand Hyatt resort fronted about four hundred meters of shore, the hotel buildings set back about a hundred meters away from the water, separated by expansive grounds full of paths, palm trees, and landscaping. The small rocky beach abutted a five-foot seawall that rose to the grass above, and while there wasn't a fence, there were abundant shrubs and flowers to prevent a guest from falling over. The only route to the beach was a set of stairs from the dock about halfway down the seawall—the same dock Manjit wanted to approach. Just beyond it to the south was the drainage cut they were planning to use for infiltration. The one with the grate.

They had found a larger beach just north of the hotel grounds with plenty of small sailboats, kayaks, and windsurfers on the shore. Originally, Kamal had planned to land the boat there, leave Manjit behind, and skulk down the seawall for the mission, returning the same way— hopefully with the billionaire in tow. After finding the dock at the resort, Kamal had decided to split the mission: drop off at the beach, then call Manjit forward to the dock, escaping from there instead of trying to run back down the sand with a prisoner who would likely be fighting them the whole way. Worst case, they might be carrying him unconscious.

Manjit said, "What are you going to do if you can't get through the grate?"

Kamal trained his binoculars on the cut, seeing a wrought-iron structure threaded with a chain and a simple padlock. He said, "The only thing that will stop us is if it's rusted shut. We should be good."

He lowered the binos and said, "Let's take it back to Baga. I've seen enough."

Varsha said, "About time. I'm getting hungry."

Kamal gave Manjit the side-eye at the comment, and Manjit hit the throttle, bringing the bow out of the water and causing Varsha to grab for the gunwales. Kamal smiled but said nothing.

The rest of the trip was spent in silence, as the outboard and wind made it impossible to talk without shouting. They went around a rocky point, the top crowned by Fort Aguada, the bottom housing the jail where Sidak had died, and Kamal was happy for the silence, not wanting to talk.

They reached a section of flatland, the sand stretching for kilometers, and cruised past multiple beaches, the surf shacks of each shuttered, waiting on the tourists yet to come. In another month, each of the beaches would be jammed with sunbathers and swimmers, but with monsoon season fading but still threatening, just a few beachcombers could be seen. Another plus for the mission.

Manjit cut the throttle and they motored into the section of shore known as Baga Beach, the small hamlet of Baga just beyond. Kamal could see Tito's Lane standing out as the beating heart of the town, the lane of bars and nightclubs dead-ending right at the beach.

Manjit cruised into the shore, lifting the outboard as the surf grew shallow, the bow crunching into the sand a good four feet from shore.

Kamal said, "Varsha, we'll get this."

Varsha leapt out of the bow, splashing into the ankle-deep water and trudging to shore without a word.

Manjit said, "Why'd you do that? This damn thing is heavy, and we could use his muscles. It's not like he does much of anything else."

Kamal hopped out and steadied the bow, letting Manjit lash down the outboard. He said, "Because I wanted to talk to you alone, before we get back to the room with the rest of the team."

He waited until Manjit had finished and leapt into the water, then they both heaved the heavy wooden boat farther up to shore, resting the bow in damp sand.

Manjit let go and said, "What's up?"

"We're going to have to do something about the Thugees." Kamal used the nickname Manjit had given the two men Mr. Chin had provided.

"What do you mean? You don't think they'll be with us?"

"No, I don't. They're only in this for the money. They're not going to be too happy when we kill Mr. Chin and they lose their paycheck."

Kamal could see that Manjit wasn't comfortable with the idea. He continued, "We can't take the chance that they try to prevent us from removing Mr. Chin and stealing his boat."

"So you want to kill them too? I already told you I wasn't good with killing any civilians on this mission, and this is pretty close. I know they're not innocent, but it doesn't mean I want to start slaughtering anyone who might stop us. We need to maintain our honor. For the cause."

"I understand that. I don't want to kill them either, but I don't see a choice here."

Manjit nodded, thinking, then said, "Mr. Chin has threatened us. He's basically said we do this or we get tortured as terrorists by RAW, so he has become an enemy. We don't know if these two men are the enemy. Maybe we should broach what we're trying to do. Maybe they'll join us. We could use the help."

Kamal shook his head, saying, "If they don't agree, they'll immediately tell Mr. Chin. We'll be done. We can't take that risk. They aren't Sikhs and don't care about our cause. In fact, they may want to harm us *because* we're Sikhs. We've both seen that before."

They walked in silence for a moment, entering Tito's Lane, the nightclubs and bars closed and looking shabby in the sharp light of day, each of them waiting for the sun to set before starting life again, when the neon lights would hide their scars.

Kamal said, "How about this? We don't kill them. We just push them overboard within sight of the shore. Let them swim out."

"They'll be caught by the police looking for us."

"So? That'll help the mission, and we aren't harming them. All they can do is lead the police to Mr. Chin, and after we reach his boat, he'll be dead."

Mr. Chin had dictated that once they had successfully captured the billionaire, Thakkar, they were to rendezvous with him just like they had on the Sidak rescue failure, but this is where Mr. Chin's plan would end. Kamal intended to kill him, throw him overboard, and then take Thakkar for exploitation in support of the Sikh cause.

Exactly what that exploitation would be was an open question. Kamal honestly hadn't thought the endstate all the way through yet.

Manjit thought about it for a moment, then nodded, saying, "That would work. I can live with them swimming to shore."

Kamal smiled and patted him on the back, saying, "Good, because I need your mind right for this. I'm sure Mr. Chin will call tonight."

CHAPTER 13

Sitting with Jennifer at the outside patio restaurant, I was glad for having worn a rain jacket. Not for any rain, but because the temperature had turned cool enough to want it once the sun had gone down. The restaurant was apparently oblivious to the cooling weather, the overhead pavilion roof having multiple ceiling fans still spinning as if it was the heat of the day.

Jennifer zipped her jacket up higher and said, "How long are we going to wait until we run the test?"

I looked at my watch and said, "Knuckles is checking the southeastern camera now, the one at the road. Brett's hitting the northern garden entrance in thirty minutes. We'll go thirty after that, at nine."

We had our infrared cameras set up around the perimeter, but we needed to test them in actual conditions—in this case during darkness—so I'd split the team into a time schedule, with Veep up in the TOC monitoring the cameras as we went by them, letting us know if we needed to make any modifications to the field of view or infrared beam.

Jennifer and I were going to check out the three on the beach—one at each end of the property, and the third at the drainage cut—by taking a nighttime stroll along the shore.

Jennifer pointed at a sign and said, "We're going to have to leave here before then."

I turned and saw the same little tripod I'd seen last night, "Patio Reserved for Private Party at 8:30 P.M." I said, "Again? That guy takes over the breakfast room each morning, and now he's cramping my style out here next to the pool?"

Jennifer smiled and said, "I guess when you're as rich as he is, you can get away with it."

I heard my earpiece crackle, then Knuckles came on, saying, "How'd that look?"

Veep came back: "Good. Really good. No issues."

We each had our operational comms on, both to conduct the tests but also to conduct a communications check. Bostwick wasn't arriving until tomorrow, and the meeting with RAW and the billionaire wasn't until the following day, but I wanted to ensure everything was working with enough time to fix any problems.

Knuckles said, "Great, so I'm good on this end?"

Veep said, "Yep. You're off the clock."

He said, "Just what I wanted to hear. Headed to the pool for a beer."

At that, I clicked in, saying, "You'd better be quick about it. Thakkar has taken the outdoor bar for himself again."

Cryptically, he said, "I've got an in. I'm good."

I looked at Jennifer, but she just raised her eyebrows. Two minutes later, he came sauntering in with Nadia by his side, her wearing the same outdoor clothes she had on when we saw her earlier at the church in Old Goa.

I said, "Should have known."

They walked over to us, and I said, "We meet again. If I didn't know any better, I'd say you were following us."

She laughed and said, "You just happened to go to the same place I wanted to on my day off. I'd never seen the ruins before."

We'd woken up this morning and made our trek to the UNESCO heritage site that was providing our cover, the Saint Augustine church ruins in the town of Old Goa.

Once the heart of the Portuguese empire, it was built on a swamp and had been abandoned, not because of an invading force but from rampant disease among the population. Cholera and dysentery had taken enough of a toll that, eventually, smarter heads had prevailed and moved to higher ground, but not before several magnificent Catholic churches and convents had been built.

The village itself was what you'd see from an American town midway through the last century, when the interstate was built and passed them by—full of original buildings the locals were proud of, but mainly just living in stasis as if the future hadn't taken a detour around them. In an effort to stop the passage of time, they'd actually entombed one of the bishops in a church on the main square, and tourists were now allowed to come on by and see the body, like it was a mummified American Indian on Route 66, designed solely to get people off the very freeway that had left them behind.

It was still the heart of Catholicism within India, with its last splash on the world stage being when Pope John Paul II visited in 1986—something that was heralded in every building within the town nearly forty years later. The area even still had a connection to Portugal, so much so that if one could prove one's lineage, one was permitted to apply for Portuguese citizenship and a passport.

After setting up our bona fides in the town, we'd traveled to the church ruins, ostensibly to check out road conditions and access routes, but I'll be damned if it wasn't pretty cool.

Because India hadn't done a whole lot of conservation, it looked like something out of an Indiana Jones movie, and Jennifer loved it. We traipsed around the site, with her checking out every little corner, and then we'd bumped into Nadia, all by herself.

Which was strange.

She'd expressed surprise to see us, and was friendly enough, but I thought it had been something else. Nobody from this area would come visit the ruins of a church they'd supposedly grown up next to on their day off from work.

Knuckles had struck up a conversation, and I'd let him, because Nadia could still be a useful conduit of information, and they'd gone traipsing about the ruins on their own.

And now they were in the bar together.

Jennifer said, "Well, we'll all be leaving here soon, because they're about to close us down."

Knuckles said, "Not if you don't want to. Nadia knows Thakkar's daughter. If we want to stay, we can."

She said, "That's true. I do, and I'm off tonight. I'm supposed to have dinner with him, so if you want to, you could join us."

Knuckles knew we would say no, because he knew what we were about to do with the cameras, but it was pretty smart to get himself at the table.

I said, "Thank you, that's very nice, but we've already eaten, and I was going to take Koko here for a walk on the shore."

Jennifer scowled at her callsign, but Nadia smiled, saying, "I get it now. Sorry if I was rude the other night. Knuckles told me he gave it to you. It's a tease from the people you work with, not you as a woman. Right?"

Jennifer nodded and said, "Yeah, but I'd like a different joke."

She looked at Knuckles and said, "I wonder what name he'd give me."

I could see the spark between them and once again wondered at the source of his charm on the opposite sex. Yeah, he was good-looking enough, in a hippy crossed with a Hells Angel sort of way, but he had some effect on women that was just unworldly.

I stood up and said, "Enjoy the dinner. I'm sure Mr. Thakkar will make it worth your while."

Knuckles smiled and said, "Enjoy the walk. I'm sure it'll live up to your expectations. Mine did."

CHAPTER 14

We left the lights of the pavilion restaurant and entered the darkness of the grounds, the only illumination emanating from small solar lights along the concrete paths.

I said, "I don't know about her."

Jennifer took my hand and said, "What do you mean? Are you jealous she didn't come on to you first?"

I chuckled and said, "No, that's not it. I'm still amazed that *you* came on to me, back in the day."

She inched closer and said, "Not how I remember it, but I do like pirates," which, honestly, was the best way to describe me. At over six feet, with close-cropped brown hair and an inconvenient scar that ran through an eyebrow and into my cheek, I *did* look like a pirate. I was the guy at a party you'd take one look at, and if you didn't know me, you'd wander off to converse with someone else. But that wasn't what I was talking about.

I said, "That's not what I meant. Didn't you think it was unusual for Nadia to bump into us at the church today? Didn't that raise a hair on your neck?"

"No, not really. It was her day off. What do you mean?"

"Yeah, so she's supposedly worked here for years, and on her day off—in an area she supposedly grew up in—she went to see the ruins of a church by herself?"

Jennifer turned to me, saying, "What are you implying?"

I realized we'd walked all the way across the grounds, the ruins of an old Portuguese chapel to our front—something the resort was quite proud of—and the drainage canal just beyond. Small and made of stone, it was about fifty by seventy feet and covered in vines.

I stopped, pretending to read the plaque outside, which was a little ridiculous because it was dark. I said, "I think she's either RAW or she's the enemy. I think she's been tracking us since we entered the resort, trying to uncover why we're here and determine if we're a threat."

Jennifer said, "Pike, that's insane. She's just a waitress who was being friendly. You're getting paranoid."

I said, "Yeah, maybe, but her trip today makes absolutely no sense. When's the last time you went to Fort Sumter—by yourself—in Charleston? Her going to see a tourist attraction in her own hometown just reeks of a coincidence that doesn't stand up."

I saw her wheels turning and continued, "Last night I just thought it was Knuckles being Knuckles, but when she showed up at the church, I began to wonder. Now she's with Knuckles again. He thinks she's attracted to his natural charms, but I think she's using him for information just like he's doing with her. Either she's with RAW, or she's a sleeper that RAW missed."

We heard Brett come on the radio, doing his camera check with Veep. Jennifer ignored it and said, "So what do you want to do about it?"

"Honestly, I don't know at this point. But I'm damn sure going to dedicate Knuckles to be with her during the meeting. We need eyes on her the entire time."

Brett and Veep chattered about his check, and Jennifer said, "I hope you're wrong. I can't stand how this job makes us think the worst of people. I don't want to start questioning everyone who asks me for the time."

I said, "Well, if she's RAW, I'm not thinking the worst at all. In fact, I'm a little impressed with the thoroughness. We are, after all, just an archeological company from the United States, not a bunch of Muslims from Qatar looking for investments."

"And if she's not?"

"Then she's just a waitress who's fallen for Knuckles. Or she's a terrorist."

Jennifer said nothing. I took her hand again and said, "Look, this is supposed to be a walk in the park, and I'm just trying to keep it that way. Let's go to the beach and take our stroll."

She nodded and we went back toward the restaurant, the incandescent lights of the dock beckoning about halfway down. Brett kept up his chatter on the radio, listening to Veep give him directions on the angle of the camera, and we reached the dock, which was really just a thatched-roof gazebo with stairs leading down to the sand and a thin wooden walkway jutting out into the water. A guard was stationed at the entrance, and I thought for a minute he was going to block us from going down.

I said, "Hey, can we go for a moonlight walk?"

He appeared embarrassed, and I realized his English wasn't good enough to understand what I wanted. I started to say something else, and my earpiece came on again, this time for me.

"Pike, Koko, it's not your time yet. I'm still working Blood's camera."

Jennifer backed away out of earshot of the guard and clicked on, saying, "We're still up top. What are you talking about?"

One ear listening to the conversation, I said to the guard—more with my arms than my voice—"Can we go walk on the beach?"

The guard smiled and nodded, and I knew he didn't understand me. The only way to find out was to walk past him to the stairs. If he stopped us, we'd have to come up with another plan to test the cameras. On the net, I heard, "Never mind. I got a group walking by the camera at the north end. Five of them. At first I thought it was you guys."

So much for the walk on the beach. I smiled again at the guard, said, "Thank you," and walked to Jennifer. She was looking at me in confusion, saying into the net, "Five guys on the beach? Right now?"

I heard, "Yep. Just went past. You don't need to check that camera. It's working fine."

She said, "Roger that," and I motioned to her. We began walking back to the chapel, and I said, "We can't do anything until those guys are gone, so we've got some time."

This trip we went past the chapel to the drainage ditch. It had two wooden bridges that crossed it, one near the chapel and the other closer to the buildings of the hotel. I stopped between them, right near the edge of the canal, and said, "Got any ideas to kill the time?"

She said, "Not really. We could go back to the restaurant and talk to Knuckles."

I said, "It's sort of dark right here."

She said, "Yeah, it is. Let's go back to the restaurant."

"I mean, it's *really* dark right here. I can think of better ways to kill the time."

I saw her face me in confusion, then felt her slap my stomach, saying, "Yeah, it'll be a cold day in hell before I'm caught in the bushes out here. Save it for tonight."

I laughed, took her hand, and turned back to the restaurant, saying, "Couldn't hurt to ask."

My earpiece came alive, Veep saying, "Pike, Pike, second camera's feed is fine as well. That group is working on the grate."

What?

Jennifer looked at me the same way I felt, and I said, "Working it how?"

"They've got bolt cutters and they're cutting the chain."

What the hell?

I looked back toward the dock a hundred meters away, thinking about jogging to the guard and letting him know that he had some intruders. Veep's next words shut that idea down.

"They're through the grate. They're coming up the cut at a run. Pike, they've got weapons. I say again, they have guns."

CHAPTER 15

The radio call sent a bolt of adrenaline through me, pushing my decision making into overdrive. In a nanosecond I realized that we were about to have a repeat of the 2008 Mumbai attack, and there was no way I could reach the guard at the dock before these guys made it to the hotel grounds. The only way to prevent them from committing a massacre was to stop them from getting out of the cut. It was now my own private Thermopylae, with Jennifer and me acting like the Spartans.

Since our official duties wouldn't start until Bostwick arrived, I'd decided that the risk of the discovery of our weapons outweighed the negligible reward we'd get by carrying them around, so we were both unarmed, our Staccatos locked in a Pelican case with Veep in the TOC.

I turned to the cut, racing to the wooden bridge over it, Jennifer to my right farther down. On the net, I said, "Veep, alert the hotel, Blood/ Knuckles, get your ass to the drainage ditch."

I heard Knuckles say, "On the way," just as a man came over the top of the canal directly in front of Jennifer. He had a strange-looking pistol in his right hand, his face registering absolute shock upon seeing Jennifer in front of him. She slapped her hands onto his shirt at the chest and dropped backwards, planting her foot into his stomach and flinging him over her head.

A second man scrambled up the side of the cut, this time in front of me, and surprise registered on his face upon seeing me no more than a foot away. He swung his pistol toward my head and I immediately trapped his wrist with my left hand. Before he could react, I rotated my body until my back was to his chest and wrapped my right arm over his shoulder, sliding my right leg past his. I whipped my body downward, flinging him over my back to the ground and landing hard on his chest.

I felt his ribs crack, the blow causing him to drop his pistol. I rolled off him, snatched it and spun around, praying the thing was loaded. I put the front sight on his skull and broke the trigger, the gun making a muted spit, but the damage to his head was viscerally apparent. I heard another suppressed round and saw the first man shooting at Jennifer as she dove behind the old stone chapel for cover.

I snapped a bullet his way, missed, then heard the boom of an un-suppressed weapon, seeing his body flung backward from the impact. Two people came running around the side of the chapel, one with a pistol out searching for a target. I dropped my weapon and raised my arms. The barrel came my way and I shouted, "No, no!"

The pistol spit fire and I felt the crack of the round break the sound barrier right next to my head. I heard someone behind me scream and dropped to the earth, my arms out, shouting, "American! American!"

The two came running toward me, the one with the pistol still firing into the drainage cut. It was Nadia, Knuckles right behind her. I heard what sounded like a stampede of kangaroos running back to the beach, and then it grew quiet.

I rolled over and shouted, "Jennifer!"

Knuckles said, "She's okay."

I heard, "Here!" and she came around the corner of the chapel, looking no worse for wear. I looked up at Nadia and said, "Did you learn how to shoot while exploring old churches by yourself?"

Knuckles hoisted me to my feet, and she said, "I could ask you people the same thing."

* * *

Riding back to the mother ship, Kamal couldn't believe the debacle that had just occurred. Everything had gone perfectly, right up until they'd passed through the old iron grate on the beach.

Kamal had snaked behind the two hired guns, trying to remain quiet, third in the line of men. He'd felt confident. In charge. The grate had fallen just like he'd said it would. It had taken less than four seconds for them to cut the links in the chain, and then another minute to break the grate from the rust that had set in, the only concern being the groan the grate let out at being opened after a long rest.

Once it was freed, the five of them squeezed through, then squatted for a moment on the other side, waiting to see if anyone at the resort had noticed. The walls of the cut were only about three feet at the entrance but grew larger the farther it went in, until it was about seven feet at the buildings themselves. The trick was to go deep enough in to get past the outer edge of the guard force, but not go so far that they'd have to use each other to get on the grounds.

In a crouch, he said, "Okay, let's go. The Thugees lead. When we get to the first bridge, we go up."

Varsha said, "What did you just call me?"

Kamal slapped him on the shoulder and said, "It's a compliment. You guys lead and we'll follow. Get up top and run to the pavilion. We'll be right behind you. You kill any security in the way, and we'll get Thakkar."

Mollified, Varsha looked at the other hired muscle and said, "Let's go."

They jogged, crouched over, waiting until the walls gave them enough height to avoid discovery, and reached the first bridge.

Kamal stopped them and said, "This is it. You ready?"

Varsha brandished his integrally suppressed Makarov and said, "Yes. You'd better be right behind me."

"We will be. Go."

Varsha and his friend turned, grabbed some foliage on the edge of the cut, and hoisted themselves onto the grounds of the resort. Kamal looked at his men and said, "This is it. No backing out now. No surrender."

Randeep and Agam nodded, and Kamal turned to the wall of the cut, starting to climb out. Kamal heard a suppressed round and immediately thought, *We're shooting already?*

He heard a grunt, some shouting, then an unsuppressed round splitting the night. He reached the top of the cut and saw one man on the ground and another rushing to him. He grabbed a thatch of vines and hoisted himself to the edge of the lawn, then saw a shadow aiming a pistol. It spit fire, tearing into his left ear and splitting apart their entire assault.

He screamed and fell into the drainage ditch, but the bullets kept coming, peppering the far wall of the cut. He shouted, "Back! Back!" and they all began running the way they had come, to the grate on the beach.

They went through it, with Kamal calling Manjit just offshore, screaming into the small handset, "Come now! Come now! We're on the run!"

They raced down the beach until they reached the dock, hearing a guard shout at them from above. Kamal ignored him, saying, "Get to the end of the dock, right now."

They scuttled down the small wooden pier and dove into the water, swimming out, away from the resort. Manjit met them in the open water, helped them aboard, and then rotated the direction of the boat, swinging it away from shore. He hit the throttle so hard the bow rose above the surf, the boat racing away.

Working the outboard, Manjit screamed above the noise, "What happened?"

Kamal said, "We failed. Get us to the boat."

They rode out into the sea in silence, eventually conducting a rendezvous with Mr. Chin. He counted the people in the boat and knew the mission had been a true failure.

After getting everyone on the larger craft, Mr. Chin said, "What happened?"

Sitting on a bench, his head in his hands, Kamal didn't want to talk about it. Not only had they failed in Mr. Chin's mission, but in so doing, they'd failed in *his* ultimate mission.

Mr. Chin said again, "What happened? Where is Thakkar?"

Kamal looked up and said, "They were lying in wait. They knew we were coming."

"What? How?"

"I don't know, but as soon as we assaulted, we were stopped. Right at the cut, right where we entered the grounds. Like they were waiting on us."

Mr. Chin leaned in and saw the blood leaking out of Kamal's head and onto his shirt. "You've been shot?"

Kamal leapt to his feet and said, "Yes, I was shot! They almost killed all of us. Something you promised wouldn't happen."

He touched his ear, brought his hand back and saw the red. In a lower voice, he said, "They almost killed me."

Mr. Chin let the accusation slide and said, "I need specifics. Who? Who was it? RAW?"

Kamal heard the question, then realized how badly he'd been duped on this mission. Mr. Chin knew more than he was saying. With steel in his voice, he said, "They were American. What have you not told me about this billionaire? Why were Americans waiting on us?"

Mr. Chin ignored that question, instead asking, "How do you know they were Americans?"

"Because they were shouting, 'American! American! Don't shoot!'"

"Wait, so the Americans who stopped you weren't part of the Indian response?"

Kamal considered for a moment, then said, "No, I guess not. They stopped your two men as soon as they exited the cut but then seemed to be afraid of getting shot themselves."

"What about my men? Where are they?"

Kamal said, "I have no idea. They were the first ones out of the cut, and they were both down by the time I got to the top. They're probably dead."

"Probably, or for certain?"

Kamal looked at him in disgust and said, "Probably. But you'd rather they be dead, wouldn't you?"

Mr. Chin said, "Only if it affects this mission."

He turned and nodded at another Chinese person in the cockpit of the yacht, and the vessel began heading north. He said, "What makes you sure they were sent to stop you, other than them just being there?"

Kamal took a seat on a cushion and said, "Because they eliminated your muscle as if they were children. The Americans weren't tourists in the wrong place at the wrong time. If they were, they'd be dead instead of your men."

Mr. Chin nodded and said, "Okay, well, it looks like we have to switch to Plan B. Instead of capturing Thakkar, we kill him."

The door to our little "holding cell" opened, and Knuckles entered the room. The man in civilian clothes pointed at Jennifer, and she rose, glancing at me. I said, "Just tell them what happened."

He let her exit the room, then closed the door, leaving me alone with Knuckles. So far, they hadn't rounded up Brett or Veep, even as they had to have ascertained we were all together. Especially since Nadia knew that. Maybe she wasn't going to drag us into this and was letting our pathetic story of "just a couple of lucky tourists" stand.

If she was, then she was most definitely covering for us, because there was no way to explain how Knuckles knew we were being attacked at the drainage cut, leading to her following him and saving the day. She knew we were something other than an archeological company. The question was: Why didn't she tell anyone else?

I said, "How'd it go?"

"Same questions, same answers." He glanced around as he said it, then looked at me, asking without asking if the place was bugged.

I said, "Don't think so. They didn't have time. If it was someone's office, I'd wonder if it was wired for sound from the management, but it's just a break room."

After the shoot-out, Nadia had begun talking into a radio she'd had hidden somewhere, and the drainage cut became overrun with a swarm of various Indian authority figures. One man came up to Nadia and she spoke to him in Hindi, then pointed at us, saying, "If you don't mind, please accompany this man."

We did, acting as if we were over-shocked tourists from the action, and the man took us to the lobby of the hotel, a sweeping area with a veranda that opened to the grounds outside. We walked past the desk we'd used to check in, then down a hallway to another room, this one sparsely furnished with a folding table, several metal chairs, and a bulletin board with hotel news tacked to it, the only other fixtures a refrigerator, a sink, and a small coffeepot.

It was clearly the first place they could find to isolate us, and so far, we hadn't been accused of anything nefarious, but I knew Nadia held the key to prevent this from turning into a shit show. Knuckles had been taken out first, then Jennifer, then me, the questions pretty normal—just name, rank, serial number stuff, with a blow-by-blow of what had occurred. We'd stuck to our cover of Grolier Recovery Services, showing them our letter from both from the university that had hired us and the invitation from the government, and so far it had held up. Knuckles had been taken a second time, and I expected the hammer to drop, but apparently it hadn't.

I said, "So they didn't ask anything new?"

He said, "Not really."

Usually when under interrogation, the interrogator will separate the people being questioned so they can't cook up a story—which is why Knuckles was sure the place we were in was wired for sound. Actually, with his answer, I had a moment of doubt, because the only reason I could see to ask the same questions was that the real interrogation was happening inside this room, giving us time to talk in "private." But the room was barren, with very few places to hide a surveillance device—

particularly on short notice—and I was pretty good at finding such things. Especially since it was my job to emplace them.

No, I was sure it wasn't bugged, even with the questions. The local authorities were killing time to keep us from demanding to be released while they figured out what to do with us. My only concern was Nadia.

I said, "They didn't press for more information?"

Knuckles said, "I mean, a little bit. Pinning down times and that sort of thing, but it was really just a rehash. Who was I, what was I doing there, that sort of thing."

"What did you tell them about running to me?"

"That I'd just seen you in the restaurant, you'd left, and I heard you shouting out on the lawn, so I went to help. I laid it on a little thick about being an American and not used to lawless places. That put them on their heels a little bit, with them now talking about how India wasn't lawless, blah, blah, blah."

"They didn't ask about how on earth you could have heard me shout from two hundred meters away?"

"Nope." He paused and said, "What did you give them?"

The hardest part about living a cover was that everyone had to say the same thing to back each other up. It wasn't unlike two bank robbers who'd been arrested on suspicion of doing a heist. You *had* to say the same story to escape suspicion, but living a cover was a day-to-day trial, not a single event. The story had to be the same between members even if you weren't involved in a crime.

Like us.

It went without saying that we'd both collapsed into our GRS cover. That wasn't what he was asking, though. He wanted to know what I'd said about the point of the spear, in case it had contradicted what he'd told them.

I said, "I just told them exactly what happened and that I was thankful they'd come as fast as they had. I asked who Nadia was, sing-ing her praises, and of course, acted like a blubbering mess of fear over my near death."

He chuckled and said, "Well, it was a damn miracle they popped out right in front of you two. Ten feet either way on that ditch and you would have had to close the distance. They'd have dropped you immediately."

I'd already thought about that, and it had sent a little bit of a mix of emotions through me: fear, anxiety, relief, but ultimately satisfaction and thanks to the gods of war. I'd always been good in a gunfight, and it wasn't solely because I was a better shot. I couldn't explain it, but for some innate reason, the universe always put me in a position to win. Maybe it was because I was quicker on the draw, or better at snap anal-ysis, or just too damn stubborn to quit, but it wasn't just luck.

The fear and trepidation came because I realized that wouldn't al-ways be the case. Sooner or later, the marble would roll onto red when I'd picked black. It was just the way of combat.

But that marble hit black tonight.

I said, "Who do you think those guys were?"

"I don't know. If it was because of the meeting with Kerry Bostwick and RAW, their intel was way off. A day early and a dollar short. I'm leaning to a coincidence."

"So you think they're Lashkar-e-Taiba? Muslim terrorists who were attacking just to attack?"

"Yeah. LeT did it once before in Mumbai, and after Hamas stole the headlines last year, maybe they're just copycatting to regain the spotlight."

I nodded, as that was an Occam's Razor answer, but the little things niggled at me.

I said, "Probably right, but they only had five guys, not dozens. And they didn't have any long guns, just those same old exotic integrally suppressed Makarovs like was found in the prison. Wouldn't you come boiling out with AK-47s and hand grenades if you intended to slaughter a bunch of people? Start out with shock and awe?"

"Yeah, those weapons are weird, that's for sure. Seems like it would be a hell of a lot easier to get AKs than those pistols, and why use a silencer anyway? They didn't need stealth."

I thought about it, then said, "On the other hand, maybe they intended to eliminate the guards quietly before starting the big show once inside. And maybe they had more men coming. They might have been just the advance force, preparing the battle space."

Knuckles tapped the table and said, "Well, two things are for sure: One, Bostwick's meeting will be the most secure in history, as this place will probably go into lockdown from local Barney Fifes. There's no way whoever it was will try a repeat now."

I said, "And two?"

"And two, these guys should be giving us a medal for saving their ass. Thank God we put in those cameras."

I laughed and said, "Jennifer did pretty well, didn't she?"

He nodded and said, "She's got the same luck as you. When she sent him over her back, he hammered his skull into the chapel wall. I saw it running in. He stood up and did a Scooby Doo shaggy-dog shake, like he was clearing his vision before shooting. Gave her time to get behind cover, and time for you to eliminate your guy."

I let out a rueful grin and said, "I missed Jennifer's guy. Couldn't believe it when I saw the bullet go wide. Thank God Nadia was armed."

I glanced at Knuckles and said, "Did you know that before?"

"No way. No idea. Came as a complete surprise. I was just as shocked as you were. I was yelling at her to get behind me as I was running. I knew she hadn't heard the radio call of guys with weapons."

I nodded and said, "Well, she can shoot." I turned in my chair, stuck my feet out, and said, "Why isn't she telling them her suspicions about us?"

He ran his finger in a circle on the table for a second, then said, "I think she's afraid of saying she was with me. I think she's protecting me and, in so doing, herself."

"Awww, bullshit. She was targeted against you. She's here collecting just like we are."

He grew incensed, saying, "She was *not*. We just hit it off."

I shook my head and said, "Don't become blind. She saw you were interested, and she used that to target you."

I saw him getting wound up and held out my hands in a gesture of surrender. I said, "Don't get me wrong, I have no issue with it, since it saved my life, but she was just doing her job."

He shook his head again, saying, "No, she wasn't. I'll give you she might have targeted me initially, because I came on to her. That's probably true, but we really connected. She might have been trying to glean information, but she was enjoying my company. She's a good egg."

"Oh, come on. Take off the blinders for a second. What you're saying is exactly what I'm saying. You followed her around the pool, and then she followed you around the church ruins. Then you took her up on the invitation for dinner. It's not like you boinked her or anything."

He said nothing. Just looked at me. I said, "It's not like you boinked her or anything, right?"

He kept his eyes on mine, remaining silent. I said, "Are you shitting me? You slept with her? When? How?"

I stood up, waving my arms and saying, "Did you do it in the rental car? In the broom closet? What the hell, man?"

He said, "Keep your voice down. If this place isn't wired, you don't need to announce it to the people outside. Yes, I slept with her, but it's not what you think. We just clicked. It was at her place, after we came back from the church, before the camera tests tonight. Did you think she gave me an invitation to dinner on the lawn?"

That just made me more aggravated. "In *her* room? She's probably got a tape of the whole thing. What the hell were you thinking?"

"She doesn't have a tape. That's not what this was about."

"How do you know? You're doing your thinking with your dick instead of your brain."

"Because I *know*, that's how."

"Did you check the bedroom before you got under the sheets? How do you *know*?"

"Because if she was going to film anything, it would have *been* in the bedroom."

"Yeah, so?"

And then it dawned on me before he even said it: "We didn't make it to the bedroom."

I rubbed my face, at a loss for words. Finally I said, "So you think she hasn't said anything because she's afraid you'll spill the beans about sleeping with her?"

He smiled and said, "Well, I'd like to think it's because she realizes I'm just a wonderful human being who couldn't have anything to do with the attack, and therefore sees no reason to include us beyond getting specific details, but you might have a point."

Before I could say anything, the door opened. I expected to see Jennifer, but it was Nadia. In her hands was a small Wi-Fi surveillance camera.

Just like the ones we had emplaced and were testing last night.

CHAPTER 17

N adia entered the room and set the camera on the table, saying, "Don't worry, I'm not going to ask who you guys work for."

Uh-oh.

I tried my best to look perplexed, saying, "I'm not sure what you mean."

She said, "We found this on the old grate to the drainage cut. The hotel says it's not theirs. It's an IP camera, and we're tracking who it was talking to tonight, right now. If it's the terrorists, we'll have a location to check out."

Mental note: Shut down the other cameras.

I said, "Okay?"

"If it was talking to someone in this hotel, that's another wrinkle we'll have to explore. We'll know soon, unless you want to spare me the trouble."

I absolutely wanted her to stop looking, but I wasn't too worried, because I knew how we operated. Veep's connection to those cameras would have been layered and spoofed by about fourteen different addresses, to the point that they'd find out someone from the Republic of the Congo was the initiating terminal.

I said, "You do what you think you need to. We'd like to stop them as much as you. We don't really like terrorists."

She circled around the table, saying nothing. Hoping the pregnant silence would get us to talk. Unfortunately for her, I'd been in her shoes with real bad guys on the other end, and I was trained not to take the bait. Never, ever answer a question that wasn't asked.

She stopped walking and said, "It was a little bit of a miracle that you and Jennifer managed to stop that assault. A couple of ditchdiggers from an 'archeological company' thwart a well-trained group of assassins right at the point of entrance. Don't you think?"

At that point, I decided to turn it back on her, since we were all doing doublespeak. She hadn't given her superiors her suspicions, or we'd be in a much more secure location, and I was sick of the bullshit.

I said, "Yeah, that's true. We were extremely lucky. But not the least because a lowly waitress from Goa managed to find a pistol in her panties she'd forgotten about. I'll give you that. If I didn't know better, I'd have thought Knuckles here had taught you to shoot it when you were together. Maybe dry firing in the kitchen instead of the bedroom."

I saw her face grow red, like I'd literally slapped her. She spluttered for a moment, then picked up the camera on the table and hurled it at my head. I dodged it, hearing it splinter against the wall. She looked at me with pure venom, and I could see the restrained rage. She wanted to attack me, literally, but I wasn't sure if it was because of my comment about Knuckles or whether she didn't like the turn of events in general. I did, however, like the emotion.

And the restraint.

If she was willing to go mano a mano with me, she was confident in her abilities, and I had no doubt I'd be in for a fight. But if she was holding back because of her mission, she had the focus of someone I'd want on my team.

Knuckles leapt up, glaring at me, saying, "Whoa, whoa, let's all calm down here. We all want to solve this problem, but we don't know what you want. We're nothing but registered guests of the hotel. There's no reason to get in a fight here."

She went from him to me, locking eyes and saying, "Okay, Mr. Nobody, if you were to say who did this, with your complete lack of experience in such matters, who would you say did it?"

I looked at Knuckles, he nodded, and I told her everything we'd just discussed about the types of weapons, the method of assault, and the timing. I ended with, "But what do we know? We don't deal with this on a daily basis."

I saw a small grin wanting to leak out, and she said, "I know that, but it's good to get a separate opinion. And I see you're thinking the same thing I am."

I glanced at Knuckles, because what I'd told her was an either/or thing, just like we'd talked about, and said, "What? I just said we don't know."

"You said you didn't think this was a random, LeT rage attack."

"I said we thought it *was,* most probably," and then hastily followed up with, "Although I'll also say I don't know what LeT is."

She smirked and said, "No, you said you *believed* it might be them, but you also said there were indications it wasn't, and this was targeted."

We were going in circles, and I didn't see the reason why. I said, "Okay? So what?"

She glanced at the door, then said, "Knuckles, lock it."

So the room isn't wired for sound. Now we were getting to the meat of this thing.

He did, and she laid all her cards on the table, saying, "Look, I'm sure you're not here for some archeological dig. I'm not going to make you say it, but you and I both know that there's a meeting happening tomorrow between Riva Thakkar, the CIA, and RAW. I think that attack was against Thakkar. I think they wanted to kill him. I don't think they intended to come onto the resort and just massacre whoever they saw. They were after *him*."

I took that in but wasn't ready to capitulate the entire cover just yet. I said, "So tell your guys. Let them hunt the terrorists. What do we have to do with this?"

She sighed, looked at the closed door, then said, "Because they don't believe me, and really, because if I'm right, there's a leak on my side."

"What's that mean?"

She took a breath, as if she was considering what to say next, then let it out. "If they were after Thakkar, they had to know he was eating outside in real time. The only way to know that was from somebody on my team. If I'm right—and I'm not really sure I am—but if I'm right, somebody on my team let them know."

Which was intriguing. This little beach vacation was starting to look like fun. I'd wanted to leave India as soon as our babysitting gig was over, not liking playing second fiddle to the CIA, but this was something else. I could hang around a little bit longer to see where it went.

I said, "But everything you guys found was from LeT and Pakistan. The weapons, the original guy who was captured here, the entire thing."

She took that in, and I saw recognition dawning on her face. I knew I'd said too much. She said, "Yes, that's true. But it's beyond me as to how you'd know that."

I started to say something but she held out her hand, shutting me up and saying, "No, no, I'm sure they brief every company who comes to India about any loose risks. I understand."

She paused, seeming to do an internal battle within herself. She turned in a circle, then faced us, saying, "The two guys who were killed tonight were tied in to D Company, which is an organized crime syndicate here in India. They're bad guys, but not ideological. They have no association with Pakistan, the ISI, or LeT. D Company writ large does, however, purely for monetary reasons. Which is to say it could go either way, but I don't think it does. They were here for Thakkar, and they were working for someone other than LeT or Pakistan."

The words settled on the room like a pesticide fog floating down from the ceiling, both Knuckles and me reassessing why we were here.

She flicked her head to Knuckles and said, "Look, I believe you're the good guys, mainly because of him, but I'm in a bit of a quandary here. I think this attack is targeted, but I can't convince anyone else of that. They don't like females telling them their suspicions."

I heard the words and knew exactly what she was saying. Once upon a time, I'd lived that very thing with Jennifer, and it had almost cost me my life. I didn't know if she was playing me, but she hit the right notes.

Even so, I said, "I don't know where this is going here. I have a female on my team and so . . . what? You now trust us?"

She looked insulted and said, "No, that's not it at all," but I could tell there was a grain of truth in what I'd said. She continued, "I don't *want* to convince anyone else, because I think we have a leak. I need some help. It's not just about me being a female, it's about them not wanting to see what's in front of them."

Knuckles echoed me, saying, "Which means, what?"

She hesitated for a moment, wondering if she wanted to jump over the cliff, and then she did. She pulled a key out of her pocket. It had a large plastic fob on the end, looking like a Holiday Inn key circa 1985. She held it up, looked at me, and said, "I searched the guy you killed, before anyone else showed up. He had nothing on him other than this. It's a hotel in Baga."

I took the key and said, "So? What do you want us to do, as an archeological research company?"

She exhaled at my continuing the subterfuge and said, "As Knuckles would say, 'Cut the shit.' Is that right? Did I get that right?"

Knuckles laughed and said, "Yeah, that's a pretty good go. Just tell us what you want."

She turned to him and said, "Do I have to spell it out? Are you two that obtuse? Go break into the damn thing and tell me what you find."

She locked eyes with me again, knowing she'd just put her career on the table. I quit with the pretending and said, "You, and you alone?"

"Yes. Me alone. If I'm right, then anyone else could be compromised. If I'm wrong, then who cares?"

I said, "Why do you trust us to do this? We could be in on the plan."

She looked at Knuckles, and he smiled, believing he knew what she was going to say.

She said, "Because of Jennifer. Because of how she reacted to her nickname. She's pure, and there's no way she would be involved in anything like this."

Knuckles' face fell, and someone knocked on the door. Nadia unlocked it, and Jennifer walked in.

She saw the group of us and said, "What did I miss?"

CHAPTER 18

Mr. Chin finally saw the monument known as the Gateway to India and crossed the street right in front of it, entering a pressing crush of people. Families with kids, couples taking selfies, and seedier groups of young men all swarmed around the giant granite structure, street vendors interspersed throughout selling photographs, soft drinks, and plastic toys for kids.

Built when India was still an English colony, the archway was right on the water adjacent to the original Mumbai city center, and it encompassed both Hindu and Muslim architecture, but that wasn't why the locals liked it. Constructed as a supposed grand entryway into the British empire, it was also where the last British troops left the country after independence.

Mr. Chin snaked through the throngs, trying to be inconspicuous, but it was pretty much impossible. At a short five foot six inches, he was the only Chinese person within miles. In fact, he was the only person of a separate ethnic group he could see, period, among a sea of Indian nationals, and because of it, he drew stares. He had planned for that, of course, outfitting himself as a tourist, complete with backpack and camera. It was why he always contracted out locals for any leg-breaking work he did, only using ethnic Chinese operatives for sensitive work when it was absolutely necessary. Repeatedly employing personnel from his homeland anywhere but in the heart of New Delhi was a recipe for exposure.

He'd worked in India for most of his professional career and had always been envious of his counterparts in the United States. At least there, a Chinese person could get away with *looking* Chinese, making operations much easier. Here, while it didn't necessarily generate suspicion, it would definitely generate curiosity, which might as well be suspicion when it came to executing his missions. To make matters worse, unlike the United States, there wasn't a large Chinese diaspora within India for him to leverage, forcing him to find local talent, which is what he was hoping to do today.

Mr. Chin's real name was Jianhong Zhang, and while he was technically employed by a Chinese conglomerate, it didn't pay his salary. Like every company within China, the conglomerate was used as a tool for the Chinese Communist Party, and Mr. Chin only leveraged it for his real work, as an operative for the Ministry of State Security.

The MSS was massive—one of the largest intelligence organizations on earth—and had its tentacles into everything, from psychological operations through social media to industrial espionage stealing cutting-edge technology to the traditional world HUMINT collection against foreign adversaries. Mr. Chin's portfolio was India, and he was but one small cog in the machine executing the CCPs orders—in this case, preserving China's monopoly on rare earth elements.

Mr. Chin crossed the pavilion in front of the gateway, making it to the far side without succumbing to the incessant hawking of street vendors. He walked to a counter at the dock, buying a ticket on the next ferry to Elephanta Island, the location of his planned meeting. He paid the foreigner price—which is to say about triple what the locals paid—then passed through a metal detector along with a stream of locals, the magnetometer beeping on every other person, the guards ignoring it all. He went through with no issues, and then entered the queue for the ferry, seeing a younger Caucasian couple in jeans and loose shirts, the only other non-Indians waiting to board.

The ferry arrived, a two-story open-aired boat billowing diesel fumes, the chipped paint fighting a losing battle against the encroachment of rust, looking more like something Humphrey Bogart would use on an African river than a safe vessel to cross the bay.

The locals didn't seem to mind. Once it docked, they surged forward, cramming into the small craft until there was standing room only, the benches lining the sides smashed together with bodies. Mr. Chin wormed his way forward through the crowd until he reached the ladder to the upper deck and saw it was chained off. He was stuck with the crowd and smells of diesel.

He pretended to be interested in the view and lifted the camera around his neck. He was just about to take a picture when a man tapped him on the shoulder and pointed. He saw a sign in English and Hindi reading, "No Photography." He had no idea why the rule was in place, but he hastily dropped his camera. The last thing he wanted was to be remembered as some subversive tourist breaking the rules.

He leaned against a stanchion in the middle of the boat, resigned to being upright for the hour-long trip but using the time to review what he was going to say to the man he was scheduled to meet.

His contact was an underboss in what was known as D Company, one of the most powerful transnational criminal organizations in Southwest Asia. Run by a Muslim kingpin living in exile in Pakistan, the syndicate had operations in locations as far-flung as the United Arab Emirates, and had branched out from pure criminal work to supporting terrorists groups like Al Qaida, the LeT, and the Taliban, which is how Mr. Chin had acquired the incriminating Pakistani ISI/ LeT information he'd originally given to Sidak.

D Company had been implicated in several spectacular attacks, including the 1993 Mumbai bombings that killed more than two hundred and fifty people and the Bali resort bombings in 2002 that killed another two hundred. It was an open secret that Pakistan was protecting the leader of the organization, and Mr. Chin needed to keep that in mind. He wanted pure pay-for-play muscle, removed from ideology, but would leverage whatever he could if it would accomplish the mission.

Up until this point, Mr. Chin's dealings with D Company had been handled through local cutouts, utilizing crypto currency for pay and the dark web for solicitation, all solely for manpower that he could direct. Basic leg-breaking tasks when he needed it, like the two men he'd required for Kamal's assault. He had never used D Company for an actual end-to-end mission, as he was about to do here, but after the briefing from his two contacts in Thakkar's security, he felt it necessary.

The defeat of Kamal's attack had raised significant concerns, not the least of which was that the two security men had been completely unaware of the potential threat. They'd made the call to Chin about Thakkar's patio dinner, saying they were going to clear out any civilians and that the guard force was as lax as the night before. Because Mr. Chin had trusted their judgment, that intel had set Kamal's assault plan in motion.

The two bodyguards were trained to protect their principal—trained to identify threats—and had seen nothing amiss, which meant it really *was* a group of lucky tourists, or more likely something else. From Kamal's description of how the assault had been defeated, Mr. Chin was leaning toward something else.

Due to Riva Thakkar's prestige, prior to his arrival his security detail had been given access to the personal information of everyone slated to stay at the hotel, and Mr. Chin had used that to analyze who the mysterious "tourists" could have been.

Since it was the tail end of the monsoon season, the resort was still in a lull and nowhere near booked to capacity, making his job somewhat easier. There was only a smattering of Americans, most easily eliminated for various reasons, such as being retirees. Only one group stood out: a company called Grolier Recovery Services, which had shown up the day before. He'd googled the company and had found a website dealing with archeological work, complete with a rash of quotes from universities and other academic institutions as to its pedigree. Mr. Chin dismissed them and was going to move on, right until he'd pulled up the passport scans they'd used to register, the pictures giving him pause.

The woman was attractive but unremarkable. The men, however, were a different story. They were all hard-looking, without any academic air about them. He'd dug deeper into the company and had learned it was ostensibly here in preparation for a U.S. university to visit the ruins of a church in Old Goa. It sounded completely on the up and up, but then again, so did Mr. Chin, as a respected member of a mining conglomerate. His company had a webpage too.

He knew it might be nothing more than paranoia, but he'd learned to trust his instincts. It was how he'd survived as long as he had, and his instincts were telling him that the Americans were using the same methods as the Chinese. The same methods *he* used, hiding as a businessman. If he was wrong, then it wouldn't matter, but if he was *right*, he needed to interfere with their ability to operate. He didn't believe in coincidences, and if he *was* right, they were here because of Thakkar. He didn't know why, but that missing piece of information was irrelevant—because he was also here for Thakkar.

He knew Thakkar's next stop in his travel itinerary, thanks to his own security detail, and had already sent Kamal and his team to the next location, wanting to get them away from any investigations that might arise. Kamal hadn't been exactly happy about the redirection but had acquiesced. They were now on the way across the country by train, heading to a safe house in Old Delhi.

Mr. Chin had his reservations about Kamal, but he'd proven resourceful and resolute. Having worked many sources in the past, Mr. Chin understood both the risks and the rewards of employing Kamal. So far, the rewards had outweighed the risks, even with the mission failure. Kamal was on the edge, but he had agreed to continue, and that was all Mr. Chin could ask; but when it was done, the entire group would have to be eliminated.

Mr. Chin didn't relish that part of the mission, but it was necessary to protect his masters. The local operatives would have to disappear, which, given their lowly status in society, should be easy enough.

He was brought out of his thoughts by the ferry slowing, the Elephanta Island jetty just ahead. They docked, the island hills blocking the wind and causing the diesel smoke to billow inside the open cabin, the fumes noxious.

A dockworker threw a small wooden plank across the gap to the boat, and he waited his turn to exit. He followed behind the lone Caucasian couple, stepping onto a thin concrete walkway. He passed by a few stands selling water bottles and fruit smoothies, then was accosted by a lone Indian man begging to take him on a tour of the island's famous caves. Mr. Chin looked down the walkway and saw the Caucasian couple being attacked the same way, with all the indigenous visitors seemingly not worth the trouble.

He waved his hand, saying, "No thank you," but the man was persistent, following him down the concrete pier until it reached land. Mr. Chin saw a small train that looked like a child's ride, with each carriage seating only four people on facing benches. He watched some of the locals begin boarding and talked to a man standing near the last carriage. The man told him it was a quarter of a mile to the base of the mountain, and that he could walk or pay to ride. He handed over some rupees, not because he didn't want to walk, but because he wanted to escape the relentless tour guide.

The tour guide continued talking even as he boarded, begging Mr. Chin to reconsider, until the train conductor finally waved him off. A local sat next to him, saying in English, "They can be aggravating, no?"

Mr. Chin smiled and said, "That's true. I just want to wander on my own. I don't need a guide."

The man said, "You're from America?"

Mr. Chin inwardly chuckled, the man's English so poor that he couldn't determine an accent. He said, "Yes, that's right."

"Where? I have a cousin who lives in New York. Are you from New York?"

Mr. Chin instantly regretted engaging the man in conversation. He said, "No, no, not New York."

"Have you been there?"

Mr. Chin pulled out a guidebook and said, "I really want to read before we stop."

The man nodded and focused on the rock-strewn shore, the eddies of water filled with the flotsam of plastic bottles and other debris. Mr. Chin studied his guidebook, as any normal tourist would, and in so doing, he learned why his contact had chosen Elephanta Island.

He only knew the man as Peanut, and they'd never met in person before. He knew that Peanut was wildly paranoid, as all of D Company were hunted men by the Indian state, and now he saw why he'd chosen this roundabout way to come together.

The island was home to several caves turned into temples for the god Shiva, with intricate carvings dating from the fifth century, but that wasn't what Mr. Chin noticed. In order to get to the caves, one had to take a ferry, then walk or use the train on a narrow path, then traverse up several thousand steps just to reach the entrance to the site.

It was the perfect choice to prevent anyone from disrupting the meeting, as Peanut could positively own the route, providing early warning. Mr. Chin realized he'd probably been identified entering the ferry, then upon exiting at the dock, and would be eyed his entire route up the stairs. If Peanut saw anything awry, he'd simply disappear.

CHAPTER 19

The train came to rest a short distance from the base of the stairs, and Mr. Chin exited behind his chatty friend. He walked to the broad staircase, seeing both sides flanked by restaurants not yet open for lunch. Looming in front of him was a seemingly endless string of granite stones rising steeply up the side of a small mountain. He paused to get his bearings, noticing the man from the rail car doing the same. Mr. Chin glanced at him, then began climbing the stairs. The man followed, a few feet behind. Mr. Chin stopped at a shop selling trinkets and souvenirs, and the man stopped as well.

This isn't going to work.

Mr. Chin engaged the stall owner in conversation, hoping the train companion would continue on. They haggled over the price of a stone façade depicting the famous carvings up top. The train man simply took a seat on the stairs, waiting.

Mr. Chin began to believe he worked for Peanut, but it presented a quandary. If he didn't, Mr. Chin most certainly couldn't lead him to the meeting site. If he was just a local attempting a clumsy robbery of an unsuspecting tourist, then Mr. Chin would have to deal with him.

He continued up the steps, and the man finally came abreast saying, "Is this your first time here?"

Mr. Chin said, "Yes, it is. And you?"

"No, no. I come here all the time. I like to practice my English with people like you."

Mr. Chin nodded, and they walked together, the man continuing with small chitchat until they finally reached the top. Mr. Chin was at a loss as to how to lose the guy. He couldn't outright demand he leave without drawing attention to himself, and he now wished he'd taken the local tour guide up on his offer, only to tell him to screw off at the top after one tour of a cave.

He paid the entrance fee and the man did the same, following him into the historical site, strangely just tagging about two feet away, saying nothing. It was odd, to say the least.

There were five different caves in the complex, but only one was worth the trip—the main cave. It was first on the path, and the reason that everyone came to visit, being large enough to traverse inside, with pools and sculptures in bas relief throughout. His meeting site was at cave five, which was little more than just a jagged hole in the rock, with little to see.

Mr. Chin decided to walk straight to it, leaving his straphanger to the tourists at cave one, hoping he'd find someone else to talk with. Mr. Chin walked briskly down the path, passing caves two through four, then stopped to assess his surroundings. He'd been so involved with the local, he hadn't thought about his own safety.

The path dropped down a flight of stairs with a toilet facility on the left, a cliff beyond it. He saw two security guards wandering about, but no other tourists. Clearly, this area wasn't worth the extra effort to see. He waited a bit more, settling into the rhythms of the area, and felt a touch on his elbow.

Startled, he turned and saw the local from the train. He said, "You didn't want to see the main cave?"

Now aggravated, Mr. Chin said, "Leave me alone. I want to enjoy this by myself."

The man's face curled into a smile, like he'd proven something to himself. He said, "You *are* by yourself."

For the first time, Mr. Chin saw a little bit of a predator. A small slice of who the man was. And he knew the local wasn't practicing his English. Now Mr. Chin had a choice: eliminate this man and go to the meeting, or lead him to the site. If he *was* with Peanut, he couldn't very well kill him. But if he wasn't, he most certainly needed to be eliminated.

Mr. Chin eyed the public bathroom and said, "If you insist on walking with me, at least let me go to the restroom by myself."

He walked down the steps and tipped the cleaning man outside some rupees, saying, "Paper?"

The man unrolled some toilet paper and handed it to him. He went inside, but instead of going to a stall, he went to the corner, waiting. If the interloper was with Peanut, he'd wait outside, as there was nothing to be gleaned by following him in. If he intended something else, then Mr. Chin would be waiting.

He reached down and pulled a small dagger out of his boot, controlling his breathing. Thinking of the last time he'd done this. Thinking about the mechanics of taking a life. Getting ready for the explosion of violence.

Nobody came in after him.

He exhaled and went to the toilet, now needing to urinate. And felt a shadow in the door. He turned, and the local was there, saying, "I really am practicing my English, so, is it 'Give me what you got' or 'Hand over your wallet'?"

Mr. Chin turned, glad he hadn't opened his pants yet, now smiling. He had no qualms about killing, only about killing the wrong person. He said, "Did you send the man outside away? Because I'll shout and he'll hear."

The local said, "Of course I did. It cost me some money to do so, but you'll pay that back with the camera you're carrying alone."

Mr. Chin said, "Thank you for making this easy. I appreciate it. Do you understand that English?"

The man looked confused, and Mr. Chin struck, his arm working like a jackhammer with his blade, stabbing the man in the chest over and over, as if he was chopping an ice block.

The man let out a single scream and then fell to the floor, Mr. Chin over him, continuing to stab holes in his body, letting out the air in his lungs like a deflating balloon.

The man quit moving, and Mr. Chin wiped the blade on his body, then dragged the carcass into a stall, closing the door. He went to the sink and washed his hands, cleaning off the blood. He stopped and checked his pulse, timing it with his watch. He was getting old, and was interested in how it affected him. Ninety-eight beats per minute.

Not as good as he had been in the past. But still not shabby.

The fact that he'd just killed a man never entered his mind. Only the mission mattered.

He exited the toilet, looking for the cleaning attendant he'd talked to outside. He didn't see him. He spotted one of the local security guards and said, "Where's the final cave?"

The man smiled and pointed to a path leading around a bend. He took it, walking in a measured pace. He rounded the corner and saw cave number five, two men on a bench outside of it. One of them had a head that looked like it had been squeezed at eye level, with the top popping out like an hourglass.

So that's why they call you Peanut.

He went straight to the bench, not wanting to remain any longer than necessary. The man with the misshapen head stood up and Chin said, "Mr. Peanut? I'm Mr. Chin."

Peanut said, "What was the stop at the toilet, and who was the man with you? Where is he?"

So he was *watching.*

"He was a crook. I tried to get rid of him, but he was persistent. I had to eliminate him."

Peanut nodded, not even reacting to the words. He turned to the man to his left and said, "Check it out."

The man left, and Peanut said, "If he's not in the toilet, you won't leave here alive. Do you understand that?"

"Of course. I understand."

They waited, and the man returned, saying, "He's dead. We need to leave."

Peanut said, "We're good for a little bit." He turned to Mr. Chin and said, "So, what is this about? I give you some men and that's not enough?"

Chin knew this was a break point. He had to handle it delicately. He said, "Your men were exactly what I needed, and I appreciate it, but they weren't enough. It's why I asked to meet you in person."

"What do you mean, not enough?"

"They didn't execute the mission as envisioned."

Peanut stared at him for a moment, then said, "What does that mean? I give you men because you pay well, but I don't control how they'll be used. What did they do wrong? Was it them, or was it you and your plan?"

Mr. Chin nodded and said, "It's exactly the second thing. They executed well, but my plan ran into something unforeseen, and I need to prevent it from happening again. I need more men."

"More? Those two weren't enough?"

Mr. Chin paused, then said, "Those two are dead."

Mr. Chin saw Peanut's eyes squint. He said, "What? Dead how?"

Mr. Chin held up his hands and said, "We ran into some Americans. I didn't know they were there, and I honestly don't know if they were there on purpose, but they caused the death of your men. And I need to stop them from interfering in my mission. It's still in play."

"Why should I give a shit about your mission?"

"Other than the pay, you mean?"

Peanut moved closer, towering over Mr. Chin. He said, "Don't toy with me. Those were two of my best men, and you got them killed. I'm not one to throw good money after bad. Or good men."

Mr. Chin said, "I know, I understand, but the Americans are a concern. The local police have the bodies of your men, and the United States FBI might become interested. I regret it immensely, but their death might bring you more pain. That's all I'm saying."

"Pain how?"

"Well, my mission was thwarted, but I don't believe they know what my mission was. All they have are the bodies. They were the only two who died."

"So you didn't get that fuck Thakkar, and instead just brought heat on *my* organization? I ought to throw you to the wolves. Nobody here likes the Chinese. Not me, not the Americans, not the RAW."

Mr. Chin said, "But you like my money and my influence. You want to continue supporting your Muslim friends under the protection of Pakistan? You want to keep your business going here, in India and the UAE? I'll allow that by having my country turn a blind eye, but if you threaten me again, I'll make sure you're crushed."

Mr. Chin took a step toward him, and even through the discrepancy in size, Mr. Chin's venom leaked out. He stared Peanut in the eye and said, "You still function because we haven't joined in the effort to stop you, but trust me, if we did, you would cease to exist. UAE is our friend now, and Pakistan has always played a double game. They care more about China than they do about your little business."

Mr. Chin backed off and said, "Don't ever threaten me again."

Peanut took a breath and then said, "What do you want?"

Mr. Chin said, "I don't need you to do anything for the mission. I have that. All I need is for you to interdict this group."

He swung his backpack around and pulled out a file folder, opening it to a Grolier Recovery Services cover page. He said, "I'm not even sure if these guys are against me, but I need them interfered with."

Peanut took the folder, saying, "Interfered with, or eliminated?"

"At this point, just interfered with. Give them enough trouble to be stuck with a police investigation. Mugging, robbery, whatever. Just trip them up. They might simply be tourists, so I don't want them harmed enough to draw an investigation by the United States."

Peanut flipped through the file, saying, "And if they aren't tourists? How will you know?"

"If they follow my men, if they track Thakkar, then I'll know."

"Track to where?"

"Delhi. Thakkar is going to New Delhi, and then headed to Agra for a visit to the Taj Mahal. He's basically rented half of the Taj for himself, under the rubric of 'security concerns.' If they go to Delhi, I'll know. But you'll prevent that, because I want them out of the hunt before they even have a chance to follow."

CHAPTER 20

Jennifer took a sip of her frozen daquiri and said, "We're going to look out of place if we keep drinking virgins."

Brett pulled the tiny umbrella out of his virgin piña colada and said, "You want to climb after a little juice?"

Jennifer said, "Not particularly, but I figured you'd at least get the real deal, being how this is supposed to be a walk in the park and all."

He grinned and said, "There's nothing that's a walk in the park. That's literally not a thing in our line of work."

She smiled back and said, "You regretting coming with me or something? I could have asked for Veep or Knuckles."

He took a pull through the straw and said, "I'm regretting having to sit in this bar for an hour, that's for sure. But I'll never regret playing backup for you. If you weren't here, it would be me climbing, and I hate that shit."

That brought out a full smile. Outside of Pike, he was the one she felt the closest bond with. On the surface they were an odd couple—an athletic blonde woman paired alongside a fireplug of muscle with black skin—but anyone looking would see only the cover of the book, having no idea what was inside the pages.

When Pike had introduced her as an equal to the team, Brett had been the first to accept her, never questioning her sex and focusing only on her abilities. He liked to say it was because they both hated their designate callsigns, but she knew it was more. She wouldn't admit it to Pike, but Brett understood her at a level different from the rest of the men. The closest before that had been Decoy, but he'd been killed right next to her on an operation. It still haunted her with feelings of guilt. She was constantly second-guessing what she should have done differently, and because of it she had built a wall. Brett had instinctively understood, which conversely made her connect with him. He never tried to penetrate her armor, and never played the man-card, respecting her skills simply for what they were.

She said, "How long should we wait?"

He looked at his watch and said, "At least until it hits twenty-two hundred. We want to attack the lull between people getting ready to party and people coming home from the party."

Nadia had shown them the room number on the key she had recovered but hadn't let them take it. She'd told them that she couldn't hide the existence of the key completely, as she was part of the investigation, but she could delay its "discovery." All she wanted was for Jennifer and Brett to inventory the room, complete with photographs, but not remove anything. Nadia planned on comparing what the official investigation found with what they found. If their findings were the same, then her fears about an insider threat would be unfounded. If they were different, she'd have to deal with it somehow.

Nadia was going to hold the key until the following morning, then make an excuse that it had been overlooked in the initial confusion. Once the key was introduced, there would be an official race to search the room, so they only had a single night to get in.

To complicate matters, Kerry Bostwick had checked in to the Hyatt today, which meant the real purpose of their mission had begun. Pike had decided that since the actual meeting wasn't until tomorrow, he could handle securing the principal with Knuckles and Veep, letting Brett and Jennifer conduct the break-in.

The initial plan had been to simply go into the hotel like they were staying there, then pick the lock. In and out in thirty minutes. Easy, breezy. They'd reconnoitered the hotel and realized that plan wasn't going to work.

The Beachcomber Inn wasn't a resort like the Grand Hyatt, to say the least. A four-story wooden structure a couple of blocks off of Tito's Lane, it was painted a garish blue and white, with each room having a wooden balcony complete with carved railings painted like a circus tent. Surrounded by a fence, there was a single entrance with a tiny lobby mostly taken up by the reception desk, and nobody was allowed past the desk without a key, apparently because the manager had had enough of people coming to sell either drugs or their bodies.

As the tourist season hadn't truly started yet, the hotel was nearly empty, and they'd toyed with simply renting a room and using that as a lily pad for the break-in, but decided against it, as they didn't want their names and passports associated with the blitzkrieg of the investigation that was coming the following day. There'd be no way to explain why they had a room in the hotel when they were known to be staying at the Grand Hyatt. That coincidence, coupled with the fact that they were witnesses to the assault, would put GRS squarely in the crosshairs of the investigation, something that most definitely couldn't be allowed.

They'd left the hotel, with Jennifer forcing Brett to circle the property, snaking through the narrow alleys that ran up both sides and taking a circuitous route back to Tito's Lane. They'd returned to the Hyatt and told Pike their findings, whereupon he'd just tried to call the whole thing off, saying, "Not our mission, and I'm not spending any more time on it."

Jennifer had said, "We don't have to go in from the front door. There are other ways."

"How?"

"The building is set back from any major roads. Outside of the road that goes by the entrance, there are only little alleys. Easy to get to the side without being seen."

"But you still can't get past the front desk. Who cares who sees you coming to the building?"

"Every room has a balcony, all the way to the top."

Jennifer had already discussed her plan with Brett, and she knew just by mentioning the balconies, Pike would guess what she had planned.

He raised his hands and said, "Whoa, whoa, slow down there, Koko. You want to scale the building and break in from the outside?"

"Yeah. Our guy's room's on the third floor, with a large balcony like all the others." She knew Pike wasn't hesitant because she was talking about climbing the outside of a building. He understood her skills and had forced her to use them on much worse structures than this hotel. More so than anyone else on the team, she was a bit of a savant when it came to climbing, and the balcony ascent would be easy enough. No, Pike's reticence was from something else.

When he didn't immediately answer, she said, "Pike, it's a cakewalk. Brett can pull security, I climb to his room, do the inventory, then get back down. Like thirty minutes max."

He said, "Look, I get that you can do it, but we have a mission here. This is Nadia's problem, not ours. Let's focus on the meeting tomorrow and let the RAW find the terrorists. We stopped the assault, and that's good enough for me."

"What if she's right? What if it wasn't a random LeT terrorist attack? What if it was something more? Something to do with the meeting tomorrow?"

She saw the wheels spinning in his head and waited. Pike finally looked at Brett and said, "You're good with this? You think it's worth it?"

"Yeah, I looked at the building. Jennifer could do that handcuffed, and I'm bored sitting around this place."

Pike smiled at that, turning back to Jennifer and saying, "And you?"

A little defensive, she said, "And me, what?"

"You *never* volunteer for anything. In fact, you're always telling me to stop when I want to stretch things. We have absolutely no sanction from the Oversight Council here for this, and you know it."

She grew a little miffed and said, "Since when do you care about that?"

He laughed and said, "Since when do you *not?*"

She started to retort but he held up his hands in surrender, saying, "Go, go. Get your climbing jihad on. Far be it from me to squash your initiative."

Six hours later, she was sitting with Brett in a seedy beach bar with neon lights and watery daiquiris.

Brett glanced around the room and said, "I don't know why anyone calls Tito's Lane the hot spot for nightlife. Looks more like Tijuana. You'd have to be living on spare change to party here."

Jennifer smiled and said, "I agree. I doubt nice Indian girls are coming here on spring break."

"Is that from the looks you keep getting?"

She said, "Well, I *am* the only female in this place."

"And I'm the only black guy. Looks like we'll be remembered here."

The waitress came over and Brett asked for the check. Jennifer waited until she'd left, then said, "You want to leave? It's still too early."

He took the check, dropped a pack of rupees on the table, and said, "I don't like the stares. Let's go find a donkey show."

She stood up and followed him out of the bar, saying, "Donkey show? What are you talking about?"

He exited onto the street, laughing. He said, "You don't want to know," and he turned left down Tito's Lane, toward the hotel alley.

She followed him, saying, "This place looks a heck of a lot better at night, I'll say that. Can't see the scars."

Brett glanced down the street, seeing bar after bar interspersed with tattoo parlors and tobacco shops, all lit up with colored string lights or neon, the music from each establishment competing for attention. Most of the bars were only half full, if that, the patrons all locals, not a foreigner among them. The people at each followed them with their eyes as they went past.

He saw the continued stares and said, "This town must not get crowded until the monsoon season's over. It's like they've never seen a foreigner."

They passed a booth with what looked like a large aquarium about waist height, the water full of minnows. Brett did a double take, seeing a local man and woman sitting on a bench, their pants legs rolled up and their legs in the water.

He said, "What on earth are they doing?"

Jennifer looked closer and said, "Believe it or not, it's a pedicure place. The fish are eating the dead skin off their feet."

"You're shitting me."

She chuckled and said, "Nope. It's supposed to exfoliate the skin. Maybe we can do that to kill some time."

He shook his head and said, "No damn way." He looked at his watch and said, "No time to kill anyway, let's go get this over with."

Jennifer felt her adrenaline rise at the words, knowing what was coming. Brett saw her take a breath and said, "We can always go back. This isn't our mission."

She said, "No, no, I want to do it."

They turned into a narrow alley, a trickle of water running down the dirt surface. Unconsciously, Brett cleared his shirt away from the Staccato he held in an appendix holster.

He said, "Why is that?"

She said, "Because I think Nadia's right. Something wasn't kosher about that assault. It made no sense to attack that place with so few people and silenced weapons."

She looked at him and said, "You don't want to do it?"

She was afraid of the answer. She needed his confidence in both the purpose and the execution of the mission. She trusted his judgment and was searching to see if she was making a bad choice.

"No, no. I'm game, it's just that Pike was right—you *are* the person who always wants the T's crossed and the I's dotted. The Oversight Council would shit a brick if they knew we were out here. Bostwick alone would have a coronary."

She'd actually thought about her decision after her conversation with Pike, and honestly didn't have an answer. She knew she'd chastised Pike for doing things outside the scope of their orders on multiple occasions, and this time *she* was the one initiating the break, but she sort of liked it.

She realized her time in the Taskforce had changed her view on the inherent infallibility of the chain of command. That, and like Knuckles always said, she was starting to enjoy the high adventure.

She said, "I don't know. Just seems like the right thing to do. It's not like we're out here running an Omega operation and putting someone's head on a spike. We're just helping a terrorist investigation."

He chuckled and said, "Pike's rubbing off on you. That's what's happening."

She said, "Well, hopefully it's working both ways."

CHAPTER 21

They reached the end of the alley, seeing the hotel directly to their front, rising beyond a pile of rubbish and a small iron fence. Brett took a knee and Jennifer slipped off her backpack, pulling out a pair of black Mechanix gloves and a set of Vibram Five Finger shoes. She removed her blouse and stepped out of her cargo pants, revealing a black sports bra and black Lycra yoga pants. She strapped on a fanny pack, tucked her hair under a black knit cap, replaced her hiking shoes with the Vibrams, then shoved everything she'd taken off into the backpack and handed it to Brett.

He took it, saying, "You look like you're going to a Pilates class."

Glancing at the balconies, she said, "That would be harder than this."

He said, "No weapon?"

She put in her earpiece, saying, "Yeah, I've got a weapon."

Brett followed her lead, setting in his earpiece and saying, "Where is it hidden?"

She said, "My weapon is you. Test, Test . . ."

He smiled and said, "I knew there was a reason I was here." He nodded at her and said, "I got you, Lima Charlie. How me?"

She nodded back, saying, "Comms up. Pike, Pike, you copy?"

"I copy. Koko, you don't have a weapon?"

"I have nowhere to conceal it. If I get caught, I'd rather talk my way out than shoot my way out. Holding a gun will cause problems."

"Unless it's the damn terrorists who catch you. Hang on before you execute. Blood, Blood, what do you think?"

Jennifer scowled at Brett, not liking having her judgment questioned one little bit. He smiled at her and said on the net, "It's a good call. I'm here, and I'm armed. If she gets in trouble, I can react."

Jennifer heard, "Roger all. Koko, you're cleared to breach."

She came back, saying, "Seriously? I have to get permission from Blood for *my* assault plan?"

Brett turned away, moving to the entrance of the alley, muttering *Here it comes* while pretending to provide security. He took off the thread protector of the Staccato and screwed on a suppressor, then put on night-vision goggles, looking up and down the walls of the hotel while Pike got his ass reamed on the radio.

He said not a word on the net. The radio went silent and Jennifer came up behind him, squatting down and saying, "You ready?"

He chuckled and said, "Uhhh . . . yeah. Nothing better than running ops with two bickering lovers."

She said, "Being his wife has nothing to do with it. I was right and you know it. If Pike was here instead of you, I would have made the same call."

"Unless I have to use my weapon. Then Pike will say it was *my* fault."

She smiled and said, "Then I guess I'll have to make sure you don't use your weapon. But I see it's all tricked out now."

He held up the Staccato and said, "Yeah, it is. This thing is sweet. Gonna be hard not breaking the trigger if you screw anything up."

Then he became serious, saying, "Target room is on the fourth set of balconies down from the front. Second floor has lights on, and I've seen someone moving. Third floor—target room—is dark. Which means we might have beat them to it. No IR cameras spotted with the NODs, which means probably no cameras at all. No movement on the grounds."

She took a couple of breaths and said, "Okay, then. I'll get across the fence and up against the wall. You spot for any movement, then follow."

He nodded and held out a fist, saying, "Get some."

She bumped it, then took off, a black shape moving through the night. She scaled the iron fence and slinked next to the courtyard on the ground floor, taking a knee and saying, "In position."

Brett reached her a few seconds later, looking up and saying, "Second-floor light is still on. You want to wait?"

She looked up as well, then said, "No. He could be up for another four hours. I'm headed up. If something goes wrong, I'll be coming back down to you."

He said, "Roger that. Be careful."

She grinned in the night, feeling the adrenaline course through her. She bounced up and down for a second, shaking her arms and rolling her neck. She stopped, now in the zone, and said, "Catch me if I fall?"

He smiled and said, "Of course."

He turned around and put his back to the wall, his knees out at a ninety-degree angle, holding the pistol with one hand, his other held in the air like he was stopping traffic. She put her left foot on his knee, took his free hand in hers, then sprang up until she was standing on his shoulders. He stood, raising her into the air against the wall. He felt her tense up, push off, then the weight leave, and looked up, seeing her holding on to the scaffolding of the second-floor balcony.

Jennifer deadlifted her body up until she reached the top of the wooden rail, finding it six inches wide. Big enough for someone with her skills to sprint down it like a road. She stood up, seeing the third-floor balcony above her, this time with no help to get to it. It would require a leap of faith, springing up to the lower carving. If she missed the hold, she'd have to land on the narrow beam or fall all the way back down.

She scuttled to the end overlooking the courtyard, then turned around. She gathered her courage, focused like a laser on the far wall where she'd plant her foot. She caught a shadow and saw a man in a bathrobe at the French doors, his belly hanging out from the open front. She felt a blast of panic, saw his hand on the door handle, and sprinted, launching into the air, planting her foot on the wall and springing upwards and back.

She turned in the air, snagged the lower beam of the third-floor balcony, and swung her legs up, cinching them on the beam. She froze, seeing the man exit onto the deck, scratching his belly. She hugged the beam like a barnacle, silently cursing under her breath and praying he wouldn't look up.

Her radio came alive, "Koko, Koko, you okay? I have the guy on my front sight."

She said nothing, snaking her hand to her earpiece and giving it a quick double click. She heard, "I copy. Stand by."

The next thing she heard was a racket out on the lawn, near a trash pile rising to the level of the fence. The man heard it as well and turned, then went to the opposite corner of the balcony, leaning over and shouting something in Hindi.

Jennifer used the distraction to scramble up the railing, flipping over it to the floor of the balcony. She took a knee, trying to control her breathing. She said, "Blood, Blood, at breach. Thanks."

She heard, "No problem. Circling around back to the launch point."

She went to the French doors of the target room, pulling out a penlight and studying the lock. She withdrew a tension wrench and pick, and in thirty seconds she was through the lock. She said, "Breach, breach, breach, going in."

"Roger all. Standing by."

The space was a simple one-room affair, with a queen-sized bed and a wooden dresser. Nothing else, not even a television set. Off to one side was a bathroom the size of a closet holding a sink, toilet, and clawfoot tub, a cheap plastic shower curtain around it.

She paused for a moment, ensuring the place was empty, then flicked on the overhead light, seeing a suitcase on the floor, some dirty laundry next to it. She went to the suitcase and took pictures with a digital camera, then laid out everything on the floor, taking time to go through the pockets on the clothing. She found a small notebook and flipped it open, a passport photo of a man falling out. She took photos of each page with writing on it, all of it in Hindi Devanagari script, then took a picture of the photo. She laid both next to the clothing, and then recorded it all again on her camera.

She replaced everything in the suitcase, utilizing the photos on her camera to ensure she left the clothing next to the suitcase just like she'd found it, then went to the dresser, opening every drawer but finding them empty. She entered the bathroom, seeing nothing but a toothbrush and some toiletries. She took pictures anyway. She was pulling open the shower curtain when she heard a scrape at the door.

A key going into the lock.

Uh oh.

She threw her camera into her fanny pack and jumped into the tub, closing the shower curtain. She began breathing through an open mouth, trying to stifle the noise.

She got on the net, whispering, "Blood, Blood, compromise. I say again, compromise."

She heard, "Status?"

"I'm hiding right now, but there's a seventy percent chance they'll find me. If they do, I'm coming out hot."

"Roger all. Standing by."

She peeked through a gap in the curtain and saw four Asian men come into the room, all in suits. They began to rapidly search it, cleaning all exposed surfaces and shoving everything on the floor into the suitcase. One man went to the dresser, repeating Jennifer's search but finding nothing of interest. Another sprayed the likely areas of contact with a bottle and wiped them down like he was polishing wood.

Jennifer prayed they'd want to get out before scrubbing the entire place down. A man entered the bathroom and she held her breath. She heard him slide all of the toiletries on the counter into a bag, then flush the toilet.

Bad sign.

If he was that dedicated in eliminating traces of the occupant, she was going to be found. She crouched, getting ready. She heard him spray from the bottle on the sink and begin wiping. When the noise stopped, she balled her fists.

She heard nothing for a moment, just waiting behind the curtain. Waiting to explode. She saw the shadow of a hand beyond the curtain, a blurry thing. She saw the fingers curl around the edge of the curtain and tensed on her back foot, cocking her hip. The curtain slid open and an Asian man appeared, his focus on the tub. He saw her feet, looked up, and his mouth dropped open. She pivoted with her hips, driving the punch with her legs, just like Pike had drilled into her, and slammed her fist into his face with all of her weight behind it.

His nose flattened with a spray of blood, his head snapped back, and he dropped like he'd been axed in the head, his skull bouncing off the sink as he collapsed. She leapt out, shouting into her earpiece, "On the move! On the move!"

And sprinted into the room.

She saw the other men snap upright at the action, all of them bewildered. She pivoted to the left, running to the glass of the French doors.

She saw one man pull out a pistol and shout at her, and realized she didn't have the time to pause and use the door handle.

She wrapped her arms around her head and launched forward, using her body to shatter through the glass and wood of the door. She spilled onto the balcony and leapt up, wrapping one arm around the railing and launching over it. She hung for a split second, until the momentum of her body swung back, and then let go.

She hit the railing below her perfectly, like a cat, and rolled off onto the balcony below. The man above her began shooting through the balcony floor, the rounds peppering around her body. She scampered away from the bullets, saying, "Contact! Contact on the second-floor balcony!"

Brett came back, "I have no shot! I have no shot!"

She leapt up, her brain screaming to get out of the funnel of fire, and the rounds shifted to the edge. The man with the pistol continued shooting into the night, blocking her escape. She turned and sprinted to the door, finding it locked. She saw the man in the room looking at his phone and pleasuring himself, his erection wilting at the commotion. He saw her outside and closed his bathrobe, his face registering shock.

The bullets kept coming down and she backed up a step, lowered her shoulder, and smashed through the glass and flimsy wood like she had done above, spilling into the room.

The man simply stared at her. She ignored him, running to his door and shouting into the radio, "New plan, new plan. I'm exiting from the inside. I'm exiting from the inside."

She flung the door wide and turned toward the stairs at the front of the hotel. She saw an Asian man burst out from the stairwell, blocking her route, and turned the other way, sprinting flat out.

Brett came on, saying, "Give me a lock-on, give me a lock-on."

She kept running, saying, "Back door. Back door. Front is blocked." She heard a shot fly by her head.

Jesus Christ, they want a thief that bad?

She hit a stairwell, jerked the door open, and began taking the stairs four at a time, tumbling down them. She heard the man behind her, then a round hit the concrete wall to her front.

She screamed, "He's behind me and shooting!"

She heard, "I'm here, I'm here. Keep coming."

She looped around the landing, glancing back and seeing a man with a gun hell-bent on stopping her. He fired again, the round smacking off the concrete next to her head. She leapt down the final stairs, hitting the ground floor, and burst out next to a swimming pool.

She didn't see Brett and began sprinting toward the darkness at the rear of the hotel. She heard the door slam open behind her and then a man scream. She turned around and saw Brett standing over a body, his fists working in tandem like a jackhammer, bouncing her pursuer's skull against the ground.

After the body became still Brett stood up, racing to her and saying, "I have the exfil. Follow me."

He took off at a sprint and she fell in behind him, both of them running flat out. He dodged around a small courtyard and she saw two people sitting on a bench, both watching them rush past, their mouths open. They reached the back of the facility, and he jumped over the iron fence. She followed, and within seconds they were in another narrow alley. They kept going until they reached Tito's Lane, spilling back into the neon and blaring music.

He slowed, then stopped, looking behind him before sagging against a building. She did the same.

He said, "Well, I didn't use my weapon, so this can't be my fault."

She laughed, letting out the emotion, feeling the adrenaline leak out.

She said, "I told you this was going to be a cakewalk."

CHAPTER 22

Kamal heard the wheels of the train start to brake, then saw everyone around him begin shuffling to the open door. Calling this a passenger car was giving the train too much credit. More like a cattle car. Yes, they could move in between the cars, and yes, there were benches to sit on, if one were lucky enough, but they were cattle, nonetheless.

It was no different from any train in India. It just was what it was. The trains were efficient by modern standards, making their stops exactly when they said they would, but were also incredibly deficient in any sort of amenities. Just an open box crammed full of people, with some riding outside the carriage itself, hanging on for dear life.

His car was a jostling mass, all surging toward the door. He let the initial explosion of people leave before he followed, stepping onto the platform of the Sadar Bazaar train station and getting swept away by the crowd like a leaf in a stream, moving with them to avoid being trampled.

He reached the main platform and the crowd thinned. He took a moment to get his bearings, then waited for his men to catch up. When they did, he said, "Follow me," then pressed through the crowd, exiting outside the station and onto the street.

The heat was oppressive, the outside of the train station no better than the claustrophobia inside, the open-air terminal itself having no climate control at all. They ignored the beggars and children all clamoring for a handout, Kamal flagging down two rickshaws. He waited until his men were loaded, then gave the driver an address: the Jama Masjid Mosque in Old Delhi.

The rickshaws wove through the Delhi congestions like masters, ringing their bells as if it would make a damn bit of difference within the absolute chaos of the traffic. Eventually, they were in a back alley full of vendors selling everything from silk scarves to mango smoothies. They pulled up to the front of the mosque's eastern gate, the men exited and Kamal paid the drivers, then watched them return to a line of other rickshaws, awaiting their next passenger.

Kamal waited until they were out of earshot and his men were around him, then said, "This is supposed to be the meeting site."

Manjit said, "The Jama Masjid Mosque? Seriously? Sounds more like a setup. Maybe the RAW's waiting on us inside, trying to prove we're LeT?"

Built in the seventeenth century, the Jama Masjid Mosque was the central locus of all things Islamic in Delhi, having a rich history that stretched back centuries. It was also a major tourist draw, which Kamal knew allowed Mr. Chin to enter it without any additional scrutiny.

Kamal said, "Chin picked the location, not me, and if anyone's getting arrested, he'll be one of them."

Kamal saw the reticence and said, "You guys go get a smoothie. I'll go in myself. I'll get the information and return."

Manjit said, "And if you don't?"

"If I don't come back out, if you see a rush of police, then you'll be free and clear."

Manjit said, "That's not what I meant. We can't let you go in alone."

Kamal said, "You, Agam, and Randeep are the last of us. Screw

Mr. Chin. He wants Thakkar dead. I want Thakkar alive for our own ends. For Sidak. For our families. For every Sikh who's been persecuted. You know what to do. You have the numbers of Thakkar's security. If I don't come out, call them. Continue the mission."

Manjit nodded, but Kamal could see he didn't like it. Kamal said, "Look, the mission takes priority. If this is a trap, you continue. Bring our demands to the world, and bring Chin down with you."

Manjit looked at Agam, then said, "What *are* our demands? What are we seeking to do here?"

Not liking the question, Kamal turned to the eastern gate, saying, "I'm not sure yet, but it'll be spectacular."

He turned and left them, entering the gates of the mosque without another word. He passed through a security checkpoint and then blended into the crowd. His meeting site was the western end of the prayer hall, an area roped off to allow true believers to avoid the tourists.

He walked across a large courtyard, then entered a long hallway, staying on the tourist side of the ropes. He didn't understand any of the intricacies of Islam and didn't want to be called out because of it.

He reached the far end of the hallway, the arches to the courtyard filled with tourists coming and going. He stopped for a moment, not sure what to do, and then felt a hand on his elbow. He turned and saw Mr. Chin wearing a large-brimmed hat and sunglasses, a backpack over his shoulder.

Mr. Chin said, "So you made it out of Goa without any problems?"

Kamal barked a half-hearted laugh and said, "Yeah, *we* made it out okay. I can't say the same for Sidak and your other men. And I also have no idea if we're being tracked. I didn't have the time to break into your men's room. I have no idea what they had in there that could lead to us."

"Don't worry about them. I had others clean it before the authorities arrived. If you weren't stopped in Mumbai, you're good. Nobody's tracking you to here."

Kamal nodded and said, "So what now? You're ready to pay us?"

Mr. Chin smiled with little warmth, the gesture coming out more as a grimace. "No, the mission isn't done. We talked about this. Nobody's tracking you right now, but if you defy me, they will be. I told you I went through the room of my other men, and I'll release all that evidence to the RAW in a heartbeat. Do you understand?"

Kamal said nothing, simply staring at Mr. Chin. He said again, "Do you understand? The mission isn't complete, and I'm feeling heat to get it done."

"Done for whom? You've never said."

Growing aggravated, Mr. Chin said, "Done for the people paying you. You never cared before, and you won't start caring now."

Kamal nodded and said, "So, like I said, what now?"

Mr. Chin handed him an envelope, saying, "This is a key to a safe house. The same one that my other men used. It's vacant now, for obvious reasons. Go there with your men. Inside, you'll find a laptop and some equipment. The next mission parameters are at that location."

Kamal took the envelope and said, "What's the next mission? I don't need the secret spy stuff. Just tell me."

"It's easier for you to read the parameters, but rest assured, it's a standoff attack. No more capture missions. We want Thakkar killed."

"How? I only have four men, and he has massive security."

"Yes, but two of those security are on your team. You'll coordinate with them, but like I said, it's a standoff attack."

Mr. Chin removed his backpack and handed it to Kamal, saying, "In here are five clean cell phones and four watches. Four of the phones are already programmed with the numbers of the others, along with the two security men and a contact for myself. Only use them to talk to yourselves and me. The fifth phone has nothing. Use that for any calls you need to make outside of our circle. Hotels, taxis, Ubers, or whatever. Understood?"

Kamal opened the bag, seeing boxes labeled Samsung and Garmin. He said, "Watches? What are those for?"

"They're GPS smartwatches attached to the phones. They're for the mission."

"For the mission, or for tracking us?"

Mr. Chin said, "Both, but for your protection. Do not turn them off, and make sure each man gets the phone that's linked to the specific watch."

Kamal zipped up the backpack and said, "Do I need to go back to the train station?"

"No. The safe house is near here, in the Chandni Chowk spice market. You can walk."

"Am I supposed to guess where it is?"

Mr. Chin smiled and said, "Put on your watch. It's in that. It'll show you the reason I want you to wear them."

Kamal did so, strapping on something called a Garmin Instinct 2X Tactical. A huge thing with buttons all over the place. He turned it on and said, "What now?"

Mr. Chin manipulated the menus until he found a saved location labeled "house." He pressed a button and the watch began showing an arrow and distance to the location.

He said, "Good for you to test it, because you'll be using it on the mission. The passwords to the computer are in here as well, on the notifications. Make sure you don't clear that."

Kamal worked the buttons on the watch, saw the notification, and said, "You actually sent it to this watch instead of just giving it to me?"

Mr. Chin smiled and said, "Yes. I wanted you to learn the utility. There's another one I want you to learn. You see that heart rate at the top?"

Kamal looked and indeed saw the rate of his beating heart. Mr. Chin said, "Don't let that go to zero. I want to see a heart rate on each of your team for the next mission. Put the watches on as soon as you leave here."

Kamal realized he was being boxed in, captured by Mr. Chin as surely as if the RAW was in the room. He shouldered the pack and thought about his next words. He said, "I'm not sure I'm doing the next mission. I'll have to call my men and see if they're still willing, since you haven't paid anything yet."

Mr. Chin said, "Call them? Why would you need to do that? They're all out front eating mangoes at a smoothie stand and waiting for you to come back out."

And Kamal realized the extent of his dilemma. They'd been under surveillance, probably since they'd stepped off the train.

CHAPTER 23

I popped an olive in my mouth, turned to Kerry Bostwick, and said, "We couldn't do this in your suite? If I didn't know better, I'd think you were trying to get some meals on the government dime."

He'd asked us to meet at a restaurant called the Fisherman's Wharf, an eclectic little place in the town of Panaji, the "new" capital of Goa, where the Portuguese had fled after disease had ravaged Old Goa centuries ago. It was a little gem of a town, complete with riverside casinos like one would see on the Mississippi Delta, but held nothing for my mission other than a meeting site.

Bostwick had chosen the restaurant's outside patio for our sit-down. The only people around the table were my team, as the CIA/RAW/billionaire meeting had gone off earlier in the day, with both Riva Thakkar and the head of the Research and Analysis Wing long gone.

He laughed and said, "Well, I sure as shit couldn't meet you at the resort. You guys are not associated with me in any way."

I said, "Yeah, but let's be honest, having the billionaire meeting here would have been better than that shit show location you used at the hotel—a known target site."

Bostwick had arranged for a suite at the hotel for the meeting, which would have been incredibly easy to secure, but Thakkar had other ideas. For whatever reason, the billionaire had decided he wanted the meeting in a public place, not in a hotel room—even if it was a suite—I guess to protect himself from enemies he couldn't see. They'd agreed to host it in the workout facility on the grounds, a stand-alone building with a single entrance and exit, which I thought was absolutely idiotic, but I wasn't calling the shots. I was only reacting to them.

They'd used a small conference room on the second floor next to a vegan coffee shop and climbing wall that stretched up from the first floor, the room itself having windows that anyone could see through inside. It didn't do much to camouflage the fact that someone was meeting, but it did allow Thakkar's robust security to be able to see out, giving them the ability to react if something went wrong.

Not that it would have mattered at that point, as the attackers would have been able to kill everyone through the glass outside of the room and there was nowhere to seek cover inside. Wouldn't have been my choice, but luckily for the stupid billionaire, I had the outside covered with Knuckles and Veep.

Jennifer and I had dressed like we were just coming from the gym downstairs and had purchased a couple of horrible vegan smoothies, sitting at a table in the lobby and in constant contact with Knuckles and Veep outside.

Across from us, at another table, were two Sikh bodyguards, both looking extremely competent, complete with full beards and turbans on their heads. One had a scar on his cheek that traced through his beard and the other had a milky eye, as if he'd taken some shrapnel or other damage in the past. They glowered at us like something out of a Gunga Din movie. I'd ignored them, sipping my vegan smoothie like I was here just for the rancid amenities.

They most certainly *looked* like they knew what they were doing, but they couldn't have been that switched on if they'd agreed to this junior varsity setup.

In the end, it didn't matter, because the meeting came and went without any drama whatsoever. We'd called it a wrap and now we were conducting a final debrief with Bostwick before we flew home. Only his idea of what was coming from the debrief was a little different than mine. I still had to tell him about Jennifer's little adventure.

Bostwick said, "The meeting location wasn't my call. I'd have had it inside my room if Thakkar had agreed to it, but he demanded a neutral site. Seems he was a little scared after that attack the other night. He's paranoid. He thought either RAW or the CIA had something to do with it."

I looked at Jennifer and said, "Yeah, about that attack. We need to analyze it."

He put down his coffee and said, "Why? You guys stopped it, and we got what we wanted. They didn't kill a bunch of civilians and we got Thakkar to agree to bankroll the rare earth mine. It's a win-win."

I said, "Well, we're not sure it's over."

"What's that mean? The RAW went to the hotel the attackers had been staying at this morning. They found nothing. Nothing from the hotel, nothing from the room, and nothing about any bigger plot. They were a few LeT guys that wanted to kill some people, and that's it."

I looked at my team, getting some nods. Originally, I'd hated the tasking as some contract flunky doing nothing but guarding a CIA meet, but I believed that Jennifer had turned up something interesting, and it was right up the Taskforce alley. I'd wanted to flee this country on the first thing smoking after the meeting, but now I had a sense that our true skills could be used. I only had to convince Kerry.

I said, "We don't think it was a random attack. We think they were after the meeting. Yeah, we stopped it, but they weren't here on an attack for Islam. They were here on a targeted attack for something else."

As much as he wanted to be cheering about his success in his latest covert action construct, he was a good enough man to take a pause. Instead of telling me to pack sand and go home, he said, "What do you mean?"

I said, "Well, sir . . . we went to that hotel room last night. There's a reason they didn't find anything."

I saw his mouth drop open. He was incredulous. He said, "You did what?"

I held up my hands and said, "Wait, sir, it's not what you think. We were contacted by a member of the RAW while we were in holding. They asked us to do it. They don't trust their own men."

He leaned back in his chair, his hands in his scalp, then came back to me, saying, "You *broke into* the terrorists' room last night? Without authorization? What. The. Fuck. How did you know where it was? How did you even have the intel to do it?"

He appeared more concerned about the mission than what we'd found, which aggravated me a little bit. I said, "Like I told you, we had some help from RAW."

He leaned forward, slapped the table, and said, "Pike, you had *no* Omega authority for offensive actions."

I'd already debriefed my team the night before and was now supremely happy that Brett had had the presence of mind not to break the trigger on his weapon, which would have made things exponentially worse. A dead body would have led to the police being involved. As it was, there was just a fight at a hotel known to cater to dubious Russian tourists, and I knew the other side wasn't going to the police. This was the difference between a true Operator and a gunslinger who just wanted to use the label. Ninety percent of the U.S. intelligence community would have smoked those guys to get Jennifer out of danger, but my team had not.

I came back at him, saying, "Bullshit. You told me I had Omega to protect the meeting, and that's what I did: proactively protect the meeting."

I told him everything that had transpired, only leaving out the name of our RAW contact.

Incredulous, he said, "So this RAW contact doesn't trust his own people, and he asked *you* to penetrate the hotel, taking an inventory so he could compare it to what the RAW found?"

I obviously didn't tell him my contact was Nadia. I said, "Yes, sir, and we don't have any proof that there is something rotten in RAW, because the place was scrubbed while Jennifer was there. Someone came in to clean their tracks, and they weren't a bunch of Muslims from Pakistan. They were Asian."

"Asian? Indians are Asian. What's that mean?"

I wasn't sure how to spell it out in a professional manner without using racial slurs. I said, "They were not Indian Asians. They were . . . Asians."

"What the hell does that mean?"

Brett leaned over the table and barked out, "Come on, man, do we have to spell it out? They weren't Indians. They were Chinese, Japanese, Vietnamese, or some other -*ese*."

Bostwick turned to him and said, "How do you know?"

Jennifer said, "Because I saw them. And if you ask me, the men who chased me were Chinese."

"Why?"

"Because they *looked* Chinese. They didn't look like they were from

Southeast Asia. They weren't Cambodian or Thai. They were tall, bigger than someone Vietnamese, and they spoke what sounded like Chinese."

Bostwick said, "You speak Chinese?"

Insulted, Jennifer said, "Well, Kerry, I also don't speak French or German, but when I hear it, I know the difference."

He held up his hands and said, "Okay, okay, so what are you saying here? China directed a terrorist attack on Indian soil? Come on, that's a little bit much. They do a lot of gray zone stuff, but it never rises to the level of bullets flying. Maybe you're misreading who came in the room. Maybe you had the *wrong* room."

I said, "We didn't have the wrong room. We had the key of the guy who was killed on the lawn. We went to *that* room, and while we were in it, a bunch of *Asians* came in and cleaned it out, speaking Chinese."

Bostwick took a breath and said, "The RAW thinks it's an Islamic terrorist attack, and they *own* this country. The head of the organization told me that to my face. Don't build this up into some conspiracy. You did your job and they did theirs. The meeting was a success, and our covert action is in motion. It will take much more than a terrorist attack to stop it now."

"The head of RAW may think that, but the rank and file don't. I'm telling you there's something more here. Those guys were on the hunt for a body, and we know it wasn't you, because nobody knew you were coming. It might be the head of RAW, because my contact thinks they might be compromised from the inside, and that's something we should look at. They take him out, and it'll throw this whole covert action into the trash bin, since he's making it so close hold. He's a single point of failure."

My bringing up the long-term success of his plan gave him pause. He said, "So how do we figure out if it's an insider threat? Do you have anything to prove that?"

"No. Not from what we found, but we *did* find an address for further exploration, and I need your approval to go check it out."

"Where?"

"It's an address in Old Delhi. I have no idea what's there, or why it was in the room, but I want to check it out."

"What's your RAW contact think? What's he saying about a Chinese connection?"

"I have no idea. I'm meeting the contact tonight. They have the information we gave, and I'm waiting on their analysis."

He nodded, then said, "Okay, see what they say, but they'll have already slammed that address by the time you talk. They have no love of the Chinese. If the RAW is involved, they're probably dead by now."

I said, "I don't think so. My read is my contact wants this close hold and wants plausible deniability if they're wrong. The contact has no power in RAW, but really believes in the mission. They're going to want me to check it out to protect themselves."

He smiled and said, "That's what I would expect. They want you to hang it out. If you're right, then they'll take credit. If you're wrong, then we'll get the blame. But if you're right, I need to know."

"So I'm good to check out this address? I get the Rock Star bird for a five-day vacation with my team? Cover development after the meeting? You'll sell it that way to the Oversight Council?"

He exhaled, knowing he was putting his own ass on the line. He said, "Yeah, go for it. But watch your back. I don't trust the RAW any more than I trust the KGB. They have their own agenda."

CHAPTER 24

K erry paid the bill and I let him exit separately first, just in case anyone was outside watching. After he was clear and on his way back to the resort, my team stood up and left the restaurant. Once outside, I said, "We've got the meeting tonight with Nadia. Jennifer, Knuckles, and I will handle that. Brett, you and Veep pack our kit up and get the Rock Star bird ready to travel. Get us a hotel in Delhi."

Brett said, "Why do we get the scut work? How about Jennifer and Knuckles do the pack-up and we conduct the meeting with you?"

"Nope. Nadia knows Jennifer and Knuckles already. I'm not dragging you two into the circle."

Veep said, "Come on. You know she's already done her due diligence. She's probably got all of our passport photos taped to her wall."

Which was true, but I wasn't budging. "Just do the scut work this time. Jennifer's female and I want her there."

I turned to go to our SUV and Brett said, "What about Knuckles?"

I said, "He's banging her. He's coming to the meeting."

Jennifer's mouth dropped open and Knuckles said, "Hey, come on!"

I said, "What? Is that a secret? Quit your bickering, the tasks are the tasks. Let's get back to the resort."

I turned without another word, hearing Brett chuckling and Knuckles muttering behind me.

Knuckles, Jennifer, and I split away, the others heading north to their vehicle as we walked to our SUV down the lane. Jennifer took my hand and gave it a ferocious squeeze. I looked at her and saw the death glare.

Gonna be hearing about that comment later . . .

I leaned into her ear and said, "Give me a break. Remember all the shit Knuckles used to give us when we were sleeping around? Before we were married? Payback is a bitch."

She said, "Payback doesn't mean being an asshole. That wasn't necessary."

I chuckled and said, "Oh, yeah it was. He deserves it."

She squeezed my hand again, this time more lightly, and I was focused on her affection. Focused on what was good in my life instead of what could go bad. Because of it, I missed the group of men who coalesced around us. Ordinarily, I'd have seen them a mile away, but I was too fixated on my team's cohesion and—if I was honest—my wife's acceptance.

We'd almost reached the SUV when Knuckles said, "Pike . . ."

I immediately widened my aperture outside of my little circle and saw three men walking toward us. I looked back up the street at the restaurant, seeing it empty. In the time it took to do that they had closed on us. We were in a narrow alley with no sight radius to anyone who might help.

The first man spoke English, which surprised me, saying, "Give us your phones and wallets."

I sensed the beast rise, an uncomfortable feeling, but something I secretly craved, like a heroin addict seeing the needle. I *wanted* them to push it. Inexplicably, my rage began to grow molten. Even so, I owed it to my team to at least try to defuse the situation.

I held up my hands and said, "Whoa, hey, we don't want any trouble. We just want to go home."

He said, "You don't get it. You're not going home."

Jennifer saw my face and squeezed my hand, saying, "Pike, don't."

Knuckles said, "Pike, let's go back. We can go back to the restaurant."

The man looked confused, wondering why everyone in my circle was acting like we had a choice of what we were going to do. He said, "You give us your phones and you can go. You don't, and you'll end up in the hospital—if you're lucky."

My brain was working at twice the speed of light, and the situation didn't make sense. *These guys are going to rob us for our phones on the street in broad daylight? Next to a famous restaurant?*

I knew this was about more than money and settled in for the fight. Letting the molten rage flow, I said, "We're going back to our friends, and you're going to stay here."

I knew that wasn't going to happen, but at least I could tell Jennifer I tried later.

They all looked at each other like they couldn't believe what I was saying. The main guy jumped forward, pulling a knife and saying, "Give me your phones and wallets."

I saw the blade and felt a sliver of sadness because of what it would mean for him. *So much for just beating his ass.*

To my team, I said, "Lethal force."

He waved the knife in confusion at my words, and I went to work, feeling the beast break free, the rage taking over. I trapped his knife hand high and wrapped his body, kicking his legs out from under him and slamming him to the concrete on his back with my full weight on top. I felt the bones break in his ribs and hammered him in the temple over and over, using a force that was driven by a bloodlust I had difficulty controlling. He went lifeless, a bloody rag doll beneath me, and I jumped up, seeing Knuckles and Jennifer engaged in combat.

Jennifer had a man on the ground with a rear naked choke, him flailing about like he was trying to get to the surface from underwater. Knuckles was dancing around in front of a guy who was still on his feet, a knife in his hands.

The man stabbed at him and Knuckles trapped his wrist and head-butted him in the face. I leapt forward, grabbed him by the hair, and bent his head back, then drove an elbow into his skull, turning out the lights, the beast running wild and looking for something else to eat.

Knuckles let his body fall and we turned to Jennifer. She was cradling the man's head, but he was clearly almost out, the fight having left his body. The sight infuriated me anew. I ran to her just as she released him, his head hitting the ground. I hammered his face, my arm working like a piston, my fist trying to reach the concrete beneath his skull. Jennifer grabbed my arm, shouting, "Pike! Enough!"

I stopped, seeing his bloody pulp of a face, breathing hard.

Knuckles said, "That was a bit much."

I looked at him, then at Jennifer, both of them wondering if I'd lost my mind. I don't know why it had happened, but something about these guys had tripped a wire in my brain, uncorking a rage I hadn't felt in a long time. Maybe it was my subconscious trying to tell me something, or maybe I was just mad at myself for letting them get within striking distance before I'd realized the danger, but either way, I'd overreacted.

I tried to project calm, as if my actions had been normal, saying, "Let's get out of here before the cops show up."

I heard the unique sirens of an Indian police car, and Knuckles said, "Too late."

I said, "Well, shit. We're not getting out of Goa tonight."

CHAPTER 25

K amal exited the mosque, glancing surreptitiously left and right in a futile attempt to locate Mr. Chin's men. He knew it was impossible, as Chin wouldn't be employing Chinese and the surveillance could be anyone.

He found the team right next to a smoothie stand, just as Mr. Chin had said. They gathered around him, Manjit saying, "So? What happened?"

"We have a safe house, and he wants us to do another mission. He called it a 'standoff attack.' I don't know any more than that."

He felt a vibration on his wrist and raised the watch face. Randeep said, "Where'd you get that watch?"

Kamal ignored him, surprised to see a text message on the watch: *Give them their phones and watches. I want to see a heartbeat.*

Kamal whipped his head left and right but saw no sign of Mr. Chin. He felt anger at being cornered like a mouse in a barn, but unslung the backpack.

He started handing out the boxes, two to a man, saying, "These are watches Mr. Chin wants us to wear. The other box is the phone it's tethered to. Do not use the phone to do anything but talk to each other. If we need to make any other calls, I have a separate phone for that."

Randeep held up the Garmin box and said, "What is all this?"

"According to Mr. Chin, it's to help us with the mission, but I'm sure it's to keep track of us, like a GPS tag for someone just out of prison."

Manjit said, "And you agreed to this?"

"I had to. What else was I going to do? He told me he had evidence from the botched hit, and that he'd give it to the RAW. They'd find us in less than a day. It was better to make him think we were still on his side."

Agam turned on his watch, saw his heartbeat, and said, "Well, honestly, it's pretty cool. I could never afford this in real life."

Randeep pushed him and said, "It's a set of handcuffs, man! That heartbeat tells him it's on your wrist, and the watch will tell him where you are."

Miffed, Agam said, "Doesn't mean it's not cool. If we must do the mission, might as well get something out of it."

Kamal smiled and said, "I'm glad you think it's neat, because I want you to figure out how to defeat it. You're always messing with such things."

He nodded, saying, "Just give me a computer."

"There's one in the safe house."

Manjit said, "Where is this safe house, anyway?"

Kamal grimaced and held up his own watch, showing them a breadcrumb trail and an arrow with a distance and heading. He said, "It's about six hundred meters away as the bird flies."

"So we're going to follow that thing like a fish chasing a lure?"

"I guess so." Before he could say anything else, his wrist vibrated and another text message came through: *I see all four. Good. Now get to the safe house and study the mission. Use the computer to contact me with any concerns. You have a single day to get ready.*

He had to press a button, scrolling down in order to see it all on the watch face, Manjit looking over his shoulder. Manjit said, "He really *is* tracking us. This is ridiculous."

Kamal said, "It's the price of admission. We'll only do it as long as we want. Agam will figure out how to defeat it. Let's go."

He held his wrist out, took a bearing from the arrow, and began walking, the men following behind him. In short order, Kamal became frustrated. The watch wasn't giving turn-by-turn directions. Instead it just showed the arrow pointing unerringly in one direction, but soon enough they found themselves in a maze of narrow alleys, all selling various goods.

They went through a textile area selling cloth and linens, a stone market, a vegetable and meat section, then entered what clearly was a tourist area, with the vendors all selling cheap trinkets most likely made in China. They hit one more dead end, the arrow pointing through a wall as if they could fly over it, and Kamal cursed.

Manjit said, "This is ridiculous. We're like children out here getting toyed with. Why didn't he just give us a damn address?"

"I don't know. He wanted me to use the watch. Wanted me to know it was working."

Manjit scoffed and said, "Well, it's not."

They went down the alley, moving away from the GPS location, found another alley headed at least parallel to the endstate, and then exited into the sunshine on a two-lane road, this one large enough for vehicles to come and go. Kamal had no idea where they were, but he could see the arrow showing them the safe house less than seventy meters away.

He followed the bearing, fascinated with the meters ticking down, enjoying the hunt for the safe house despite himself. He went past another alley going back into the markets, and the distance started getting longer.

He stopped, retraced, then entered the alley, walking down it for about fifty feet before stopping outside of a roll-up metal door with a padlock, a sign above it proclaiming a spice store. The watch told him he was at zero meters.

This must be it.

The spice storefronts left, right, and behind him were all open, the air pungent enough to make Kamal feel like he needed to sneeze.

The vendors of the other stores looked at the group curiously, but Kamal ignored them, acting as if he belonged. He pulled out the envelope Mr. Chin had given him and removed a key, putting it in the padlock and holding his breath.

The lock sprung open and he exhaled, raising the roll-up door and entering the safe house. He waited until the men had followed, flipped an overhead light, and slid the door closed. He turned and saw a narrow storefront no larger than a passageway, the entire area maybe twenty feet wide and sixty feet long, with empty shelves and cabinets on each side and a wooden ladder at the rear leading up into darkness.

While his men explored the downstairs he went up the ladder, feeling along the wall until he hit another light switch. It blazed into existence, revealing four mattresses on the floor and a wooden table with a laptop computer, a MiFi cellular data device attached to the back.

He went to it and opened the lid, seeing a sign-in screen. He went back to his watch and pulled up the notifications menu, retrieving the instructions. He typed in the login and password and was met with a screen that had a single document in the center. He opened it and began reading. As he read, he couldn't believe what Mr. Chin wanted them to do.

He heard clattering on the ladder and Agam appeared, holding something above his head, saying, "There are four of these downstairs. What's that about?"

Kamal looked closer and saw he held a small commercial drone. A folded quadcopter. He returned to the screen, studying the instructions, and it all became clear.

The rest of the men made it up the ladder, each of them standing around the entrance, looking at him expectantly.

He said, "We're supposed to attack the day after tomorrow. Thakkar is doing a pre-wedding party. A small group of prestigious people from around the world. Chin wants us to kill him there with a drone."

That set them back a bit, Agam saying, "He wants us to fly a drone into him? That won't kill him. Even if we fly all four from downstairs. At most, it'll knock him to the ground. Is Mr. Chin hoping for a heart attack?"

Kamal returned to the screen and said, "According to this, those are for practice. The real one will have explosives."

Manjit said, "Explosives? Like we're in Ukraine? Like it'll hunt him down on camera and kill him?"

Kamal continued to study the screen, absently saying, "Yes. Exactly like that."

Randeep said, "This is getting out of control. He wants us to flat out assassinate the billionaire on camera?"

Kamal turned from the screen and said, "Yes, he does, but that's not the worst part."

"Seriously? What's the worst part?"

"He wants us to do it on a visit to the Taj Mahal. He's visiting there the day after tomorrow. Thakkar's apparently locked down the locals' gate and purchased a block of time for him and his entourage to tour the place. There will still be some foreign tourists there, but no locals. I guess he doesn't want his entourage mixing with the real world. They'll be out front of the Taj, taking pictures during a span of time."

Manjit said, "You know how I feel about that. I'm not going to kill a bunch of civilians because Mr. Chin said to. I'm not doing it."

"The drone is embedded with facial recognition. We fly it above the site, and it'll go straight to him. It'll kill him, and only him."

CHAPTER 26

I handed the key to the valet at the Grand Hyatt resort and walked inside like it was just another day. Which, of course, it wasn't. The sun had gone down during our time at the Panaji police station, and I still wasn't sure if we were good to go. Our cover of GRS appeared to have held up well enough, and the event had been chalked up to a random mugging, but you never knew who was looking at what. The last thing we needed was a foreign government digging deep into our company.

As for me, I was sure it wasn't a random mugging. Those men were after us for a specific reason, and that reason had something to do with the meeting between the RAW, the CIA, and Thakkar. I had no proof of that, but the circumstances were too coincidental, and the leader of the group had made that strange statement before I crushed his ass, telling us that we were "not going home."

Not something a mugger who was out for a score would say but something a team on a mission would let slip out. A mugger would have wanted compliance, telling us sweet nothings that would make us feel that if we gave him our stuff, he'd let us go. Threatening to kill us right off the bat didn't fit. I was convinced that they weren't after our valuables but instead were after us, specifically. The police didn't care about any of that, and in the end, I thought they were more concerned with us posting a negative review on TripAdvisor than they were about solving the crime.

Jennifer and I had gone back to our room to clean up, getting ready for our meeting with Nadia, and she'd finally cornered me. Something I knew was going to happen.

"What was that back there?"

I said, "What? Back where? You mean when you were having trouble with your guy?"

She put a finger to my lips and said, "No lies. What was that? I haven't seen you like that since Amena was in danger. Actually, since we first met and *I* was in danger. You lost it for a minute against some guys you *knew* we could handle. Why?"

I took her hand in mine, moving it away from my face, and said, "I didn't 'lose it.' I did what was necessary."

In truth, I didn't have an answer, and that alone scared me. I had gone from zero to a thousand miles an hour over three guys I could have handled in my sleep. She was right. That had never happened unless someone I cared about was in extreme danger. Something had slithered out from my soul, and I didn't control it.

I didn't know why I had reacted the way I had, like an old man trying to cut an apple, only to find he didn't control the knife, the hand tremoring and doing something outside of what the brain said it should do.

I really had no answer.

She said, "What you did wasn't necessary. It was primeval. You know it and I know it. Why?"

I held up my hands and said, "I don't know. For whatever reason, those men cut into my scab. The one that keeps me normal. I just . . . wanted to smash them."

She stared into my eyes for a moment, then said, "Can you control it? Like you did before?"

"Of course I can. I always have."

She continued staring, her eyes boring into mine, and it was disconcerting, because she knew I was lying. She said, "I used to think I had the ability to keep you from going berserk. From letting the beast go free. Now I'm not so sure."

She and I had had long conversations about my inner demons, and we'd labeled my inability to control myself "the beast." It was something inside of me that she tried to understand. She knew intimately about the death of my family and what it had done to my psyche. She'd seen up close and personal what I could do when I let the beast free, but she'd been able to keep it contained simply by trusting me, which led to me trusting her and the beast going back into its cave. It really hadn't reared its head again until Amena, and when it had, it had been brutal. The men it was directed against deserved it, but my actions had frightened even me.

Every time it showed its head, I wondered if I was a hero saving lives for the greater good, or simply a psychopath leveraging my position to kill. And whether such a distinction even mattered.

I didn't want to admit it to myself, but the beast was still there, looking for a release, poking at the cage walls to find a seam. It scared me that it had come calling during a simple mugging, but I wasn't going to let Jennifer know that.

I said, "Honey, come on. It's not like that. The assault ended up okay. I didn't kill anyone, for Christ's sake."

She kept staring at me for another heartbeat, then said, "You have issues, and you're too big of a coward to admit it. Your brain saw something else in that mugging, and your body followed. You're letting the beast control your actions."

Without saying it, she was telling me I had PTSD, and that aggravated the hell out of me. I wasn't like the average soldier. PTSD didn't factor in my world. At least that's what I told myself.

I snapped, "That's bullshit and you know it. All I did was keep us from getting mugged, and you're turning it into some psychobabble bullshit, like I need to go to a head farm or something."

She heard my tone and said, "Okay, Pike, okay. But when you feel the beast breaking free, when you want to satisfy it, I want you to look at me."

"What the hell does that mean? 'Look at you,' like you're some sort of Buddhist sensei?"

Now completely serious, without an ounce of humor, she said, "Yes, that's what I am. Can you promise me you'll do that?"

I wanted to tell her to pack sand, that I didn't need any help controlling my demons, but I knew she was right. She'd been telling me to seek counseling for years, and I hadn't. Now she was the one doing the counseling.

I said, "Yes. I can do that."

She smiled and said, "Good. Maybe I'll keep you out of a prison."

She went to get her purse and I said, "There *was* no prison, damn it. Nobody locked us up. It was just a mugging."

She slung her bag over her shoulder and said, "I'm not talking about one with physical walls."

I heard a knock at the door, and she said, "We're not done here."

Relieved, I went to it, saying, "Okay, okay. We're done for a little while anyway."

I opened it to see Knuckles standing there, out of his T-shirt and flip-flops, now wearing a pair of khaki pants and a loose button-up short-sleeve shirt.

I said, "So you can meet with the head of the CIA looking like a beach bum, but when it comes to Nadia, you have to shave?"

Indignant, he said, "The Hyatt Club has a dress code. That's all it is."

I smirked, turned to Jennifer, and said, "You ready?"

She nodded and said, "I wish you'd take the time to change clothes for me."

Jesus Christ. Can I do anything right?

We left our room and wandered through the grounds, dodging the golf carts driving around until we reached the Hyatt Club. Like before, we had to show our room key to prove we were allowed to enter, and took a seat in the corner. Unlike before, I never had to tell anyone what we wanted to drink, as Nadia came over with a tray, dressed yet again like a Hyatt employee.

She set the drinks on our table, then said, "You guys had a little trouble today, huh?"

I said, "How would you know that?"

She pointed next to me, at an open space on my couch, and said, "May I?"

I nodded, saw Knuckles scowl, and smiled at him. She took a seat and said, "People talk here. It's a small town. Tourists getting mugged spreads like wildfire."

I said, "People talk? Or you're tied into the police here? If I went to the other waiter over there, would he have any idea that we were mugged?"

She smiled and said, "Probably not, but he's not that smart."

I chuckled and said, "Sure. He probably sees so many random muggings it doesn't even register."

She said, "Your mugging wasn't random. I think you were targeted."

CHAPTER 27

The upper room of the safe house was becoming cloyingly hot in the midday sun. That, and hearing the method of attack, did nothing to calm Manjit. He grew agitated, saying, "Facial recognition for an assassination? And how does that help us? How does that help the Sikh? I'm willing to kill for a cause, but I'm done with this killing for China."

Kamal turned from the screen and said, "I am too. Are you really committed to helping the Sikh? If it comes to killing innocents, can you do it?"

"What's that mean?"

"It means I've seen what Chin wants, and it gives us an opportunity. We can pretend to do what he wishes, but accomplish much more. I need to know if you're willing."

Kamal paused and looked at the rest of the men, saying, "I need to know if all of you are willing. We can strike a blow against the government for what they've done to us in the past, but it's not without sacrifice. Some innocents will die, but only because they support the regime Thakkar represents. If they come to his daughter's wedding, then they come supporting him, and he's the devil that props up the government we hate."

He looked at each in turn, knowing he held the mettle to continue, but unsure of them. He said, "I want a commitment, right now, before we continue."

Manjit said, "What is this? You want me to promise to kill innocent people, for China?"

Kamal grew cold, remembering his past. Remembering the arrest that had destroyed his life. Remembering what had brought him to this point.

Feeling the fury.

He said, "No. We're not going to kill Thakkar at the Taj Mahal. I'm not doing anything for China."

He turned back to Manjit and said, "Do you remember the jail? Do you remember crying to me after your interrogations? Do you remember asking why they were so cruel, when you'd done nothing wrong?"

Taken aback, Manjit looked left and right at the other men, having never told them of the trials he'd faced, or the way he'd dealt with the pain. Something he was embarrassed about.

Subdued, he said, "Yes, I remember. I haven't forgotten what you did for me there."

"Well, it's time we took that anger to the enemy. Revenge for Sidak. Revenge for *all* of them. In the end, we're done because we were stupid enough to take the pay of Mr. Chin, but we can make that right. Make it pure. We're probably dead either way on this. If we do what he wants, Chin will kill us afterwards. If we do it wrong and fail, he'll still have us killed. He can't allow us to live either way."

He tapped the screen and said, "The answer is right here, and I say we do it wrong. Bring his ass down with us while shining a light on the Sikh travesty."

The room went quiet, nobody saying a word about the true threats being spilled out loud. Each man had continued looking only at the five-meter target, first for the money, but now for survival. None of them wanted to hear the truth: that they were dead no matter what they did.

Manjit said, "How is killing Thakkar going to shine a light on our travails?"

"Because we're not going to kill him." Kamal pointed at the screen again and said, "Mr. Chin gave us his complete itinerary. He's going to the Taj in two days with a limited group of people, but he's attending a pre-wedding celebration in Jaipur with hundreds of people from all over the world."

He turned to them and said, "We're going to invade that party, and use China's bullshit on the Taj Mahal to camouflage it. We're going to attack those rich bastards at their own ceremony and take what they value most, all in the name of Khalistan."

He stood up and his voice grew stronger, saying, "Are you with me? Are you willing to avenge what you've been through? Or has all this talk about Khalistan been just *talk*?"

His men shuffled from foot to foot, shocked at his words, and he realized they were just now coming to grips with the danger they were in.

He whispered, "You're already dead. Each and every one of you, because of Mr. Chin. If we do what I say, we might live to see Khalistan."

The silence hung in the air, and Kamal thought he had lost. Then Manjit surprised him, saying, "What do you think we can do? We have these watches, and we're all being tracked. What can we do?"

Kamal smiled and said, "I've been thinking about this for a while, ever since Gaza made the world stage. We can do a lot. We might die, but at least our deaths will be for our people and not China."

He turned to Agam and said, "You need to figure out how to spoof these watches. They're tied to a phone, which means it's all software. We need to break ourselves from that. But you can't do it until after we're supposed to attack at the Taj Mahal."

Manjit said, "Why? Why not just do it now?"

"Because that asshole Chin has given us the method of attack. If we break from these watches now, he'll know and come hunting us."

Agam said, "None of these drones have any explosives. And where is the facial recognition?"

Kamal gave a half-hearted laugh and said, "These four are for practice. He wants us to go to a field and practice killing the guy, driving the drones into the ground."

He took the quadcopter from Agam's hand and said, "He's pretty good, I'll give him that. The real drone is hidden in the Agra Fort, right next to the Taj Mahal, and the waypoint for it is in our watches. That's how we'll find it. Just like we found the safe house."

Manjit said, "So what do we do? How do we alter that?"

"We show him we're going to do the attack. One man goes there for the mission, letting him know we're doing it by the heartbeat and location on the watch, but we don't do the kill. We launch the drone after Thakkar's gone, but before our real attack."

"How's that going to do anything?"

"Because we're all going to Jaipur. To the big party. We're going to attack that celebration and seize Thakkar, killing anyone who stands in our way."

Manjit said, "Wait, wait, I've told you before, I'm not going to do that. Even if we could."

Kamal grew incensed and advanced on him, saying, "Is that what Sidak would utter? As he was hanging on a rope? I'm sick of your bullshit. This is the way. Hamas and the Palestinian fight in Israel has shown it."

Manjit recoiled, saying, "You want to associate yourself with those murderers? You hold *them* in high esteem? You want *me* to become *them*?"

Kamal poked him with a finger and said, "Yes, that's *exactly* what I want. You can't win this war playing by the establishment's rules. Yes, the Hamas attack was horrible. Abominable. But what happened after it? Israel attacked with overwhelming force, and then the world changed."

He turned to the rest of the men and said, "Now *everyone* talks about the Palestinians. Hamas murdered more than a thousand people, and nobody cares. All they care about is the plight of the Palestinian people. The highest institutions of learning in the United States started protesting. All because Hamas did an attack. Nobody cared about the murders. You don't see that happening with the Rohingya in Myanmar. They get slaughtered wholesale, and nobody cares. Terrorism *works*, and we're going to use it here."

Manjit said nothing, and Kamal softened his tone, saying, "I'm not talking about raping people, like Hamas did. I'm not saying we need to go totally crazy, just that an attack on a wedding party for an Indian billionaire will hold weight, just like it did for Israel. India will take notice. And so will the world."

Manjit sighed and looked at the other men. He went back to Kamal and said, "When does death become a thing that advances our purposes? If we've gone that far, we've left the principles of being a Sikh. Yes, Chin can kill us, but killing in exchange? Why do I wear a dastaar? To kill?"

Kamal saw he was losing Manjit—and in so doing, losing the rest of the men. He said, "The dastaar doesn't define you. You're not even wearing it now. What defines you is what you do to advance the purpose of the cloth. Wear it after this and you can do so in pride. Wear it if you quit, and you'll only do it in shame."

He could see Manjit was on the edge, and he drove home the knife. "Sidak wore the dastaar every day of his life, striving for a better one. You can give his family that."

Manjit looked at the floor for a moment, then looked up, saying, "I'm in. But we don't kill anyone unless they're part of the state."

Kamal nodded, then said, "Do you consider Thakkar and his family part of the state?"

"Yes, I do."

CHAPTER 28

N adia's comment about us being targeted on purpose took me aback. I said, "I sort of feel the same way, but why do you think so?"

"The men who attacked you are from the same organization as the two guys you killed here the other night. I've seen the police reports, and they're tied into D Company, and that coincidence is just too convenient."

I said, "Why? What does D Company have to do with the assault here? And why would they try to kill us after the fact? What good would it do?"

She said, "I honestly don't know, but either you're the most unlucky man on the planet, or they were hunting you."

She glanced at Jennifer and said, "I don't think you're unlucky."

I smiled and said, "I don't think I am either. What does your command think about last night?"

"I haven't told them."

Knuckles finally perked up, saying, "Seriously? You didn't tell your boss that you had some Americans break into the suspected terrorists' hotel room, and that while they were there, they were ambushed by a bunch of Chinese?"

She turned to him and said, "Yes, seriously. Something is rotten here, and I still don't know if it's my own people. I had hoped to confirm or deny one way or the other, but the men you saw short-circuited that. I can't prove that someone was hiding terrorist connections when all the evidence is gone. I have no idea what our search team would have presented, because they literally had nothing to present."

I said, "So where does that leave us? The meeting's over, and from what we're hearing it was a success."

She smiled and said, "How do you know that? Does the CIA routinely talk to archeological firms?"

I said, "Spare me. We're beyond that now."

She nodded and said, "Yes, I think we are."

She looked at Jennifer and said, "I've run the documents you took pictures of, and most of it led nowhere. The passport photo didn't ping anywhere in our database. We have no idea who it is. The journal itself was mostly a bunch of random notes. Really just a collection of to-do lists the man kept. That address you found, however, is real. It's a spice shop in Old Delhi."

I said, "And have you checked that out?"

"No. I have no sanction to do that. I don't have anyone I can direct to the address. I don't have a team working under me. I *am* the team."

Knuckles said, "Surely you've used Google Earth to take a look. I know you've studied it. What do you think?"

"It's a spice shop, just like a hundred others in the area. The only thing that's odd is that it hasn't been open for a couple of weeks. Someone's paying the rent, but not opening the storefront."

"Meaning you think it's a D Company front?"

"Meaning I think it's odd. The lease is washed through a host of cutouts, so yes, it could be the Mafia, but it could be something else. Something more sinister."

"Like what?"

"Like an influence operation from another country. After what Jennifer saw, maybe Chinese influence, but it's more likely Pakistan."

"Well, that's not unheard of. We've uncovered a ton of Chinese influence in the United States, all the way down to bagel shops that are actually undercover Chinese police stations used to keep track of the Chinese diaspora."

"That's exactly what I'm thinking. If China is behind this, then the RAW is going to want to know, but I'm leaning more to Pakistan. I can't see China being this brazen, but Pakistan has proven their willingness through past history, and all the evidence points to Islamic terrorism and the ISI. I just need the proof."

And I knew the crux of the entire meeting was about to come out. I said, "Then go check it out."

She shook her head and said, "I'm still not sure someone inside of RAW isn't tied into this. It wouldn't surprise me if the Pakistani ISI were paying someone. Those attackers the other night were focused, and I think it was because they had inside information. I was hoping to see if the search of the hotel room would pinpoint someone, but you know how that went."

I cut to the chase. "So you want *us* to go check this place out?"

"That's what I'm thinking. You and Jennifer."

I glanced at Jennifer and said, "Have you wandered around for a single day in your country? Jennifer here sticks out like a whore in church."

Jennifer glared at me and said, "You're not blending in any better."

I smiled and said, "The point is there's no way we can do a B&E without getting caught. I won't even be able to conduct surveillance on the site without compromise. This isn't a hotel that caters to Russians."

"Yeah, I know the problems, but it's in a touristy area. A bazaar that all the Westerners go to in Old Delhi. You won't stick out as bad as you think."

"Am I supposed to work this with you, or just do it on my own, giving you the results? Do we get any support here?"

"Well, you're not getting any official support from RAW, but I can provide what little I have. I actually know the owner of the spice stall down the alley from the target. He's a family friend, and he trusts me. He can get you an observation point on the second floor. He's already told me he's seen some men coming and going from the place."

"And how are we supposed to coordinate this? Just walk up and say, 'Nadia told us to come in and spy around'?"

Nadia gave me a sour look and said, "I'm not stupid. I *am* RAW, but just like them, you don't believe a woman. You don't believe what I'm telling you because I'm female."

That hit an open sore. I had done more to get Jennifer into the Taskforce than anyone alive. Being female had *nothing* to do with it. Being stupid did.

I stood up and said, "Spare me the women-of-the-world-unite bullshit. I have no time for it. What I *do* have is a *team*, and I'm not willing to sacrifice them on a mission just because you have an axe to grind as a *female*."

She looked like I'd slapped her, which, I suppose, I had—at least verbally. She said, "Why did you even come here to talk?"

I sat back down and said, "Because I think you might be right, but now I'm worried that you're doing this as a way to get back at some asshole chauvinists in RAW. I'm not into that, and I won't use my team to validate it."

She leaned back in her chair and said, "There might be a little bit of that in here, but it's not why I'm doing it. I honestly think there *is* an inside threat, and I have no way to expose it myself. I'm not going to burn your team, I promise. I'll be in just as much trouble as you are if you're caught."

"And *if* we get caught? What's the backstop to this? Just you?"

She looked at Knuckles and said, "Well, you have your assets to help, no? I'm assuming that since you're even entertaining this, you've spoken to your command."

I chuckled and said, "Okay, you're a good read, I'll give you that, but I'm not getting any help to execute, I promise."

"But you'll get help if it goes sour?"

I sighed and said, "I suppose that's true, but it's not ideal."

"Just pretend you're here on a mission sanctioned by the United States, and you happen to have a person on the inside of RAW to help. Can you do that?"

I looked at Jennifer, and she gave a slight nod. I went to Knuckles and he said, "You know me, I'm always up for some high adventure."

Nadia said, "You won't be getting any high adventure, I promise."

I said, "Okay, let's just take this one step at a time. Why did you specify Jennifer and me for this?"

She acted surprised and said, "What do you mean? Do you have someone else here?"

I laughed and played the game, even as we both knew it was ridiculous. "No, no, I just meant I have Knuckles, but you specified Jennifer and me."

She said, "Well, you wanted to coordinate with me, so he's going to do that. He'll be our liaison."

Knuckles scrunched his brow and said, "How? What am I going to do?"

She leaned forward and said, "I told you I'm friends with the bride. I'm invited to the pre-wedding party in Jaipur. It's going to be the event of the year, with a who's who guest list. You're going to be my date."

I saw Knuckles' eyes shoot open, and I glared at him. He held up his hands, stammering, "Pike, I swear, I didn't set this up."

CHAPTER 29

Jianhong Zhang—aka Mr. Chin—walked into the lobby of the Mumbai Four Seasons hotel and went immediately toward the elevator, pressing the button to go up. He had a room in the Four Seasons, though he had no time to go to it. His meeting was at 5 P.M. sharp, and it had taken him longer to return to Mumbai from New Delhi than he had planned. After meeting Kamal at the mosque the day before, he'd toyed with immediately returning, but decided he had all the next day to travel and had chosen to relax in New Dehli for the night. That had proven to be a mistake, as his flight was delayed long enough that he barely had enough time to make the designated update with his control in the Ministry of State Security.

He entered the elevator with two Englishmen, both discussing some business meeting or other. He gave a perfunctory smile and pushed the button for the thirty-fourth floor, looking at his watch. They pushed the twenty-fourth and twenty-fifth, one man saying, "I guess it's close enough to five to go topside."

Mr. Chin smiled and said, "I want to go early enough to get a seat for the sunset."

The other man said, "That's the ticket. Save us a seat."

They exited and Mr. Chin continued to ride to the rooftop. He exited into a narrow, unassuming hallway, following the light from the windows on the far side.

AER was known as one of the best rooftop bars in all of South Asia, with spectacular views of the Mumbai cityscape and the coast, the scenery marred only by the ubiquitous blue tarps of the slums sprinkled throughout the landscape. Mr. Chin had picked the location. If he was to meet his masters, he'd rather do it there than in some dark alley.

He went to the hostess and asked for a table for three, peeking beyond her shoulder and relieved to see the bar was fairly empty, with only a smattering of people. That would change when the monsoon season officially ended and the glass roof and walls opened up. At that point, there would be a line to get onto the rooftop, the bar open to the air and filled with those who wanted to see or be seen. Now, with the rains still threatening, its retractable roof was in place, with no open-air ambiance, a chrysalis that would evolve into a butterfly in a month, something the Mumbai jet set would demand to experience.

But the chrysalis stage suited Mr. Chin, as crowds always represented a threat to his operations.

The hostess led him to a curved couch right next to the glass overlooking Mumbai, a small table in front and a single chair on the opposite side. He took the chair, facing the entrance, leaving the couch for the men he was meeting, reviewing in his mind what he would say. So far, the mission had been a mess. Salvageable, but a mess.

He caught movement at the door and saw his control enter. Two Chinese men, one tall, close to six feet, the other shorter, both with close-cropped bristle hair and wearing business suits. Because they supposedly worked for the same mining conglomerate as Mr. Chin.

He stood and waved his hand at the couch. They sat and he took the chair, wanting to project confidence. He said, "Thank you for the meeting. I know it's unorthodox, but I wanted to convey the danger we are in for completion of the mission and ask for some additional assets."

The taller man said, "I don't understand how this hasn't been accomplished already. It was a simple task, and you were given incredible back-stopping to execute it. All you had to do was capture a man or kill him. That's it. Kill him and stop the mining of rare earth elements in India. You didn't even have to make sure anyone on the team survived, as you were going to eliminate the ones who did it as well. How difficult is that?"

Mr. Chin realized this was going to be harder than he wanted, but he'd been in such situations in the past. These clods had never been at the sharp end of the spear. Party functionaries who spent their time kissing the CCP ring to get ahead, all they wanted was a win in their column and they had no ability to articulate what that win would mean to China. He had little time for them, but realized they held the fate of his mission in their hands.

He said, "We were blocked from our first attempt by a penetration from the RAW. They captured my mole. I could not predict that. I did manage to cauterize the damage and continue."

The shorter one said, "But the second attempt—"

A waitress arrived and he ceased talking. Mr. Chin understood why, but also knew that the chance of anyone in this bar speaking Mandarin Chinese was about as likely as getting struck by lightning. Even so, people *did* get struck by lightning, so he remained mute as well. They gave their drink orders in English, waited for her to leave earshot, and the man continued, saying, "But your second attempt was thwarted as well. It doesn't bode well for your acumen. It was a simple mission."

"Yes, it was, which is why I contacted you. The mission was simple, but I believe the forces who thwarted it are not. Did you trace the company I gave you?"

"Yes, we did. It appears to be a real company, with concrete results. A niche American archeological firm that's worked all over the world."

"Did you trace the travel of the company personnel after I left Goa? Did they fly to Delhi?"

"Why are you tracking Americans? We do not want to involve the United States in this operation. Your mission is Indian only, understand?"

Mr. Chin knew that the "we" in that statement meant the Chinese Communist Party. For all of its bluster, it was very reticent about upsetting the status quo between China and the United States.

Mr. Chin said, "I believe they are already involved, and that company—Grolier Recovery Services—is a front. I don't know who they work for, but I believe they are the reason we haven't succeeded so far."

The shorter man leaned forward, now interested. "Why do you say that?"

Mr. Chin said, "The GRS personnel are the ones who stopped the attack at the resort. They just happened to be at the right place at the right time. It was too convenient to be true."

"That's it? They happened to be at the right place and time, and your attack was stalled? Given your plan, it could have been anyone who did it."

"No, my men were trained and ready to kill with weapons out. Those men had some type of early warning and were waiting. I'm sure of it. If it had been just a bunch of tourists, they'd all be dead."

"That doesn't prove they were actively targeting anything. It could have been just dumb luck, and it would be a mistake to do something against them if you're wrong. Every action leaves a trail and we don't want an attack against a civilian company from the United States to lead back to us. Maybe your men weren't as trained as you say."

Mr. Chin leaned back, choosing his next words carefully. "It wasn't dumb luck. I already took the liberty of using local talent against them, and the local talent failed as well."

The tall man looked shocked, saying, "You did what? You had no authority for that. *Especially* against a different foreign asset."

"My authority was to accomplish the mission by any means necessary, as long as it didn't reflect on our organization. I hired some local talent to simply rob them, maybe rough them up a little, in order to get them tangled with the local police. It would have been—in fact *is* being—treated as a local crime problem. If they were truly an American company, they'd just get an experience to tell their co-workers, or maybe become tied up with the police or hospital. Neither happened, which is why I'm more convinced than ever that they're not just a U.S. company but are an intelligence asset targeting our mission."

"What did happen?"

"Three men were annihilated by those Grolier people, just like what occurred at the resort. Three rough men, I might add. Recruited from the largest criminal organization in India. They weren't local muggers. Their specialty is intimidation and neutralization of opponents, and all three were sent to the hospital. I'm telling you, Grolier Recovery Services is not just a typical U.S. company."

The short man, whom Mr. Chin took to be the one in charge, said, "Maybe they're just good at fighting."

Mr. Chin said, "One of the targets was a woman. And yes, she was good at fighting, and she didn't learn that getting an archeological degree. But you might be correct, if they're still in Goa or have flown home. Where are they now?"

Mr. Chin saw a flicker of belief in the short one's face. He said, "They went to Delhi. They're at a hotel in New Delhi. How did you know that's where they'd be?"

"Because that's where my team is. Somehow, they're following my team. I don't know how they tracked them, but they did."

Now convinced, the short one said, "So what do you want from us?"

"I need a Condor team from the MSS. Experts at interdiction. I know you have one stationed in Delhi, and I don't want to rely on the local talent anymore."

The short man looked at the taller one, then said, "Okay. That can be arranged, but I don't want them executing unless you're certain the Americans are interfering. Right now, I don't see enough evidence of that, but I'll release a team. What is the status of the mission and your team?"

"Luckily, the RAW is still focused on Islamic terrorists. The pocket litter and phone numbers seemed to have worked. They're still clean."

"You'll have to ensure they get killed in the attack or kill them later to keep that cover. You know that, right?"

"Yes. I have a plan in place for that. They want to get paid, and when they show up for their money, I'll give them something else. I'll leave more evidence with the bodies pointing to Pakistan and Muslims. That won't be a problem."

"What are they doing now?"

"I gave them instructions for the mission, and they're practicing with the drones. Thakkar is taking selected VIPs to the Taj Mahal for a pre-wedding event tomorrow. That's where the attack will be."

The taller man said, "How do you know they're following your instructions? Do you trust them?"

"No, I don't trust them, but I can follow what they're doing."

He withdrew a small tablet, then tapped on it for a moment until a satellite map appeared, showing a field with four icons. He laid it on the table and said, "They're currently south of Delhi right now, practicing for the mission."

CHAPTER 30

Agam watched the drone turn into a speck in the distance, then come racing back as he controlled it with his smartphone clipped into a plastic harness. It zipped overhead and began hovering directly above them, the camera on the drone showing their bodies on the screen. Kamal could see he was really enjoying the technology.

Kamal said, "Can you reach the Taj from the old fort?"

Agam continued focusing on his phone screen, manipulating the drone and saying, "Watch this. I can plot a grid and get it to fly there without doing anything."

He pushed an icon on the phone and the drone zipped off overhead like an angry bumblebee, soon lost from sight. Agam said, "See the target out there?"

Kamal looked out at the field and saw a section of a cardboard box painted white with a red crosshair on it, standing in the field like a scarecrow.

Agam said, "This is how we'll attack the Taj Mahal."

He manipulated the screen again, setting some other parameters, then used his thumbs on the joysticks of the controller. Kamal saw the drone fly away, then come back at incredible speed, slamming into the target in a spray of plastic and metal.

Agam shouted, enthralled by the display. He turned to Kamal and said, "This stuff is top-notch."

Kamal, much calmer, repeated, "Can you hit the Taj Mahal from the fort?"

Adam bent over to the ground and began preparing another of their test drones, saying, "Oh, yes. That's easy. Like I said, I can set a grid and just let it fly. I don't even have to be around for the fireworks. Aim it at a minaret, and then hit the street while it does the work."

Kamal nodded, but said, "I'm afraid you're going to have to watch it fly."

Agam quit fiddling with the next drone and looked up. He said, "You told Manjit no unnecessary deaths. You said that hitting the building itself would cause the necessary police response."

"I know what I told Manjit, but he doesn't understand. We need the deaths to get the police to overreact. Just hitting the building will generate interest, but nothing like killing some tourists visiting. Tourists from as many countries as we can. We need a complete lockdown of the Taj. We need everyone focused on that attack while we do our own."

Agam, always the loyal follower, took that in and said, "Are you sure? You want to step across that line? Become Hamas?"

"We're going to become Hamas at the Jaipur party. That's a foregone conclusion. If we aren't willing to commit . . . if we do half steps while the government responds with full force, we're going to lose."

"But the wedding party is full of Thakkar's people. This will be complete innocents just visiting the Taj."

Kamal nodded and said, "That's true, but the Taj Mahal represents the Indian state. It's necessary."

"Have you told Manjit this?"

"Of course not. He will follow his heart. I just need to make sure he believes his heart is pure. There's no reason for him to know."

Agam said nothing, getting the next drone ready and launching it. He began to control the flight, this time with less enthusiasm. He said, "Are you sure we're on the right path here? I trust you, but I need to know."

Kamal said, "Yes. You see what the prime minister is doing. You see how he's crushing any dissent. It's not only the Sikhs. He does it to anyone who's not a Hindu. That needs to be stopped, and we have the means to do it."

He put a hand on Agam's arm and saw regret in his eyes. Kamal said, "I'm sorry for the deaths to come just as you are, but it's necessary. By visiting the Taj Mahal, they are supporting our persecution. Remember that."

Agam nodded, then raced the drone into the target again, shattering it in a small hurricane of plastic and metal. He turned to Kamal and said, "I'll do my part, but don't let it be in vain."

Kamal smiled and said, "It won't be, as long as you've fixed this watch problem."

Agam bent down for the next drone, saying, "It was actually easy. The watches are tied into our phones. Right now, he's seeing four men here instead of just two."

"How is that? What did you do?"

"I slaved all of Mr. Chin's phones to mine through the Garmin app. It was easy once I did a jailbreak on the phone and got to the root of the app. The watches talk to that app alone, and all I wanted to do was make sure that data was sent to my phone first, before anyone accessed it. I'm sure Mr. Chin is watching my phone, but what he doesn't know is that he's seeing all of our watches through my phone. Where I go is where you go."

"What about the health reports? The heartbeats? I mean, the watch is transmitting how many steps I take."

"I couldn't do anything about that. All I could do is spoof the location. Your steps and your heartbeat are still transmitted, albeit to my phone, so I suppose he could say that you took more steps than were shown in the history of my geolocation, but he's not looking at that. As long as your heart is still beating, it'll show him you're wearing the watch. It just won't show him where you are."

"So he thinks there are four of us in this field right now?"

"Yes. Unless Manjit and Randeep have a heart attack, they'll show up as living and breathing right here."

Kamal considered that, then said, "So when you do the attack tomorrow, it's going to look like all four of us are at the fort?"

"Yes. Is that a problem?"

"I don't know. He might become suspicious if we travel in a group for the next day. Sometime, somewhere, we'd separate."

"I can turn it off when Manjit and Randeep come back. Revert it to individual use."

"They aren't coming back. They're getting the launch point in Jaipur and talking to the security people."

"What security people? The ones on Thakkar's detail?"

"Yes. Apparently, our little team has grown. Thakkar has twelve on his security detail. Six are Sikhs, and four have now joined our mission."

Agam said, "What about the men controlling us? The Chinese? Do you really think they'll let this happen?"

"They will, because they do not know what we have planned. They make the mistake of assuming we're just vassals for them to manipulate. Just like the Hindu state. We will prove them all wrong."

"And the Americans? What about them?"

"The Americans? What do you mean?"

"The ones who stopped the assault at the resort. Mr. Chin thinks they did it on purpose. I could tell by the way he reacted."

Kamal scoffed and said, "They were just lucky. America has no fight here."

CHAPTER 31

I went down the street with Jennifer feeling as if we stood out like circus clowns attending a funeral, everyone in the afternoon sun gawking at us because we were the only gringos within five miles. Under my breath, I said, "Tourist area my ass. This is absolutely stupid."

Jennifer said, "It's a tourist spice market. We're fine. We belong here."

I chuckled and said, "Where are the tourists?"

"It's the end of the monsoon season. They aren't here yet."

"Well, that'll be something we can say when we're arrested. 'We're blending in. It's not our fault we did it two months early.'"

We'd flown the Rock Star bird to New Delhi late last night, getting a room in an incredible establishment called the Imperial Hotel. I suppose I should have put some price constraints on the team, but had not, and now we were getting five-star amenities. Veep and Brett, of course, had done this just to poke me in the eye about giving them the work. I only hoped the Taskforce would cover the bill.

Right after breakfast, Brett, Jennifer, and I had traveled to Old Delhi, finding the suspected address after a little bit of searching down the alleys, finding a nondescript space with a roll-up metal door, nothing else. We continued on, locating Nadia's spice market friend about seventy meters farther down. The bazaar was pretty much deserted at this time of day, with most of the proprietors just now opening up, but we were already drawing stares as the only Westerners around.

I'd called Nadia, she'd phoned her "family friend," and a man had come out, looking furtive. He'd waved us into his little shop and said, "I don't know what this is about, and I don't want to know."

I said, "Don't worry, we're not here to cause trouble. Nadia is just doing us a favor."

"What is this favor? Is it about that shop down the street? Because a lot of strange stuff has happened there."

"Like what?"

"Like they never sell anything, but there's always someone coming and going. Four men went in there yesterday afternoon, but not before wandering around as if they didn't know the address. But they had a key to open the door."

Which was an indicator. I said, "That's what we want to check out. Nadia said you had a second story where we could see the front?"

He nodded and said, "I do, but I don't want any trouble. Why are Americans doing this? Why isn't Nadia? I know where she works."

Jennifer smiled at him, disarming his angst. She said, "Your country wants to be completely silent on this. We asked her for a favor, and she is facilitating. Trust me, we won't be giving you any trouble. This isn't something that concerns you or the neighborhood."

He nodded, his wife at his side, and said, "If it's Muslim terrorists, I'll do whatever I can. Just don't let it lead back to me."

I said, "You have my word. All we want to do is observe."

He'd given us a little perch in his apartment on the second floor, and we'd started a rotation, keeping eyes on the roll-up door across the way. We saw two people leave later in the morning, getting photos of both, and waited. Eventually, the final two exited, both of them carrying backpacks. They left the market and we continued watching, just to make sure.

Nobody else appeared, and I decided that it was time for the break-in. I left Brett upstairs to give us an early heads-up if anything suspicious happened while we were inside, then exited to the street, walking down it like I owned it, Jennifer by my side.

As it was almost noon, the market had picked up considerably with shoppers, but every stall owner seemed to ignore the locals and zero in on us, encouraging us to come inside. Even the beggars began to follow us, like we were the Pied Piper of the homeless. Jennifer was stopped twice by random locals, asking if they could get a selfie with her.

Brett came on the net, saying, "Man alive, you guys look like Taylor Swift just showed up. Why is everyone crowding around you?"

I said, "I have no idea. Probably because they know any Westerner that comes in here didn't do so for daily shopping, and if we have enough cash to fly to India just to be looky-loos, we must have some spare money to give to them."

The alley we were in was small enough that the only motorized conveyances were mopeds, and they came zipping by with all manner of things strapped to them, the swirl of people almost claustrophobic. Every five feet some beggar would grab Jennifer's hand, pleading for money. It was almost as if word had spread that a rich pair of Westerners were walking around, and everyone wanted a piece of us.

After another few feet, I made the call. "Blood, I have a mission for you. This isn't going to work."

"What's that?"

"We're going to stop at the stall, and I'm going to start flipping money in the air while Jennifer picks the lock. Then we're going to lead the caravan away, and you're going to roll up the door after we're gone. We'll circle the block in a rickshaw, breaking free from them, and come back to your stall."

"What makes you think I'm not going to have the same problem?"

"Uhhh . . . you're black?"

"Seriously? I stand out here just like you do."

"Yeah, well, I honestly think it's Jennifer who's standing out. If I gave them the side-eye with a little Pike behind it, they'd probably leave me alone, but they all want a picture with her."

Jennifer glared at me and came on the net, saying, "That's bullshit."

Off the net I said, "Is it? Really? You think we'd have this caravan of deadbeats asking us for money if it was me alone? All I'd have to do is raise a fist and they'd all flee."

Brett came back, saying, "Yeah, you probably have a point. Let me know when you want me to execute."

Jennifer pursed her lips because she knew we were right. She said, "So how am I going to pick a lock in front of everyone?"

"Just bend down to tie your shoe. I'll be raining dollars like a gangster at a strip club and they'll be focused on that."

She shook her head and muttered under her breath, but snaked a hand into her purse, pulling out a neat little device called a Lishi padlock pick. It was a self-contained unit that gave Jennifer the ability to provide tension while she set the pins, all in a single device, allowing her to crack a padlock in seconds, if it had the right keyway. If it was some weird Indian lock, we were out of luck.

We kept walking, stopping occasionally to check out a stall, until we were finally at the spice shop right next door to the target. I sampled the goods, with the crowd around me looking on expectantly. Jennifer stood next to me, acting interested, but really focused on the padlock about six feet away.

She leaned in and said, "I can pick it."

I said, "Showtime."

I thanked the proprietor and we continued on, reaching the front of the roll-up door. I purposely stepped on the heel of Jennifer's Solomon shoe, pulling it off her foot. She stutter-stepped forward, then turned, bending down to put it back on her foot.

A woman holding a baby tugged my sleeve and I said, "Okay, okay, I give up."

I pulled a wad of rupees out of my pocket and began handing them out, shooing away each person after I'd doled out their cash. I ended with a guy who was literally pushing himself along on a wooden trolley.

Jennifer stood back up, nodded at me, and we continued on, reaching an intersection with a major road. The beggar crowd kept following us, and I flagged down a rickshaw, getting in back and saying, "Just go around the block. Show us the bazaar."

The driver nodded, and we were off, racing through the narrow alleys so fast that I had to duck my head from the pipes and electrical cables dangling about, Jennifer gasping every time someone jumped out of our way. We left the beggars behind, and I gripped the metal pole holding the awning over our head like it was a ripcord, grimacing with every pothole the driver powered through.

The guy weighed about a hundred and five, but he was pedaling like he was Lance Armstrong. We went through a linen section of the market, something that looked like a wedding dress area, then some sort of industrial space with sparks flying and blacksmiths banging away, the images appearing and disappearing so fast I wasn't sure I'd seen them. Brett finally came on, saying, "This is Blood. I'm in."

I leaned forward, tapped the driver, and said, "Back to the start."

He nodded, and we continued through one claustrophobic alley after another, and I began to wonder if he was lost—because I most assuredly was at this point. Before I knew it, he'd re-entered the spice area above the location of Nadia's family friend. I had no idea how, because we'd left much lower, but apparently he knew what he was doing.

I tapped him again and he stopped. I gave him a wad of rupees, much more than necessary, and dismounted quickly, before the beggars could home in on us like mosquitoes in a swamp.

We hurried the hundred meters to the target and entered without getting accosted anew. I turned and closed the roll-up door, then said, "Brett? You in here?"

"Yeah. Upstairs. Not a lot here."

I flicked on an overhead light and threaded back to the rear of the narrow space, the walls lined with shelves, all empty, the air swirling with dust. At the very back, next to an abandoned crate full of empty soda bottles, I spied a bunch of new boxes on the ground. I picked one up and saw it was a box for a DJI Mavic 3 commercial drone, something that had been used in Ukraine to deliver death to the Russians with great effect.

Not good.

Jennifer had gone up the ladder to the top floor and said, "Pike, we have a computer up here."

I went up and saw an Apple MacBook Pro on a simple table in an otherwise empty room. The only other items were four small mattresses and some blankets, with water bottles and soda cans scattered about.

No backpacks or other luggage. No personal items.

They aren't coming back.

I turned to Brett and Jennifer around the computer, their faces lit up from the screen. "What do you have?"

Brett said, "Nothing yet. It's password protected."

"What's on the back?"

Brett leaned over and said, "A MiFi internet connection."

"We need that number."

"You want to just pack it all up and go? It looks like they're not coming back."

"No. Someone's coming for the computer. There will be a cleanup crew. Get an octopus on it. Drain it."

Jennifer said, "That'll take some time to crack the passwords. We could be here for hours."

I said, "I know. Don't worry about breaking it open right here. Just mirror the hard drive and clone the SIM card for the MiFi. We'll crack the passwords later, when we have time."

Brett reached into his backpack and pulled out a device with multiple cables coming out of it, looking like a small octopus. He plugged a USB C cable into the port on the side of the computer and hit a button. A light went green, then another, with five more to go.

Jennifer removed the MiFi from the Velcro on the back of the computer and accessed the SIM card, pulling it out and inserting it into another device that looked like a small flip phone. She hit a button, and in thirty seconds, it went green. She replaced the SIM card, reattached it to the back of the computer, and said, "What's the octopus status?"

Brett said, "Maybe another minute, but I can't say we're getting it all. I'd prefer to crack it here, then we know it's all open and we're not missing some hidden drives or something else."

I said, "Can't be helped. Cracking it with the octopus might take two hours on a good day. We get what we get, because I don't want to be here when the cleanup crew shows."

The octopus lights went to five and then began flashing. Brett unplugged it and we went back down the ladder. I said, "Brett, you exit last. Jennifer and I are going to the right. You lock up and go left. We'll meet you back at the vehicle."

He nodded, looked around the space one last time, and said, "Man, I'd really like to know what these assholes are up to."

CHAPTER 32

Manjit pulled off the dusty asphalt to a dirt parking lot next to a collection of ramshackle buildings, one advertising Indian cuisine with pictures of the various dishes, another selling souvenirs. In the distance he could see a temple, the pillars crumbling as if it had been abandoned long ago. Across the road, in front of the temple, was a ticket counter leading to the entrance of one of the largest stepwells in India, the Chand Baori.

Built between the eighth and ninth centuries, it was thirteen stories deep, with over 3,500 steps leading to a massive tank of water at the bottom. Situated about an hour and a half east of Jaipur, it was originally a way point for weary travelers, but had long ago lost its usefulness and was now relegated to a lesser-known archeological site.

Kamal's Sikh contacts on Riva Thakkar's security detail had picked the location, not wanting to meet anywhere in the city of Jaipur itself. Manjit had agreed, as it was easy to find on a map and on the way to their new safe house. He and Randeep had awakened early, starting the five-hour drive south from Delhi before Kamal and Agam went to test the drones. They'd had little trouble on the trip, and he hoped Agam's watch trick was working. If it wasn't, their whole plan would be compromised by Mr. Chin.

Randeep surveyed the parking lot, seeing a smattering of cars, but only one van. A white two-seat cargo van, without windows. He said, "Is that ours?"

Manjit shut off the engine and said, "I don't know. We'll find out when we meet them inside."

Randeep started to open the door, but Manjit put his hand on his arm. Randeep turned, and Manjit said, "Remember, this will be our only chance to talk to them, so if you have any questions, now is the time to ask."

Randeep nodded and said, "I know. The next time we see them will be behind the barrel of a gun."

They exited the vehicle, crossed the street, and went to the ticket counter, each buying a day pass for the well. Walking through a modern anteroom, they gave their tickets to a lackadaisical guard sitting behind a desk, and crossed the threshold into the stone architecture of the ancient world.

They found themselves on a covered walkway surrounding the well, the gaping hole looking like an inverted pyramid that had been bored into the earth, the sides of the walls covered in steps zigzagging to the bottom tank. A railing prevented anyone from using them, but Manjit could see laborers six stories down working on the masonry of the stone.

The upper deck had a smattering of tourists, but not many. Manjit surveyed the walkway around the pit and saw an open-air room on the far side, the stone roof held up with columns. He could make out some figures in the shadows, and recognized they were wearing dastaars.

He said, "Over there."

They walked around the well, the depth and the zigzagging stairs giving Manjit vertigo even as he stayed away from the edge. Leaving the sunlight and entering the stone room, Manjit saw various statues and carvings situated about, with plaques describing their heritage.

Manjit ignored them, walking to two men sitting on a sandstone bench in the back, both hard-looking and wearing the dastaar of the Sikh. Middle-aged, they were older than Manjit, with one having a milky eye, the other with a white line of a scar tracing through his beard.

Looking up at him as he approached, he said, "Do you know a man named Kamal?"

The one with the scar said, "Maybe. Where would we know him from?"

Manjit didn't reply. He pulled a keychain out of his pocket, a broken half of the Hindu god Shiva dangling from a chain. The man reached into his pocket and pulled something out. Manjit saw it was the other half of the keychain. The man took Manjit's Shiva statue and matched it to his own, forming a whole.

The man looked up and said, "I'm Jaiden. And you, I presume, are who I'm putting my life on the line for."

Manjit said, "You're not putting your life on the line for me. We're both putting our lives on the line for the Sikh. If you feel otherwise, then I'm talking to the wrong man."

Jaiden scowled and stood up, towering over Manjit. Manjit did not back down, locking eyes with the bodyguard. Randeep stepped in, saying, "Hey, hey, we're all on the same side here, and we don't have a lot of time."

Jaiden flicked his eyes to Randeep and said, "You two don't look like you could fight your way out of a primary school."

Manjit said, "Looks can be deceiving. We can fight, and we will. Now, what's the plan for this?"

Jaiden pointed to his companion and said, "This is Rakesh. We're the principal security for Mr. Thakkar. For tomorrow's party he's hired a bunch of secondary security. We've managed to get two hired who are with the cause. All four of us have served in the military, and all four have heard shots fired in anger. Have you?"

"Yes. We both have, in fact recently. We can shoot, but more importantly, we can shoot when under fire. Don't worry about us."

Jaiden nodded, appraising them anew. He said, "Kamal told me he had good men, and I trust him. He was someone I could always trust back in the Punjab, before he was arrested."

"He's *still* someone to trust. I do. What can you do for us?"

"There's a van in the parking lot. It has weapons, ammunition, and hand grenades. It also has two cell phones to coordinate. Those are the only two phones you will use to contact us."

He held out a thumb drive, saying, "There is a map in here for you to follow. Thakkar has taken over the entire Oberoi hotel in Jaipur. The security will be incredibly tight, with guests arriving by helicopter and through the front gate, with the entire staff on hand to facilitate. There is no way to do a frontal assault, but the back of the property has a wooden fence with a simple gate. I'm in charge of the security for the greater perimeter, which means I own this gate. I'll make sure it's open. The two other true believers I've recruited will be on that gate."

Manjit said, "How big is this hotel? Is it like a five-story building or what? I get I can drive on the grounds, but we need to hit the actual party."

"It's not a hotel like that. It's big, but there are no buildings over one story. It's spread out over acres of land, and all the rooms are villas scattered across the grounds. The party will be held by the pool and the ground-level temple. It's all on the map. You'll enter the back gate and be driving across a makeshift golf range. You will not have to storm a building. They'll all be outside, in the open."

Manjit said, "How will we coordinate the assault? We need to take

Thakkar with us. That's important. We want to cause mayhem, but we need to take Thakkar."

"Rakesh and I are in charge of his personal security. You attack, and we'll take him. You do what you're going to do, and we'll get him to the van. Once we're in the van, we exfiltrate, no matter what. The killing must stop, and we need to leave."

Manjit nodded and said, "We can do that."

"What are the follow-on steps? How are you going to leverage this? Where are we going to go?"

"Kamal has a plan. We'll leave Jaipur and go to Mumbai. Kamal has a safe house in the slums. From there, we start talking."

"The slums? That's perfect. Thakkar living in the same conditions I grew up in is a just reward. What about the follow-on?"

"Kamal has already set up a website. We were hoping you would be able to give us a conduit to the government, since Thakkar deals with them daily. Maybe someone in the foreign ministry or even the RAW."

"I can get it, but why? The government isn't going to tell anyone what you want. They aren't going to broadcast our demands. They're going to hunt us."

"Because we need to both project to the population, which we'll do through the website, but also let the government know we're real. They need to know that *they* are the target, not the population. The website will get the press that we need, but it's the government we want to stick with a knife."

Jaiden leaned back, reflecting on his words. He looked at his partner, then said, "Okay. We're in." He handed Manjit the keys to the van and said, "But one final question."

"What?"

"What about Mr. Chin? What about the Chinese?"

"He no longer thinks you're in play. He has his own plan that doesn't involve you, which we're going to pretend to execute. By the time he knows we didn't follow his instructions, it'll be too late."

Jaiden slowly nodded, thinking about what he'd said. "You know he's not going to stop. We'll have both the RAW and the MSS on us the moment we attack. You'll no longer be Islamic terrorists, and you have the ability to implicate China in the attack."

"Mr. Chin won't find us."

Jaiden laughed and said, "You clearly haven't worked for him long. He *will* find you, and when he does, he will kill you. China is his priority, and he'll do anything to protect that. You need to remember his reach."

Jaiden motioned to Rakesh and they both stood up, Rakesh's milky eye floating over Manjit. The man hadn't said a word the entire time, and his eye was unsettling.

They turned to go, and Rakesh finally spoke. "You need to understand what Jaiden has just said. When you start on this path, there is no turning back. I believe in this mission. Believe in Khalistan. When this is done, we'll all be the most hunted men on the planet. If you think about running when it gets hot, I'll kill you myself."

CHAPTER 33

Knuckles followed Nadia out of the Jaipur airport baggage claim area, saying, "How are we getting to the hotel?"

She turned to him, now dressed in a traditional Indian sari, sandals on her bare feet, her hair spilling out all over, and bangles on her arms. She looked incredibly sexy, which made him internally take a step back. He had a mission here, something Pike was skeptical about, but Knuckles took seriously. He was Pike's control with RAW for their actions, even if the RAW component was someone to whom he was attracted. Honestly, he still wasn't sure if Nadia was playing him for something else, a possibility he'd have to guard against.

She smiled at him and said, "We have a car."

He smiled back, then thought, *Stop it. This is a mission.*

Knuckles understood Pike had agreed to this arrangement on purpose, because he was a sadist deep down. Pike knew Knuckles would accomplish the mission, but he also saw the connection between Nadia and him and had decided to leverage it.

It wasn't the first time Pike had done this, and, while Knuckles was definitely smitten with Nadia, Pike recognized he could separate the difference between a pre-wedding party and an actual mission.

Knuckles said, "Who's paying for that?"

"It's courtesy of the Thakkars. Trust me, this is all going to be first class."

Sure enough, they went out into the street and a man in a suit advanced, saying something in Hindi. She answered, and the driver led them to a black Suburban, the interior outfitted in leather, with a screen between the driver and the passengers, tablets in the headrests, and a cooler between the seats outfitted with champagne.

They settled in, and Knuckles said, "I could get used to this."

Nadia smiled at him and said, "Me too. Honestly, it'll be the last time. Once Annaka is married, I'll probably never see her again."

He looked at her and said, "Seriously?"

She grew a little wistful and said, "Yeah. We were friends in school, and from what she told me, it was a battle to even invite me to the wedding. Her father was against it. I came from a different world, but we bonded at uni. She got to be herself there, but now she's in her father's environment. Once she's married, she won't see people like me again."

He said, "That's terrible."

She said, "It's not so different in your world. She's the daughter of one of the richest men in the world. I just happened to go to school with her. I doubt Elon Musk's kids in preschool will have anything to do with their friends after they leave. It's just life."

Knuckles had no reply to that.

They rode in silence for a moment, then he started to say something but stopped, glancing at the screen separating them from the driver. She grinned and said, "Don't worry. It's soundproof. All of Thakkar's rides are like this. He does a lot of business in the back of these beasts."

He said, "Good to know."

"You were going to say something?"

"Yes. Do you really think the RAW had something to do with the attack at the hotel?"

She said, "I don't know, but it's really screwing up my weekend. I was going to have a blast, and now I have to deal with you and a possible terrorist attack."

He scowled at the words and she laughed again, a tinkling like a bubbling stream that crumbled his fragile bulwarks. She said, "I'm just kidding. Look, I don't know if it's the RAW, but something's going on. I'm convinced those men are going to attack somewhere else. Pike finding a bunch of drone boxes and a single computer in a safe house is not a good sign."

As the designated "liaison," Pike had told Knuckles what he'd found in the spice market as soon as he'd left, along with the fact that they had no further information. They'd mirrored a hard drive but hadn't exploited it yet. The drone boxes alone, however, were concerning.

He said, "You still believe they're Islamic terrorists?"

She turned to him and said, "Well, yeah. Who else would they be?"

He said, "I don't know who they are, but I've seen plenty of bad things done by people other than Muslim fanatics. It's easy to blame them, but I'm not so sure these guys are fighting for Allah."

"Why do you think that? Every indication is they're LeT run by the Pakistan ISI. That's what the ISI does."

He remained silent for a moment, then said, "The men with Jennifer in that hotel room were Chinese. The ISI doesn't do China's bidding. If China is behind this, then all bets are off, because they're probably implicating the Pakis to cover themselves. We don't know why they're doing it, but we do know they have the capability to introduce whatever evidence they want. The Ministry of State Security is no joke. It's the largest intelligence organization on earth. Maybe they *want* us to believe it's Islamic terrorists. I mean 'we' in the sense of both the U.S. and India."

She remained silent for a moment, then said, "That may be true, but I have to go with what the evidence shows. The cell phone data was connected to an ISI number, and the pocket litter was from Pakistan. All of that could have been planted, but we have no evidence of it."

"We *do* have evidence. Jennifer saw Chinese men in the hotel room. The Islamic thing is just too pat. The supposed terrorist you guys found on the hotel staff at the resort had a lot of incriminating stuff from Pakistan but very little to show he was a Muslim. No prayer rugs, no Quran, nothing. If he was a devout Islamist, he had a shitty way of showing it. He was seen drinking booze every night, never acting like a Muslim the entire time he was on the resort grounds, and when you interrogated him, he couldn't even say if he's Shia or Sunni. The only actionable intel he had was a cell phone with contacts to the ISI. Like they wanted you to find it."

"Well, maybe he acted that way before he was detained to throw us off. I mean, a true terrorist wouldn't wear a keffiyeh with 'Kill the Infidels' scribbled on it."

"Yeah, that's a good point, but I still think China is behind it. The Pakistan ISI angle is a red herring."

"Red herring? What does that mean?"

He laughed and said, "It means they're trying to misdirect us from the true plan. They want it to look like a random terrorist attack, but it was targeted. I agree they had some help, but I'm not so sure it was from the RAW."

"Who do you think the target was?"

"Well, I *would* say it was the head of the CIA, but that doesn't make any sense because nobody except the head of the RAW knew that he was coming."

She said, "Maybe that's who they wanted, the commander of the RAW."

"Maybe. They're in Delhi right now, and that's where the RAW headquarters is, but it doesn't explain why they attacked when the commander of the RAW wasn't on the resort grounds. If someone from RAW was helping them, you'd at least think they'd get that right."

The SUV pulled into a circular drive, and he quit talking. The pavement turned to brick, and Knuckles saw a line of people waiting on them, reminding him of the old *Fantasy Island* TV show. Each had some trinket or drink to hand to them, all with huge smiles on their faces. They exited and he went to the rear to get their luggage, but was told not to worry about it, that by the time they arrived at their room, it would be there.

He leaned into Nadia and whispered, "Am I supposed to tip someone?"

She shook her head and said, "They'll be well taken care of. Don't worry about it."

A Ricardo Montalban look-alike with an iPad asked for their passports, and then Knuckles was ushered through the line, receiving a glass of champagne, then a mala garland of flowers. The final person had him lean toward her and she put a dot on his forehead, saying it was for good health and luck.

He accepted it and waited on Nadia to finish. Eventually, the Ricardo Montalban look-alike asked them to follow, and he half-expected a midget to jump out shouting, "The plane! The plane!"

He leaned into Nadia and said, "I thought the dot was only for women."

She smiled and said, "It's called a tilaka, and it's a greeting for you, welcoming you into their home. You're thinking of a bindi, which is what women here wear, but it's usually much more ornate."

They were led through the massive doors of the entrance, passing by the front desk, through a breakfast area, then past an oak-paneled English bar, their guide explaining the amenities as they walked. They exited onto an outdoor seating area for a restaurant and kept walking, causing Knuckles to wonder where the elevators were. How far did they have to go to get to their room?

They crossed a stone bridge over a moat, the water blanketed in floating flowers, then continued on a gravel path. To their left was a large swimming pool, with fountains spraying into the water. To their right was a small temple of some sort, with a sign stating that all faiths were welcome to attend ceremonies. The grounds spilled out for acres, with brilliantly colored peacocks roaming about like a fantastical petting zoo, and Knuckles began to understand why the place had been chosen for the party.

There ended up being no tower of rooms. Instead, the rooms were all villas spread throughout the landscape. Wannabe Ricardo Montalban led them down one path, then another, ending in a circle of small buildings with a fountain in the center. He crossed a small pond and said, "This is your room."

On the stoop was the word "Welcome," spelled out in rose petals. Wearing his usual blue jeans and 5.11 shirt, Knuckles began to think he was underdressed for checking in.

The man led them into the room and he saw a large king-sized bed with a faux mosquito net, a plate of fruit accompanied by more champagne, their luggage on separate stands, and a garden outside beyond the French doors. The man began a perfunctory explanation of the amenities, and Nadia cut him off, saying, "I think we can figure it out. Thank you."

Ricardo Montalban smiled, had Nadia sign something on the iPad, and left them.

Knuckles said, "I can't believe I'm getting paid to spend the night here."

Nadia laughed and said, "Well, it pays to be a spy when you know me."

Wanting to be professional, and honestly confused by the conflict of being here with her while conducting a mission, he threw his back-pack on the bed and said, "I should probably check and see if Pike's done anything with that hard drive."

She put the backpack on the floor and said, "I'm pretty sure Pike hasn't done anything with that hard drive yet. And we've already made it past the entryway."

CHAPTER 34

I heard my phone start bleating and wanted to just turn it off, but it was a special tone, meaning it was from the Taskforce. I groaned, looked at the clock, and saw it was just before five in the morning. We'd made it back to the Imperial Hotel in New Delhi a little late, and I wanted my beauty sleep. Jennifer rolled over in our bed and climbed across me, snatching it up and saying, "Did you think it would stop if you ignored it?"

I said, "Well, yes, it would. Let it go to voice mail."

She put it to her ear and said, "Hello?"

I saw her nod, then nod again, and I knew it wasn't going to be good. She hung up and said, "That was Creed. They did a deep dive on our mirror of the drive and apparently whoever set it up put in some trap doors. Brett was right. We should have cracked it in the safe house."

I leaned up on an elbow and said, "So they got nothing?"

She said, "No. They got something, but it wasn't a smoking gun. He's sending the data."

I said nothing, rolling over and burrowing into my pillow. This sort of crap just aggravated me. You never knew when you'd get to sleep next, and I was getting mine.

She set the phone back onto my bedside table, her arm draped across my body, and leaned over me, saying, "So you don't want to know what he said?"

I said, "Does it matter? Can I do anything about it right now?"

"No. Not immediately, anyway."

That got my attention. I sat up and said, "What's that mean?"

She said, "Me leaning over you doesn't get a rise, but Creed giving us a call does?"

I grinned and said, "Don't test me. If the choice is between you, Creed, or this pillow, you might not like the results."

That brought a smile, because she knew the answer. She said, "The computer was firewalled with Trojans, but Creed found some random numbers and a time. Ten thirty A.M. today."

"That's it?"

"Apparently so. As soon as he started to drain it, it started to wipe itself. He got five hundred gigabits of gobbledygook, and all of it was triggered because we bypassed the password. We really should have risked staying in that safe house and cracking it first."

"Too late for that. So all we have is a time?"

"Yes. Well, Creed got one other thing. Someone cut and pasted a bunch of numbers to a document in the hard drive. The document is corrupted, but the cut itself was still in the memory, which was outside the firewall."

"Numbers for what?"

"Don't know. Creed's sending the data now."

My phone pinged, and I snatched it up, seeing a text from Creed. All it had was 44RKR0484009823, followed by the number 10:30 and today's date underneath it.

Leaning over my shoulder, Jennifer said, "Well, that's not a lot of help. Looks like just random trash."

I stared at the numbers and said, "No. This is something. Get your computer."

She didn't question me, sliding off the bed to fire up her MacBook. Once it was online I said, "Pull up Google Earth."

She did and said, "What do you see?"

"That first bit of trash is an MGRS grid. I'm positive. Put it in the computer and see what happens. If it ends up in Africa, I'm wrong, but I'll bet it doesn't."

She did so, and Google Earth spun, then zeroed in to India, showing a fort in the town of Agra, south of Delhi, within spitting distance of the Taj Mahal.

Now I was really engaged. I took the laptop from her, saying, "Didn't Nadia say that Thakkar was going to the Taj Mahal? He was going to stop all tourist traffic for his little party?"

Jennifer slid in next to me to see the map and said, "She did, she did."

I pointed at the screen and said, "Something's at that grid. That he also found a time means it's fleeting. We need to get there before the deadline to see what's happening."

"But why is there a grid reference at all? What's that about? Why go into a fort that's a tourist attraction?"

"I don't know, but I'm sure it's a thing. Maybe they're meeting their contact for follow-on operations at that grid at ten thirty A.M. Either way, I don't think the RAW commander or Kerry Bostwick was the target. I think it's Thakkar."

She looked at the Google Earth map and said, "Why not just meet outside the fort? Why go inside, past security? That makes no sense. If they're using drones, they already have them, and they won't be able to get them past the checks."

I hated it when she used logic. I said, "I don't know, but we can only judge the information we have. Get Knuckles on the phone."

She dialed and I kept looking at the map. I said, "We might be able to get there before ten thirty if we move out now."

Jennifer started talking, and I saw her pause. She waited a second and then said, "Are you awake?"

I squinted and said, "Is he in her bed right now? Is that what's going on?" Knuckles was my 2IC and I'd trust him with my life—had, in fact, trusted him with my life numerous times—but sometimes the fairer sex caused him to think with his little head instead of his big one. I honestly didn't think that would happen here when the plans were made, but maybe I was wrong.

Jennifer shook her head, which was women-speak for "Let me handle this because you embarrass me when you do it," and I started demanding the phone. She batted my hand away and said, "We have some intel on Thakkar's visit to the Taj tomorrow. We need Nadia to get some assets in place."

He said something, then Jennifer said, "Look, we need to speak to Nadia. Is she with you?"

I got sick of the back-and-forth and said, "Put it on speaker."

Jennifer looked at me, then reluctantly did so. I said, "Knuckles?"

He said, "Yeah, Pike, I'm here."

"Where's Nadia?"

"You're on speaker here as well. She's right next to me."

I really wanted to poke him in the eye, but I let that slide. Instead, I said, "We have a MGRS number that's located at a fort up the river from the Taj Mahal."

I heard Nadia say, "The Agra Red Fort."

I looked at Google Earth, saw the label, and said, "That's it."

She said, "What's MGRS?"

"It's the military grid reference system the U.S. uses. It's a location via GPS. It was in their computer we hacked. There's a meeting at that location at ten thirty this morning. Isn't Thakkar going to the Taj Mahal today?"

"Yes, he is. That's not good."

"Can you get someone on this grid? Some police to be there before whoever is supposed to meet shows? Break the whole thing up?"

I heard nothing and said, "Nadia?"

"Pike, I . . . I can't get that done in time. I don't think you understand this country. There's no way I can get a police response in Agra from my position in the RAW. We don't talk to each other. It's just not going to happen. I would have no idea who to even call."

"What about Thakkar? You're in the pre-wedding party. Can you tell him to wave off the Taj Mahal visit?"

"That might be easier. But I'll let you know right now, he doesn't like me. I'm here because of the bride, not him. Let me call her."

I said, "That's not good enough. We're packing up and heading to Agra. I'll be at that grid before ten, and I need you to give me backup."

She said, "Wait, what does that mean?"

I was already shoving clothes into my carry-on, Jennifer one step ahead of me, calling Brett and Veep. I said, "It means I need the RAW to keep me from being arrested, because I'm almost positive I'm going kinetic on their ass."

CHAPTER 35

Mr. Chin took a sip of coffee at a table, remaining mute, waiting for the last man to come back from the breakfast buffet, the New Delhi Imperial Hotel providing a selection for any diet. He returned and took a seat next to the three other men. They were all younger than Mr. Chin—probably twenty-five or thirty—but Chin knew that they had spent an inordinate amount of time in selection and training to be anointed a member of a Ministry of State Security Condor team. They were the highest-skilled men the Chinese Communist Party had to offer.

When the final man sat down, Mr. Chin handed the leader a folder with the passport photos he'd gleaned in Goa and said, "Your target is in this hotel. I honestly don't know if they're working against the CCP, but if they are, you'll eliminate the threat."

The leader said, "Lethal action? Here in India?"

"Yes, but only if they indicate they're attempting to thwart our plans. If they are just conducting tourist activities, then let them be. If they go to Agra, take them out."

"Agra is the location of the Taj Mahal. That's literally the biggest tourist destination in India."

"I know. The key will be if they ignore that 'biggest tourist destination' and go to the Agra Red Fort. I have an operation there this morning, and if this man goes there, it's a red line. Take them out."

"What are our parameters? We don't blend in very well here. When you say 'Take them out,' what do you mean? If we do an overt direct action here, we'll have to leave the continent, and it took a long time to get us in place under cover."

"I understand, and so does your commander. This is how important the action is. It isn't about India. It's about competing with the United States for technological superiority. You eliminate them, and then you flee the continent. We'll deal with the loss of the team here in India later, but this is precisely why you were created."

* * *

Agam woke up a little disoriented, not sure where he was. He shook his head and remembered. He was in a small house in Agra, and he had a mission. He rolled over and saw Kamal packing his backpack.

Kamal glanced at him and said, "I guess your phone hack worked."

Agam sat up and said, "Why do you say that?"

"Mr. Chin called me on the contact phone this morning. He only wanted to know if we were good. He doesn't suspect anything."

Agam nodded and said, "But he will after midday. One of his minions is planting the drone with the explosives at ten thirty, and I'm supposed to launch it when Thakkar's party is taking pictures in front of the Taj Mahal. He'll know that didn't happen by noon, as there will be no news stories."

Kamal smiled and said, "I have the phone. I'll handle that, and I'm looking forward to his panic."

He zipped up his backpack and said, "I have to go. It's a four-hour drive to Jaipur. Are you good?"

The question held more than it seemed. Agam knew he was asking if he could kill.

"Yes. I'm good. I'll get the drone and use it, don't worry."

Kamal nodded and said, "It has to be a big enough attack to cause the state to freak out. I want every police officer from a hundred miles to collapse on the Taj."

"I'll do it. Trust me. How did Manjit's meeting go?"

"Apparently pretty well. He has the entire plan for the attack, and there are now four insiders. Two who will let us through a back gate, and the two that I knew from home who are now Thakkar's primary security. Manjit has weapons and explosives and a van now. It's going to work."

He stood up and said, "When you're done, when the attack is over, ditch the phone and the watch and disappear."

Agam nodded and said, "I'm going north. Up to the Kashmir. I'll call you from there."

Kamal hugged him, squeezing harder than he intended, the path they were on now set. Agam said, "Good luck. I'll see you in Khalistan."

Kamal smiled and said, "I will like that." He turned without another word and left the room. For the first time, Agam wondered if he'd ever see him again.

He sat on the bed and stared at his own backpack. He looked at his Garmin watch and saw he had a little over four hours before he had to be in the fort. Time that would slowly leak out like blood from a wound, continuing to drain no matter how much pressure he used to stop it.

Resigned, he stood up and shouldered his pack.

* * *

I gave the valet my ticket and waited on our SUV to arrive, tapping my feet and feeling the press of time. Behind me, Brett was talking to Knuckles on the phone, trying to get some limited response at the Agra Fort but obviously having no luck. Veep was working a Taskforce GPS, which had satellite imagery instead of Garmin or Google Streetview roads, trying to pinpoint the exact location of the grid. Jennifer was working to find us a hotel in the area and coordinating for the Rock Star bird to be on strip alert.

I'd debated flying to Agra with the Rock Star bird, but it was close enough that I'd decided not to introduce the signature of a private aircraft into the area. If what I thought was about to happen came true, and I missed stopping it, I'd rather be leaving on a dusty highway instead of boarding a private plane at the Agra Airport with all the history and documentation that entailed. Better to get them sitting in the cockpit ready to pick us up wherever we ended up.

The SUV pulled into the drive and we loaded up, Brett behind the wheel and me in the passenger seat. Veep leaned over and showed me what he'd found.

"The grid is on the northern edge of the fort, next to the river. Doing a little research on the place, there are catacombs and tunnels that run the length of the fort at that location, along with walkways on the walls that surround the fort, so our problem is that the GPS grid is a 2D fixed focal point. It doesn't show locations in three dimensions."

I said, "Meaning what? The grid is useless?"

"No, no, not at all. Just that we can go to the grid on the surface of the fort, and the meeting could be below us, in a catacomb, or above us, on a wall. When we get to the location, the GPS is going to say 'arrived,' but it doesn't know if the meeting is below or above us."

I turned to Jennifer and said, "Get me a map of that fort. Start looking at it from a place that you'd like to meet."

She pulled out a tablet and started doing the research, and I glanced out the window as we exited the hotel grounds, seeing another SUV loading up, all of them young Asian men.

Which, if I wasn't so worried about finding the terrorists, would have been an indicator that we weren't the only ones on the hunt.

CHAPTER 36

A gam watched the security line for the fort. Everyone had to pass through a magnetometer and have their bags checked, but the guards were lackadaisical. They did their job perfunctorily, without any serious effort.

The fort was huge, stretching out for more than a hundred acres, with what appeared to be a small contingent of the Indian army on a compound attached to the walls. That was a surprise. Mr. Chin had said nothing about any official government presence here.

He'd gone out into the streets of Agra after Kamal had left, buying some breakfast from a roadside stand and patiently waiting. After a couple of hours of walking the dusty lanes, he was inexorably drawn to the fort. He walked to the long road leading to the entrance, conducting a reconnaissance of the security posture. Like a lot of the locals around him, he sat on the curb, just observing.

He had conflicting emotions, torn by the pressure of the mission. On the one hand he wanted the attack to be done immediately, the adrenaline coursing through his veins making it hard to breathe. On the other, he wanted the seconds to quit ticking by. Quit drawing him to the moment when he had to act. At nine thirty, he decided to go in, getting in the line with the rest of the locals.

He had his bag searched, went through the metal detector, and was inside the fort, the crowd breaking from the linear entrance line and spreading out. Agam breathed a sigh of relief, moving into a large courtyard with a huge bowl that appeared to be carved out of a single block of stone.

He went to it, seeing two men, both with chipmunks in their hands. One of them reached out to hand him one, but he knew better. All they wanted was an unsuspecting Westerner to take the rodent, and thereby earn a tip. He waved them off.

He sat outside the bowl and looked at his watch. He clicked the navigate function, pulled up "Saved Locations," and picked the only one in it. The screen came up and he saw an MGRS grid. He went to his phone and pulled up WhatsApp, checking a message he'd sent himself.

When he'd read the instructions for the location of the drone, it had involved a lot of different things, but the one aspect that was concrete was the grid. He'd copied and pasted the grid in the instructions and sent it to himself. Now he wanted to see if the grid on the computer in the safe house was the same as the one on his watch.

He compared the two and saw they were the same, giving him confidence. He hit "Navigate" and waited for the GPS to lock on.

The instructions had told him there were catacombs underneath the castle, including a set of gallows that were used to execute unfaithful concubines. The drone would be in the well below the gallows.

Like the quest to find the safe house, the GPS watch would point unerringly to the location, but he would have to find his way.

The watch vibrated, and he saw he had a GPS lock. He walked to the interior of the fort, following the watch and ignoring the various attractions scattered about the grounds. He passed through the clusters of crowds taking pictures and reading plaques, and reached the far wall, right on the Yamuna River. Off in the distance, he could see the

Taj Mahal. He looked to his right and saw a tower with tourists coming and going. He went to it and found why it was an attraction: the Taj was framed in one of the open windows of the tower, the grounds spilling out around the monument.

He could see the crowds at the Taj and, in that moment, he realized it would be his attack point.

He studied the grounds of the monument, not staring at the Taj itself but to see if he could recognize faces of the tourists there from this distance. He could not, and was relieved. Whoever he killed would still be a mystery to him.

He left the watchtower, bumping into a child with her parents. He mumbled an apology and walked back the way he'd come, following the watch. When it vibrated, telling him he'd arrived, he began looking for a small marker engraved with the history of the catacombs.

He found it and scanned to the left in accordance with his instructions, seeing an iron door behind a small barricade. He crossed the barricade and found the door closed by a padlock, preventing entry. He looked left and right, saw he was alone, and pulled the lock. Just as Mr. Chin had said in the instructions, it popped free. He swung the iron door, wincing as it groaned open, and saw a narrow set of stairs leading down.

He entered rapidly, closing the door behind him, the clang reverberating on the stone. He began walking down the stairs, the small bit of light from the sun coming through the door cracks rapidly disappearing, leaving him feeling his way in the darkness. Halfway down, he remembered the flashlight on Mr. Chin's watch. He double-clicked the upper button and a beam stabbed out in the darkness, lighting the way.

He continued down until he reached a tunnel dimly lit by slits in the castle walls. He looked at his watch to get a bearing, and it told him he needed a GPS fix.

He shook his head, incredulous that Mr. Chin had given him a grid based on a GPS watch that had to have a view of the sky to work. He was a little embarrassed that he himself didn't realize this plan wouldn't work.

Maybe Mr. Chin isn't as good as he seems to think he is.

The thought brought Agam both confidence because of what Kamal intended, and trepidation because if Mr. Chin was that stupid about using the watch, maybe the drone wasn't even here.

He went to the first slit in the wall, the light spilling in from a sliver of open air about ten inches long and five inches tall. He stuck his hand out, letting the watch see the sky. He felt the watch vibrate and pulled it inside, seeing he had about a hundred meters to the location.

He returned to walking down the tunnel, using the watch's built-in flashlight to see, and reached another slit. He looked at the watch, saw it no longer had a fix, and stuck his hand out again.

He felt the vibration, pulled his hand in, and saw he was within thirty feet of the grid. He continued on in the darkness, entering an open area, feeling the space open up around him beyond what the small watch flashlight could show.

He advanced forward, using the light on his wrist to show the way. He saw an ancient gallows, a macabre remnant of the punishment for the concubines who had lived here during the time of the Mughals. He sidled up to the edge of a pit, seeing a glint of something in the darkness. He bent down and reached a hand into the hole, searching by feel alone, and his hand brushed a box. He stuck his other hand in and managed to get the box out of the hole.

He set it on the ground and used the light from the Garmin watch to study it. It was for a DJI Mavic drone, just like he'd tested. He carefully opened the box and saw the device, only this one had some type of metal harness on the bottom. He shined the light back in the hole and saw a small backpack. He pulled it out, opened it up, and found a canister about the size of a quart bottle with a mating connection for the harness on the bottom of the drone.

The explosives.

He removed the drone, then the controller underneath it. He mounted his phone into the controller and set the drone on the ground, running a test sequence. The drone's four lights above each propeller blinked red and green, the four blades spinning and stopping while the drone talked to the phone. The lights went from green and red to white, and it ceased to move. It was synced to the controller.

He picked up the drone, seated the explosives to the bottom, and was complete. All that was needed now was to launch it.

CHAPTER 37

We reached the city of Agra in record time, having little traffic to deal with. I wasn't sure how India monitored speeding, but I bet it wasn't with police cars and radar guns like you'd find in the United States, so I'd told Brett to punch it.

We left the highway at just over three hours and crossed into the city of Agra proper, now bogged down by the insanity of Indian traffic, which included donkey carts. Veep said, "Next right, next right," and I looked at my watch, seeing it was now past ten in the morning.

"We've got less than thirty minutes. Get us to the fort. Veep and I will get out. You guys find a place to park and follow."

We found the road leading to the entrance, the fort still about a hundred meters away, and Brett tried to pull over. A policeman blew his whistle and started waving his arms, demanding we come to him. Brett continued forward, his window down, and the cop waved us to keep going, not addressing Brett at all.

We drove past the entrance, with me cursing. I looked to the left and saw a shopping area, the lanes not as narrow as in Delhi but still dense. I said, "Take a left into that area. Find a place to park. We're running out of time."

He did so, tooting his horn and moving through the crowds, at one point using the bumper to clear a lane through the people. They didn't seem to mind, which was crazy to me. Apparently, if you didn't show you would aggressively plow someone over, the locals would just ignore you.

He began to pass a narrow alley, and I saw a bunch of cars behind the buildings. A parking lot. I said, "There, there!"

He turned, and we were riding forward on a lane that barely cleared our rearview mirrors. In about seventy meters, it opened up to a dirt lot full of trash barrels, mopeds, and larger vehicles, the area surrounded by the back walls of various shops, and unlike the street outside, it was empty of people.

He inched forward and said, "There's no parking spot."

I looked at my watch and said, "We're out of time. The meeting is in fifteen minutes, and it'll take us at least ten to get tickets and enter. Just double-park this thing on the far side and we'll run to the fort."

He reached the far side, pulled parallel to another car, and put our SUV in park, and I turned to open the door, hearing Jennifer shout, "Watch out!"

I saw a black SUV coming straight at me. I slammed back into Brett in the driver's seat and the vehicle hit us head-on, crunching my door and spraying me in glass, our SUV rocking violently. Time slowed, my brain trying to process what was happening.

I looked out the shattered window, saw their SUV back up about twenty meters, then all four doors open, and the same Asian men I'd seen at the Imperial Hotel started spilling out, all of them armed. Brett opened the driver's door, grabbing his pistol at his waist, Jennifer rolling to Veep's side while he flung his own door open.

It was all out of time, in slow motion, my body simply reacting, flooding with a reptilian fight-or-flight response.

Before I had even processed what had happened, I'd jumped over the separation between the passenger seat and the driver and rolled out, Jennifer diving out from the back seat, Veep and Brett already on the ground, scanning for threats. Then the gunfire started, the men in the SUV plastering our vehicle with rounds. My ears felt like they were full of cotton, my body instinctively trying to protect my eardrums from damage from the exploding gunshots as rounds ripped through the steel of our vehicle.

I slammed against the side of our SUV and saw Veep rise, shooting to try to suppress the enemy. He took a round, his body spinning behind me.

Mother fucker.

My brain went into overdrive, which was both fast and slow. I rose, pulling my pistol from its holster, seeing the front sight of my barrel and placing my other hand on the grip. I focused on the red dot and started killing.

One man was to my left, hiding behind a vehicle door and shooting through the window. I split his head apart with a single shot. Another was running to my left. I tracked him for a millisecond, snapped a double tap his way, but missed. A round smacked the frame of our SUV right next to my head and I rolled to the front of our vehicle, peeking around the bumper.

I saw two more men coming out of the SUV and crouched back down behind the vehicle. I turned, finding Jennifer treating Veep, Brett on a knee with his own pistol out.

The entire action had happened in the blink of an eye. Brett shouted, "Left, left!" And I turned, seeing the man I'd missed earlier darting into the parking area, going behind a civilian vehicle.

I said, "There are two more out there. Three on the loose."

He nodded and faced away from me, toward the rear of our vehicle. I turned to Jennifer and said, "Status?"

"He's got a through-and-through on his shoulder. Nothing vital hit, but he's bleeding."

I nodded, and Veep said, "I'm fine, I'm fine. I just can't use my strong arm. I'll have to shoot from my weak hand."

I said, "Well, we're in trouble then, because I've seen that shooting."

He smiled, and I realized he really was going to be okay. I turned to Brett and said, "We need to end this. Brett, I'm going after the guy on the left. He's trying to flank us. Keep your eyes on the rear, that's where the other two will be coming from."

He nodded at me and said, "They have to finish this soon, or leave. They've made a lot of noise."

I said, "Let's help them leave."

I rolled out and started hunting the loose man in the car lot. The other two saw my movement and focused on me instead of Brett, taking a couple of shots as I ran, the bullets smacking ineffectually around me. The muzzle blasts gave away their position and Brett started firing, forcing them behind cover. I kept moving and made it across the open ground to the row of cars.

Behind me, Brett and the other two kept exchanging rounds, with neither getting the upper hand. I squatted down, listening, trying to hear the third man on the move. I leaned around the bumper of a car, looking down the row, and then heard a clatter on the roof.

I whipped my eyes up and saw the barrel of a gun aimed at my skull. My body reacted without thought, first slapping his weapon aside with my own, like we were dueling with swords, then grabbing his wrist behind the weapon with my other hand and jerking it violently to the ground.

The weapon discharged harmlessly into the metal of the car and his body slammed into the earth. I stomped a foot on the hand with the weapon and raised my Staccato, trying to put the red dot on his forehead. He whipped his legs around, hitting me just below my calves and sweeping me off my feet. I landed hard on my back, my weapon still held in front of my body, and he leapt up, raising his own pistol. I fired twice, hitting him once in the neck and once right in the middle of his face, splitting his eyes apart.

His head slapped against the car, then slid to the ground. I shouted, "This one is down! This one is down! Coming back!"

I heard Brett shout back, "Keep going deeper! Jennifer and I have them pinned, get around them!"

I thought, *Easy for you to say* . . . and shouted, "Roger all. I'm moving."

I crouched over and ran up the line of the cars, the remaining two enemy ineffectually spraying rounds at my movement only for Jennifer and Brett to force them to drop back down.

I was making ground, and they knew it. Soon they would be in a crossfire with no cover to use. I reached the end of the line of vehicles and began moving perpendicular to my line of march, toward their vehicle. I saw them on the open ground, fired one round at them, and they slid into their SUV. Brett rose, pumping rounds into the windshield, and the driver crouched down, putting the car into reverse and punching the gas. I began peppering the vehicle with my own rounds and it slammed into a parked car, went into drive, then raced back up the alley to the main road.

I ran back to our vehicle, seeing Brett helping Jennifer load Veep in the back seat. I said, "You think this thing will still move?"

Brett said, "Yeah. Just can't open the doors on the passenger side, but the engine should be okay. If it doesn't start, we're screwed, because even if nobody heard this gunfight back here, someone's going to show up sooner rather than later and see the bodies."

We got Veep settled, him bitching about how he was fine, Jennifer next to him in the back keeping pressure on his wound. I slid across the driver's seat to the passenger side, and Brett got behind the wheel, saying, "Moment of truth."

He pushed the start button, and the SUV roared to life. He smiled and said, "Where to?"

"Out of here, first of all."

We went back down the alley we'd used to enter, and I was amazed at the normal activities happening around us. Nobody had registered the life-and-death struggle that had just occurred.

I said, "Unbelievable. We're going to drive away from a gunfight and these locals have no idea."

Brett said, "The question is, 'Drive where?'"

I looked at my watch and saw it was just after eleven. We'd missed the meeting, and I had a wounded teammate in my vehicle from an unsanctioned mission for the RAW. The correct choice would have been to call it a day and exfiltrate, getting the hell off the Indian continent.

But I wasn't known for doing what was correct.

I said, "Jennifer, you're going to take Veep back to Delhi. Call Kerry Bostwick. I'm sure he has a doctor in New Delhi for things like this."

She said, "Not the Taskforce? You want me to call Kerry at the CIA? We can get a Taskforce medical team here. That's what they do."

"No, that'll cause too many problems. George Wolffe will lose his mind, and he'll have to notify the Oversight Council about a medical emergency. Call Kerry and tell him you're coming in. Worst case, meet him at the U.S. embassy in New Delhi. Let him deal with the problem with CIA assets. If he gives you any shit, threaten to call Wolffe. He'll play ball, because he sanctioned this and doesn't want the headache either."

Brett said, "What are we doing?"

"We're going into that fort to find the grid."

"The meeting's come and gone. What's the point?"

"Thakkar's coming soon. If they plan on attacking him from there, we're going to stop it."

He said, "What about what just happened? Those guys weren't Indian."

"Yeah, I'm pretty sure they're Chinese, and they have something to do with this attack. All the more reason to go in before Thakkar arrives."

Jennifer looked at the time and said, "Thakkar's already there. Nadia said he leaves at eleven thirty."

I said, "Then pull over, because we really need to get moving. And call Knuckles. Tell him to let Nadia know she's probably going to get some bad news."

CHAPTER 38

M r. Chin sat at the Imperial Hotel bar, surrounded by dark oak walls and artifacts from the time of the British empire. He was the only patron on a stool, the bar having just opened, the bartender serving him a bourbon old-fashioned.

Dressed in a red uniform with a Sikh dastaar, his beard shaped in a V sharp enough to carve beef, the bartender said, "Watch it with those, because they'll bite you if you aren't careful."

Mr. Chin took the drink and said, "I will, trust me, but I have no work today and you make the best ones I've ever had."

The bartender nodded in thanks and Mr. Chin pointed at the television, saying, "Can you put that on the local news?"

The bartender picked up a remote and changed the channel from a cricket match to a local New Delhi channel, saying, "Do you speak Hindi?"

"No, I just meant national India news, in English if you don't mind."

The bartender clicked through the channels, found one, and disappeared in the back. Mr. Chin saw a breaking news story and waited with bated breath, not wanting to show his interest. It was a bus crash in another Indian state. He relaxed and waited again. Any minute now his operation would make the news.

He sipped his drink, not really liking it at all, and then it came: a breaking news report from the Taj Mahal. He leaned forward, seeing a smiling reporter discussing Riva Thakkar's unprecedented closing of the monument for twenty minutes. The clip was obviously recorded and not live, the video showing them walking around the grounds with the reporter giving a voice-over. The video showed armed security pushing back the regular tourists, then the group taking pictures in front of the façade before moving into the monument proper.

The reporter continued talking about the unprecedented nature of the event and spent his time discussing the juxtaposition of Thakkar's wealth allowing him to do such a thing with the average tourist's "trip of a lifetime" stalled because of it, focusing on the inherent inequality and castigating the government for allowing it to happen.

The story ended with the glaring excess of a helicopter landing on the Taj Mahal grounds, Thakkar's party entering it, and all flying away. Mr. Chin was dumbfounded. He looked at his watch and saw Thakkar had been gone for at least thirty minutes, maybe even an hour.

He reached into his briefcase and removed a tablet, booting up his tracking software. He saw all four heartbeats at the Agra Fort, right next to the Yamuna River. A perfect location for the drone attack that had not occurred.

His first thought was, *Why are all four there*? Kamal had shown himself to be smart, so why put the entire team inside the fort, past security? What did that give them when only one man could control the drone?

His next thought was, *Why hasn't the attack occurred?*

He removed the contact phone from his backpack and dialed Kamal, tapping his fingers on the bar, waiting on an answer. None came, the phone going to an automated voice mail system.

Growing a little alarmed, he looked at the tablet again, seeing the four rectangles on the satellite image of the fort, all stationary.

What are they doing?

He pulled up the history of their movements and saw that the triangles had been within five feet of each other for at least twenty-four hours. That made no sense. He checked the health tab for each watch and feared he'd see the same numbers, but they were all different, with different step counts, different heartbeats per minute, and different stress levels.

The watches were working, because it would have been inordinately hard to fabricate that data, but the locations couldn't be accurate. Especially with the step counts being different. How had they all been together for the last twenty-four hours, and yet some had walked twice as far as the others? He began to worry, and then his other phone rang. The one from the Condor team.

He answered and heard, "Go secure."

He pulled the phone away from his face and pressed a sequence of buttons, initiating an encrypted handshake with the far handset. After the handsets synched, he could talk without anyone listening, the conversation encrypted end-to-end. If either he or the Condor team were being tracked, someone could still get the location data, cell tower history, and everything else with a call, but they would hear nothing of what was said.

It was a double-edged sword: while it protected the conversation, it also alerted any state agency that was doing routine monitoring of him because of his Chinese affiliation that he was something beyond what his cover said. What businessman has a phone that encrypts? Only drug dealers, organized crime, or state intelligence.

Something he couldn't help, and he desperately needed answers.

He waited, saw the lights in the display change, and put it to his ear, saying, "Secure. What is your status? Did the Americans stay in Delhi?"

"No. They went to the Agra Fort, just like you suspected they would. When they did, following your instructions, we committed. You didn't tell us they were armed."

That didn't sound good.

"I told you I thought they were an arm of United States intelligence. That should have been enough. What happened?"

"I took that to mean they were like you, living here under cover but without any particular skill at fighting. They aren't just intelligence people like yourself. They're a Condor team in their own right."

Mr. Chin listened to the after-action report and realized he had touched a tiger, something his masters in the Ministry of State Security would have to understand now. Although he was sure he would get the blame.

The man finished his report, ending with, "We had to break it off, as there was no way to eliminate the threat and still escape. We were at a stalemate, and we needed to exfiltrate."

Mr. Chin said, "What's the status of the men left behind?"

"They're dead."

Mr. Chin spit out, "I know that. That's not what I'm asking. What will the police find? Are they clean?"

"Absolutely clean. The weapons are untraceable, and they have no identification on them. They have never conducted any operations here, so there's no way to match up fingerprints or DNA, and we have the vehicle, so they can't trace that."

"What damage did you do to the Americans?"

"Vehicle severely damaged, one member hit, but unable to discern how bad. Most definitely out of action."

"In your estimation, can they continue?"

He waited, the man considering his question, then heard, "They can continue if they don't care about the one who's down. If they want to evacuate him with whatever infrastructure they have, it will require them to focus on that mission."

"So that team is now committed?"

He heard nothing for a moment, the man reconsidering. He came back and said, "No, not fully. There was one man who was a devil, and if he wants to continue on his own, he'll do so, and he'll be effective. The most I can say is they've been slowed, but not stopped."

CHAPTER 39

Kamal looked around the room and said, "Not bad, not bad. I thought we'd end up sleeping in some abandoned building."

It was spartan, but clean, with four low wooden bedframes housing a thin foam mattress, a desk, and a four-drawer dresser, but nothing else. Not even pictures on the walls.

Randeep smiled and said, "We lucked out. This place caters to students and is usually full, but they had a room big enough for all of us, and we can come and go from here without anyone questioning us."

Called the Kami Boys Hostel, it was located just off the main campus of Jaipur National University, the area around the campus teeming with men their age.

Kamal said, "How'd you find it?"

"We went for a drive-by of the Oberoi and it was on the way. The hotel is a few kilometers down the road."

"Good. Good." He turned to Manjit and said, "What did you think of Jaiden and Rakesh?"

Manjit said, "They were really trying to test us. Acted like they were stone-cold killers and we were babies, but in the end it worked out."

"Do you think they'll follow through?"

"Absolutely. If anything, they'll think they're in charge, which may be a problem. You need to be ready for that. If we succeed, they might fight you on your plans for how to execute the follow-on exposure. Especially Jaiden."

Kamal nodded, saying nothing. Manjit said, "How do you know them?"

"We're from the same village. They were older than me, and they looked after me when I was a boy, after my father died. I used to work for Jaiden, back before he went into the Army. My mother never really cared for them, but they knew my father well. We got along as friends then, but it's been years. I went to jail and they went to work for Thakkar's security. I'm glad to hear the meeting went okay."

"As far as the plan goes it did, but keep what I said in mind."

"I will."

Randeep said, "How is Agam? How did that go?"

Kamal exhaled and said, "I honestly don't know. He was fine when I left, but I've been on the road for hours. I have to assume it's going okay."

"You didn't call him?"

"With what? I can't use the watch phone because I'm afraid it'll screw up his spoofing software, and I most surely can't use Mr. Chin's contact phone. That's probably being recorded in Beijing."

Manjit said, "But at least the spoofing is working? Right?"

Kamal nodded. "Yeah, it is. Mr. Chin called me earlier this morning for a check-in, but didn't act like he suspected anything. That's not going to last for too much longer. He called again as I was driving to you, but I let it go to voice mail."

He held up his Garmin watch and said, "Agam showed me something about these things. It has what's called a 'kill switch.' When you hit it, it stops transmitting everything and wipes itself of all memory. Before we do the mission, we hit that switch."

Manjit smiled and said, "Only Agam would figure that out. I'm sure he's fine. He loves tinkering with technology, and he'll hit one of those minarets at the Taj."

Kamal remembered what he'd told Agam and changed the subject, saying, "Where's the van?"

"Outside, a little bit down the road. Don't worry. It's safe. We parked it next to a little mechanics shop and asked them to watch it."

"That's probably not so smart. Especially at night."

Randeep said, "The owner lives there. It's okay. We checked it this morning, and it was fine."

"I don't like that. It's been there for twenty-four hours now. Enough time for someone to become interested."

Manjit said, "It doesn't matter anymore. Nobody's going to mess with it in the daylight, and we're not staying another night."

Kamal nodded, the words reminding him of what was to come. He said, "Let me see it. I want to check out the equipment."

Manjit stood and said, "Let's go, then."

He led them past the other dorm rooms and down the stairs, looping around from the front entrance, going past a lounge area until they reached the back door. Through the window, Kamal could see four men going at it on a volleyball court.

Manjit opened the door and passed by the court, saying, "We could get in a game to let off some adrenaline before we leave."

Randeep gave a half-hearted laugh, and Kamal said, "Let's just stick with the mission."

Manjit led them down a narrow dirt lane, passing concrete buildings interspersed with weed-covered lots, until they reached a machine shop, the interior showing sparks from someone working. In the front was a white panel van.

Manjit unlocked the back and Kamal crawled inside, seeing two duffel bags on the floor. He unzipped one and saw three AK-47s, a stack of magazines, and a wooden crate. He opened it, finding six Chinese Type 86 hand grenades. He lifted out the tray and found six more. Meaning four apiece.

A lot of death and destruction within the bag. It made Kamal physically sick thinking about it, but he had to show strength.

"What's in the other bag?"

Randeep opened it like a child ripping into a present, saying, "It's full of body armor."

He pulled out a vest festooned with Velcro and put it on, cinching down the elastic waistband. He held out his arms and said, "We'll look like commandos when we attack that place."

Kamal tapped his chest, feeling the ceramic plate inside. "I don't care what we'll look like, but I do appreciate the protection. Come on, let's lock this back up."

They did so, and then walked back to the hostel. Kamal said, "I want to see the Oberoi. I want to find the gate in the daylight so we aren't searching around after dark."

Manjit said, "We've already done that. I know right where it is."

"What was the security?"

"There was nothing yet. It's a chain-link gate set into a wooden ten-foot fence that surrounds the entire compound."

"I want to see it for myself. See what's happening now."

"If we drive that van back down the road it might cause suspicion. There aren't a lot of buildings out there. It's in the country, and the people who are there look at you as you go by."

"We'll take my car."

Manjit nodded and said, "Let's go, then, I'll drive. Where's your car?"

"In the front of the hostel."

They reached the back of the building, the volleyball game now finished, and retraced their steps to the front, this time moving through the lobby to the entrance. Kamal led them to his beat-up Hyundai, tossing his key fob to Manjit.

Randeep got in the back seat while Kamal went around to the front. Manjit started the car and turned it around, driving north. They went for about five minutes before Kamal said, "How far?"

"Another ten minutes."

"Have you mapped out a route to Mumbai?"

From the back, Randeep said, "I have. I know the way. We'll want to stay off the main highways, and it's about a twenty-four-hour trip, so we'll have to switch out drivers."

"We'll take both the van and the car. If we have at least five people out of the seven, we can do it."

"Five? What's that mean?"

Kamal said, "It'll take two per vehicle, one driving and one sleeping, with one left over to guard Thakkar in the van."

"I meant why not seven? Us three and the four bodyguards?"

Kamal's face went grim. He said, "I'm not sure how many are coming out of the Oberoi."

They rode the rest of the way in silence, Manjit taking turns on the roads by memory. Twelve minutes later he said, "There's the entrance."

Kamal looked, seeing a side road leading to a circular drive and the front of the hotel. Manjit continued on, now driving down a dirt lane next to a tall wooden fence painted green. He said, "That's the compound to the right."

"The gate?"

"It's on the back side."

He reached an intersection, the fence taking a right. He turned, following it, then midway down slowed. He said, "There's the gate just ahead."

They drove by it slowly, Kamal seeing two armed men wearing dastaars and uniforms on the inside. Manjit said, "They weren't there yesterday."

Kamal said, "Let's hope those are the two Jaiden found."

They reached the end of the fence, which wrapped around to the right, and Manjit continued straight, finally pulling over next to an abandoned building surrounded by fields.

He said, "So? Back to the hostel?"

Before Kamal could answer, they heard the thumping of rotor blades, a helicopter flying low overhead. It crossed the threshold of the fence and began to sink to the ground, lost from sight behind the fence.

Kamal said, "That's Riva Thakkar. He's here."

Kamal watched the cloud of dust raised by the helicopter, then heard the whine of the rotors begin to die, thinking what it meant. Finally understanding the mission was going to happen.

He was brought out of his thoughts by his phone ringing. He realized it was the contact phone and pulled it up, his face draining of color.

Manjit said, "What?"

"It's Mr. Chin."

He let it ring out, then said, "He knows his mission is now fucked. He's calling to find out why Thakkar just flew here."

Randeep said, "But he thinks we're in Agra, right?"

"Yes, but not for long. It's time to use the kill switch."

We drove by the same policeman who'd seen us entering, everyone in the vehicle holding our collective breath, but he continued blowing his whistle and waving his arms ineffectually at the insane
traffic, ignoring us completely. I couldn't believe he didn't recognize us
and wonder what the hell had happened to our SUV.

We rolled past him, then turned into the drive leading to the fort.
Brett pulled over and we did a fire drill, Brett and me spilling out the
front and Jennifer jumping in the driver's seat.

Veep was in the back, sitting upright, conscious but in pain, his
wound covered by a rain jacket. I said, "Can you use a phone?"

He nodded and I said, "You're going to have to coordinate your
medical treatment while Jennifer drives."

He let a weak grin slip out and said, "I would expect no less."

I patted him on the arm and closed his door, moving to the front
and leaning in Jennifer's window. "Don't stop for anything. You've got
about a three-and-a-half-hour drive to New Delhi, plenty of time to
coordinate for Veep, but remember, those final two assholes are still on
the loose. Keep an eye out for them."

Jennifer flicked her eyes to her Staccato on the seat next to her and
said, "We'll be okay." She returned to me and said, "You remember the

same thing. We're driving out of the blast radius. You guys are still in it. Don't do anything stupid."

I smiled and said, "Probably a foregone conclusion."

She put the car in gear, saying, "Don't forget what I said about the crypts. That's where I'd go for a meet."

I said, "I got it, now get out of here."

I turned, nodded at Brett, and we began jogging up the road, entering the line for the fort. I'd told Jennifer it was "probably" a foregone conclusion that we were going to do something stupid, but it was more than that. It was an absolute certainty because we were both carrying our pistols concealed in our waistbands and we were going through a security checkpoint with a metal detector.

I'd been through multiple metal detectors while in India, as they were in just about every hotel, train station, metro, ferry, or museum, and in all of them, no matter what happened, the security guards just let the person continue on. Nobody ever emptied their pockets, instead going through the detectors with cell phones, keys, change, and whatever else, and because of it, the machines consistently went off. The men manning them, when confronted by a mass of people trying to enter or exit, just let the offender go on, wanting to facilitate the flow of people more than the art of security.

I hoped it was the same here but wasn't sure. The line went swiftly, and as we approached, I relaxed. Security was treated just as important here as it had been everywhere else—the magnetometer flashing red and buzzing, and the person just being waved on. The only thing extra was that purses and backpacks were searched.

We reached the end and I went through, hearing the detector go off. I looked around, acting surprised and confused as to what to do next, and was waved forward by the guard.

Brett was next, and he received the same treatment, only having to have his backpack searched, but that was fine, as it had nothing incriminating in it. He caught up to me and we swiftly began walking, me saying, "Get that GPS out and let's get a lock."

He did so, saying, "What do you hope to find here anyway? If it was a meeting, it's long over."

"I was thinking about what Jennifer said to me, about how a meeting past security makes no sense when they could have it right outside the gate—or in a hotel room, back alley, or whatever. Back then, I figured it was to ensure that neither party was armed, like conducting a personal meet past security in an airport, but after what we just did, that's probably not it either."

He said, "I got a lock. This way."

We started moving again and I said, "Now I'm thinking it was a cache. A dead drop for one of them to find."

We speed-walked by two weirdos with chipmunks crawling all over them, one coming my way holding out the ball of fur. I waved him away and Brett said, "But that's the same problem. Why not just do that outside?"

"I think because the attack is going to be launched from here and they couldn't get a drone past the security line. It has to be in a backpack, and all of this area, to include the Taj Mahal, is a 'no drone zone.' It would get confiscated."

"But they already had the drones. We saw the boxes in the safe house in Delhi. Why a dead drop?"

"Yeah, I know. But it's something like that. Whatever it is, I think the Chinese set it up. They would have the expertise and capability to do it, and I don't think they trusted their chosen killers to be able to execute the mission by bringing the equipment in on their own."

We went through a large arch, finding ourselves in a courtyard surrounded by a large stone wall with turrets on the corners.

Brett stopped, getting a bearing with the GPS and saying, "It's in the far wall according to this satellite image."

"Inside the wall?"

"The dot is centered on the wall, but I don't know if it's up or down."

I looked up at the wall and saw people walking back and forth along it, looking at the view of the river on the far side. I said, "It's not up. It's got to be down, in the crypts."

We went to the location on the wall, and he said, "It's about twenty feet in front of us, right through the brick."

I said, "We need to find a way down. Let's start walking the wall."

We'd gone about seventy meters and came across a marker titled "Subterranean Apartments and Gallows (1569–1658 A.D.)." The description described a gallows, separate rooms, and how they ran all along the fort wall, with slits for ventilation and lighting, concluding that everything I'd just read was speculation, and it was a mystery as to why they'd been built or how they'd been used. It ended by saying they had been closed to public viewing.

I said, "This is it. The marker is probably placed near the entryway. We need to find it."

Brett pointed to a small iron door on the other side of a barricade, looking not unlike a basement entrance on a farmhouse in the Midwest. I looked closer, seeing a padlock on the ground next to the latch. I said, "That's it. Let's go."

We quickly crossed the stone barricade, crouched down, and pulled open the door, and it screeched in anger at being disturbed. In front of me a set of narrow stone stairs led down into the darkness. I glanced around, saw nobody paying any attention, and said, "Go, go."

Brett pulled his pistol and entered, flicking on the weapon light to see. I followed quickly, bringing the door down behind me.

Brett led the way, stopping every few meters to listen. We heard nothing. In short order, we were on a dirt floor, Brett saying, "The GPS isn't any good down here."

"We know the grid is back the way we came, and there aren't multiple levels. Start that way."

He turned and started walking, our weapon lights splitting the darkness, showing a narrow, arched passage made of stone. Eventually, the tunnel opened up into a room with a wooden beam crossing a black pit. Brett shined his light in and saw it was only two feet deep with a dirt floor. His light caught something and he bent over, pulling out a box. He shined the light on it, seeing the label for a DJI Mavic drone just like the ones in the safe house.

I saw something else in the pit and reached down, removing an empty canvas bag. I said, "I'm betting that drone is armed, and he's after Thakkar right now. We need to find him."

Brett said, "We know he's got to hit the Taj Mahal, and there aren't too many vantage points for that here at the fort. All to the southeast."

CHAPTER 41

Sitting on a broken folding chair in a stone structure shaped like a minaret, Agam stared at the expansive grounds in front of the Taj Mahal, seeing them still clear. He looked at his watch and knew the time for the attack was coming. Soon the crowds would return and he would have to launch the drone.

The minaret was basically a stone gazebo on top of a large palace at the south end of the fort, and it functioned more as decoration, serving little defensive purposes. Having a small open hole for an entrance, a low wall, and narrow pillars holding up the dome of the top, it now protected Agam from being seen by anyone down below.

The roof of the palace, like many sections of the fort, was off-limits to tourists, but there wasn't any way he could launch the drone from a lower level. He'd initially planned on launching the drone from either the lower walls or the original tower where he'd seen the Taj, but they were both constantly clogged with tourists. He'd walked around and seen the stone minaret on the roof of the palace, thinking about how he could get up there. He entered the palace, pretending to take note of the various markers, but really looking for stairs. He found some on the eastern side, deep in a dark narrow hallway that led to various royal chambers. It had a simple rope blocking access, a sign outside stating "No Entry," but he could see light coming in from above.

He waited until the hallway was clear and then crossed over, running up the stairs and breaking out onto the roof. The first thing he saw was the Army compound across the courtyard at the back of the fort, and he immediately crouched down, scuttling to the tower.

Inside, he found a broken metal folding chair surrounded by cigarette butts, a sign that workers likely came up routinely. Not ideal, but he didn't have long enough to figure out their schedule, and decided to risk it. He took a seat, unzipped his backpack, removed the drone, and set it on its canister. He clipped his phone into the controller and sat down, staring out at the empty grounds of the Taj Mahal.

The waiting was eating at him, as was the thought of harming someone he'd never even met. He remembered Kamal's words and endeavored to remain strong. If someone was visiting the Taj Mahal, they were providing money for the state that oppressed them, and in so doing had become the enemy. It rang hollow, but he focused on the words. Wanting to believe.

He heard a noise and saw the groups of tourists on the wall pointing out over the river. He looked that way and saw a helicopter approaching, the rotors growing louder. It circled the fort, coming right over his head low enough for him to feel the wind and see the pilots' helmets, then flew to the Taj Mahal, hovering over the expansive grounds, then landing in a grassy area south of the monument.

Kamal stood up, watching a group of people enter the helicopter.

Thakkar.

The rotors spun back up and the helicopter lifted off, retracing its flight path over the Agra Fort, once again flying so low that Agam could feel the wash and see the people inside.

It disappeared, and the air grew quiet. Agam sat back down, knowing his time had come. He repeated in his mind that everyone who had paid for entry into the Taj Mahal had enriched the government that oppressed people like him. A mantra stated over and over: *They pay the government, and the government kills the Sikh. They pay the government, and the government kills the Sikh.*

He kept his eyes on the expansive Taj Mahal courtyard, waiting on the ordinary tourists to begin entering the grounds. He saw a trickle of individuals, presumably the ubiquitous guides allowed to pester anyone who visited without one, then clusters of four or five tourists. He waited until at least fifty were on the grounds, most gathered in the middle of the courtyard around a pool of water, the single best spot for photographs with the Taj Mahal in the background. That group would only grow, as nobody was leaving the Taj without a picture.

Resigned, he glanced back at the Indian Army compound, then exited the temple, moving to the edge of the roof. He set the drone on the ground and conducted the rotor test again.

When the lights went from flashing to solid, he hit the lift button, watching the drone move to eye level. He checked the camera and saw that it worked flawlessly. He left it in the air for a moment, not wanting to launch it on its deadly mission.

CHAPTER 42

I stopped on the upper walkway of the wall, realizing we were wasting our time. Because the Taj Mahal could be seen in the distance from this vantage point, this section of wall was a magnet for tourists compared to the rest of the fort.

I said, "There's no way he's going to try to launch the drone from here. He'd get stopped immediately."

We'd already gone to the tower viewing area down below and, while it appeared to be a good launch point, it had the same problem, only worse: throngs of tourists trying to get a picture with the Taj in the background.

Brett said, "Maybe he's outside the wall now, on the moat or something."

"How would he get there? Rappel down? He's here, somewhere. We're just not looking in the right place."

Before he could answer, a civilian helicopter with some sort of company logo on the side came right over the fort, circling around and then flying to the Taj Mahal. We both watched it settle onto the lawn and thought the same thing: *Thakkar*.

We were too late. If the drone was going to launch, the location of the helicopter was a perfect target, as hitting it would cause a massive explosion that would kill everyone around it.

I said, "Look for the drone. This is it."

We leaned over the escarpment of the wall, searching the sky. I saw nothing, even scanning back on a line of sight from the helicopter to the fort. I said, "You got anything?"

"Nope."

I looked back at the helicopter and saw a group loading. *Maybe he's going to miss.*

The rotors spun back up and the helicopter lifted off the ground, retracing its flight path over the fort. It came across the roof of the palace across the courtyard, zooming just above it, and I saw a man appear out of one of the decorative towers, watching it go by.

It flew over our heads, across the river, and was a speck in the distance in seconds.

Brett said, "Looks like mission accomplished without any drama. Wherever he is, he missed. Maybe the drone malfunctioned."

I returned to the man on the roof and saw him go back into the tower, disappearing from view. He came back out, but this time he had something in his hands.

A drone.

What the hell?

At first I thought Brett might be right: he was the terrorist and his drone had failed, and now he was just trying to escape the scene. Then he went to the edge and placed the drone on the roof before fiddling with something in his hands.

Jesus Christ. He's going to launch, after Thakkar's gone.

I said, "Brett, the roof. Look at the roof."

He did and said, "Holy shit, let's go!"

We raced back toward the stairs at the tourist tower, then took them two at a time to the base of the wall. We reached the bottom and sprinted across the courtyard, ignoring the attention we were drawing. We leapt from the grass to the low parapet, me shouting, "Find a way up. I'll take the right side."

The palace was a rectangle with a cavernous anteroom, then a single hallway stretching the length of it. Brett took the hallway to the left and I went right. I jogged down the corridor, slowing at each opening, finding room after stone room with various artifacts scattered within and tourists milling about, but no stairs. I heard Brett shout and raced back to the center, then ran down his hallway. He pointed up and jumped over a rope, disappearing into an opening.

I reached the stairwell just as he cleared the top, a few seconds behind him. I leapt over the rope, scrambled up the steps, and broke out on the roof, seeing Brett with his pistol out, shouting at the man with the controller.

I ran around to the far side of him, seeing the drone crossing the gap between us and the Taj Mahal, the grounds now teeming with people. It looked like a pregnant bumblebee, and I knew the bottom of the drone was an explosive charge.

The man was tall and gangly, and was focused on Brett, a look of shock on his face. He didn't even realize I was there until I shouted, "Bring it back, or you're dead!"

He whipped his head to me and I thought he was going to faint. Instead, he ignored me, staring down at the camera feed and manipulating the controls.

More calmly, I said, "Bring it back, now."

He shook his head, said something in Hindi, and I saw his hands shaking. I went back to look for the drone, but could no longer find it. I figured I had about ten seconds. I took two steps forward, taking the slack up on my trigger. He caught the movement, saw the death in my eyes, and fell to his knees, letting out an anguished shriek. He said, "No, no. I'll bring it back."

I eased off the trigger and Brett said, "It's coming back. I can see it now."

I said, "Good man. Good. Just land it here nice and soft."

He nodded again, the tears running from his eyes. He returned his gaze to the controller and I saw his face grow rigid, a snarl coming out. Brett said, "Pike, that thing is hauling ass right at us."

I said, "Slow it down! Now!"

He looked up at me and I saw what he intended. I pulled the trigger twice, hitting him in the chest. He fell, the controller underneath him, but the drone kept flying on its last trajectory, heading straight at us. I shouted, "Go!" and took off running toward the stairwell, praying the device had no shrapnel built into it.

Brett was in front of me and made it into the stairwell just as the drone slammed into the stone roof of the minaret. My peripheral vision saw the light from the explosion, like a strobe had gone off, then I felt the blast pressure, the wave flinging me into the opening behind him. I hit the stone steps and tumbled twice before being grabbed by Brett, still upright, protected from the blast by the stairwell.

The echo of the explosion rolled across the valley and I stood up a little unsteadily, checking my limbs, my ears ringing. Brett said, "You okay?"

"Yeah, I think so."

"We need to get the fuck out of here."

"We need the phone in that controller."

Without another word he took off up the stairs and disappeared from view. I tested my legs, seeing they functioned, and I realized I hadn't been harmed in any meaningful way. It was a miracle.

In seconds he was back, saying, "Got it. Can you run, or do I need to carry your ass?"

"I'm good. Go, go."

We made it to the bottom before anyone arrived to come up, but they would soon, and if we were caught in the stairwell, we'd have some explaining to do.

Brett paused, took a glance out, then shook his head. A group of tourists raced by, all chattering in Hindi. He flicked his head out again, then leapt over the rope. I followed and we were in the hallway again. Brett went right, away from the entrance to the palace to avoid the initial scrum of authority that he knew was coming. The hallway ended in a little alcove with a window overlooking the valley, and we stopped there, listening to the shouts echo through the stone.

I heard the sound of boots thumping toward us and we waited until a horde of security guards and men in Army uniforms went up the stairs, then started walking back like we were confused American tourists. A guard was shouting and waving his arms, telling everyone to get out of the palace. We, of course, followed his instructions.

We reached the courtyard and I saw the army side of the fort starting to boil over, a wave of uniforms coming toward us like someone had kicked over an ant pile.

In two minutes we were back with the chipmunk men, only they were no longer looking to hand them off. They, like everyone else, were being directed to leave the fort, a steady stream of people forced back toward the entrance.

We went past the metal detectors in a growing mob of tourists and reached the street where we'd left Jennifer. We walked away from the fort on the main road, toward the Taj Mahal, and Brett said, "Well, that didn't go like we'd planned."

I chuckled and said, "We're out and free, so I'll take it as a win. Let's see if we can't get a cab before they're all taken."

"What's the next step?"

"Get to a hotel with Wi-Fi and get this cell phone connected to Creed. He needs to drain it for information, because that attack made no sense whatsoever."

CHAPTER 43

The bartender asked Mr. Chin if he'd like another old-fashioned, and Mr. Chin said, "No, you're right. Another one will bite me. May I have a glass of water and a menu, though?"

The bartender smiled and slid across a menu, then went to get the water. Another couple came in, taking a seat two stools away. Mr. Chin nodded at them as if he was enjoying his time, but he most certainly was not.

He pretended to study the menu, giving him a reason not to engage with anyone, while his mind furiously tried to determine what had become of his mission.

The Americans were more formidable than he had envisioned, but they'd had nothing to do with stopping the attack on Thakkar. From what the Condor team leader had said, they wouldn't have had the ability to execute. Given when the team had engaged, there wasn't enough time to unravel what Mr. Chin had planned. They would have had to know the precise method and timing of the mission in order to stop it, and if they had known that, they could have simply had someone waiting to catch Kamal or his men. Or told Thakkar to skip his visit to the Taj Mahal.

But they *did* know something about the Agra Fort, or they wouldn't have gone there. First they went to New Delhi while Mr. Chin's team was there, then followed them to Agra, but always a step behind.

How?

Somewhere, there was a leak. But it couldn't be anyone on Kamal's team, or they'd all have been rolled up by the RAW immediately. And Kamal's team were the only ones who knew. Somehow the Americans were getting breadcrumbs and successfully following them.

And then he remembered the two hardened men on Thakkar's security detail, Jaiden and Rakesh. They were friends of Kamal and maybe they'd talked. Maybe Kamal had given generalities of what they were doing without specifics. Enough for them to tell the Americans, giving them a vague outline to follow.

But that theory also had holes. They were both willing to kill Thakkar in Goa, and had, in fact, set him up for it. Why would they try to stop it in Agra? They worked purely for money, and Mr. Chin had paid them well over the years. They didn't care what occurred, as long as the money was right. And then he remembered: Goa was where that attack had been thwarted by the Americans.

Maybe those two were playing a double game, taking his money while also working for the Americans. The more he thought about it, the more likely it seemed. Thakkar was their meal ticket, and with him gone, they'd be out of work. Maybe they'd been taking Mr. Chin's money all along while doing whatever they could to keep their benefactor alive. It would explain why they didn't just insist Thakkar not go to the Taj Mahal, as they'd have to explain how they knew something was occurring. It would also explain why they let him have dinner on a patio at a resort in Goa when they knew a kill team was coming. They'd already told the Americans to prevent execution.

He felt the anger build, convinced he was right. Those two would have to be dealt with, but not before he completed his mission against

Thakkar. He'd have to carefully construct his plan in such a way as to use their ability to get close while foiling any ability to thwart it.

He was brought out of his thoughts by a breaking news report. He turned to the screen and saw the outside of the Agra Fort, the same newsman who had been at the Taj Mahal giving a report. He was no longer calm and smiling, but sweating, his face a mask of serious concern, the area around him swirling with uniformed personnel and police cars with lights flashing.

Mr. Chin focused on the closed captioning coming across the screen, seeing that a terrorist attack had occurred at the fort itself, not the Taj Mahal.

He said, "Could you turn that up?"

The bartender did so, and Mr. Chin heard that an Islamic terrorist had tried to launch an explosive-laden drone from the roof of a palace on the grounds, but it had misfired, killing the terrorist.

So that's what happened.

The reporter continued, saying it was a single man who initiated the attack, and authorities didn't suspect any further danger. Authorities were trying to determine how the terrorist managed to smuggle explosives and a drone into the compound, suspecting he had inside help, and vowed to get to the bottom of the mystery.

Mr. Chin thought, *Good luck with that.* Then, *A single terrorist?*

Kamal and the others must have escaped. He woke his tablet and flicked to the Garmin tracking application, wanting to see where the other three had fled.

The screen showed no information at all, simply saying, *Connection lost.*

He furrowed his eyes, closed the application, checked the cell connectivity, then booted it up again. The same screen appeared. All four of the watches were no longer transmitting, meaning the persons wearing them were dead, or they'd been shut down intentionally.

No more than thirty minutes ago, all four were at the Agra Fort, each transmitting a pulse rate and location, and now all four were gone?

He heard the television say Thakkar's name and returned to the news report. The anchor was now saying that government sources had confirmed that Riva Thakkar's visit to the Taj Mahal was purely co-incidental, and that he was not specifically targeted, as the incident occurred a full ten minutes after the billionaire had left the grounds.

What? That made absolutely no sense.

The reporter continued, saying authorities believed the terrorist had no knowledge of Thakkar's visit and was forced to wait until after he left for his attack, convinced he intended to kill more people than Thakkar's group provided.

What on earth is going on?

CHAPTER 44

Kamal and his men stood in the back of the downstairs lounge, every student staying in the hostel now crowded around a single flat-screen television, listening to a report of a terrorist attack in Agra.

When the story was over the group split up, all chattering nervously. Kamal led his men back to their room, not saying a word. Once the door closed, Kamal spoke in a whisper, saying, "Agam's dead."

Manjit said, "What do you think happened?"

"I don't know. Maybe the drone was faulty. Maybe he turned it on, and it exploded. There's no way to tell."

Randeep said, "Do we continue?"

Kamal looked at both of them, seeing the loss of Agam had driven a stake in the heart of their will. The loss of Sidak in Goa had been a motivator, but for some reason, unlike for him, Agam's death was having the opposite effect on his men.

He said, "Yes, of course we continue. I spoke to Agam before I came here. He knew the risks and was willing to accept them."

"But *we* put him on that path."

And Kamal saw the issue. Manjit and Randeep blamed Mr. Chin for Sidak's death, but blamed themselves for Agam. He had to put that to rest.

"That's not true. What happened at Agra would have happened whether we had come here or not. If the drone was faulty, it would have blown up whether we were trying to kill Thakkar for Mr. Chin or whether we were using it to further our goals."

He saw his words held weight, and understood they wanted to believe him. He decided to focus on the mission. He looked at his watch and said, "We have about nine hours until the attack. Instead of sitting here mourning Agam, I want to take the van to that abandoned building next to the Oberoi. Get it parked inside the garage and start familiarizing ourselves with the weapons and gear. Fit the body armor, load the magazines, double-check the grenades, that sort of thing."

He stood up and Randeep said, "Wait, wait. I understand what you're saying about Agam's death, but there's more to it than just him getting killed. Agam failed in his mission. He didn't hit the Taj Mahal, and you said that was necessary for us to be able to escape from here."

"No, that's not true. What I said was we needed a diversion large enough to draw away national assets. I only want to deal with local police when we escape, without any national police or the RAW coordinating efforts. We have a long drive to Mumbai, and we won't make it with a coordinated response. Agam accomplished that. The Agra Fort is close enough to the Taj Mahal, and his death was enough to cause what we needed."

"How do you know? How *can* we know?"

Kamal scoffed and said, "Did you not see what I just saw? It was a local news station here in Jaipur talking about an explosion 'near the Taj Mahal.' Every station in this country is going to be talking about that, which means the pressure to solve it will be enormous. Every police and intelligence agency in the country will be descending on Agra, if only to show they're trying. Do you think an explosion at an old fort in Goa would generate that? No, Agam's mission worked."

Manjit said, "What if it worked too well? What if they *do* solve it and somehow attach us to Agam? His death might have given them the clues to find us before those ten hours are up."

"That won't happen. If anything, they'll unravel Mr. Chin's involvement, but the true hunters will be focused on Agam and Agra. They won't be looking for us."

* * *

I hung up the phone and turned to Brett, saying, "Veep's going to be fine. Kerry's got him patched up through an embassy doc."

"What's the damage?"

"Basically, it's stitches and a hole through his shoulder. Didn't hit a bone, so he'll only be in a sling for a while with some muscle loss in his lat. He'll come out of it with a cool scar to show his grandkids someday."

He smiled and said, "That's good news. When he went down, I thought for sure he'd been hit bad. What's Jennifer's status?"

"She's dealing with the rental car agency and a 'hit and run.' I told her to let the insurance company handle it and to load up our luggage on the Rock Star bird. Basically, get her ass down here so I don't have to stay in this hotel with the same pair of underwear."

He laughed, and I said, "Don't worry, I told her to bring yours too. Did you get anything more from Creed?"

He looked at the tablet on the table and said, "Nothing yet. Let him do his work."

We'd finally found a cab in the sea of people either flocking to the scene of the explosion or trying to get away from it. We'd had to walk about a mile before we found one, and by that time, Brett had gotten us a reservation at a hotel and convention center called the Jaypee Palace just outside the city center, but they only had one room left. At least it had two queen beds. Apparently, every government agency and reporter was descending on the Agra Fort and rooms were getting scarce. The cab got us to the hotel in record time, as it was just south of the Taj Mahal, and we checked in looking a little worse for wear.

The receptionist asked if we were on a tour, and Brett said yes, only to realize she was asking if the tour was going to pay for our room. When she asked for the company, he fessed up and told her no, that we were doing our own tour, and she checked us in, probably thinking we were a couple. Luckily, she didn't ask where our luggage was.

We went to the room and Brett immediately slaved the phone to his tablet, then the tablet to the hotel Wi-Fi. He called Creed, Creed did his magic through the miracle of the internet, walking Brett through instructions on the tablet, and then we sat back and waited.

That was six hours ago, and after getting the update from Jennifer, I was getting a little antsy.

I said, "That attack was something out of left field. I really want to know what he found in that phone."

Brett stood up and said, "Well, he's working as fast as he can. Let's go get some dinner at the 'grand buffet.' Maybe he'll have something by the time we get back."

I agreed and we left our room, walking through a labyrinth of hallways until we reached the reception area again, having missed the entrance to the buffet. Out the windows of the entrance I could see the sun was setting, the splash of orange impressive against the low skyline.

I asked the receptionist for directions, and she told me it was one floor down, but we'd have to charge it to our room since we weren't on a tour. Apparently, this place stayed in business with tour busses. We followed her instructions, and sure enough, entered a giant room full of tables, food stations liberally sprinkled throughout, all with different choices. Chinese, sushi, Indian, Western, you had your pick.

We separated, going through the lines, then found a table. I started shoveling food in my mouth, my body finally realizing it hadn't had nourishment in a long while. After the adrenaline of this day, I had expended quite a bit of energy, first with the Chinese, then with the terrorist.

In between bites, I said, "What do you make of that attack in the parking lot?"

"I honestly don't know. I mean, clearly it's the Chinese, but what the hell? Why are they attacking us? Is it some organized crime thing, or is it the government? What do you think?"

"I think it's the government. I think it's the MSS and they're behind these so-called 'Islamic terrorists.' I think they zeroed in on us when we stopped the attack in Goa, and they're still worried we're a threat."

I took another bite, reflecting, then said, "I originally thought they were trying to kill Thakkar, but I'm not so sure now. They're calling that attack in Goa an Islamic copycat of the 2008 Mumbai slaughter, but after Jennifer saw the Chinese in the hotel, I believed that was just a cover to eliminate him. After today, I'm not so sure."

"You don't think they're behind it now?"

"No, no, I still think China has something to do with this, but I'm not so sure it's Thakkar anymore. He was on the grounds for over thirty minutes before we even arrived. That terrorist could have launched the drone at any time while he was walking around, and most assuredly could have done so once he saw that helo come in to pick Thakkar up. He didn't."

"Well, they *are* calling him an Islamic terrorist, and if that's true, maybe he's just crazy. You can't control crazy."

"He's not a Muslim."

Brett looked at me in surprise and said, "Why do you say that? It's all over the news that he is."

"It's also all over the news that he was killed by the drone in a misfire. And yet we both know he has two bullet holes in his chest. They know that too. They're just saying something to placate the public."

"So how do you know they weren't Muslims?"

"You already said it. Because China knows Islamic terrorists are fanatics. Because they know they can't control a man whose sole identity is ideology. They'd never do it, just like we'd never do it."

"We *did* do it. In Afghanistan during the Soviet occupation."

"Yeah, well, we learned that lesson the hard way, didn't we. Trust me, China's not tying their wagon to a bunch of fanatics. This is something else."

"Maybe that's the answer. Maybe they're learning the same lesson we did."

"What's that?"

"They tied themselves to a bunch of fanatics, and now those guys are running loose, looking for their own version of success."

I heard that and thought he had a point. Maybe the masters had lost control of the slaves. I said, "China would only use someone who was motivated by money."

I took another bite and pointed my fork at him, saying, "But maybe the ones they think are motivated by money are using China just like China thinks they're using them."

Brett said, "So where does that leave us?"

I laughed and said, "On the first flight out of here, which should be arriving soon, unless Creed has found anything."

CHAPTER 45

We went back to our room and along the way I called Knuckles, letting him know the state of play.

When he answered, I said, "So, you getting a lot of work done?"

He said, "Well . . . that depends on what you call 'work.'"

I laughed and said, "What did Nadia say about our actions here?" I'd spoken to him just before talking to Jennifer earlier, letting him know that we might need some help from Nadia. It turned out we were okay, but I'd given her a secret squirrel update through Knuckles to see if she was hearing something different from the RAW, which would bolster her theory that they were somehow involved.

He said, "The official word on the street is a lone wolf that was killed by his own bomb, but she's being told it's a conspiracy, and that someone had killed the man with a gun. It's not being hidden from her."

"So there's no cover-up inside the RAW?"

"Well, there's no cover-up, but that may be because someone else saw the body first and it was too late to deny it. I *will* say they think it's Muslim terrorists. They haven't backed off of that, and they aren't looking at China."

"Bullshit. They aren't Muslim. Well, they *might* be Muslim, but they aren't doing this for Islam. The Taj Mahal is an Islamic shrine.

Why would they choose to attack that instead of some Hindu temple? It makes no sense."

"Because it's a symbol of Indian power? Because it's the number one tourist destination in the entire country?"

He had a point, but I wouldn't let it go. "Fanatics don't think that way. They want to attack what they despise, not what they revere. The Muslims in this country all know it was a Muslim who built that place. They wouldn't attack it even if it was the number one tourist destination."

"So what are you thinking?"

"I'm thinking those assholes from the safe house are still on the loose, and I think China's lost control of them. Tell Nadia that, because we're leaving here tonight."

"Wait, what?"

"Look, we had a gunfight today we barely survived, Veep's arm is in a sling, and we had no sanction for any of it. Brett and I stopped a damn terrorist attack today against the state of India, and while I don't know what it was about, I don't really care at this point. One free terrorist prevention per month is all I'm authorized, and we're now fresh out."

"Okay, okay, I get it. I understand. What else do you want me to tell Nadia?"

"You mean about us leaving, or my thoughts on the attack?"

"On the attack, you ass. I'm pretty sure I don't need to explain us leaving."

I paused, collecting my thoughts. He said, "Pike?"

I said, "Nadia needs to get the RAW to start looking at China. They're running amok around here, and they're the thread. They're doing this for something other than just trouble. They could pay Pakistan for that, but they're here, on the ground. Which means it's something directly important to them. I thought it was Thakkar, but now I'm not so sure."

"Pike, Nadia's going to say all those guys had Pakistani ISI ties."

"That's bullshit Chinese disinformation. She needs them to start looking at people motivated by money, not Islam."

I heard nothing to that and said, "You still there?"

He said, "You and I think exactly alike. I said that to her earlier today. I'm just glad to hear *you* say it, because I think you're right."

"Well, get her ass on the thread. I don't think the RAW is corrupt, but I *do* think China's trying to bite them in the ass, and they're using guys they've lost control of. There's going to be another attack, somewhere, for something we haven't figured out, but it isn't driven by Islam."

"I will, I will. She's getting ready for the big party right now. We're supposed to leave in an hour. You wouldn't believe this place. It is out of control. There are peacocks all over the grounds, they have rose petals at our door, and we have our own butler. It's insane, but I'll give her our evaluation and then head to the airport to meet you in Agra."

I said, "What are you wearing right now?"

"Some weird-ass Indian man-dress with leggings. Everyone has to wear it. I look pretty good in it, but I'll change before I see you, I promise. I wouldn't want to get Jennifer all hot and bothered."

I chuckled and said, "I'd never be so cruel. Enjoy your time with Nadia. She seems nice, and you'll never get to see an Indian pre-wedding party like that *ever*. Take a commercial flight home when it's done, but I'm taking the team tonight."

I could almost see the smile on his face. He said, "You got it. Sorry I wasn't there for the gunfight."

I said, "You didn't miss much. I had Veep take the bullet instead of you."

Brett and I reached our room and I called Jennifer to find out her status. She told me she was at the airport and would be here in about an hour. She also said she had Veep with her, and asked if we had enough space. I looked at Brett and mouthed, "We need another room."

He shook his head and said, "There are no rooms. It's here or no-where."

I went back to the phone and said, "We have plenty of space. Veep's going to sleep with Brett, and you'll sleep with me."

Brett snapped his head to me and said, "No way am I sleeping with some guy who has to lie on his back and groan all night every time I move. I'll sleep with Jennifer. You're sleeping with Veep."

I looked at him and mouthed, "Shut it."

Into the phone I said, "Just get down here, we'll figure it out."

Jennifer said, "I'd better have a bed when I get there."

I started to reply when Brett said, "Creed's responded."

I said, "Gotta go. Call when you're in the air."

I hung up without another word, turned to Brett, and said, "What did he find?"

Brett was going through the tablet, saying, "Absolutely nothing, apparently. The phone was never used for a call, texts, or email. Never used to surf the web. It apparently did nothing but control the drone."

I said, "It took *that* long to get us nothing?"

He said, "Wait, wait. Here's something. There was a Garmin watch attached to it. And some gobbledygook about spoofing."

I said, "Enough of this shit," and dialed my phone to DC. I looked at my watch and saw it was now seven P.M., did some quick math, and realized Creed had been working all night for nothing. It was nine thirty in the morning his time, and I hoped to catch him there.

I heard the switchboard answer, did a dance of bona fides with the woman on the phone to prove who I was, and then was connected to the network operations center. A man answered, and I said, "Get me Creed."

There was a pause, then: "He's not in yet. He'll be here later."

Which was a mistake on his part, as I knew Creed had been there all night. The NOC wasn't waiting on him to arrive. Creed was likely waving his arms, telling the man on the phone to say that so he could leave.

I said, "Tell him it's Pike, and put his ass on the phone."

A second later I heard, "Pike, I did like you asked—outside of any orders from George Wolffe, I might add. There was nothing on that phone. It's like it was opened and never used for anything other than a Garmin watch and a Mavic drone."

I said, "That's what I want to ask you about. You said something about spoofing. What did you mean?"

"Apparently, the phone was tied into a Garmin watch—specifically an Instinct 2X Tactical—and it transmitted all sorts of data to an application."

"Yeah, so?"

"That's what I said: 'Yeah, so what?' I can tell you wherever that watch went, which isn't that big of a deal, because I could do that with the phone alone, but this phone had been modified. There were four watches that sent it data, and someone modified the app to appear as if all four watches were with this phone."

"You're speaking Egyptian. Can you tell me what that means?"

"It means that wherever those other watches were, they were transmitting from their phone to this phone, and this phone was recording them as all being in the same place. That's all. I know, I get it. It's nothing. That's what I was trying to say."

"Wait, are you saying someone was trying to hide their location through this phone?"

"No. Their own phones would still have the data from their watches. If you found their phone, you'd see where they'd been. They weren't hiding anything."

"Then why do it?"

"I don't know, Pike. That's why I said it was nothing. I'm not sure why they did it."

"But this phone was transmitting that data?"

"Yeah, like they all were. If you had access to the phone, you got the data."

"Wait, slow down. You said that the other Garmin watches, tied to other phones, were sending their data to *this* phone?"

"Yeah. That's what I meant by 'spoofing.' Why?"

"Can you show me where the other watches are located? Can you give me a history of their movements from this phone?"

"Yeah . . . I think so. The phone recorded it all."

"Get me that, right now. Send it to the tablet."

I hung up and turned to Brett. He said, "What was that all about?"

I said, "We just found the other terrorists. I think the Chinese were tracking them, and they found a way to get around it. He's sending the data to us right now, and when we get it, we send it to Knuckles for Nadia to sort out."

We gathered around the tablet display and I saw Creed halfway around the world working a cursor on the screen. It was like magic. He punched one button, highlighted something else, and the phone lit up, pulsing. The cursor kept working, and four icons appeared on the screen, along with a ton of breadcrumb trails tied to numbers, so much that the screen was overridden with them.

Brett said, "What the hell is that?"

I called Creed back and said, "We've got a mish-mash of shit over here. I can't see anything."

He said, "That's the complete picture for the last forty-eight hours."

"But there's not even a map, just a bunch of dots and numbers."

"The dots are the trail the GPS recorded. The numbers are the lat-long."

I gritted my teeth and said, "That's no fucking help, Creed. I need this on a map, so I can see."

"So you don't want to know the actual grid?"

"I will after I see a map."

He huffed and said, "Hang on."

Five minutes later, the screen cleared, showing a map of India, the dots and icons tiny in the center. He came on the phone and said, "Now?"

"Yeah, I have the whole continent, but the icons are microscopic."

"So zoom in. You want me to do that too?"

I felt a little embarrassed and picked up the tablet, putting the phone on speaker. I hit the plus button on the map, and it started closing in on the trail. It showed all four moving from Delhi to Agra, then two to Jaipur, followed by a third, with one remaining behind.

Jaipur? That's not good.

I said, "Can I separate this by last known grid for each? No trails?"

He said, "Hang on."

The screen cleared, showing a single icon in Agra, and three in Jaipur. I hit zoom on Agra and it came down to earth right above the palace in the Agra Fort. It was the terrorist we'd killed today, his last recorded grid being where he'd died and the time of death.

I looked at the last recorded time for the other three and saw it was about thirty minutes earlier. So they'd all ceased transmitting about the same time. Weird. Like they knew that guy was going to be dead soon and no longer needed his phone.

I zoomed in on their location, getting down to the granular level. They were all together, right outside the Oberoi Rajvilas Resort.

Holy shit.

I said, "Get Knuckles back on the line, right now."

Brett heard the steel in my voice and said, "What, why?"

I tossed the tablet to him while dialing Jennifer with my own phone, saying, "Those fuckers are outside the wedding party. They're trying to kill Thakkar after all."

CHAPTER 46

Kamal tossed his half-filled plastic bowl to the concrete floor, took a drink from a water bottle, and said, "Maybe we should have waited for that final meal at the hostel. Beef curry and melon slices from a roadside stand isn't what I wanted for our victory dinner."

Manjit chuckled and said, "You're the one who said we had to come out here this early. We could have waited."

On Kamal's orders, they'd driven both his sedan and the van back to the abandoned building they'd parked next to earlier in the day. Kamal had no idea what it had been in the past, but now it was just a hollowed-out concrete husk, two stories of empty rooms full of trash, with a one-story garage large enough for four vehicles.

All three of them were on the second floor, sitting on their haunches using an old wooden crate as a table. Manjit and Randeep still wore their body armor. Kamal had taken his off, finding it stifling.

They'd been out in the house since just before sundown, checking out the weapons, loading magazines, and fiddling with the body armor. They adjusted the fit, loosening and tightening the Velcro straps and playing around with the pouches. The only snag was Manjit. He refused to load his four grenades into his vest.

Kamal said, "Manjit, that's the way we're announcing ourselves. We throw two when we enter and we'll shock the security with the explosion, then we throw two when we leave to keep them from following. We talked about this."

Manjit said, "I'll kill if I have to. If someone is charging me, shooting at me, or trying to stop us, but I'm not throwing a hand grenade into a pre-wedding party. I'm just not."

"You said you agreed they were the enemy. Agam agreed for his mission."

"Agam was going to hit a piece of carved rock at the Taj Mahal. It's not the same thing."

Manjit saw Kamal's expression and said, "He was going to hit the stone, not human beings. Right?"

"No. He was going to strike a blow for the Sikh people, just like you."

Manjit's expression clouded over, his eyes squeezing shut. He said, "You were going to have Agam kill innocents? People just visiting?"

Kamal stood up and said, "We agreed that there are no innocents in this fight."

Manjit rose as well, saying, "What has happened to you?"

Randeep looked between them like a child deciding between his parents. He said, "Hey, hey, come on. If he doesn't want the grenades, I'll take them."

Kamal ignored him, locking eyes with Manjit. He said, "This fight is not going to be without sacrifice. Some of us sacrifice our lives, like Sidak and Agam. Some of us sacrifice a piece of our soul. But we're all going to sacrifice."

Manjit broke eye contact first, spitting on the ground and saying, "I'll do this mission for Sidak and Agam, but I'm not going to hell by murdering women and children. If someone from Thakkar's security threatens us, I'll kill him. And that's it."

Kamal nodded, putting his hands around Manjit's neck and bringing him so close their foreheads touched. He said, "You and I have seen the injustice, and I'm proud that you maintain your honor. Khalistan needs people like me, but more so people like you. We will do the distasteful work. You are my brother, as you were in prison. Follow me now and I'll follow you when we build Khalistan. When your honor will matter."

Manjit looked him in the eye and nodded, saying, "So be it."

They broke the embrace and Randeep relaxed, saying, "If we have to sit here for another four hours, we're going to go crazy."

Kamal smiled for confidence, feeling the stress of the mission straining the seams of his team. He said, "We're just waiting on the call. Waiting on them to finish dinner and move to the open area, when the rest of the guests arrive. Once they're watching the show by the pool, that's when we go in. Shouldn't be more than a couple of hours."

He felt Jaiden's contact phone vibrate in his pocket, the sensation no less startling than if it had been hooked to an electric current. He snatched it out, looked at the screen in confusion, then answered.

"This is Kamal."

"You need to come, right now."

"What? Are they done with dinner? Are they out in the open?"

"No. They're still eating dinner. They're in the first building you will see on the back of the compound. It's split into three sections, two rooms with an outdoor patio between them. Thakkar will be in the room on the right. You come in from the patio, killing the patrons. I will take Thakkar out from the right as if I'm trying to protect him. You keep killing, moving to the left room, then out the side door. I'll meet you at the back of the building on the way to the gate. No more than a minute on target."

"Wait, wait, what? That's not the plan. We were going to wait for them to finish dinner precisely because it's in a building, with security arming the strong points. And it's only half the guests. You told me the size of the target would double by the pool because not everyone was invited to dinner."

"They know you're coming."

That caused Kamal's head to spin. "They know? They know what?"

"They know there's an attack planned. They told me as the head of security, and now I have to tell everyone else on protective duty here, to include the celebrities who brought their own security. I can't sit on the information for long. You need to come now, before the security posture here is heightened."

Now afraid, Kamal said, "How do they know? *What* do they know?"

"Look, it's just a general thing. I was told that an attack was possibly imminent, and that it was possibly tied into the attack at the Agra Fort. They have no specifics, but I'm supposed to get everyone on a war footing. You have about ten minutes before I'm questioned. Get your ass here. Now is the time."

"But we don't know anything about that building. We've planned everything on the pool and temple grounds. We'd studied the maps, looked at Google Earth, seen all the pictures, and planned the route in and out. We didn't focus on that building. I was supposed to come in and go straight to the pool area after the other guests arrived, and I'm prepared for that. I'm not prepared for this."

"This is even easier. The building is the closest one to the back gate. I'll send you pictures. I'll go around on a security check and take them. You get them, and you come here. My men are waiting at the gate."

"Pictures? I'm supposed to look at them for five seconds and assault?"

"I have to go. It's too late. Either commit, or back off, but I can't stay on the phone."

And he hung up.

Manjit said, "What was that all about?"

Kamal picked up his body armor and put it on, cinching the Velcro cummerbund tight. He picked up his grenades and began shoving them into individual pouches, saying, "We have to attack now."

Randeep began stowing magazines in his pouches, but Manjit said, "Why? What's the change?"

"Somehow there's been an alert. Jaiden was told to increase security for a possible attack. He hasn't done that yet, because he's waiting on us, but he can't wait forever."

Randeep stopped loading his kit, saying, "An alert? For us?"

Kamal said, "Yes, well, maybe. It might just be because of the attack in Agra and it's a general thing, but right now it's like nobody knows, because the head of security is Jaiden. He's responsible for giving everyone the word to increase their security posture, and he hasn't. Which is why we need to go now."

Manjit said, "But the plan is the same?"

Kamal began shoving AK-47 magazines in his pouches and said, "No. We attack them at dinner. In the first building."

Randeep said, "During dinner? Only half the guests will be there, and we didn't plan for that. We don't know that building."

"We will soon. Jaiden's sending pictures."

They finished loading their vests in silence, and then the pictures came in. It was just like Jaiden had said, a U-shaped building with a patio and two large rooms left and right, split by a center area with a bar. Both rooms were crowded with people, all wearing traditional Indian dress and all clearly having a good time. Kamal could see the bride in the room on the left talking to some celebrity or other, and the photo sent from the right room showed Riva Thakkar talking to someone of importance, the security man with the milky eye named Rakesh dutifully standing behind him.

Another load of pictures arrived, showing the outdoor patio and the route in from the gate, followed by a text saying, "Now."

Kamal said, "We'll enter the patio, causing destruction, and move to the left room when everyone starts running. Jaiden and Rakesh will take Thakkar from the right room out the side door, ostensibly to protect him, but really to get him to the van. We're in for thirty seconds, one minute max, and we leave, collapsing back to the van. Understood?"

Randeep nodded and Manjit said, "How will we start the attack?"

Kamal said, "I'm sorry, but we're going to lead with hand grenades. Once those go off, we'll follow onto the patio."

Manjit turned away, thinking. He turned back and simply nodded, saying, "Okay."

Kamal said, "It's necessary. This is for what the state did to us. What the prison guards did to you. If I could do it to them, I would, but this is for them and the government that paid them. For the RAW."

Manjit began shoving in his own magazines, saying, "I know. I don't like it, but I understand."

Forty seconds later they were pulling out of the garage, Kamal and Manjit in the van and Randeep in Kamal's sedan. It took less than a minute to reach the gate, Kamal slowing down when he saw it. He pulled up to the edge and flashed his lights, waiting. Halfway hoping nobody showed up.

He saw a light flash from behind the fence and tensed, knowing it was time. He looked at Manjit and said, "Are you ready?"

Manjit nodded and Kamal rolled down the window, waving his arm for Randeep to come forward. He saw the headlights turn off and the door open. Randeep jogged forward and entered the back of the van just as the chain-link gate opened.

Kamal turned off his own lights and rolled forward with the parking lights alone. He passed a man in a dastaar and red uniform and slowed. The man said, "Turn it around and aim it back this way. We'll protect it."

Kamal nodded and did as he was told, turning off the ignition and sitting, the engine ticking in the darkness. Manjit said, "What's wrong?"

Staring out the windshield, Kamal said, "Nothing. Just enjoying the quiet. But the clock continues ticking, doesn't it."

Manjit said, "It's too late for regret. That was spent when we sent Agam on his way. Let's go."

He flung open the door and stepped out, surprising Kamal. Manjit turned back to the driver's seat and said, "This is our path now. No turning back."

Manjit's words gave him confidence. If Manjit was committed, they would succeed.

Kamal exited, met him and Randeep in the back, and they each put a magazine in their respective weapons, racking a round. Kamal waved over the gate security and said, "We'll be coming back on the run. You two will be driving the car outside."

"Jaiden said we'd get in the van."

"No. Randeep, give them the keys."

Randeep did so, and Kamal said, "When you hear the explosions, open the gate and go to the car. When we leave, you follow."

"What if you don't come back?"

"Then take the car wherever you want. It won't matter, but they'll know you let us in."

Kamal turned without another word and led his men through the darkness, the laughter and tinkling of glasses faint in the distance. He could see the light of the building no more than fifty meters away, imagining the celebration he was about to destroy.

CHAPTER 47

Knuckles tried to be engaging and relaxed, but he honestly ran out of steam after meeting the fifth person whose life was so outside the realm of his own. Celebrities, hedge fund managers, sports icons, tech industry titans, you name it, they were all here, and these were only the select ones who'd been invited to dinner. He was dreading when the crowd doubled in size and everyone got liquored up. Three hours of trying to find something in common to talk about with these people was going to be a trial.

Pike's phone call earlier hadn't helped matters. Knuckles thought he might as well have simply said, "Danger, Will Rogers, danger!" for all the information he'd been able to relay. Apparently, the final three terrorists had been geolocated near the Oberoi grounds, but that was all they had.

Nadia saw him standing alone and came back to him, saying, "I thought you'd enjoy talking to Sledge. I figured he'd be right up your alley, but you spent more time talking to his security guy than you did with him."

Sledge was an aging American musician who'd made a mint more than two decades ago. He'd been the epitome of an American rock star, partying and hedonistic to his core, but then one day, when he was on the tail end of his fame, he'd decided to use his clout for good. He'd done a concert in India and had been touched by the poverty divide, specifically when he'd seen women washing clothes in the Ganges River. He'd dedicated his life to getting clean water to impoverished areas around the world, and had spent the remainder of his career doing just that. He seemed to be genuine about the work, and was nice enough, but Knuckles wondered if he wasn't just trying to buy his way into heaven.

Knuckles smiled and said, "I have more in common with the security guy than his boss."

"Did you tell him about Pike's call?"

"No. How could I? I'm here as your guest, not as some secret counterterrorism agent. I'd have to do serious tap-dancing to explain how I knew intelligence like that. Anyway, me telling everyone the sky is falling will only undercut the actual security. Jaiden's in charge of that, and he seems pretty capable. I'm not going to step on his toes by running around behind his back whispering to the individual security teams of the guests here."

She grinned and said, "But you asked to see his gun."

He chuckled and said, "Yeah, I acted like I was fascinated by his job, but really I just wanted to see if he was armed. He is."

"And you think he can use it?"

He turned to her and said, "What's with the interrogation?"

"I just know that you didn't ignore Sledge because you're bored. You did it on purpose, checking Sledge's security guy's abilities. Just like you did earlier with the Silicon Valley guy's security."

Knuckles laughed and held up his hands in surrender, saying, "Okay, okay. You caught me. But they think I'm a neophyte just captivated by their guns. To answer your question, yeah, they're good to go. Sledge's guy is ex Special Forces. The Silicon Valley guy's security is retired Secret Service. They both know how to use their guns, trust me."

"You're worried about Pike's call."

"You're damn right I am. They had an armed drone set to kill civilians at the Taj Mahal. That's not firecrackers in the garage. That's serious."

"I know, but if their mission is to kill Thakkar, why did they wait until he'd left the Taj Mahal?"

"Yeah, that doesn't make a lot of sense. Why miss him there only to attack him here, where the security is as tight as a presidential inauguration?"

He glanced around at the multiple different protective details and said, "I'm not too worried about an attack tonight. They'd get shot dead trying to breach the perimeter, never mind Jaiden and his boys here in the party itself."

She said, "I agree. Let's go get a drink before dinner starts."

"That's okay. I'm good."

She squinted her eyes and said, "You're still worried."

"Not worried. Just prudent. We can get a drink after the party, back in our room."

She kissed him on the cheek and whispered, "I don't think we'll have time for that."

He smiled and then felt a tug on his sleeve. He turned, finding the bride and groom standing next to him. The groom said, "Annaka wants me to meet the man who's smitten her old friend. She says Nadia has impossible tastes. I fear I'm in competition with you in this room."

The groom was handsome, with sharp, angular features and a way of gliding about as if he was the most important man in any conversation. Which he probably was. The bride, Annaka, looked like a twin of Nadia, which was to say she exuded confidence and personal charm irrespective of her innate beauty. She should have been aloof, given her stature in India, but from their initial meeting Knuckles had found her fun to be around, and wondered how she was so irresistibly optimistic after having lived with Riva Thakkar as a father her whole life.

He was the complete opposite of Annaka. Taciturn and demanding about everything. It *did* explain how Nadia, from a lesser station in life, had connected with Annaka. Neither of them, unlike Annaka's father, saw a person based on class. They judged people by who they were, not on what pedigree they held. Knuckles had liked her immediately, and hoped her groom wasn't a Riva Thakkar in the making.

The groom stuck out his hand and Knuckles shook it, saying, "Well, I don't know about competition in here. You're the man with the bride. I just met Nadia a week ago in Goa."

The groom said, "A week?" He looked at Nadia with a smirk and said, "Annaka told me you were fast on the uptake."

Knuckles saw Nadia's face cloud over, but before she could answer, the groom said, "Mr. Thakkar would like to meet you. He's in the other room. Come, come."

The man began tugging on Knuckles' sleeve, so much so, Knuckles thought about smacking his hand away, but Nadia gave him a look and he said, "Sure, sure, hang on a second."

He turned to Nadia and pulled her away, saying, "What's the protocol here? What should I do when I meet him?"

"Just be yourself. Thakkar's still aggravated by my having been invited. He's looking for a reason to be mad. To tell Annaka I'm a bad influence."

Knuckles grimaced and said, "Are you shitting me? I'm not playing these games. I'm not a hired date. He can take me as I am, and I'm sorry for your loss."

She laughed and said, "That's perfect. Annaka sees in you what I do. She likes you. Which means he'll probably hate you."

Knuckles returned to the groom and said, "I'm all yours."

They walked outside of the northern room onto the patio, the guests swirling around, waiting on the call to dinner. The groom said, "You want a drink before we go in?"

"Do I need one?"

The groom laughed and said, "Annaka said you were a pistol. But I'd like one. Wait here."

He went to the bar and Knuckles remained behind alone, watching the various partygoers enjoying their time, feeling detached from it all.

The groom came back, drink in hand, and said, "Are you ready to meet the host?"

Knuckles nodded, saying, "Sure."

The groom himself seemed to be nervous, as if meeting Thakkar made him skittish. He clearly didn't want to be associated with Knuckles, but Annaka had forced him, and now he was worried that Knuckles could impact his future solely because he was the one to introduce them. Or maybe Thakkar had no idea Knuckles even existed, and the groom was just nervous about being in his presence.

It was his first indicator that the people here looked at Riva Thakkar as something more than simply rich. In a room full of people with just as much money as he possessed, his position was somehow higher. At least in the eyes of the Indians at the party.

The groom led him into the southern room, and Knuckles saw a line of people waiting to talk to Riva, the man politely greeting each party.

Knuckles waited his turn, studying him. He was about sixty-five years old and slight, but his mannerisms didn't reflect that of an older man. With a manicured beard and wearing a diamond-encrusted watch that was twice the size of his wrist, he clearly relished his position.

The groom left him, moving down the line talking to other people, and Knuckles thought about returning to the other room, convinced that Thakkar hadn't asked to meet. The line inched forward and he felt his phone vibrate. He pulled it out, saw it was Pike, and answered.

"Hey, what's your status?"

Pike said, "We're in the air right now. We'll be in Jaipur in about thirty minutes. What's going on there? Did you lock it down?"

"Pike, trust me, it's locked down. It has been since before you called. Nobody is going to attack this place unless they have an armored personnel carrier. There is security all over the place, and that's just Thakkar's guys. Everyone else that's been invited has their own security. They'd be crazy to try anything here. How's Veep doing?"

"He's fine. Sitting here bitching about his sling. Look, I think those guys are up to something. They aren't in Jaipur for the tourist sites. We're missing a key somewhere. I don't know what it is, but we're missing it."

"Well, it's not happening tonight. Maybe they're going to try to kill Thakkar after he leaves here, but they aren't doing it at this party unless they're crazy."

"Did you tell Nadia what we found?"

"Yes, of course I did. She told the head of Thakkar's security, and he's taken appropriate measures. He's a scary dude, Pike. He's not going to let anything happen."

"Does the RAW have anything to do with the security there?"

"No, they don't. Wait, what? Do you think they're involved?"

"I have no idea, but if those assholes are going to try something it's because they have an insider, and the RAW is the only group that's under suspicion. They have nothing to do with the security?"

"None at all. It's all Thakkar's men, and they don't look like they'd tolerate any bullshit."

Knuckles heard a pop on the other side of the building, then a woman scream loud enough for Pike to hear through the phone, followed by more pops. He said, "What was that?"

"I don't know. I'll call you back."

Knuckles took one step toward the patio, saw a flash of light, and then felt the shock of an explosion. He hit the floor just as another explosion shattered the air on the patio. He saw multiple bodies thrown back by the force, the wounds glaring through the festive clothing, and then the gunfire started, sounding like firecrackers thrown by a child, but the damage wrought was anything but childlike.

He turned into the room, knowing they were coming for Thakkar, and saw the head of security dragging him toward a side door. He saw the groom grasping at a second security man, begging to be protected, the others in the room diving left and right, trying desperately to escape.

The security man aimed his pistol at the groom's head and pulled the trigger, his skull splitting open like a melon. He then aimed his pistol into the room and began firing, hitting the guests who were running about. Knuckles dove behind a table and scrambled forward, not wanting to give the man a sitting target, and threat crystalized like he was staring at a three-dimensional painting, the hidden picture appearing like magic.

It's not the RAW, it's Thakkar's own security.

The gunfire stopped. He rolled upright, seeing the men dragging Thakkar out the French doors at the side of the room. They disappeared in the darkness, other guests following them out the doors, and he gave chase, exiting on the run. He looked right, seeing a hodgepodge of people fleeing deeper into the Oberoi grounds, but didn't see

Thakkar. He looked left and saw the two security men fighting Thakkar, forcing him to run down a path to the rear of the building. One hit him in the head with the butt of his pistol and the other turned, hearing Knuckles coming toward him.

Knuckles dove into him like he was blindsiding a quarterback, slamming him to the earth hard enough to jolt his pistol free. He punched the man once in the head, snatched the pistol up, and heard the other man begin shooting. He rolled away, took a knee behind a small shrub, and fired back.

He saw Jaiden drop Thakkar and duck down, trying to find cover. Jaiden fired blindly toward where he believed Knuckles was and then began running, disappearing behind the building.

Knuckles scuttled to Thakkar in a crouch, keeping his weapon up, but checking on the vitals of the billionaire.

Thakkar batted his hands away, trying to sit up, saying, "I'm fine, I'm fine."

Knuckles drove him back to the earth, saying, "Shut the fuck up and stay down."

Thakkar looked at him in fury, but did as he was told. The air grew still, the screaming and chaos from the party behind him overshadowing his ability to hear Jaiden, still on the loose. Knuckles took a deep breath and held it, listening, but all he heard was the patio going berserk.

He hoisted Thakkar to his feet and said, "We need to get back inside, now."

Thakkar pointed at the security man he'd knocked unconscious and said, "Kill him, right now."

Knuckles said, "I don't roll that way. Let's go."

CHAPTER 48

Kamal reached the back of the building and took a knee, letting Manjit and Randeep gather around him. He said, "From here, it's game on. Randeep and I will lead. We'll toss a hand grenade from the darkness, and when they go off, we'll storm the patio. Shoot long and loud. Hit whoever you can, but I'm not looking for a body count. The entire point is to cause panic, allowing Jaiden and Rakesh to pull out Thakkar."

Randeep said, "Do we go in? Do you want us to assault, or just shoot and run?"

"Once the grenades go off, we go in. Just carve a path through the crowd with your gun, go to the northern room, and then out the side door. We'll run from there back to the van and meet Jaiden."

Kamal looked from Randeep to Manjit and said, "Are we good? Ready?"

They both nodded. He said, "Let's go," and he turned the corner of the building, running up the path that snaked along its side.

He dodged around a tall shrub and ran smack into a man and woman in a heated embrace, knocking them to the ground. The man shouted and Kamal shot him twice in the chest. The woman leapt to her feet and began running, letting out a vociferous shriek that split the night air.

Kamal shot her in the back, causing her body to tumble to the ground. He hissed, "We lost surprise! Get out the grenades!"

He dropped his AK-47 on its sling and frantically ripped at the Velcro of a pouch while running forward. He reached the light of the patio with the grenade in his hand, saw partygoers staring into the darkness from the woman's scream, and pulled the pin.

He waited until Randeep reached him, then lobbed the grenade into the crowd, the overhead string lights making the spoon gleam as it flew off.

He stumbled back, unsure how big a blast the grenade would cause. Randeep tossed his own grenade and followed. They both dove on the ground in fear as the first one went off, smacking their ears with a thunderclap like a lightning bolt that had hit next to them.

Kamal slapped his hands over his ears and the second one exploded, the overpressure racing past him. He stood up, raised his weapon, and charged forward onto the patio. He reached the light and was astounded at the carnage. Torn bodies were lying all about as if a giant axe had swept through the crowd, some completely ripped open and dead, others groaning from various wounds.

He stumbled to a stop, shocked at what he'd wrought, fixated on the carnage. He was brought out of his trance by Randeep firing into the crowd inside the building.

Kamal raised his weapon and began shooting as well, blindly spraying the brick walls and windows. He began moving to the northern room, the chaos swirling around him, guests running to escape. He reached the stone arch, paused until Randeep and Manjit were behind him, and swung his weapon up, entering.

He took one step and felt like he'd been hit in the chest with a baseball bat. He collapsed on the ground, the wind knocked out of him, seeing one of Thakkar's uniformed security in the room with a pistol out.

Manjit unleashed a string of automatic fire, cutting the man down. Just then, two more security guards, both Caucasian and in suits, began shooting.

Randeep grabbed Kamal's vest and began dragging him out of the line of fire, through the carnage the grenade had caused, Manjit suppressing the bodyguards by wildly shooting until his weapon locked open on an empty magazine.

They reached the edge of the patio, the overhead lights illuminating Kamal. Randeep said, "Oh shit, Kamal's been hit! He's bleeding all over the place."

Kamal took a breath and rolled to his knee, rubbing his chest. He said, "That's not my blood. You dragged me through it. I was hit in the vest."

He stood up unsteadily and said, "We need to go."

The security men came to the archway and Randeep fired at them, causing them to jump back inside. Kamal started jogging the way they'd come, gaining strength with each step. Soon he was running flat out to the van, Randeep and Manjit two steps behind.

They reached it, finding only Jaiden. Kamal said, "Where's Thakkar? Where's Rakesh?"

Jaiden said, "We had trouble. Rakesh is captured or dead. Thakkar escaped."

"What? You don't have Thakkar?"

Jaiden spit out, "No! I told you, we had trouble. Some American broke up the extraction. We need to get the hell out of here. Who has the keys?"

Manjit said, "I do."

"Let's go."

Kamal said, "Wait, we're not going anywhere without Thakkar. This entire mission will be a failure without him."

Jaiden turned to Kamal, pushed him against the vehicle, and hissed, "He's under armed guard now. It's too late. Get in the van."

Kamal shoved back and said, "No. We're taking someone from that party. If not Riva Thakkar then one of his relatives."

"Get in the van, now!"

Kamal raised his rifle, pointed it at Jaiden, and said, "You know what his daughter looks like. You're coming with us."

Jaiden saw he was deadly serious and raised his hands in the air. Randeep said, "Kamal, maybe it's too late. We can try again another time."

"No! They're still in confusion up there. We go to the northern room and enter it from the side door. We kill the security that was shooting at us, grab his daughter and whoever else is around, and then leave."

Manjit said, "We barely made it out when we had surprise. They'll be waiting for us."

"They're going to be dealing with the wounded. They won't be expecting us to come back. I've read about that tactic in other attacks. I'll go alone if I have to."

He started walking back toward the building, glancing at Manjit. Manjit said, "Randeep, let's go."

Jaiden said, "Give me the key to the van."

Manjit shifted his weapon and said, "You heard Kamal. You're doing the identification. You're supposed to be the battle-tested one."

CHAPTER 49

Knuckles half dragged, half walked Riva Thakkar to the brick wall next to the French doors of the southern room, then took a knee, listening. The firing had stopped and almost anyone who was ambulatory had fled the dining area, running across the grounds to the main hotel building.

He glanced into the room and saw two of the hotel's red-uniformed security and the rock star's bodyguard aiding the wounded. He knew they'd be on edge and he didn't want to attempt to enter without announcing himself first, but couldn't remember the man's name. Tony? No, Troy.

"Troy, Troy, I'm outside here with Riva Thakkar. We're coming in."

Troy whipped his pistol up, but lowered it when Knuckles waved. Knuckles entered, dragging Riva behind him. He sat Riva in a chair and turned to the uniformed men, both looking a little sick at the carnage around them. He said, "Were either one of you hired by Jaiden?"

They both shook their heads, one saying, "We work for the hotel. Not Mr. Thakkar."

Knuckles said, "Are either of you armed?"

They shook their heads no. *Shit. So much for protecting Riva.* He said, "Go out that door and down the path toward the back of the property. You'll find one of Thakkar's security men down there, unconscious. Bring him back here. If he tries to fight you, knock him out."

They left the room and Thakkar said, "If they bring that traitor in here, I'll kill him with my bare hands."

"No, you won't, if you want to find out what's going on. He's the only key we have. You kill him and Jaiden gets away."

He turned from Thakkar without another word, saying, "What do we have, Troy?"

Troy said, "A group of nuts attacked the party. We've moved everyone who's ambulatory into the northern room. There's another protective detail in there providing security, and it's the most secure space right now. The hotel's been alerted and police are on the way."

He paused, then said, "Look, you need to get in there with the rest of the civilians. I can't protect you out here and deal with the wounded."

Knuckles bent down, checking the pulse of a woman and finding her dead. Troy said, "You have medical experience?"

Knuckles said, "A little. Just basic first aid stuff I had to learn for a previous job. You?"

"Yeah, I was an eighteen delta in the Army."

Knuckles feigned ignorance, and Troy said, "Special Forces medic."

Troy continued working on a wounded man, then said, "Take Mr. Thakkar to the other room, then come back here. Being able to triage is better than nothing. It'll save me time."

The two hotel security men returned with the bodyguard Knuckles had knocked out, carrying him by his arms and legs. They dropped him on the floor and Knuckles said, "Troy, this asshole is involved in the attack. I'd recommend flex-cuffing him to a radiator or something."

Troy finished applying a compress to a wounded man and said, "Flex-cuffs? You ever work with them in your 'previous job'? And how did you know where that asshole was outside?"

Knuckles said, "Look, I used to do something a little like your job, but I'm just here on a date. I'll get Mr. Thakkar to the safe room and come back. Don't let that man get away."

Knuckles turned back to Riva and said, "Mr. Thakkar, he has a point. Let's get you to the safe room and wait on the authorities to sort this out."

Thakkar stood up and kicked the unconscious guard in the leg. Knuckles said, "Sir, that's not necessary now. The fight's over."

The words were barely out of his mouth when gunfire exploded on the other side of the building. Troy said, "What the fuck?"

Troy drew his pistol and started running to the northern room. Knuckles shouted, "Thakkar, stay here!" He pointed at the hotel security and said, "You two protect him!" and followed right behind Troy.

They ran past the bar area, Troy shouting, "Can you shoot that pistol?"

"Yeah, I can shoot."

"Aim for their heads. They have body armor."

* * *

Kamal reached the French doors of the northern room, staying just outside the light. He crouched down and saw that the men and women they'd killed earlier had been moved to the patio, stacked next to the grenade casualties. Neat lines of corpses all in a row.

Two private bodyguards were inside trying to get the guests who hadn't fled to remain calm, both armed with pistols.

He looked at Randeep and said, "Single shot. I'll take the man on the left. You take the one on the right."

Randeep nodded and Kamal turned to Jaiden, saying, "There are two women in the room. Which one is Thakkar's daughter?"

Jaiden pointed to the one on the left, saying, "The one with the blue flowers in her hair."

Kamal nodded and said, "We're going to kill those two security men. When we do, Randeep and I will go inside and snatch her and that old white guy in the rear. You and Manjit cover us. Shoot anyone who tries to resist."

Jaiden nodded, saying, "Just be quick. I'm sure the police are on the way, and if we get stopped on the road, we might as well have gotten killed here."

Kamal raised his weapon, taking aim. Out of the side of his mouth, he said, "Randeep, do you have your man?"

"Yes."

Kamal squeezed the trigger, felt the recoil, and saw his man drop. Randeep fired right after him, killing his target, and they both leapt up, kicking in the doors. Randeep ran to the older man in the rear, now cowering on his knees, his hands over his head. He reached down to grab him, and Kamal saw Randeep's body jerk, then his head snap back, his arms flying wide as he fell straight back, his AK-47 clattering to the floor.

Kamal turned to the arched entry door and saw two men shooting, one in a Western suit, the other wearing Indian garb. He returned fire, hitting the suit and causing the one dressed like a local to duck behind the entrance wall. He screamed, "Manjit, Jaiden, get the hostages!"

Jaiden ran into the room and grabbed the older Caucasian, jerking him to his feet by his hair, then dragging him back out the door. Manjit ran to Thakkar's daughter but another woman jumped on her, covering the daughter with her own body.

The bodyguard Kamal had hit was rolling on the ground. Kamal whipped his weapon to him, but before he could fire, the other man had snatched him back behind the wall, snapping rounds as he did so.

Kamal fired, missing him, then turned, wondering what was taking so long.

Manjit was standing over the two women, his weapon raised, but not shooting. Kamal screamed, "Kill her and take the daughter!"

Manjit aimed, but he didn't squeeze the trigger. He lowered his weapon and grabbed the woman on top, shouting, "No, we take them both."

Kamal cursed, emptied his remaining rounds at the door, then turned and snatched Thakkar's daughter by the arm, snarling, "You'd better run, or I'll kill you."

She began screaming but let him lead her out the door.

They reached the path, Kamal seeing Manjit in front of him with the other woman. Manjit turned to make sure he was there, and Kamal screamed, "Don't look! Run! Run!"

Kamal dropped his weapon on its sling, keeping one hand on the daughter's arm while his other hand reached for a grenade.

* * *

Knuckles pulled Troy out of the line of fire and said, "Where are you hit?"

"It creased my chest. I'm okay, I'm okay."

Knuckles rotated back to the entranceway and Troy rolled upright, aiming low underneath Knuckles' firing arm, both of their barrels sticking into the room.

They were met by a fusillade of automatic fire driving them back, the bullets chipping the stone around the door. The firing ceased, Knuckles waited for a second, then whipped his weapon back into the room, Troy following his lead. Outside of dead bodies, it was empty.

Troy said, "Shit. They took my principal."

He stood up, running to the open French doors. Knuckles shouted, "Wait! Not straight behind them!" but it was too late. He muttered, "Shit," then launched himself through the room and dove out the door, expecting to feel a bullet as soon as he exited.

He rolled upright, his pistol at the ready, and saw Troy running down the path ten feet away. He leapt up, trying to catch Troy and get him to pause a moment instead of running willy-nilly after a group of terrorists wearing body armor with AK-47s and a propensity to kill.

Knuckles shouted, "Troy! Stop!"

Troy said, "I see them! I see them!" and Knuckles heard a faint springlike twang, then a small thud in front of him, like a rock had been thrown. Remembering the patio, he hit the earth, screaming, "Grenade!"

It went off, launching Troy in the air and hammering Knuckles with overpressure. His ears ringing, he crawled forward, finding Troy's body split almost in half, his innards splayed on the ground, his eyes open, lifeless. Knuckles stood up, took two faltering steps forward, then took a knee, shaking his head to clear the fog.

He heard a vehicle start, then the squealing of tires, with a final flash of brake lights disappearing in the night.

CHAPTER 50

The sun began cresting the horizon, and Kamal felt like he was becoming a danger while driving. He simply couldn't keep his eyes open and had caught himself swerving to the side of the road twice. Manjit was asleep in the passenger seat next to him, Jaiden in the back, his head nodding down while he was supposed to be watching the hostages.

They'd made it out of Jaipur by the skin of their teeth, literally a miracle that Kamal attributed to Agam's attack at the Taj Mahal. If the authorities hadn't been occupied six hours away, they would have descended with a blanket of steel, locking down the entire city.

Because they were otherwise committed, the response was haphazard. The local police had tried to implement road closures with little success, none of them being fully informed of what they were attempting to accomplish. One checkpoint they'd passed through was using the checkpoint order to fleece everyone who was unlucky enough to be on that road. Kamal and his follow car were that unlucky, but they made it through for a few rupees, and then they were free, racing away from the city limits.

From there it was a comedy of errors to find a safe route to Mumbai. Randeep had mapped the original path after three hours of research, but he was dead, and Kamal found out quickly that smartphone mapping applications didn't have an option for "back roads to avoid the police."

Randeep's planned route off major thoroughfares was supposed to take just over twenty-four hours. Now, after eight hours of driving down one wrong highway after another, they were way behind, and Kamal was starting to fall asleep at the wheel.

He saw Jaiden shift in his seat and said, "I'm going to pull over. I need to swap out with Manjit." Jaiden said, "I have to use the bathroom anyway. Find a spot to stop."

Kamal said, "Yeah, I'm with you. The follow car probably needs a change-out as well."

Jaiden said, "We need food too."

Kamal looked at Manjit sleeping next to him and said, "I'll pull over at the next place."

Four minutes later, Kamal saw a roadside stop with signs begging drivers to come in for food and tourist trinkets. He put on his turn signal and drove into the parking lot, the sedan behind matching his exit. He parked, waiting for the follow car to come next to him. When it did, Jaiden exited, said something to the two in the car, then went inside. Kamal looked at the hostages in the back of the van.

They were lined in a row, blindfolded and flex-tied on both their wrists and ankles. The two women were trembling, even after eight hours of driving, their fear evident. The man appeared to be passed out.

He crawled through the front seats to the back of the van and checked the man, not sure Jaiden even cared if they were alive or dead. He touched his neck and the man jerked awake, batting Kamal's hands away with his own flex-cuffed ones and shouting in English.

Kamal trapped his arms and, in English, said, "Shut the fuck up, right now, or you're dead. I don't need you. I have Thakkar's daughter. You're just extra baggage at this point."

He saw fear on the man's face, even behind the blindfold. The man said, "I'm famous in the United States. You don't want to kill me. I'm worth something."

Kamal said, "We'll see about that."

One of the men driving the follow car came up, and Kamal exited the back of the van. He closed the doors, saying, "Just watch them from out here. Let them roast in the heat for a little bit. If we aren't back in thirty minutes, open the door and give them some water, but don't let them move otherwise."

The man nodded and Kamal went to the passenger side of the van, waking up Manjit.

When the fog cleared from his head, Kamal said, "It's your turn to drive. Bathroom break."

They walked into the shop, finding an outpost for truckers who routinely drove these roads. Full of various automotive accessories and sprinkled with trinkets, it was surprisingly clean, and even had a cooler in the rear filled with sodas and water.

The back of the station held a little fry-grill with a limited menu, an older man sitting on a stool watching a television, looking like he didn't get too many customers. They walked to the counter, ordering eight bowls of rice and chicken, three with zero spice. Kamal knew that "zero spice" only meant the food wouldn't burn your intestines, and the last thing they needed was for the hostages to come down with diarrhea in the back of the van.

As they waited, Kamal finally asked what had been bothering him for the last eight hours. "Why didn't you shoot the woman in the van? Why did you give us this extra complication?"

Manjit remained quiet for a moment, then said, "She was protecting the bride. Willing to give her life for another. It is what we strive to be. I couldn't kill her."

Kamal grew aggravated but couldn't raise his voice in the store. "She's going to die anyway. We can't keep all three. It's too hard to do that logistically. You've just made someone else do the dirty work for you."

Manjit said nothing. Kamal continued, "When that time comes, it'll be *you* pulling the trigger. You need to learn the price of what we're doing."

Manjit hissed, "I told you I wouldn't kill innocents for this. I'm not Hamas. *You* might be, but I'm not. We have Thakkar's daughter, and that's enough."

Kamal looked at him, saw the steel in his face, and changed the subject, saying, "The older guy is an American. He claims he's famous, which will work to get our word out to the world. This wouldn't make American news without him, so that's good."

Manjit said, "Well, maybe I should have killed him instead, since a death is just a death."

Kamal saw the anger and said, "Okay, okay, I hear you. I didn't mean what I said. It's just that we can't keep three hostages. It's exponentially harder."

"Then let her out on the street. When we get to Mumbai, just let her go. She's a nobody. We don't have to kill her."

"We can't let her go now. The minute she surfaces, whether it's here, where they'll know our path, or later, once we're in Mumbai, it's not going to happen. She's with us for the duration. Or she's dead."

Kamal looked to see the reaction of his words, and he saw Manjit staring, his mouth open. He said, "What?"

Manjit hissed, "Look at the TV."

On the screen was a story about the attack, and in the left corner was a picture of Jaiden.

Kamal said, "Sir, what's that story on the TV?"

The cook said, "Some attack in Jaipur from a bunch of Muslims. Apparently, the head of security tried to prevent it and was taken. I hope he's giving them hell."

Kamal nodded and said, "Yeah, I hope he is too."

The man returned to the grill, and Manjit said to Kamal, "Muslims? They still think it's a LeT attack from Pakistan."

"I know. I'll initiate the webpage once we have cell service. They won't believe that for long. The bigger issue is that Jaiden's face is now on the news."

He saw Jaiden exit the bathroom and went to him immediately, saying, "You need to get to the vehicle. You're on the television."

Jaiden ducked his head and began walking to the door, saying, "So they know I'm involved?"

They exited, and Kamal said, "No. They think you've been kidnapped. But your face is on the television. You need to hide."

* * *

Inside the back of the van, Nadia waited a beat after the outburst from the American. Sure they were now alone, she said, "Annaka, are you okay?"

Annaka jerked at her name, saying, "Yes, yes, I am. Is that you, Nadia?"

Nadia smiled behind her blindfold, saying, "It is. Thank you so much for inviting me to the wedding celebration."

The man who'd been taken with them said, in English, "Shut up! You're going to get us in trouble."

294 / BRAD TAYLOR

Nadia switched to English as well, saying, "They're outside the van. If we keep our voices down, they won't know we're talking. But you can keep yelling if you want."

The man said nothing, and Nadia continued, saying, "We need to escape sooner rather than later. While we're driving. I don't know where they're taking us, but once they arrive, our chances of survival drop significantly."

The man said, "Most hostage situations like this end with a payment. If we try to escape, they'll kill us. The only reason they took me was for money. Don't do anything stupid."

Nadia said, "You think they took *you* for money? Just a minute ago you were telling him you were famous. These men have no idea who you are, but since you've told them you're famous, they're going to use it, and I promise it isn't for money."

Annaka said, "Nadia, what should we do? Will your people come looking for us?"

Nadia took a deep breath, knowing she meant the Research and Analysis Wing. She said, "They will, but I'm not sure they'll do it to protect us. They're going to be concerned with eliminating the people who did this, not rescuing us. The government is going to want a statement, and we're going to be the price of that."

She heard Annaka start to weep and said, "What about your dad? Will he bring pressure to bear?"

Annaka choked out, "He's the same way. He's going to kill these men no matter what. He'll hunt them to the ends of the earth, but he won't care if I'm gone. If I die, it'll just give him a reason to continue."

Nadia heard that and felt her world begin to crumble. They were all going to be corpses in a field somewhere, all for the politics of India. She banished the thought, knowing she had to keep them confident. She said, "Shush. Quit crying. We aren't dead yet. There are others looking for us, and they care about our lives."

"Who? The RAW? Your bosses? You just said they were no help. They want a reason to blame Pakistan. They're loving this."

"Not the RAW. The Americans."

"Why would they care? They're just as bad as the RAW. They've been paying the Pakistani ISI for years. After Afghanistan, they want nothing to do with our part of the world."

Nadia closed her eyes behind the blindfold, wanting to believe her next words. "My date to the party cares. And he's more than I told you. He's going to come."

I entered our villa, threw my suitcase on the bed, and turned to the man who'd let us in, saying, "We've got it from here."

He looked nervous, which, given what had just occurred at this hotel, was understandable. He said, "Sir, I need to scan your passports."

I thought about telling him to pack sand, but Jennifer handed them over, saying, "Sorry. Here you go."

He scanned them, then said, "Would you like me to show you the amenities of the room?"

I said, "No. That's not necessary."

He understood that we weren't here for the amenities and left without another word. I turned to Jennifer and said, "This is not going to end well."

I could tell that Knuckles wasn't going to be on an even keel the minute I'd met him in the lobby. He was too close to this one. We'd separated when a guy in a golf cart came to take us to our room, and I told him we'd talk soon. The golf cart guy, wearing a historically British uniform from something out of Disneyland, took us to our villa on the grounds, about a hundred meters from the one where Knuckles was staying.

The trip was surreal, because the hotel space was completely locked down due to the attack, forcing us to spend the better part of the night just trying to get inside, but once in, everyone was acting like it was business as usual. As if more than a dozen people weren't slaughtered last night.

Jennifer said, "Kerry Bostwick is here. The Oversight Council is meeting in three hours, and they have that guy that Knuckles captured. Maybe it'll be easy."

I shook my head and said, "Nope. Knuckles is going on the warpath. And we're going to have to back him up."

She said, "Back him up how? We don't have authority to operate here. We've already—"

"We don't have authority *yet*."

"What's that mean?"

"It means we have to convince the Oversight Council to continue. We're going to find those hostages. I just need to convince the Oversight Council that it's in their interest to do so."

I opened the French doors to our little garden, saw a peacock walking around, and realized again how weird this whole thing was. I watched the bird pecking at the ground and said, "You ready for that?"

She said, "Pike, we have no standing here. We've already pushed the limits on this one. Veep's got the bullet wounds to prove it. We should let the country team solve this."

I closed the doors and turned to her. I knew I was in the right, and so did she. I just needed to remind her. I said, "Is that what you were thinking when the Chinese assassins were chasing you in Goa? Did our 'standing' help you then? You wanted to do what was necessary at that point."

Her face became truculent, looking like she did when she found me about to launch our house cat with my foot, but this time it was much more serious. What she said surprised me.

298 / BRAD TAYLOR

"*You're* going on the warpath here. Not Knuckles. Because you *want* to. You want to let the beast out, and you're using this as an excuse to run amok."

I heard what she said, and I knew she wasn't wrong. I'd been fighting the release of the demon since the assault in Goa. I thought I'd won with the action in Agra, where I'd been the steady hand like always, but the assault at this hotel had breached something in me. She knew it and I knew it. I wanted to break something apart. Or someone.

While talking to Knuckles from our aircraft on the way to Jaipur, I'd felt the scab tear. His earlier confidence about the security of the party had disappeared, and he'd told me what had happened. The price had been enormous, and I felt impotent riding in the aircraft. I was so angry I had difficulty communicating to him on the phone. Jennifer had seen it, and now she was worried, but the bottom line was I had screwed up, letting the Chinese guys intervene in Agra. They'd thwarted our ability to capture the terrorist with the drone, and that loss of intelligence had cost a plethora of lives. I should have seen them coming, but I hadn't, and because of my failure, a lot of people were dead. It was my fault, and now I wanted some payback.

She came to me, taking my face in her hands. She said, "I see what's happening. I don't understand it, but I see it. You want to let the beast out. I don't know why now, after all we've been through, but we can't go back to what you were. It tore you apart. Let the Indian government handle this. Don't go there."

I took her hands in mine and said, "Telling me not to go there is like screaming at a volcano to keep the lava inside. It does no good."

She stared into my eyes and said, "So the volcano is already erupting?"

I glanced away, not saying anything. She said, "Am I wrong?"

I wanted to tell her to stop the psychobabble bullshit, but she was right.

I said, "You're not wrong about me, but you're wrong about the solution. India doesn't care about the hostages. The government only cares about what they'll look like when it's all over."

She said, "This isn't our fight."

I said, "It is now. You saw Knuckles."

She backed off and said, "Yeah, I saw him. He's just like you, wanting to kill to alleviate the pain."

Knuckles was still processing what had happened last night, going over and over what he could have done differently, not the least because he'd failed to stop the assault. He felt like it was his fault, which was exactly how I felt.

I said, "So that makes a difference? Because he has a connection to Nadia it means we can't continue? But you'd rescue Nadia if she was some random stranger?"

She looked like I'd slapped her, saying, "What? What does that mean? Of *course* I want to rescue her, but we don't have the assets for that here. And I worry about you. When this is over, we still have to live. *If* we're alive at the end of it."

I smiled and said, "One step at a time. Let's go see what Kerry has found. Maybe it's already over."

I went to the door and she stopped me, saying, "It's never going to be over until you believe it's over. There will always be another."

"Maybe that's true, but right now, I have Nadia, and I'm not going to let that go. The next one can wait."

We walked out of the room and across the grounds to the next section of villas, where Knuckles was staying. We knocked and he opened the door, looking haggard.

He said, "Come on in. Kerry will be here in a minute. He's bringing over his kit for the off-site with the Oversight Council."

We entered, finding the villa a carbon copy of our own. The bed was unmade, and Nadia's clothes were still over a chair. I said, "Hey, how are you doing?"

"As well as can be expected."

I waited, but he said nothing else. I said, "You know this isn't your fault."

"Fault's got nothing to do with it. Nadia's been taken by those Islamic assholes and she's probably getting violated right now. We saw what Hamas did."

He balled up his fists in frustration, his imagination running wild. Like me, he wanted to punch something, but there was nothing to hit.

I went to him and put my hands on his shoulders, saying, "Don't do this. It won't help. Nadia's okay, and so is Thakkar's daughter. We just need to find them."

He knocked my hands away and said, "Those motherfuckers have her right now! They have her at their will."

He saw himself in a mirror on the wall, hated the reflection, and drove his fist into it, the shattered glass falling to the floor.

He looked at his hand, seeing the blood start to run free, and Jennifer went to him with a towel, wrapping it and saying, "Knuckles, this isn't helping. Let's work the problem."

He looked at me and said, "You know how these guys are. They aren't going to negotiate."

I said, "What makes you so sure they're Islamic? I don't think they are."

Now interested, the question tamping down the pain he was feeling, he said, "You don't think they're crazy Muslims?"

"I don't know for sure, but I know for a fact that China was paying them. They might be Muslim, or they might be something else, but either way, China's behind it. I think they lost control of the plot they'd planned, but that's where we need to focus. We find their handler, and we find them."

CHAPTER 52

Mr. Chin returned to his table with a plate full of Western food. He'd ignored the Indian offers, as they tore his guts apart, and stuck his nose up at the pathetic attempts at Chinese dishes. He sat down, trying to appear nonchalant to the other man at the table, but it was difficult. Mr. Chin was sure he would be blamed for what had happened at the Oberoi. And maybe that was warranted.

The man across the table was the Ministry of State Security's chief in India, and he was not pleased. Mr. Chin said, "I hope your room was pleasant."

They were both staying at the Hilton in Jaipur. Him, because he was coordinating with the remnants of the Condor team for damage control. The chief because the damage control had grown exponentially.

The chief said, "My room is fine. I didn't come here to see the sights. Where do we stand?"

Mr. Chin said, "They massacred over a dozen people, but Thakkar is still alive. Presumably, so is the mining deal."

The chief said, "You understand what that means, right? The mining deal Thakkar is involved in is a game changer. We cannot allow it to continue."

Mr. Chin took a sip of water and said, "How is it a game changer? I have never understood why this was so important."

The chief said, "Artificial intelligence is the new form of combat, and it relies on rare earth elements. We own the monopoly of them right now, but we won't forever. We need to prevent that loss for as long as possible before we go after Taiwan. If India becomes a player, we'll lose. They won't side with us. They'll side with the West."

Mr. Chin let his words settle before bringing up the rotting corpse in the room. "Okay, sir, I understand that stopping India from extracting rare earth elements is paramount to our global reach, but we now have significant exposure. Do you want to continue the mission of preventing the deal, or do you want me to cauterize the wound?"

"What do you mean?"

Mr. Chin took a deep breath, let it out, then said, "The men I hired from Riva Thakkar's security know what I am. I've used them for multiple different operations—much smaller than this, but still, they know I'm not a Chinese businessman. From what I can glean, one of the security men was captured during the operation. He's still alive and in the hands of the government."

The chief looked at him with his dead black eyes and Mr. Chin continued, "I can get rid of him, but if I do, I'll burn any ability to continue. It'll be too risky to kill both him and Thakkar."

The chief nodded, thinking. Then said, "How much does this man know?"

"He knows enough to compromise me. And he'll do so under intense pressure, which I'm sure he's about to experience. The CCP will be in the glare of the spotlight, which means cutting off the mine deal will be a nonstarter."

The chief reached across the table and plucked a grape from Mr. Chin's plate and popped it into his mouth. He said, "You have disappointed me on this one. It should not have been so hard."

Mr. Chin held up his hands and said, "It wasn't me. The men I hired went crazy. I couldn't predict that. I thought they were in it for the money, but it was more than that. I can still clean it up, with the Condor team."

"The last time you used them, two of them were killed. You want to try again?"

"The men they went against were the American intelligence team I've been warning about since we started this. I can't be blamed for that. I told you people that they were skilled."

"And yet you got my men killed. We've barely managed to escape scrutiny on that hit. Actually, the debacle here has helped the situation. What would have been a front-page news story is now just a couple of deaths in a parking lot. Thanks to your hired men conducting a Hamas-type attack. Paid for by the Chinese Communist Party."

"We didn't pay for this. I had no idea they were going to do what they did. They were in it for the money, right up until they weren't."

"So we have two problems. One is the man the government has in custody. The other is the idiots you paid out in the wild. They have Riva Thakkar's daughter, and the entire country is watching. How do you propose solving this?"

"Give me the Condor team. I've seen the location where Riva's security man is being held. I can kill him with a rifle shot."

"And the second problem?"

"I don't know yet. But I know where they are. They tricked me earlier, but they outsmarted themselves. One of them is still wearing the watch I gave him. They used the kill switch, but his didn't set for some reason. When he rebooted the watch, the malware started functioning again. He thinks it's not transmitting, but it is."

"If you eliminate them, can you return to the primary mission of Riva Thakkar? Blame the death on the same group? It would be a shame to waste the crisis they created. It gives us great cover to execute the mission."

Mr. Chin considered, then said, "That's certainly within the realm of the possible, and I agree with the reasoning. Waiting to reset and trying to kill him later will be much harder from a deniability perspective. Easier to use what they've done to blame them up front. First we need to eliminate the threat to us, though."

The chief popped another grape into his mouth and said, "Why did they do this? Where did you go wrong? The cover you built was for them to be Muslim terrorists, and they actually became terrorists. What did we miss? What do they want?"

"I honestly don't know. They were just a bunch of kids with computer skills. I have no idea why they did what they did. It makes no sense to me."

The chief gazed at him for a moment, then said, "It makes sense to them, and we're going to find out why soon. How on earth did you miss this?"

"I can't explain it. I've worked with Thakkar's security for years, but I hired these guys recently. I used them because of their contacts, not because of their skills. I even had to train them."

The chief laughed at that, saying, "You trained them well."

Mr. Chin knew he was on treacherous ground, despite the chuckles. The chief acted like he didn't mind, but Mr. Chin understood that he was dangerously close to being eliminated himself. Loose ends were loose ends, be they Indian or Chinese. The chief, after all, had his own bosses to answer to.

The chief took a sip of water, then said, "You can have the Condor team for the first problem, and I'll talk to the command about the second, but you failed to mention the third one."

Mr. Chin said, "Third one? What's that?"

"The Americans. The team you were adamant about eliminating because they were interfering with the mission. What about them?"

Mr. Chin shook his head and said, "I don't think they're in play anymore. Thakkar's alive, and they did their job. They don't care about the daughter."

CHAPTER 53

I heard a knock on the door and opened it, letting in Kerry Bostwick. He was carrying a laptop and looking a little harried.

He said, "Oversight Council meeting in a couple of hours. The president is attending. Where's the ethernet port?"

Knuckles led him to a desk and he plugged in the laptop, then went through a bazillion different protocols to ensure he was encrypted. I said, "I guess you didn't get to fly home today like you planned."

He chuckled and said, "You guessed right. The people who took the hostages are Sikh separatists. They just put out a manifesto on the web."

Knuckles said, "Sikh separatists? That's who took them? Not some ISIS offshoot?"

"Nope, but they want what every crazy ISIS guy does. They want their own homeland. They're demanding the government free a bunch of Sikh prisoners and grant them land and autonomy. But first they want an actual government official to read the manifesto on the air— from a government building."

Knuckles said, "That'll never happen."

Kerry said, "No shit. Absolute nonstarter."

I said, "This makes no sense. What's that got to do with China? What's their play here?"

"I don't know, but it is what it is, and now we're about to find out if we have a mission here."

I said, "We both know we have a mission. The only question is whether they approve it or not."

Kerry looked at Knuckles pacing the room and lowered his voice, saying, "Pike, I can't vouch for a mission here. Thakkar is alive and well, and he's willing to continue our arrangement. The rest of this is just collateral damage."

I looked at him like he'd sprung a horn out of his head. I said, "Are you serious here? They took the daughter. They slaughtered a slew of people."

"I hear you, but this is an Indian problem, not a U.S. one. They're not going to let us in on this, and I don't blame them. Riva Thakkar is on a blood hunt. Even he doesn't care about his own daughter."

"What's that mean?"

"I just left a meeting with him and the RAW. He wants the men who did this dead. He feels like he has egg all over his face and he's pissed. The government is listening to him, because they have a Hindu majority and fear the Sikhs. They want blood as well. Sikh separatism has a long history here. Thakkar's a power broker, and whoever took them is going to pay. Probably anyone near them is going to pay whether they're guilty or not."

Knuckles spoke up, saying, "So they're going to use a sledgehammer when we could be the scalpel?"

Kerry turned to him and said, "Yes, that's about right. I'm sorry, but like I said, we don't have any standing here."

Jennifer said, "That's bullshit. They took an American, Sledge. That gives us standing to at least be in the room for some sanity."

Kerry looked at her, then me, saying, "Who the hell is Sledge?"

I said, "Seriously? You've never heard of Sledge?"

Jennifer started humming an old rock song, and he said, "That's Sledge?"

She said, "Yeah, that's him. And he's a U.S. citizen."

Kerry took that in, and Knuckles said, "That's what we take to the Oversight Council."

Kerry said, "I get your interest in this. I understand it, but we can't just go running amok here because you've become emotionally involved with one of the hostages."

Knuckles started to advance on him and I pushed him back, saying, "Whoa, whoa. That's not helping things."

Kerry stood up, saying, "What the hell was that? Have you lost your mind?"

Knuckles balled his fists and said, "You're giving up here. And I'm going after Nadia with or without your vaunted Oversight Council."

Kerry said, "You keep that up, and I'll have you on the first plane out of here."

Jennifer stepped in and said, "Hey, come on now. Stop this. We're all on the same team."

Knuckles said, "Are we?"

Kerry looked at me, and I said, "That's a good question. *Are* we on the same team here? You keep saying we don't have any standing in India, but China is pulling the chain for this entire mess. Surely we care about that."

Kerry softly nodded, then said, "I believe you, but we don't have any proof of that."

"The guy Knuckles captured is the proof. What's he saying?"

"He's saying he's just a bodyguard and had no idea what the head of security was up to. He's claiming he did what he was supposed to do to protect his asset."

Knuckles said, "He fucking shot the groom in the head."

"He's denying shooting anyone. He's saying he was getting Thakkar out of the line of fire, full stop."

I said, "Who's he talked to? Has he spent any time with the RAW guys?"

"Not yet. Just local police."

Jennifer was looking out the French doors of the villa. She had a clear field of view to the temple in the center of the estate. It was a tourist attraction opposite the pool but had been turned into an interrogation center. Knuckles, as the man on the ground, had been through it, getting questioned by the police like everyone else.

She said, "He's going in now. I'm assuming he's facing the RAW this time?"

We all crowded around the doors, watching the poor bastard getting frog-marched across the grass to the temple. Kerry said, "Yeah, I wouldn't want to be him. They're going to apply pressure this time."

I said, "He deserves it. We should hold off on the Oversight Council meeting until he's done. I'm sure he's going to spill his guts, and it'll involve China."

Kerry said, "I can't dictate the POTUS schedule. It's not something I control."

I saw the fear on the bodyguard's face and said, "Maybe this one time we should try to delay. He's going to start talking. I can see it in his expression. He's done."

Kerry watched him walking to the temple and said, "Yeah, you might have a point."

The bodyguard's pace was lethargic, as if he wanted to stall what was to come. He had two men behind him poking him in the back and one walking in front. He reached the pool area, the temple to his left, and a crack split the air.

I saw his head snap back in a spray of red, and he crumpled to the ground. I jerked open the doors and began running, Jennifer and Knuckles right behind me. We had to cover seventy meters of ground, and by the time we arrived, his body was surrounded by what seemed like a hundred government officials, all of them screaming.

I saw his twisted corpse on the ground, his head shattered, but also saw something poking out of his pocket. It was a cell phone.

How on earth does he still have his phone? What kind of clown fest are these guys running?

Jennifer came up behind me as I was being manhandled away. She grabbed my arm, yelling at the guard to back off. They started to tussle, and I leaned into her ear, saying, "Let them take me to the ground. He's still got his phone. Get the phone."

The guard shoved her and she fell away, then another one grabbed me, both of them forcing me back. One hooked a leg underneath my calf and flipped me on my back. I hit the ground hard, seeing Jennifer dart into the body, nobody noticing her in the chaos.

She snatched the phone and then was assaulted just like me, the officials forcing her back, but nobody realizing what she'd done.

Ten minutes later Kerry was negotiating with his counterpart in the RAW, telling them to let us go. With the dead body on the ground, we were the least of their concerns, and they did so. We went back to the villa, him looking at his watch and saying, "We missed the damn meeting. I have no idea what they decided."

Jennifer pulled the phone out of her pocket and said, "Let me get Creed on the line. Whatever decision they came to, it's been made with bad information."

CHAPTER 54

Kamal awoke on the outskirts of Mumbai, the roads becoming more and more congested. He looked at Manjit behind the wheel and said, "Where are we?"

"About thirty minutes out from the city center. You'd better hope our safe house is good to go. Are you sure we can use the beds in that place?"

"Yes. It's in the heart of the Dharavi slum. Nobody will be looking for us there. It's all Muslims."

Manjit turned to him and said, "*We're* Muslims according to the police!"

"Not anymore. We're the Khalistan Commando Force now. I published the webpage."

Manjit continued driving for a moment, then said, "So we're now wanted men?"

"We were wanted before that webpage went live. Now they just know why. What time is it?"

Manjit glanced at the Garmin watch on his wrist and said, "A little after seven P.M. We've been on the road for close to a day."

Now fully awake, Kamal said, "You're still wearing that watch? Why didn't you toss it like Randeep and I did?"

Manjit looked a little embarrassed, then said, "Because it's an expensive watch and it might come in handy sometime. We hit the kill switch. Nobody can see what it does."

Kamal let it ride, having more pressing issues to worry about. They entered the cloistered traffic of Mumbai, the honking horns becoming the norm, the vehicles all jockeying for position. Manjit said, "What do you want to do with the car? We can't take it into the slum."

"We'll park it outside. Go to the Mahim Junction railway station. We'll leave it there."

From the back, Jaiden said, "They'll find it and know where we are."

"They aren't that good. It'll take them weeks to find it. And what will they know? That we entered the slum? They have no control inside there."

Manjit said, "I'm not so sure of that. They have abilities we can't comprehend."

"People leave cars in train stations all the time. It'll take them a month to figure that out."

Manjit said, "The follow car is mine. I don't want it near this van."

Aggravated, Kamal said, "Then we'll park it somewhere else. I'm not worried about the cars. I'm worried about the packages."

From the back, Jaiden said, "Who have you coordinated with for the safe house? How secure is this location?"

"They aren't Muslim, if that's what you're asking. It's a factory owner from my village. He uses illegals—mostly Muslims—to take the plastic off wrecked cars and make it into luggage."

Jaiden said, "What's his name?"

Too late, Kamal realized that Jaiden himself was from the same village. He said, "Look, you need to trust me on this. I'm not going to tell you his name, and we'll never meet him. He has a tiny factory and he's agreed to let us stay. Trust me, he's with us, but he doesn't want to get involved. He continues his work and we hold the hostages in his factory. Everyone there is illegal and won't want to turn us in."

Jaiden said, "How do you intend to get the hostages into the slum? You want to just walk them in?"

"Yes."

"You think that's smart? What if they decide to run?"

Kamal looked back into the van and saw the hostages listening. He said, "Because I'll kill them if they try anything."

Manjit pulled into a parking area across the street from the rail station, a bridge across the tracks leading to the slum. He said, "You want to just leave the vehicle here?"

"For the time being. We need to calculate the government response. They're going to come at us with everything they have, and we need a means of escape."

The sedan following them pulled adjacent in a parking spot three vehicles away, the two drivers still wearing their red and black uniforms, complete with dastaars. Kamal said, "We need to get them out of those uniforms before we enter."

Jaiden glanced at them, then turned to Kamal. Kamal saw in his eyes that something had shifted during the drive to Mumbai.

Jaiden said, "Get out of the van." He flicked his eyes to the hostages and said, "We need to talk."

Kamal did so, remembering Manjit's warning about Jaiden's propensity for wanting to take control. He met Jaiden at the front bumper and said, "What?"

Jaiden looked left and right, making sure they were alone, then said, "You take the American to the slum. I'm going to take the women."

"Wait, that's not the plan. We're going to hold them until the government reads my manifesto on television, or until we're forced to kill them."

"You can't hold them all in the slum. The only security you have is your anonymity. Once that's gone, you're dead."

Kamal grew angry, wanting to put a stop to any mutiny before it began. "We knew that before we came here. Nothing's changed in the plan since the sun's come up, and let me be clear: I'm the one who's in charge."

Jaiden said, "Calm down. I'm not trying to usurp your plan. Trust me, from what I saw last night, you're the right man for this. You have the courage of your father."

The comment surprised Kamal. He had been expecting a fight, but maybe having to be forced at gunpoint to return to the mission while Kamal's men went willingly had caused Jaiden to reflect on the meaning of courage.

Kamal said, "What's my father have to do with this?"

"You never asked me why I agreed to do this."

Now confused, Kamal said, "I just assumed you believed as we do."

Jaiden smiled and said, "What did your mother tell you about your father's death?"

"He died in a car wreck. Nothing special."

"Your father was a member of the Khalistan Commando Force, as was both Rakesh and myself. He was a cell leader, and he was murdered by the government. He didn't die in a car crash."

Shocked, Kamal said, "That's impossible. I would know. My mother would have known."

"She *did* know. After he was killed, she insulated you from any talk of Sikh nationalism. It's why she hated you hanging around with Rakesh and me. After the loss of your father our cell dissolved. Rakesh and I went into the Army, but we never lost faith in the cause. When you appeared out of nowhere, hired by Mr. Chin, it was like something sent from beyond the grave. It was a sign from your father."

He put his hands on Kamal's shoulders and said, "You are the heir of the KCF, and *that's* why I'm following you."

His mind reeling at the revelations, Kamal stuttered for words, but none came out.

Jaiden continued, "Your father would be proud, and that's precisely why I'm taking the women with me. To ensure your plan succeeds."

Kamal simply nodded, deciding to refocus on the mission, leaving Jaiden's words about his heritage behind for later reflection. He said, "But why do you need us to separate?"

Jaiden said, "I've been giving it some thought. The workers at that little factory are all going to be illegals, and possibly all Muslim. Maybe one of them wants to get on the good side of the authorities."

Kamal held that fear himself, but said, "They've been well paid to stay quiet. They'll make more in the next week than they will all year."

Jaiden continued, "That may be true, but where is the most secure spot in Mumbai? Where we can control everything? It's not in the slum."

Kamal said, "I don't know. The police station? What do you mean, 'most secure'?"

"I mean Riva Thakkar's house here in Mumbai."

Flabbergasted, Kamal said, "The mansion? That's insane."

Riva Thakkar was one of the richest men in the world and was known for a multitude of different business accomplishments, but his home outshone everything. Outside of Buckingham Palace, it was the most expensive residential building in the world, costing more than two billion dollars to build. Located on Altamount Road—colloquially known as Billionaires' Row—it was twenty-seven stories tall, with three helipads, a private car garage with 168 spaces, a fifty-person theater, two floors of workout equipment, a room that literally rained snow during the summer heat, and a permanent staff of more than three hundred. It was all to service only three people—Riva Thakkar, his wife, and his daughter—and was the ultimate example of the difference between the haves and have-nots in India.

Jaiden said, "It's not insane. I can get in there because I'm the head of security, and then I can lock it down. We could stay there for days, with all of the amenities you won't have in the slum."

"You're on the news. If you show up there, it'll raise questions. There's no way they'll let you in."

"I'll be with Thakkar's daughter, and I've watched the news reports on my phone during the drive here. Right now everyone's reporting that I'm a hostage, not a hostage taker. I'll tell the staff we escaped and need shelter. Like I said, I'm the head of Thakkar's security. Nobody is going to question me, and I can control everything they do and say."

Kamal remained silent, and Jaiden said, "Look, taking Annaka works for me, because she'll back up my story just by her presence. If she gets recognized with you in the slum, you're dead. Nobody knows the American, but everyone in Mumbai knows Thakkar's daughter. She's a liability to you."

Kamal said, "But either her or the other woman will tell the staff what's happening. They aren't going to sit still while you hold them hostage. It's *her* staff, after all."

"I can handle that. I'll implement a quarantine like we did when COVID was here. With Riva out conducting the pre-wedding celebrations, they're at a skeleton staff anyway. During COVID they were locked into the staff apartments for months on end, and I was responsible for the protocol. Nobody was allowed to interface with the Thakkar family at all, except for the security element. We'll do the same here, only I'll convince them it's for Annaka's safety. She'll not have the chance to talk to anyone, except through me."

"And then what? You'll have to contact Thakkar and say you're 'okay' or something. The staff is going to wonder what the hell you're doing there while the press goes crazy about the kidnappings. You can't keep that secret."

"I'll keep the staff from contacting anybody by saying our location must remain secret. I'll take their cell phones and cut the landline. They'll believe me, but you miss the point. I won't keep it secret from Thakkar or the RAW. I'll fortify the building and contact Thakkar myself. It will be our final grand event. They will publish the manifesto, or we kill them."

Kamal thought about it, running the ramifications through his mind like he was worrying a piece of meat in his teeth. He finally said, "That will be Thakkar's ultimate insult. First we attack his wedding party, then we capture his famous house? He'll be so embarrassed that he'll destroy the entire building just to prove a point, with his daughter in it."

"Yes, I know. It'll make worldwide news, which is exactly what we want. It'll cause so much traffic to your webpage it might crash. Look, I know all the ways in and out of the building, as well as how the security systems work. I'll know when they're coming, and I'll let him do his worst, killing his own daughter. It'll be just like the attack on the Golden Temple, when the Army killed our Sikh brethren. It will galvanize our people now just like it did then, and galvanize the world in our favor. We won't kill her—the government will."

"But they'll slaughter everyone in the building and we'll lose our leverage in days instead of weeks."

"The slaughter will be a good thing, and as for the leverage, we will still have the American, which means exposure of the Sikh abuses by the United States press. If you've managed to avoid the authorities—which you will because I'm going to take the heat off of you—you'll still have him. Hit one goes down, and when they're celebrating the success of taking down the tower, I'll come back here to you, and we'll use him for further leverage."

Kamal remained silent, thinking through what Jaiden had described. Jaiden finally said, "And we won't have to change the other security men out of their red uniforms. I can use them as they are."

Kamal nodded, finally won over. He said, "So Manjit and I take the American into the slum, and you take the van with those two to Thakkar's place?"

"Yes, and with your leadership, the Khalistan Commando Force will rise again, just as your father led us before you."

Kamal said, "My father was a good man. A strong man, but let's hope this doesn't end the same way it did for him."

CHAPTER 55

J ennifer and I made our way over to Knuckles' villa because Kerry had turned it into our makeshift tactical operations center. He figured the RAW had wired his room for sound before he'd arrived, but they hadn't had a chance to do so in Knuckles', so he got the short end of the stick. I didn't think they'd had time to do so in our room either, but Kerry wasn't taking any chances—which worked out for Jennifer's and my privacy.

It had been over twenty-four hours since the bodyguard had been killed, and the shooter or shooters had disappeared like smoke. The bullets had come from outside the compound walls, from more than three hundred meters away, and I found it hard to believe that some jihadists could have made that shot. I was more convinced than ever that it was the Chinese, and they were cleaning up loose ends.

We knocked on the door, heard, "Come on in," and found the room reordered, with Knuckles, Brett, and Veep each working a laptop at a different table.

I glanced around the room and said, "Where's Kerry?"

Knuckles turned around and said, "He's with the RAW and Thakkar right now. Be back soon."

"I thought the rescheduled Oversight Council meeting was in five minutes. Is that still on?"

"President decided he wanted to attend. It's been postponed until 1730."

I looked at my watch, saw it was almost 1700, which meant it was almost 0730 in DC. This was the third time the meeting had been delayed. Luckily, the first one had been canceled because Kerry wasn't available due to him getting us out of RAW custody after the body-guard had been murdered, but the rescheduled meeting had been de-layed twice. Earlier, it was just supposed to be the principals of the Oversight Council, but I guess POTUS figured he wanted in.

I said, "I'll bet they delayed the other ones because the Council didn't want to get out of bed. They keep this up and we'll never get authority to do anything."

I expected concurrence from Knuckles, and was a little surprised he wasn't losing his temper over the delays, given Nadia's predicament. Instead, he said, "Might be better to wait a little bit."

"Why?"

Brett turned around and said, "I'm on with Creed. He got some-thing out of that phone Jennifer took."

Now interested, I said, "What? Something we can execute?"

"Not yet. He's downloaded all the phone data and cross-checked it, creating a data constellation of every phone that handset has contacted in the last week."

"What good will that do? We don't know the terrorist numbers, so we have no idea which one to focus on."

"Yeah, that's true, and all of the numbers were Indian, but there was an anomaly: one handset was Chinese."

"Wait, are you saying it called a Chinese phone number?"

"I wish. No. The IMSI was Indian, but the IMEI was from a Chinese phone."

He sounded like he was speaking Greek, but it was actually pretty simple. The international mobile subscriber identity—the IMSI—was basically the phone number of the handset and was used by the telecoms to know how to route calls. That number could be changed simply by swapping out SIM cards, like one could do to save roaming charges when traveling to a foreign country. The international mobile equipment identity—or IMEI—was the number permanently assigned to the handset, and it detailed the make, model, and origin of the equipment. What he was saying was the phone number was Indian—because of an Indian SIM card—but the handset was Chinese.

That still didn't give me any great confidence of a breakthrough, since India was right next to China.

I said, "Why does that matter? There are probably millions of Chinese-made phones in this country. Hell, I'll bet the majority of phones here are Chinese."

"Creed's one step ahead of you. He's already done the research and he agrees with you, but most of the Chinese phones here are affordable, bottom-basement knockoffs of iPhones or Galaxy handsets. This one is an expensive handset only sold in China, and it's touched the Chinese telecom system. Whoever has that cell phone has talked to China."

Now *that* was interesting. I said, "Do we know who he contacted in China?"

"Not specifically, but Creed says that the IMEI serial number of that handset is registered to a Chinese conglomerate that ostensibly invests in mining interests here in India."

Jennifer said, "So it could just be a businessman here in India. He'd naturally call China, and he'd naturally be involved with Riva Thakkar."

Knuckles said, "Yeah, okay, we're trying to get Riva Thakkar to invest in a rare earth element mine here in India, and this Chinese mining guy is talking to Thakkar's security? The one who tried to kill Thakkar? Not likely."

I said, "I agree. More likely that company is an MSS front, and this guy is trying to take out Thakkar to prevent the mine."

Veep, staring at his screen, held up his left hand, the right one still in a sling, and said, "We have a geolocation."

He turned around and said, "It's here, in Jaipur."

That's it.

I said, "Where?"

"Hang on. Trying to get fidelity. Creed's building the map."

We all gathered around the laptop and saw a blue icon on a blank screen, then the map began to draw itself. First a satellite image from high in space, then zooming in to an overlay of what appeared to be terrain features of streams and hills. Streets began sprouting like vines, the blue dot remaining steady, until finally shaded squares of buildings appeared, the blue dot centered over one.

I said, "Where is that?"

Veep moved the cursor over the building, and it said, "Hilton Jaipur."

I turned to Jennifer and said, "Map that from here." I went back to Veep, saying, "Is this real time, or historical?"

"It's historical, but it's from this morning."

"Can we get real time?"

Before he could answer, Kerry entered the room, saying, "Man, this is turning into a mess."

I said, "Did you tell them about our Chinese theory?"

"I tried to, but we have zero proof. I couldn't very well bring up your actions here as evidence. I mean, I really couldn't say that Jennifer had been chased by Chinese agents when she was breaking into a terrorist safe house that we hadn't told the RAW about, or that you took out two Chinese assassins just before stopping a terrorist attack in Agra that they think is a misfire. That wouldn't go over very well, and other than that, we have no real proof."

I said, "Good, because we got something from that phone Jennifer took."

He rolled his eyes and said, "That phone is going to be an issue."

"What do you mean?"

"The RAW didn't trust the local police with anything they found on the bodyguard. Before their interrogation team got on the ground they ordered the locals to just conduct an inventory and store everything with him, with instructions to bind his hands in such a way that he couldn't access any of it."

I said, "Shit. I was hoping it was incompetence."

"Nope. The interrogation team arrived, and he was supposed to show up with everything he had on his body the night of the attack. The interrogation obviously didn't happen, and when they searched the body, the phone was gone."

"What do they think happened to it?"

"Right now, they're blaming the locals for being incompetent, but I've got half a mind to throw it in the bushes for them to find. The last thing I need as the head of the CIA is to be found hiding evidence involving a major terrorist attack from the RAW. The conspiracy theories and the fracture of our relationship would be massive."

"Sir, the phone had contact with a handset that's been on the Chinese telecom system. The bodyguard was talking to someone who was then talking to China. I'm right on this."

He said, "All the more reason to somehow get it into RAW hands without our fingerprints all over it. There might be something on there that we would miss, but the RAW would find."

Brett said, "Honestly, Pike, we don't need the phone anymore. Creed's done what he could."

I said, "I guess that's true, but how are you going to get it into their hands? I'm sure they've already searched the holding area he was in. It's not like you can drop it there now."

"They have, but I wasn't kidding about dropping it in a bush. They didn't search from the holding area to the spot where he was shot, and I've asked to see his cell. The RAW chief thinks it's a waste of time, but he's agreed because he thinks I badly want to find it."

"When's that supposed to happen?"

"I told him I had a meeting and I'd come back to the temple after. So probably just before sunset, after the Oversight Council. Which will be perfect."

Veep said, "You're literally going to do a dead drop with some guy walking right next to you?"

Kerry said, "Hey, once upon a time I was a swashbuckling operative. It won't be an issue. What else did you find about that phone?"

I looked at the team, then returned to him, saying, "We know the location of that handset. It's here in Jaipur. I think it's the Chinese control for this entire mess."

"And?"

"And he's the key to resolving this debacle. If we roll his ass up, we can locate the hostages."

CHAPTER 56

Abercrombie VanSant—aka Sledge—felt his first spike of fear when his captors removed his blindfold and cut off his flex-ties. The fear rose higher when he was removed from the van and separated from the women. The terror skyrocketed when the van drove away with the women inside, leaving him alone with the two lunatic killers.

He said, "Are you separating me because I'm American? I've read about that happening on aircraft hijackings."

The taller one—the leader—threw on a small backpack and said, "Yes. We're going to cross that bridge over the tracks and move to a secure location. You will feel out of place because you'll be one of the few Caucasians inside, but you are to act like you're on a tour. We're your guides just showing you around the area."

"But I look like a clown in this outfit. Won't it be insulting? Like I'm making fun of them? Won't it draw attention?"

Sledge was still wearing the outfit he'd been given for the party, a dhoti and kurta ensemble of red and gold, and Sledge had felt conspicuous wearing it even at the party. He was certain it would be out of place where they were going.

The leader said, "You'll draw stares, but just smile and talk to us, asking questions about things as if you give a crap about our lives."

Sledge said, "I don't even know your names. How am I supposed to act like we're together?"

The leader seemed to think a moment, then said, "You can call me Kamal. This is Manjit. What is your name?"

"You don't even know who I am? Why did you take me?"

Sledge saw Kamal's eyes harden, and he said, "I'm called Sledge in America. You know, the singer?"

Kamal said, "Never heard of you. Just because I gave you a name doesn't mean we're friends." He raised his shirt, showing the butt of a pistol, and said, "Get across the street, but remember, if you do anything to attempt to escape or draw attention to yourself, I'll sell you to someone else, and they won't be near as kind as me."

Having thought his name would mean something—that he would get at least a smidgen of the hero worship of his past—Sledge felt the fear return. Manjit pushed him and said, "Go, before the traffic comes back."

Sledge speed-walked across the street, reaching the covered stairs leading across the tracks. He glanced behind him and Kamal pointed up. He began climbing, reaching the top and seeing the walkway full of people traveling to various train platforms. He thought about simply running, maybe in a zigzag pattern. Best case, they'd be too afraid to shoot. Worst case, if the lunatics behind him began shooting, someone would stop them.

He felt a hand on his shoulder, then a barrel in his back, Manjit whispering in his ear. "I see what you're thinking. Don't. There's no need to die on this walkway."

Kamal moved to his front and said, "Follow me."

They passed through the crowds on the walkway, reaching the far side with only the odd person gawking, and went down the stairs. Kamal crossed the next street, and in seconds, they'd left the swirling, chaotic atmosphere of urban Mumbai and entered what Sledge could only describe as hell on earth.

Kamal led them down a small alley, the pavement slick with some type of sludge, detritus and refuse everywhere, electrical wires running chaotically above his head to each building. Every few feet a black hole in the corrugated steel or cinderblock wall would appear, and Sledge could see shirtless men working various machines for metal, pottery, or textiles.

They passed a barber shop stuffed into a cutout CONEX container, men sitting around on plastic chairs with a single barber running an electric clipper through a man's hair, then reached a corner with four men sitting around a cauldron of stew, one slowly stirring it.

Kamal, acting like a tourist guide, said something in Hindi to the men. They laughed and nodded their heads. Kamal turned to Sledge and said, "Would you like a taste of what the workers here eat?"

Sledge shook his head no and Kamal said something else in Hindi. The men around the cauldron all laughed again. Kamal continued, leading Sledge away and saying in English, "You should have tried it. That's what you're going to be eating in here."

Sledge said nothing, his mind trying to come to grips with the utter despair of the place. Kamal walked with an unerring confidence, making one turn after another, and the deeper they went, the bleaker the area became. They passed another opening and Sledge glanced in, seeing two men bathing from a five-gallon bucket, both standing, one with soap on his body while the other poured water over his head from a coffee can. They were wearing shorts for modesty, but that was it, and paid no heed to anyone walking past.

Sledge's mouth dropped open and Manjit pushed him forward, saying, "Give them some privacy. They only get water here about two hours a day, so they have to save up for a bath."

Eventually, Sledge's brain became numb to the sights, his senses overwhelmed like a soldier seeing death on a battlefield up close instead of antiseptically reading about it in a book. He put one foot in front of the other, his white Gucci tennis shoes now spackled with black goop, keeping his eyes on Kamal's back instead of looking left or right. They passed an enormous stack of plastic bumpers from wrecked automobiles and Kamal stopped outside another black hole, saying, "We're here."

Sledge looked inside the opening and saw a stack of plastic luggage, all carry-on size. The room stretched about fifty feet back to a concrete wall with men working various machines, taking the ruptured bumpers through stages, eventually turning the discarded material into the finished suitcases by the door.

One man came out and Kamal spoke to him in Hindi. The man nodded and disappeared back into the darkness. Kamal said, "Follow me," and entered through the hole in the wall.

Sledge did so, walking hesitantly through the opening, letting his eyes adjust to the dim light. He saw the floor was dirt and the men were barefoot, each of them working shirtless in the heat on a machine that looked decidedly unsafe, the air smelling of burned plastic. They stared at him with dead eyes and he hurried to catch up to Kamal.

Kamal took a left down a small hallway formed by two metal CONEX containers, stopping at a wooden ladder. He climbed up it and crouched down, disappearing from sight.

Manjit poked Sledge in the back and said, "Up."

Sledge went hand over hand up the ladder until he reached the top, the air still and hot, smelling of soiled men. He saw Kamal turning on a small electric lantern in the corner. The light spilled out, exposing four soiled mattresses, if they could be called that, the stuffing only about an inch thick. Above them affixed to the wall was a simple bit of lumber creating a makeshift shelf. On the shelf were pictures of various Indian families, and Sledge realized he was looking at the living space of the men below.

Kamal said, "This is home for you. It was supposed to be for Riva Thakkar, but you'll have to do."

CHAPTER 57

Lying in the back of the van, Nadia felt every bump in the road and tried to memorize every turn and roundabout they used. She'd heard the discussion about the train station, knew where it was in Mumbai, and was trying to determine where they were going, convinced the blindfold would remain on for the duration of her captivity.

She needn't have put in the effort. The van slowed and the man known as Jaiden said, "When we stop, you two will remain silent. I'm going to remove your bindings and your blindfolds. If you try to escape or tell anyone what is happening, I'll kill not only you, but whoever is near that can affect my escape. Remember that."

Nadia thought, *What does that mean? Where are we?*

She felt the flex-cuffs on her ankles cut free, followed by the ones on her wrists, then the blindfold was removed. She blinked her eyes, afraid to sit up. She craned her head, saw Annaka next to her, and reached out her arm, taking Annaka's hand into her own and squeezing.

Jaiden slapped the hands apart, looked at Nadia and said, "Remember, not a word. I need her, but I don't need you."

For some reason, Jaiden had a special hostility toward her. She'd feared earlier he knew she was a RAW agent, but took small comfort in the thought that if that were true, she'd already be dead.

The van stopped and Nadia could see security guards in front of a large iron gate. Jaiden exited the van and began speaking to them, pointing to the van, and the men began running back and forth. Shortly, the gate slid to one side and the van began to roll forward.

Nadia whispered, "Where are we?"

Annaka excitedly whispered, "We're home. It's my residence."

Thakkar's monstrosity? How? She saw the hope on Annaka's face, but didn't feel the same emotion. If they were somehow being miraculously saved, Jaiden wouldn't have given them a warning, and he would have removed the bindings and blindfolds as soon as Sledge had been removed.

The van stopped again and Jaiden opened the back, saying, "Annaka, please come out."

She did, and Nadia saw she recognized some of the staff gathered around, all with huge smiles on their faces. Jaiden said, "I've made them turn in their cell phones, as nobody can know you've been saved until we capture the men who did this. It's a matter of national security."

Annaka nodded, confused, and Nadia noticed the two other red-uniformed men from the party standing behind the group, both with unzipped duffel bags. She worried what Annaka might blurt out, and spoke first to prevent Annaka from making a mistake that could kill them all.

Nadia said, "Jaiden, thank you for your help, but I think Annaka has been through so much she just needs to get to a secure location."

A fleeting smile flicked across Jaiden's face, and he said, "As you wish. Follow me. The staff will take care of the van."

He began walking toward an elevator and Nadia looked up, seeing six floors of cars above her, row after row circling around the space, like a giant beehive. Jaiden pressed the call button, the two men with duffels behind them, and Nadia saw the van rising upward on its own elevator to be placed in an empty spot.

The door opened, they entered the elevator, and Jaiden stayed outside, saying something to the staff. He finally entered, and they began to go up. He said, "We're going to the residences at the top. I'll have to decide if we'll stay there or move down to the lower guest apartments."

They rode for what seemed like an eternity, and then the doors opened to an opulence that Nadia had never experienced. A ceiling twice as high as an ordinary room, artwork on the marble walls, crystal chandeliers lighting the way, the anteroom alone oozed wealth. When they entered into the first living space Nadia's breath was taken away. The far side was a wall of glass, the skyline of Mumbai falling below them. Outside the glass was an open balcony thirty feet wide, adorned with hanging gardens. Inside the room were lavish fountains, statues of Hindu gods and other art scattered about, the ceiling at least thirty feet above them, a mezzanine midway up that circled the entire space, truncated by gilded stairwells at each end near the window. It was as big as a five-star hotel's lobby, only more ostentatious, with marble and gold fittings the standard.

Jaiden waved to the sofas near the glass wall and said, "Take a seat. I'm having food brought up."

Annaka didn't move, still confused. Nadia took Annaka's hand and led her into the room, ensuring they sat together. Nadia had no idea what Jaiden's plan was, but she wanted to be close to Annaka if it came to a fight.

The other two men took up stances on either side of the room, setting their bags on the floor and each removing an AK-47.

Annaka saw that and said, "Jaiden, what is happening?"

Nadia said, "Jaiden's lying. We're his captives. He is a Trojan horse in your house."

"What?"

Jaiden said, "Look around you. What do you see? Your father funds this government, and that same government slaughters my people. All we've ever asked for is equality, and all we've ever received is pain."

Annaka said, "How can you say that? My father has been extraordinarily nice to you. You and Rakesh. We've treated you like family."

"Your father throws money at people as if that absolves him of the damage he does. I'm not 'family.' I'm simply the hired help."

He stomped across the room to her until he was face-to-face, worked into a rage. He said, "I should have taken you to the slum to see how the rest of the world lives."

He raised his hand and Annaka recoiled. Nadia jumped in front of him, shouting, "No!"

He slapped Nadia's face with an open palm and she fell to the floor. He stood over her and said, "Remember what I told you in the van. If you try something like that again, it won't be my hand I use."

He turned to Annaka and said, "You need to learn what it feels like to be powerless. I promise my friends who were arrested for nothing more than being Sikh endured much worse in the prisons your father supports with all of his government work."

Annaka started to cry and Nadia pulled herself off the floor and sat next to her, glaring at Jaiden and putting her arm around Annaka, rubbing her shoulders.

Annaka hitched out, "Why can't you be like Rakesh? He would never do this, and he's a Sikh."

Jaiden grimaced at the words, saying, "Rakesh put a bullet in your groom's head, you stupid bitch. He was with *me*, not you."

Annaka looked stricken, the enormity of the treachery coming home. She grew angry herself, saying, "I hope you both rot in hell."

The insolence infuriated Jaiden anew, and he said, "Don't talk about Rakesh. He is gone, and I won't let you spit on his sacrifice."

Trying to defuse the situation, knowing they were powerless but also knowing Annaka still hadn't grasped that fact, Nadia said, "She didn't mean anything. She's in shock. We didn't know he was dead."

The words only seemed to make him angrier. He turned to her and said, "I ought to kill *you* for him. You and you alone."

Fearful, not understanding why he was so vehement, she said, "I didn't do anything to him."

He said, "No, you didn't, but your fucking date from the party did."

The words sank in, and she fought to suppress a smile.

CHAPTER 58

I saw Knuckles scowl and open his mouth as if to speak. I glared at him and held up a finger, shaking my head.

Kerry Bostwick said, "Sir, on this one I have to disagree. Yeah, this might be outside the Taskforce charter, but we have a thread here and we have the capability to explore it."

He was in front of a laptop screen, conducting an encrypted virtual teleconference with the Oversight Council. We were sitting off to the side, and, as Operators, technically not allowed to be in the meeting. All the Oversight Council could see was Kerry's head and an empty hotel room behind him. After a lot of back-and-forth, Kerry had allowed us to remain if we stayed out of sight—and out of sound. If Knuckles blurted something out, they'd know we were eavesdropping.

I heard the secretary of defense's distinct voice, say, "Kerry, you of all people should know the state of play now. It's completely overt, and we have other assets for this. It's a DOD problem pure and simple. An American is being held hostage and JSOC has been alerted. This is their job, not yours."

I saw Kerry bristle, saying, "I get that, Mark. Trust me, I understand the state of play. Christ, I have my entire station here integrating like ticks with the RAW. The National Security Guard has turned this place into an armed camp. The hostages are all over the news. All I'm saying—"

Someone interrupted, asking, "Who are the National Security Guard?"

The SECDEF said, "That's their hostage rescue element. Special Forces guys, and pretty good. They're our link for the JSOC boys."

A little miffed at the interruption, Kerry said, "As I was saying, I get this situation is no longer covert, but Pike has a lead and it's time sensitive. He believes that the Chinese have a hand in this."

I heard Alexander Palmer, the president's national security advisor, say, "Pike? Are we taking direction from that loose cannon now? Who cares what he thinks, this is above his pay grade."

Now it was my turn to bristle. I started to say something and this time Jennifer glared at me, holding a finger to her lips.

Alexander Palmer was a little weasel I'd always wanted to punch in the face, and having him bad-mouth me behind my back was almost too much. Luckily, no love was lost between him and my boss, George Wolffe.

Wolffe said, "Sir, the insults aren't necessary. Pike's track record speaks for itself. If he thinks this is worth looking into, then it probably is."

President Hannister stopped the bickering, saying, "Let's table that for a moment. Kerry, I'm getting information from State, DOD, and your own CIA, but you're on the ground. What's your current assessment?"

Kerry flicked his eyes to us, letting us know he wasn't done with the conversation, then said, "Sir, right now we have no leads. The group that's holding them are calling themselves the Khalistan Commando Force, which is an old-school Sikh separatist group that was most active in the seventies and eighties. The RAW has gone ballistic rounding up anybody from those days, to include the ones still in prison, and they're pretty sure that this group is new and is just using the name."

"I've read their manifesto—I get they dream of a separate Sikh state—but what do they want in the short term? What will it take to get the hostages back?"

"Sir, they mention Hamas in the manifesto, not as a kindred spirit but because of what Hamas caused for the Palestinians on the world stage. If you want my honest opinion, they want exactly what we're giving them right now: publicity. The longer this goes on, the better it is for them. Hell, compare how many Americans could have found Israel on a map prior to the October 7th attack versus how many can now tell you the difference between Gaza and the West Bank, or can describe Palestinian grievances."

"So they've made no demands for the return of the hostages? I mean demands that can be met in the short term?"

"They've demanded that manifesto—which is on every news show and countless websites—be read by an official government minister."

"Is that doable?"

"No, sir. It's a nonstarter. Would you read a fatwa from Osama bin Laden if he had demanded it as a condition of return?"

President Hannister said, "No, I suppose not. What's the state of play?"

"Well, honestly, Riva Thakkar is going ballistic. He feels his honor has been impugned and he is frothing at the mouth for vengeance—and as the richest man in India, he has a lot of pull with the government. It's precisely why we chose him for the mining project in the first place. Because of it, the government is fired up as well. In my professional opinion, the hostages are taking a back seat to the destruction of the terrorists."

President Hannister turned to someone in the room, presumably the secretary of state, and said, "Bring some pressure to bear on this. Get them to pump the brakes. I'm not losing an American citizen because some rich asshole had his honor impugned."

He then said, "Kerry, do they have anything at all to go on? Any actionable intelligence?"

"Nothing that you haven't seen, which is to say, nothing. We know they left in a van, but nobody even got a color, forget about a license plate. That's it. They have the dead bodyguard's cell phone, but so far have nothing from it."

Kerry said that without mentioning the whole theft of a cell phone thing Jennifer and I had engineered. Just like he said he would, Kerry had managed to drop it on the path to the bodyguard's holding cell without the RAW agent accompanying him noticing, and then had maneuvered the RAW agent right over it on the way back. So far, they had gleaned nothing from it.

Kerry continued, "They went through the manifesto webpage, looking for IP addresses and anything else they could find, but so far it's also a bust. Every bit of it ran into a dead end. One of the terrorists is very technically savvy, that's for sure. He knows how to move through the internet undetected."

Secretary of State Amanda Croft, said, "What about the attack Pike stopped? Did they get anything from that or the terrorist's body?"

"Nope. The drone obliterated him. They have his DNA and fingerprints, but nothing has come from it yet. They're not as automated as we are and are still running it through various states and prisons to see if they can get a hit on the fingerprints. As for DNA, I doubt that will even matter. They use it in criminal cases to match a bad guy to a crime, but don't maintain any databases or do systemic DNA profiling."

"So they have nothing to go on? We're at the terrorists' mercy?"

"Well, every time they communicate, they open themselves up to being tracked. They gave their demands in the manifesto, and then sent a message about the government reading it on television through the website, but each time, the terrorist covered his tracks. Eventually—

hopefully—the terrorists begin getting worn down and start making mistakes that we can use."

"That's it? Wait on them to screw up?"

Kerry glanced at us, then returned to the screen, saying, "Well, there's Pike's theory, if you'll let him run it."

The SECSTATE said, "What is this theory?"

"You've all read Pike's situation reports. You know he's run into Chinese pipe-hitters on at least two occasions. His theory is that China set this ball of mud in motion to stop us from executing the rare earth element mine, but then they lost control of their assets. Our biggest lead to finding the hostages was the Sikh bodyguard that Knuckles captured. He tried to abduct Riva Thakkar and would have been a wealth of information, but now he's dead. The RAW thinks the terrorists eliminated him to prevent him from talking. Pike thinks the same guys who attacked him in Agra were the ones to eliminate him. He thinks it's the Chinese tying up loose ends to cauterize their colossal fuckup."

President Hannister said, "So how does that help us?"

"Through Taskforce assets we have the location of what we believe is the control for the entire operation. He's here, in Jaipur. He very well might know where the terrorists are located."

Palmer said, "Why not turn this information over to the RAW?"

"Because for one, they've discounted the Chinese connection from the beginning. They aren't going to dedicate assets against this target during the crisis. Two, if the target *does* know where the hostages are, do you really want these guys to have that knowledge before your JSOC guys get on the ground? It might be guaranteeing their death at the hands of Riva Thakkar's rage."

President Hannister said, "So you want to do this without their knowledge? Without their cooperation?"

"Yes."

"Do you have his identification?"

"No, sir, we don't. All we have is a handset that's talked to both the dead bodyguard and to China."

"That's it?"

"That's Pike's theory, and I think it's worth exploring."

Palmer said, "You can't just rip a guy off the street because he has a cell phone. It'll take a lot more evidence than that before we sanction an Omega operation. I'm willing to vote for Alpha and explore the issue, but that's too thin for an operation."

It took all of my willpower to remain in my chair. I wanted to stand up and start shouting at the stupidity of that statement. Luckily, we had a ringer in the room.

George Wolffe said, "No offense, but that's just idiotic. We don't have days to sniff this guy's ass to find out if it stinks. In my mind it's fairly easy: find the handset, and if the guy holding it is Chinese, take his ass down. It's not like Pike's going into Chinatown in San Francisco looking for a Chinese. It's fucking India, and if that handset is in the hands of a Chinese and we know it's talked to a dead Sikh who tried to abduct Riva Thakkar, then we'd be foolish not to take him down."

The computer went silent for a moment, then President Hannister said, "I'm not even putting this to a vote. Tell Pike he has Omega authority."

Yes!

I looked at Knuckles, knowing I had just as big a grin on my face as he did.

CHAPTER 59

M r. Chin pulled into the parking lot for the Amber Palace, surreptitiously attempting to spot the countersurveillance element
protecting him. He knew he wouldn't find the men conducting it precisely because their entire purpose was to identify someone following
him without being spotted themselves. He tried anyway purely out of
habit, but the growing twilight from the fading sun made the task all
but impossible.

The Ministry of State Security had authorized him to execute the
mission against Kamal's men, but in so doing had become unreason-
ably strict on how Mr. Chin would conduct himself. The leash was
growing tighter, and he wondered if he'd be sacrificed. He didn't want
to believe it, but having worked in this world for most of his adult life,
he couldn't help considering that the only reason he was still walking
around was that he had the information on the men they were tracking. Once he passed that to the Condor team, he would become just
another loose end with information that could implicate the Chinese
Communist Party in one of the most spectacular terrorist attacks on
Indian soil in a generation.

He'd suggested conducting the meeting at his hotel or in a restaurant in Jaipur, but the MSS chief had demanded he conduct a long

surveillance detection route out of the city, using a preplanned course. The chief said it was a precaution against the Americans, and given that, Mr. Chin also suggested the meeting occur in the midst of some local establishment to highlight any Westerners who might attempt to intervene, but once again he was overruled. The MSS chief wanted the meeting in an open area, with enough tourists to allow the Condor countersurveillance team to blend in, which was why he was now sitting in the Amber Palace parking lot.

Built in the sixteenth century, the fortress was a majestic construct of marble and sandstone stretching along a hill overlooking a man-made lake, a smaller stone fort providing overwatch on a higher peak behind it. Once the seat of the regional government for the Mughal empire, it was now known more for its light and sound show, a nightly occurrence that drew foreigners of all stripes, and the location for Mr. Chin's meeting.

The viewing platform for the show was on a spit of land jutting out into the lake just below the imposing façade of the palace. Called the Saffron Gardens, it had once been the crown jewel of the Amber Palace. Now it was simply a location large enough for the tourism bureau to plop down chairs for foreigners to sit, enamored by the various colored lights spilling across the front of the palace while an announcer elaborated on the history and Bollywood performers sang and danced in the background.

Mr. Chin had tickets to both the interior of the palace and light show, courtesy of the MSS, but had no intention of exploring either one. He was to meet the Condor team at a small food kiosk situated right in front of the viewing platform.

He checked his watch, seeing he had seven minutes until he had to walk to the meeting sight. He had been given specific parameters for the meet, such as the route he should take and the pace of his walk, and knew the standard was to arrive at the meeting site plus or minus thirty seconds. Anything outside of that, and his contact would be gone.

He studied a map to his destination, determining if there was anything outside of his control that could hinder his timing. He wanted to be on the far side of such an obstacle to ensure his plus or minus. There was a primary entrance that everyone coming to the palace had to go through, followed by various kiosks selling tourist trinkets, then the path split, with a road going up the hill to the main gate of the palace, and a smaller path staying low, circling the lake until it reached the viewing platform. According to the instructions he'd been given, that path should take four minutes at a normal walking pace.

He saw the line for the show starting to form up at the main entrance and decided he'd join them. He could burn off time after that point if necessary, but didn't want to be caught short if the line took longer than predicted.

He locked up his car and followed other arriving customers to the entrance. The line went swiftly, and he showed his ticket, then passed through a metal detector and had his small knapsack searched, and was finally set free with about a minute to spare before he needed to start on the path. He burned off the sixty seconds looking at tourism brochures, then began his walk.

He split off the main thoroughfare and took the small path snaking around the lake. Right at the juncture of the split were two Chinese men taking pictures of the front of the palace, ostensibly fascinated by the spotlights illuminating the ancient structure. They paid him no mind, but he knew who they were.

He continued on, crossing over to the Saffron Gardens among a group of seventy-year-old Europeans. A man was directing traffic to the stairs leading to the viewing platform but Mr. Chin ignored him, instead going left around the platform to an Indian food kiosk. He got in line for a cup of tea and casually glanced around. He saw six wooden tables, most with two or three people, then found the one closest to the lake occupied by a single man.

He recognized the leader of the Condor team talking on a cell phone. He paid for his tea and went to the table, patiently waiting until the team leader was off the call. He pulled out a chair and said, "May I?"

The man nodded his head and said, "You're clean."

Mr. Chin took a seat, saying, "I knew I would be. We could have conducted the meeting in Jaipur instead of doing this complicated dance."

"After what happened in Agra I was taking no chances."

"You called for this?"

"Yes. Well, the chief thought it prudent, and I did the planning."

"I'm sorry about your team members. I tried to convey that the Americans are dangerous."

The team leader waved his hand and said, "They knew the risks. It was combat. I don't blame you, and I have two new men. If we meet the Americans again, it will be different."

Mr. Chin was surprised at the response. The chief had told him the Condor team leader was incensed about the deaths of his members. A primordial part of his brain wondered why he would be so forgiving.

Mr. Chin said, "I don't think you'll see them again. Like everyone else here, I'm sure they're now trying to find the American hostage."

"I'm told you know where he is. Is this true?"

"I know the location of one of the watches I modified. It's still transmitting."

"But you don't know if the terrorist you've hired is wearing it?"

Mr. Chin pulled out a mini tablet, turned it on, and slid it across the table, saying, "It's watch number two, and it's tied to a new phone, but the malware the MSS used to modify the watches is still working."

Illuminated by the glow of the tablet, the team leader said, "How do you know this isn't some false image?"

Mr. Chin said, "I don't. The terrorists tricked me before and somehow managed to spoof their location through a single phone, so it might be a mirage, but it's all we have."

"Do you know the phone the watch is tethered to?"

"No, I don't. I gave them watches and phones tethered together. They ditched the phones and hit the kill switch on the watches, which theoretically reverts the watch back to factory settings. For some reason, the malware in this watch came back to life. I don't know why, and I'm not questioning it. He tethered it to a new phone, and the malware invaded that phone. It's now transmitting to this tablet. I'm sure some tech people could decipher the IMEI of the cell phone tied to the watch, but we don't have time for that. It's irrelevant with the position."

"What's this heart with a number?"

"It's his heartbeat. It means a living human is wearing it and it's not just sitting in a field somewhere."

The team leader smiled and said, "You can see his heartbeat on this tablet?"

"Yes."

"That's devious." He tapped the screen and said, "The Dharavi slum. That will be hard to penetrate."

"Nobody's going to stop you from walking in there. It's not like there's a gate or anything. Plenty of people go in there to hide from the authorities."

"Plenty of *Indians* go in there to hide. I doubt many Chinese. Getting in and out could be difficult. If the terrorists have any security, it'll be a gunfight, and I'm sure anyone in this slum is going to side with them."

"The residents will flee before they engage. Remember, most do not want to get involved in anything because they're illegal. If you wear

346 / BRAD TAYLOR

police uniforms—even as a Chinese—they'll assume you're the authority. At the worst, it'll cause confusion. Trust me, they'll run."

"What about the hostages?"

"We don't care about the hostages. All we care about is eliminating the terrorists who know of our involvement. If they're captured by the RAW, it will be a mess."

"I mean, do you want them eliminated along with the terrorists?"

"If they can identify you as Chinese, then yes. If it's night, and they don't know what happened, then no. Only eliminate them if they pose a threat of exposure."

The team leader nodded and pointed at the tablet, saying, "Who else has this information?"

"Nobody. I have it on my phone, but nobody else knows it exists."

The team leader said, "Let's keep it that way."

They heard music begin to play and saw the front of the palace bathed in a purple light. An announcer began talking, and Mr. Chin said, "Looks like the show is beginning. Do you need anything else?"

"No, this should do, but you're not going to the show."

Mr. Chin smiled and said, "I had no intention of attending. I'm going back to Jaipur."

The team leader slid across a slip of paper and said, "No, you're meeting the chief's men."

Mr. Chin took the paper and said, "Where?"

"In the palace. The area's already been cleared."

Mr. Chin opened the paper, seeing instructions to go to the bottom level of the palace at the ancient water-lifting system. "Why don't they come up here? Why am I going there?"

The team leader stood and said, "I don't know. This doesn't involve Condor and has nothing to do with my mission. I'm just passing the information. I'm taking my team and leaving."

He walked away without another word. In seconds, he was off the island and striding back to the entrance, gathering his men as he went. Mr. Chin looked at the map he'd been given, wondering about the change in plans. It was highly unusual. There was no good reason for him to conduct two separate meetings at different locations. In fact, it broke just about every rule for clandestine operations. Once a site was secure, that was it. You never left one site and went to another, giving the enemy a second shot at you.

He felt the unease rise and thought about fleeing. If he were being paranoid, he could blame the Condor team leader for confusing instructions when questioned after the fact. He thought about it, and realized if the chief *did* plan something nefarious, he could have simply ordered Mr. Chin to fly home. Or kill him when he returned to his Jaipur hotel. The chief knew where he was staying. Resigned, he realized that missing the meeting here would simply be delaying the inevitable.

He memorized the map, wadded it up, and threw it in the trash, then returned to the lakeside path.

CHAPTER 60

Jennifer and I sat in our car listening to the engine tick, waiting on an assessment from Brett and Knuckles. Finally, we heard, "Pike, Koko, this is Blood. It's not looking good."

"What do you have?"

"The security here is actual security. If the detector goes off, they use a wand."

So much for weapons. "Roger all. Get us tickets, we'll be there shortly."

I turned to Jennifer and said, "Call Veep and get a fix. Is he still on the island?"

We'd started this Omega operation basically at a sprint, without any serious advanced force work. That had simply consisted of splitting the team into two vehicles and leaving Veep behind to coordinate with Creed in the rear.

It turned out we couldn't get real-time mapping of the phone—like any civilian could with Uber or a Domino's Pizza delivery—but we *could* get a fix every time we asked Creed to ping the handset. Veep's job was to keep track of the little blue icon, pinging it every once in a while to make sure it hadn't shifted.

I'd put Knuckles and Brett in one vehicle, taken Jennifer in another, and we'd set up a surveillance box on the hotel, my original plan based on KISS—Keep It Simple, Stupid. Since we didn't have any time to set up an elaborate operation, I was going to sit out here until he left in a vehicle, then conduct a vehicle interdiction the first chance we got.

Of course, it hadn't worked out that way. We'd gotten an alert from Creed that the handset was on the move, then spotted a Chinese guy waiting on the valet. I'd asked for an immediate ping, and the handset geolocated right in front of the hotel.

That's him.

His car arrived, and we started tracking him, but he began a surveillance detection route right off the bat. Within five minutes of the follow I knew he was looking for someone stalking him and I called our teams off. We still had his handset, and I decided to follow him that way.

Honestly, I didn't have a Plan B. I barely had a Plan A with the vehicle interdiction. Even if we did roll up this guy, we had no safe house or extraction plan. I'd convinced George Wolffe to let me take him down first, before all of that was solidified. I told Wolffe I'd secure him in the Rock Star bird, letting the handwringers decide what to do with him later. Whatever they decided—fly him to our embassy in New Delhi, fly him to some safe house that Kerry Bostwick managed to procure, turn him over to a JSOC interrogation team—I didn't really care as long as I had an hour alone with him.

We backed off and let Creed do the work. He pinged the phone every five seconds, and after zigzagging around Jaipur like a tweaker on meth, the car eventually headed north on a highway called Amer Road. We started to track him in a loose follow about four miles back and he eventually stopped at some old fort.

I looked at Jennifer, and she was already working on it, saying, "It's called the Amber Palace. They have a sound and light show there at this time, first one in English, second one an hour later in Hindi."

"What the hell? Why's he going there?"

She shook her head and said, "Maybe he's just doing tourist things for his cover."

There was only one way to find out. I redirected the team to the Amber Palace and sent Knuckles and Brett on a recce to check on the level of security. Brett's call told me that we were going in unarmed.

I took out my Staccato and shoved it under the seat, saying, "What's the last ping?"

Jennifer called Veep, then said, "He's still on the island in the lake."

"Let's go."

We jogged up to the entrance of the complex, meeting Brett and Knuckles, Brett holding our tickets.

Knuckles said, "What's the plan?"

"Right now, just PID and surveil."

Brett said, "That's it? Just identify the guy and follow him around? That's the whole plan?"

"Well, right up until you guys come up with a better one."

We went through the entry point metal detector and handed our tickets to a guy at a counter. He said, "The show's already started. You should hurry."

I nodded and we acted like we cared, speed-walking toward the path that led to the island. We took about four steps before Brett pushed all of us to the shadows of a kiosk, saying, "Cover, cover, cover."

We immediately ducked our heads and turned away from the street, me saying, "What do you have?"

"Group of four Chinese moving our way."

I looked at Jennifer and she called back to Veep, then said, "Not him. He's still on the island."

I glanced at the group as they moved abreast of us and recognized one of them as a shooter from Agra. I said, "One of those guys is the asshole that tried to kill us."

Brett flicked a quick glance and said, "Yep. I recognize the guy in front. They must have gotten some replacements for the ones we took out."

Jennifer said, "Handset is on the move."

I glanced at the security point, seeing the guards all facing away and the four Chinese men disappearing into the darkness of the parking lot. I asked, "Coming this way?"

I was thinking, *Maybe we take his ass down right here.*

She said, "Unclear. He's on the path. He'll either turn left toward the palace or right toward us."

I said, "If he comes this way we follow him into the parking lot and tune his ass up. Jennifer, you distract him with a question. Brett, you have security. Make sure those other pipe-hitters don't come back to interfere. Knuckles, you go low, I'll go high. Jennifer, once we engage, haul ass to the vehicle and bring it to us."

There was no way I'd pull a mission out of my ass like that if it hadn't been my team. Anybody else and I'd have had them repeat their individual assignments using a sand table, but I knew my team could flex seamlessly to any contingency.

I asked, "Roger?"

I got an up from the team, and then Jennifer said, "He's moving left. He's headed to the palace."

Shit.

"Okay, looks like we're going to wait him out. He's got to leave here sooner or later. We'll use the same plan when he does. Let's get inside the palace."

We began speed-walking in the darkness, going higher and higher on the hill, the ancient portcullis of the palace ahead. We reached it, entering a large courtyard about a hundred meters across, the area lit up with multicolored lights blinking and shifting, making it look like a Halloween amusement ride.

I said, "Jenn, what's his status?"

She talked to Veep, and the conversation lasted longer than it should have. She turned to me and said, "He's turned his phone off."

Double shit.

I said, "Okay, let's find him the hard way. Knuckles, Blood, take left. Koko and I will take right."

CHAPTER 61

Knuckles and Brett reached the far side of the courtyard, threading through the crowds but not seeing their prey. Knuckles called on the net, "Moving into the left building."

Pike came back, saying, "Same here. Entering right building."

Knuckles and Brett continued on, searching the individual rooms for a Chinese hiding in the sparse collection of tourists. Brett touched Knuckles' elbow and pointed. "Stairs. You want to stay down and I'll go up?"

Knuckles said, "Yeah," then called Pike, saying, "Splitting low/high over here. No jackpot."

He heard, "Roger. Doing the same on the right."

He moved deeper into the building, finding a maze of hallways and rooms, some large, others tiny. He checked each one, coming up empty. He reached the far wall, a stone façade with cutouts for windows, and saw another courtyard beyond it, this one smaller and ringed with more buildings.

He said, "Blood, Blood, at the far side. Status?"

"Almost there. Stand by. When I reach it, I'll find some stairs to get back down. Got one more room to check out on the lake side."

Knuckles waited, then heard, "Jackpot. I say again, jackpot. He's in a room with some sort of wooden contraption talking to another guy."

Knuckles said, "On the way. Give me a lock-on."

"Get to the second floor and move to the lake. You'll find me."

Knuckles did so, saw Brett standing in a hallway, the changing illumination of the light show flashing into the space like he was in a cheap music video. He jogged to Brett and said, "Where?"

Brett pointed, and Knuckles saw two Chinese men talking at the top of a narrow stairwell. Next to it was some ancient wooden apparatus, a wheel with two ropes attached to it dropping into a shaft.

Knuckles said, "Pike, we have him. Don't bother coming up. Not enough room. If he leaves here, he's going down."

Pike said, "Roger that. On the ground floor of your building, standing by."

Knuckles kept his eyes on the men, seeing that the target was apparently arguing over something, his phone in his hand. The other man was pointing down the stairs, causing the target to shake his head. Ultimately, the target agreed and began going down. The other man waited until he was in front of him and then followed.

Knuckles said, "Target is going down, but he now has a trailer with him."

"Roger all. We'll pick him up when he exits. If he still has the trailer, I'll make the call on the assault."

Knuckles turned to Brett and said, "Let's get a little closer."

They walked quietly to the small room, and Knuckles moved to the stairwell, straining his ears. He heard the footsteps going down, and it seemed like a lot longer than just a single flight. He heard Brett hiss, saw him standing at the pit with the ropes going down it, and went to him.

Brett pointed at a plaque on the wall and said, "This is some sort of water system for the palace. It goes all the way down to the lake."

Knuckles glanced into the pit, smelling the overpowering stench of ammonia. The middle part of the shaft was cloaked in darkness, but the very bottom was illuminated and he could see it was about three stories down. Deeper than the ground floor. He saw an undulation in the dim glow, like the walls were moving, and whispered, "What's that?"

"Bats. The shaft is full of bats."

Knuckles caught movement at the bottom and focused on the lighted area. A figure came into the illumination. He whispered, "Someone's down there. Keep eyes on. I'm calling Pike."

He stepped out of the room, going back to the hallway, and clicked on the net, saying, "Pike, he's not coming to you. He's in some type of water shaft that goes below the ground floor."

"What's he doing?"

"I don't know, but if I were to guess, it's a personal meet. There's a man at the bottom of the shaft that I think is waiting on him."

Knuckles heard nothing for a moment, and knew Pike was deciding if the meeting was important enough to intervene. He finally came back. "Wait for them to finish and we'll stick with the plan."

Knuckles heard Brett hiss. "Get over here! He's getting his ass kicked."

Knuckles ran over to the shaft and stared down it, seeing their target in a rear naked choke, his flailing arms causing shadows to flicker on the walls.

What the hell?

"Pike, Pike, the target is being eliminated. I say again, the target is being eliminated."

"What? Say again?"

"He's being killed right now by two goons."

"Stop it. Interdict the assault."

Knuckles heard the words but knew there was not enough time.

The hold the target was in would render him unconscious in seconds, but if held longer than that, it would kill him fairly quickly. He would more than likely be dead by the time they could make it three floors down the narrow stairwell.

He saw the ropes in front of him, wondering if they were new for the exhibit or from the sixteenth century. Brett saw his focus and said, "Oh, no. Not doing it."

Knuckles ripped off his jacket and said, "Oh, yes you are."

He reached out, grabbed one of the ropes, and pulled on it. It held, for whatever good that proved. He wrapped his jacket around his hands, took a grip on the rope, and leaned out into the pit. The line held his weight. He looked at Brett and said, "Get your ass in here," and began sliding down the rope, using his feet and hands as friction points to slow his descent.

He entered the darkness and felt an explosion around him, a horde of bats bursting out of the shaft, slapping into his body in a frantic effort to escape. He tucked his head, pursed his lips, and kept streaking to the bottom. He reentered the light and saw he was right above the fight, one man directly below him, the other still holding the target.

He let go, dropping straight down onto the first man, slamming his shoulders and driving him into the ground. He rolled upright just as Brett hit the ground next to him. Knuckles turned to the man he'd landed on and punched him in the head to ensure he was out of the fight, then turned to the other one. The second man flung the target away and went into a fighting stance against Brett. The target dropped to his knees holding his throat.

Brett brought up his fists and the second man began doing something out of a kung fu movie, becoming a whirlwind of kicks and punches. Brett blocked two, caught the man with a jab, and then was hit in the shoulder with a roundhouse kick, the blow knocking him to the ground. The man turned to Knuckles, hissing and screaming like he was in a Bruce Lee movie. He attacked and Knuckles backed up, letting the flurry hit nothing but air.

He ended the routine with a spinning back kick and Knuckles batted it aside, then dove into the man, wrapping his arms around the man's waist. He lifted him off the ground and slammed him back down with his weight behind it. The man continued to fight like a wildcat, catching Knuckles with two elbows to the head that nearly rendered him unconscious.

Knuckles tied up his arms and tucked his head into his chest, knowing he didn't have to win the fight alone. Brett reentered the brawl, wrapping his arms around the man's neck just like the man had done to the target and began squeezing like a python.

In seconds, the man was unconscious.

Breathing heavily, Brett let go, saying, "I have done some stupid shit before, but that is probably a record. What were you going to do if the rope snapped?"

Knuckles rolled off, checked his forehead for blood from the elbow blows, and said, "I'd have just entered the fight a little more dynamically."

He looked around the room and saw the target was gone. He immediately got on the net, saying, "Pike, Pike, target is on the loose. He's gone back up."

Pike didn't respond. Knuckles ran to the stairwell, taking them two at a time and saying, "Pike, Pike, are you on the net?"

He got nothing. He kept driving his legs up the stairs and reached the ground level, Brett right behind him. He tried again, saying, "Pike, Koko, Pike, Koko, come back."

They jogged across the courtyard, looking left and right, then stopped, Knuckles saying, "Where the hell did they go?"

Jennifer came on the net, saying, "Knuckles, this is Koko. We have jackpot."

Knuckles looked at Brett and said, "Say again?"

"We're in the parking lot. We have the target. Pike says no thanks to you."

CHAPTER 62

I'd decided to wait until we had our target safely on the Rock Star bird before telling Kerry Bostwick we'd been successful. The last thing I wanted was to alert him about our operation only to have him say he'd coordinated for a rendition team in a tiny town on the way back to Jaipur, telling us to just pass him off in some dark alley. I wanted my time to question him, and most certainly didn't have that opportunity in the parking lot of the Amber Palace.

Jennifer and I had heard the call that Knuckles and Brett had eyes on the target, and we'd hustled over to their building, blending into the other tourists milling around in the colored lights splashed about. When Knuckles alerted me about a possible meeting, I'd really considered attempting to move in close enough to ascertain the purpose, but immediately knew there was next to nothing we could glean from the encounter, not the least because they would probably be speaking in Mandarin. It would have taken a choreographed advanced force operation with technical surveillance emplaced days prior to execute something that complex.

As much as I wanted to find out why they were meeting, I made the call to simply let it go and keep eyes on the target, focusing on the primary mission, which was to roll this guy up and quiz him on the hostages. The next thing we heard was that the target was being assaulted—which made absolutely no sense, but it would directly compromise my primary end state of an interrogation.

I ordered Knuckles to intervene, but, given the conditions, I knew there was little chance he could do anything. I gave him my intent and let him sort it out, thinking that if he couldn't do anything, he'd let me know.

Jennifer and I waited to hear something, the adrenaline flowing from a fight-or-flight response we could do nothing about, and then the target burst out of a stairwell, running right by us. If someone had had a camera, our expressions would have been the perfect viral computer meme.

We recovered quickly and I gave chase, following him out of the portcullis and down the road toward the entrance. I heard a call from Knuckles saying the target was on the loose, but ignored it, as I had him in sight. When he came within view of the entrance security he slowed to a walk, and so did we.

He left the lights of the entrance and wove through the cars of the parking lot. As soon as he was in the darkness, I sent in Jennifer to distract him, just like we'd planned. She went to him and held out a map, asking a question. He looked at her with a dazed expression, obviously overwhelmed from the last few minutes, but then engaged, focusing his entire attention on her. As soon as that happened, I struck, taking him to the ground.

I rolled him on his back, crossed my wrists over his neck, and snatched his left and right collar with my hands, ignoring his feeble attempts to fight back. I violently pulled outward, the fabric cutting deep into both carotid arteries like a closing scissor. He flailed a bit, but in five seconds, he was out cold.

Jennifer returned with our vehicle, and I heard Knuckles calling again on the radio. I hoisted the man over my shoulder and told Jennifer to answer, instructing her to poke them in the eye about the lack of help.

We stuffed him in the back of our car and waited for the rest of the team. They arrived, and I heard about the insane actions they'd taken to prevent the loss of our target. Besides the heroics—which would earn them both a beer later on, but nothing more—I was intrigued that our target's very own masters had wanted him dead.

It was something I fully intended to use once we had him in our little "safe house" called the Rock Star bird.

After an uneventful thirty minutes on the highway, we pulled into the Jaipur airport and followed the signs to the general aviation section, passing by Riva Thakkar's helicopter. I noticed a flurry of activity around it, and wondered what that was about.

We reached our rented hangar and I went inside, finding the pilots ready and waiting in a small office. I had Brett and Knuckles bring in the car, closing the roll-up door behind them, and they loaded our target into the aircraft. He had a blindfold over his eyes, noise-canceling headphones over his ears, and was flex-tied at the ankles and the wrists, but he was awake, twitching like a worm on a hook.

I let them finish getting him settled in a chair and made my call to Kerry. Once the phone went encrypted, I said, "Hey, sir, we have a jackpot and we're clamshell at the Rock Star bird. No issues."

I expected to hear the next steps for extradition of the target, or at least a congratulations. I got none of that. Instead, I heard: "We don't need him anymore. We've located the hostages. This entire place is moving to Mumbai."

Which explained Thakkar's helicopter preparation, but not what they'd found. I said, "Mumbai? Where and how precise is the intelligence?"

"It's precise. The crazy bastards have taken over Thakkar's residence in Mumbai. He has the most expensive house in the world. Twenty-seven stories, and his head of security apparently just waltzed right in with the hostages and locked it down."

That made no sense. "How did we get the intel? Is this cell phone data from the other bodyguard, an inside source, or what?"

"It's from the head of security himself, a guy named Jaiden. He literally contacted Riva Thakkar on the phone and sent a video showing Annaka. Claims he's going to kill the hostages in the next forty-eight hours if they don't read the manifesto on the air."

"Did you verify it? Make sure it's not a deepfake or some other trick?"

"Thakkar verified it. Jaiden had the daughter say certain things to prove it was real, and the call was on FaceTime using Thakkar's Wi-Fi. Afterwards they geolocated the cell phone used, and it's in Thakkar's house. I didn't see the video, but everyone here thinks its genuine."

"Just Annaka? You didn't see Sledge or Nadia on the video?"

"Like I said, I didn't see it, but the assumption is all the hostages are collocated. Look, I have to go. This place is going nuts and I still have to brief the president."

"Wait, what about my Chinese guy?"

"He's going to have to wait. He's not a priority right now. Pike, I have to go."

Great. So now I'm a babysitter.

I said, "Put on Veep."

He did so and I heard, "So you got jackpot?"

"Yeah, fat lot of good that did. What's the plan right now? Are the JSOC guys on the ground?"

"Yeah, but I'll tell you, I'm not sure how much sway they're going to have on operations here. Thakkar is losing his mind at the insult of his pride and joy being taken, and the Black Cats are leaning way forward on an assault."

"Black Cats? Who is that?"

"Sorry. That's the nickname of the hostage rescue element, the National Security Guard, and they are raring to go. They got a black eye in the Mumbai attacks in 2008, and they aren't going to let this one get any worse. One thing's for sure, nobody's reading that manifesto on TV any time soon."

"But the terrorists would know that would be Thakkar's response. They *must* know an assault is coming. Why would they telegraph their position like this?"

"Maybe they're ready to see the virgins. Maybe they knew this would make worldwide news. I don't know."

"They aren't Muslims. There are no virgins in this scenario, and Sikhs don't do suicide attacks for martyrdom. This sounds off kilter."

Something didn't smell right about the situation. It was too easy, reminding me of times in Iraq when insurgents would feed our intelligence apparatus false information for a target, then load it with IEDs in the hopes we'd hit it.

I said, "What's the press reporting? Does the world know Thakkar's place has been taken over by terrorists?"

He said, "Not at this point. They're still reporting the original story. The RAW and Black Cats are keeping everything about Thakkar's residence close hold. They aren't planning on telling the press anything, because it might screw up the assault. They're going to take that place down with overwhelming force and don't want any complications."

Meaning they didn't want any cameras rolling if this turns into a bloodbath.

I said, "What about the hostages? Are they discussing how to rescue them, or just talking about smoking that place?"

"They're talking about smoking it, but they can't come right out and say it. The RAW is concerned about Nadia since she's one of their own. They're demanding all options be considered, but they're losing that fight to Thakkar and the military. Right now, Sledge is the biggest blocking point to a scorched-earth assault. Since he's American, it's causing them to slow their roll in favor of our input for rescue."

"Tell the JSOC guys to leverage that. Get them to pause before they do a knee-jerk assault."

"They *are* leveraging it, but there's no proof of life on Sledge, and Thakkar's ranting to anyone who will listen that the hostages are probably all dead. He's given them permission to hit the place with any means necessary, and the Black Cats are taking that to heart. They aren't going to allow a repeat of the 2008 Mumbai terrorist attacks. I hate to say it, but right now the hostages are taking a back seat to national pride."

CHAPTER 63

Nadia woke up to see the two security guards from the wedding celebration, still in their red uniforms, placing what she believed to be explosive charges at selected locations around the large den, four complete, with more still to be emplaced. Jaiden was in front of them, pacing with a cell phone in his hand. While she'd had little sleep the night before, from Jaiden's drawn face she wondered if he'd had any. The strain of the capture was beginning to take a toll, and after experiencing Jaiden's anger the night before, she was worried about what would happen if he snapped.

Instead of using one of the many bedrooms in the residence, he'd forced Nadia and Annaka to stay in the den, not allowing them out of sight of him or his men. He'd managed to quarantine the staff, preventing them from leaving with a preposterous story of "protecting national security" and allowing no interactions with her or Annaka. The only exception was the in-house security, and even they were forbidden from speaking with Nadia or Annaka. To ensure the women didn't try to communicate unilaterally, whenever the local security was present, so was Jaiden or one of the two red uniformed men.

The staff seemed to buy it completely, believing their cooperation was necessary for Annaka's safety, not the least because the press was 'backing up Jaiden's story by reporting that he himself was a hostage and there were no leads to their location.

She knew Jaiden had confiscated the staff's cell phones, but last night she hoped one had been missed and someone on the staff would carelessly contact the outside world with the juicy story that Annaka was "safe." But then Jaiden had done it for them, and in Nadia's mind, that cemented the likelihood that she and Annaka were as good as dead.

Right after midnight, Jaiden had FaceTimed Riva Thakkar's iPhone, startling both Annaka and Nadia. He showed Riva the interior of the room they were in, and then put Annaka on the video, making her recite specific events that had occurred to ensure nobody believed the video was being staged. He ended by making multiple threats and screaming into the camera. By the time he was done, he'd worked himself into another rage, making Nadia and Annaka cower.

He took out his anger on Nadia, smacking her around until she'd curled into a ball on the floor, Annaka shouting at him to stop. He did, and then stomped out of the room, leaving them with the two security men from the hotel attack. Annaka collapsed into a deep sleep on a couch. Nadia slept fitfully, waking at every small noise only to find one of the security men hovering over her.

The feelings of helplessness and fear angered her, making her want to lash out, but she knew that wouldn't help their predicament. Now, seeing the security men turning the room into a death trap and Jaiden pacing with the cell phone, she knew they were reaching an endgame. Lashing out might be their only option.

Jaiden saw she was awake and came to her, expecting to see fear. She showed him defiance. He raised his hand, but she didn't flinch, and, as expected, it angered him.

He balled his fist, but held it back, saying, "You're lucky someone cares about you."

Confused, she said, "Everyone has a mother and father. Even you."

He said, "Who are you, really?"

That raised the hair on her neck. Had he discovered where she worked? She said, "I've told you who I am."

"Then why do they care about proof of life for you? They're demanding to see both you and the American. I understand the American, but why you? Riva Thakkar doesn't even care about his own daughter, but the government representative I spoke to on the phone has demanded to see you alive. Why?"

She slowly shook her head, knowing it was the RAW trying to protect one of its own. She was genuinely amazed, but realized the concern was perversely putting her in more danger. She said, "You're surprised the government is concerned about one of its citizens?"

"It's more than that. I told you before I only needed Thakkar's daughter, but apparently that's no longer true. I can't have you screwing up what I have planned."

She glanced at the security men still working around the room, now unspooling what looked like thick twine, but she knew from her training it was detonation cord.

She said, "What *do* you have planned?"

"You will find out along with everyone else. In the meantime, I'm going to give the government what they want. You show your face on this camera, tell them where you are and today's date, and nothing else."

He dialed the phone and turned the camera toward her, saying again, "*Nothing* else."

The screen connected and she found herself facing a young man in a military uniform, a scrum of other uniforms behind him. His face was stern, as if he'd prepared the expression before answering the call. He said, "This is Lieutenant Johar. Who am I speaking with?"

"This is Nadia Gupta. I was at the pre-wedding party with Annaka Thakkar and am now being held in Riva Thakkar's residence."

"How do I know that's who you are?"

Good point. She couldn't very well say, "Ask the RAW. They have my photos and fingerprints." She said, "Show this video to Riva Thakkar. He'll confirm."

The lieutenant said, "Let me speak to Jaiden."

She said, "Please talk sense into him. Get us out of this explosive situation."

She saw Jaiden's eyes widen and he jerked the camera away from her, saying into it, "You have your proof of life."

"What about the American?"

"It's coming." He hung up the phone and slapped her hard enough to bring her to her knees. He leaned over her in a fury, saying, "I told you what to say." She recoiled from him, scrambling backward to the couch. He stomped away, bringing up the cell phone again, this time using it for a voice call.

She sat on the couch, finding Annaka awake. Annaka put her arm around her shoulders and said, "What happened? Why did he hit you again?"

"I had to make a video like you did last night. I tried to warn them about what they're setting up in here."

"What do you mean?"

Nadia whispered, "They're emplacing explosives around this room. They're setting a trap, and I think we're the bait."

Nadia saw Annaka's eyes widen, and she said, "So that's why we're not in the safe room."

"What?"

"My father built a safe room in this house. It's basically a bedroom inside a vault, with food, water, and its own power source. Jaiden knows about it, and I thought for sure we'd end up in it, if he wanted to keep us safe."

Annaka glanced at him talking on the phone and continued, "But he doesn't."

"He does for the time being. That's why he had me make the proof of life video. He's trying right now to get one of the American."

"The American? I'd honestly forgotten about him. I hope they're treating him better than they treat you."

CHAPTER 64

Standing in a food kiosk line at the Mahim Junction railway station, Kamal was surprised to feel his smartphone vibrate in his pocket. He pulled it out and saw it was Jaiden.

He stepped out of line, wondering if something had gone wrong. He'd seen nothing about Thakkar's residence on the news, and it had been almost twenty-four hours, but Jaiden had said he would only call if he had a problem.

He said, "This is Kamal. What's happened?"

"Everything's good. I talked to Thakkar and the government last night, and as we expected, they have kept it secret. I'm sure they're planning a surprise assault right this very minute. How is it going on your end?"

Kamal said, "Okay. I was getting breakfast just now. The workers were elated that they get to stay in a hostel instead of the factory, and the American has been docile. Why are you calling?"

"The government is stalling about reading the manifesto on television. They want proof of life for the American."

"They want what?"

"They want a video proving he's alive. It's a negotiating tactic, but we need to do it to convince them he's in the building with me. Right now, everyone's focused on Thakkar's residence. We don't want them to start looking elsewhere because they believe the American isn't with us."

Kamal reentered the narrow alleys of the slum, saying, "I can't do a FaceTime call from in here. I can't spoof your phone from the slum, so they'll know it's not you calling, and worse than that, they'll have my phone. They'll be able to locate me."

"Well, we need to figure something out."

"You want me to come to you? I still have the car. We could film it in the parking garage and then I could leave again. Or you could come to me."

"No way. While they haven't locked this road down with sirens and armed police, I'm positive they're watching this building now. Probably from three hundred and sixty degrees. I've stayed in the primary living area precisely so they'll pinpoint it for assault. If you come to me, you might get in, but you'll never get out. They'll capture you within two blocks. Same thing if I try to leave. No, we need to plan something else."

"So that leaves me just sending you a video for you to resend. But nothing in this place looks like Thakkar's house."

"I know. I've been thinking about it. Is there a good hotel nearby?"

Kamal reached the luggage factory but remained outside, saying, "The convention center is just across the Mithi River north of here. There are nice hotels near that, but Thakkar's not going to be fooled by a hotel room. It won't have priceless artwork on the walls or gold fittings."

"I know, I know. We need one with a respectable gym. Something with modern exercise equipment."

"Why?"

"Thakkar has a two-floor exercise room in this place that's completely outfitted with the most modern exercise equipment in existence, but that lazy fucker has never stepped one foot into it. The only ones who've used it are the staff and his daughter. Get him inside the hotel gym next to some equipment, and video him close up."

"I don't think that'll fool them. They'll wonder why he's in the gym."

"I'll handle that. I'll tell them that he's been a pain in the ass and we separated him. It'll be just enough to cause them to question. They'll err on the side that we're telling the truth, and that's all that we need."

Kamal agreed to the plan, disconnected, and entered the tiny factory, the pungent smell of molten plastic burning his nostrils. The men working inside glanced over but paid him no further attention. He went down the narrow hallway, then up the ladder, finding Manjit sitting on a mattress playing with his Garmin watch and Sledge in the corner with the lantern, his hands wrapped around his knees, looking gaunt.

He said, "I really wish you'd get rid of that thing. It worries me."

Manjit smiled and said, "It has an app called the 'body battery' that tells me how tired I am. According to it, I really need more sleep. Where's the food?"

Kamal saw Sledge's face grow apprehensive at hearing the Hindi, wondering what they were talking about. He said, "We need to get the American cleaned up and somewhere else."

"What for? I thought we weren't going to move until Jaiden's mission was done. To protect ourselves."

"I'll explain on the way, but it's to make sure that we *don't* have to move. We need to ensure they're only looking at Jaiden and nobody's searching for us."

CHAPTER 65

I rolled into the hangar with breakfast sandwiches for everyone. Jennifer had wanted Indian fare, but she'd have to settle for McDonald's.

The general aviation side of the hangar was much quieter than it had been the night before, when everyone and their brother seemed to pack up and fly to Mumbai. Thakkar's helicopter was long gone, as well as a plethora of other government aircraft. Kerry Bostwick and Veep had flown out with the RAW team.

Veep had wanted to come to the hangar, cutting ties with the intel side of the house and rejoining the team, but I'd told him he'd be more valuable as a liaison with Kerry, feeding me information about what was happening. I would have liked to have had a face-to-face with Kerry before he left, but I was preoccupied with talking to our mysterious Chinese captive.

We'd searched him, finding a cell phone and a bunch of pocket litter designed to prove he was just a businessman, but nothing that screamed "I'm a spy for China." Which was to be expected. I'd turned over the phone to Brett, telling him to get Creed on it, and then had a one-on-one with our mystery man. Well, really a two-on-one. I had Knuckles in the aircraft just to look menacing, but I'm the one who did all the talking.

We'd gone around and around, and he was good, I'll give him that. He gave me nothing to grab on to for leverage. He just repeated the same tired refrain that he was a businessman and had no idea why we had him. He only wavered when I confronted him with the fact that his own "business partners" had tried to kill him, but he stuck to his story that he had no idea who those men were and that he was attending the light and sound show as a tourist.

I asked him to explain how his phone had called the bodyguard who had tried to assassinate Riva Thakkar, and he acted like I was clinically insane, telling me that he had no idea what I was talking about.

After two hours, I gave up, deciding to let Creed do his work over-night. From what I'd seen, the Black Cats weren't planning to assault during this cycle of darkness, so I had some time to get more evidence against him. And I wanted him to stew a little bit, marinating in what I'd told him, letting him know that he wasn't going anywhere and coop-eration was the best option he had.

Knuckles shut the roll-up door and I handed him a bag of food, saying, "Drink's in the passenger seat."

Jennifer stuck her head out of the open aircraft door and said, "Mc-Donald's? Really?"

I said, "Yep. How's he doing?"

"He's awake. He's asked when you're coming back to talk. He knows we're digging into his cell phone."

I looked at Knuckles and said, "How's that going?"

"Not good. I'll let Brett explain."

I went into the small office to find Brett in a headset talking to Creed on a video call. Creed looked like he hadn't slept, circles under his eyes and a day-and-a-half stubble on his face.

Brett saw me, took off the headset, and put the computer on speaker. He said, "Tell him what you just told me."

I went to the screen and said, "Tell me what?"

"Pike, I can't get anything from the phone. You said he turned it off last night, but that's not what he did. He reset it. It's basically a fresh phone right now. Like it came straight out of the factory."

"I thought that was impossible. That even if someone reset a phone to factory settings, you could still find traces of what they'd done and who they'd talked with."

"Ordinarily, that's true, but in this case he wiped it, using some sort of program that completely erased all its data. It was so good, it erased even itself, leaving just a smidgen of a trace about its presence. Honestly, it's better than the wiping program we have on our own Taskforce phones."

"So we basically wasted the night. Is that what you're saying?"

"Well, I'm saying that I worked all night and can't get anything out of this phone. Even the SIM card is wiped. But the lack of any evidence is evidence in itself."

"What do you mean?"

"I can prove the phone was wiped with a sophisticated program, not a cheap app he purchased on Google Play. And that itself is proof of something."

I nodded and said, "True. What ordinary businessman has a program to eliminate all traces from his phone?"

He said, "Sorry, Pike. I did my best."

"Don't worry about it. I'm sure you did. Go get some sleep, I might need you in top form later."

I closed out the video just as Jennifer entered the office. She said, "He's asking for you."

I looked at Knuckles and said, "Ready for round two?"

"Do I get to do something besides glare at him this time?"

I said, "Probably so, since all we have left are our fists."

Jennifer squinted, and I said, "I'm just kidding."

I grabbed the phone off the desk and we left the office, going up the short staircase of the Gulfstream jet. I entered finding "Mr. Chin"—the name he'd asked to be used—sitting in the same chair I'd left him in last night, a tray of wrappers for Big Macs and fries on a table to his front. Jennifer had let his arms free to eat, but his ankles were still handcuffed to a couple of hidden bolts in the floor, put there specifically for that purpose.

He lowered the straw from his drink out of his mouth and said, "McDonald's? That's what you give me?"

I saw a bit of humor in his eyes, and it aggravated me, a match flickering next to a fuse. I said, "You complain again and it'll be the last meal you get for a while."

I took a seat in the chair opposite him, and he said, "We both know that isn't true. You have no authority to torture me." He pointed at Knuckles and said, "His presence here is wasted on me, because I know you will not harm me."

"And how would a simple businessman know anything about what I'm authorized to do or not do?"

"I read the papers."

I said, "You know and I know that you're not a businessman. Let me tell you what I think. The Ministry of State Security somehow found out that India had located significant reserves of rare earth elements and had tapped Riva Thakkar to extract it. You were sent here—as a member of the MSS—to prevent that from happening. You chose to eliminate Thakkar as the easiest route, and you hired some local thugs to do the work, to give you plausible deniability. How am I doing so far?"

He remained mute. I said, "Okay, so here's where it gets a little iffy. Somehow, those local thugs left the chain and went berserk. Instead of just eliminating Thakkar, they torched an entire wedding party and then started screaming about the Khalistan Commando Force. Now, I don't know if that was part of the MSS plan, or if you just lost control, but that's where we are. My job is to rescue the hostages they've taken. Your job is to help me, if you ever want to see the light of day again."

He said, "We went through this last night. I told you I'm just a businessman."

I set his cell phone on the table and said, "You wiped this phone last night with a sophisticated program. Something beyond what a business-man would have. Something an intelligence service would use."

"How would you, a government flunky, know what a Chinese business-man would have on his phone?"

"I'm a businessman too, and trust me, I deal with some very sensitive information, and I don't have that on my phone."

He leaned forward and said, "Yes you do."

CHAPTER 66

His answer surprised me, as it was his first indication that he was playing a game. He was telling me he knew I had the software, because he knew what I was, and he and I were the same. It threw me off my game.

I said, "You're right, I'm not authorized to start waterboarding your ass. Yet. But maybe your own people won't be so nice. If you don't give me anything about the terrorists or the hostages, I'll have to assume you *are* simply a businessman, and I'll drop you off at the Chinese embassy."

He leaned back, saying nothing. Which was something in and of itself. Last night, he'd stated over and over that he had no knowledge of the terrorists or the hostages. Now he wasn't denying it.

I thought maybe I was on to something and said, "They seemed to not like you so much the last I checked. If I were to keep spitballing, I'd say they're embarrassed by this entire debacle, and they're cleaning up loose ends, just like you did with the bodyguard in Jaipur."

He said, "That is true. Nobody is more surprised than me. The question I have is, What are *you* authorized to do?"

Breakthrough. I was beginning to think my idea of letting him sweat his fate was paying off.

I said, "What do you mean?"

"I mean, if I were to know something about this awful terrorist attack, and I were to tell you, what would prevent you from still dropping me off at the embassy?"

Is he asking for asylum?

I said, "Nothing, I suppose, but if it were true information, I wouldn't do that. Right now, all your people know is that you escaped. They don't know we have you. They think you're in the wind, and I can keep it that way."

"You would just let me go? On my own?"

I slowly shook my head and said, "As long as we're being honest here, no, I'm not going to let you go. That, as you say, is something above my pay grade. I will, however, keep you out of your enemy's hands."

He thought for a moment, then said, "I don't know what enemies you're talking about. Those men who attacked me were complete strangers. I'm just a businessman."

He'd decided it wasn't worth it and had reverted back to his cover. We were going backwards, and he didn't care one whit about the lives in the balance. The gamesmanship cracked open my scab and I felt the rage start flowing through my body.

I said, "If you know anything about where the terrorists are, I would suggest you tell me."

He saw something had changed in my demeanor, but plowed ahead anyway. "My fate with you is sealed whether I say anything or not. You've already admitted without saying so that you aren't authorized to decide my fate. You're not going to turn me over to the embassy. That decision will be made, as you say, above your pay grade. I'll wait for them."

The words split the scab open, letting the beast run free. I snarled and leapt across the table, grabbing his hair with my left hand and punching him in the face with my right. I managed two strikes before Knuckles pulled me off him, shouting, "Pike, Pike, back off!"

We struggled for a second and I calmed down. I threw Knuckles' hands off me, turned to Chin, and said, "You ordered your men to try to kill me. Right now, I'm looking at an enemy combatant. You're right, I'm not going to turn you in to your embassy, but me killing you in self-defense is something I can justify. I just won't tell the people above my pay grade that it was in self-defense of the hostages."

Focused on Chin, I said, "Knuckles, give me your pistol."

He said, "What?"

My eyes still on Chin, I said, "Give it to me. I'm done with this shit."

He passed it butt first and I laid it on the table in front of Chin. I said, "You either grab that pistol or start talking."

He looked at the Staccato in front of him, then into my eyes, recognizing I wasn't bluffing. He said, "Let me have my cell phone."

I picked up the pistol and handed it back to Knuckles. I took a seat again and said, "Why?"

"Because I know the location of one of the terrorists, but it's in that phone."

"The phone is wiped."

"I know. I have to download an app."

Which was a conundrum. We'd had the phone off since we captured him precisely to keep any of his "friends" from tracking us. If he turned it on and it touched the cell network, it would be visible for anyone to find.

He saw what I was thinking and said, "I don't want anyone tracking the phone any more than you do. Does this aircraft have Wi-Fi? I'll leave it in airplane mode to do the download, which, given where I'm sitting, seems appropriate."

I sent Knuckles to get a pilot, since I had no idea how to turn it on, and Mr. Chin gave up all subterfuge, describing a Garmin watch and how he'd modified it to transmit to a special application designed by his "organization," which I knew was the Ministry of State Security. He went through the entire history of the device, and I didn't let him know I was somewhat familiar with it, since it was how we'd located the terrorist in Agra and also how we'd found out the rest were in Jaipur.

By the time he was done, the Wi-Fi was operational. I turned on the phone, immediately put it into airplane mode, then handed it to him, saying, "I don't have to tell you not to try anything stupid, do I?"

He took it and said, "No, you don't."

He manipulated the phone for a moment, then sat it on the table, saying, "Downloading. Understand, the watch was working before I wiped the phone. I'm not trying to trick you, but it might no longer be transmitting. I can't predict if the man is still wearing it."

"I understand, but that's just the tactical intelligence. You're going to get a complete debriefing from Jennifer, and you're going to tell her everything you know about these terrorists, to include why you're involved."

He looked stricken for a moment, as if he thought the phone app alone was his ticket out. I saw him wavering and said, "Unless you want me to put that gun back on the table."

He pursed his lips, nodded, and picked up the handset. He poked the screen a few times, then turned it to me, saying, "It's still transmitting, and it has a heartbeat, so someone's wearing it."

I was looking at a map. I took it out of his hand and saw a little blue icon in the heart of the Dharavi slum.

I turned to Knuckles and said, "You and Brett pack this place up. Kit up for a dismounted close target reconnaissance. We're going to Mumbai. Get Jennifer up here."

He left and she came in. I said, "Mr. Chin is prepared to give you a full debrief. Start in Goa and have him go all the way through the killing of the bodyguard."

She showed surprise at his turnaround, then saw his swelling eye. She squinted at me and I said, "It was his own free will. He wants a ticket to the witness protection program."

CHAPTER 67

Three hours later we'd landed at Mumbai International. I'd let Jennifer handle the debrief on the flight while Knuckles, Brett, and I planned for a reconnaissance of the Dharavi slum. We did a deep dive of everything we could find, both on the open web and using reachback for classified intelligence from the Taskforce. During the flight, the blue marble had moved to a hotel next to a convention center, but by the time we'd landed, it had returned to the slum location, and we knew everything we could without being on the ground there.

Jennifer continued her debrief as we taxied to the FBO hard stand, and I read her initial notes while waiting for the aircraft to stop. We parked in our designated slot and I let her continue, immediately sending Knuckles and Brett to get a rental car and conduct the recce. Not long after they'd left, Jennifer came up and said, "We have a problem."

"What?"

"Chin had two meetings that night at the Amber Palace. The second meeting was supposedly to meet his MSS chief, but was a setup to kill him. He thinks you're partially right. Part of it was the cleanup of loose ends, but part was punishment for screwing up so royally with the terrorists."

"And the first meeting?"

"Remember we saw those guys who attacked us at Agra leaving the palace?"

"Yeah?"

"That was the first meeting. He gave the information about the Garmin watch to what he called a Condor team. It sounds like they're our counterpart in the MSS, except they specialize in killing as opposed to solving problems. They're on the hunt for the terrorists too, to prevent them from getting captured and talking about CCP ties."

"And they have the same information as Knuckles and Brett?"

"Yes, and their mandate is to kill anyone who can implicate China, to include the hostages."

Shit. I said, "Call Knuckles and give him everything you know. I need to talk to Kerry."

"Kerry? Not George Wolffe?"

"Woffe isn't on the ground with the Black Cats. I need to know what they're doing before we execute anything."

"So you'll call Wolffe after?"

I said, "Probably not. I'm not sure we have the time to wait around for the Oversight Council's hand-wringing. We're probably going to have to go operational before they'll make a decision."

She said, "I'm not sure that's smart."

I said, "Call Knuckles. Don't worry, I'm going to blame Kerry for anything that goes wrong."

She went to get her phone and I dialed up Veep. He answered on the first ring, and I said, "Hey, we're in Mumbai and I have a lead for one of the terrorists. I need to talk to Kerry."

He said, "He's in a meeting right now, but it was already supposed to be over. He should be out at any minute. What's the lead?"

"The Chinese guy spilled his guts. He has a location in the Dharavi slum that might have one of the bad guys."

"Not at the residence?"

"No. Where are you at now?"

"A National Security Guard compound on the outskirts of Mumbai. After the 2008 massacre they made seven hubs around the country, and we're at the Mumbai one. It's pretty cutting edge, with climbing walls and an indoor shoot-house. These guys are the real deal."

I'm sure the Black Cats were qualified for all manner of operations, but being the "real deal" only went as far as the orders they were given. I said, "What's the current state of play?"

"They're in full assault mode. They have the blueprints for the building, and snipers have identified the floor where the hostages are being held. It's near the top, a primary living room with a gigantic outdoor balcony. The roof of the building has three helipads, so they're going with an air assault using all three. Meanwhile a ground force will lock down the bottom and start clearing up."

"And the hostages?"

"Not really a focus. They're still planning on going in full bore, with success defined as dead terrorists, not live hostages."

"This whole thing stinks. Jaiden isn't stupid. He knows that building inside out, and has military experience. He must have a plan for that."

"You may be right. They received a proof of life with Nadia, and the RAW thinks she was trying to tell us something. She said she hopes the government gets them out of the 'explosive situation.' As soon as she said it, Jaiden jerked the camera away from her. They think she was saying the place is rigged."

"What do the Black Cats say?"

"Well, that's the issue. In order to protect Nadia, the RAW has kept it under wraps that she's an agent. They don't even know that we know. Because of it, the Black Cats think she's just a civilian who spouted that off the top of her head. They're not putting too much stock into that threat analysis and are focusing on a hard ballistic assault."

"When are they looking at going?"

"I don't know, that's what the meeting is about right now."

"Are we having any luck focusing them on the rescue instead of search and destroy?"

"Hang on. Kerry's back."

He passed the phone and I heard, "Pike, sorry about not getting back to you sooner about the extradition of the Chinese, but you're going to have to babysit a little longer. I haven't had time to sort it out."

I said, "Sir, the Chinese—Mr. Chin—talked. My theory was right on the money. The MSS hired these guys to kill Thakkar to stop or slow the rare earth element mine. They lost control of them and now they're tying up loose ends to protect the CCP. Chin was one of the targets because of his fuckup, along with the bodyguard and now the terrorists."

"Well, good luck on them beating the Black Cats to the inside of Thakkar's residence. There's only room for three helicopters on the roof."

"He had intelligence about the location of one of the terrorists, and it's not at Thakkar's residence." I then gave him a rundown of what I knew and what I was doing, ending with, "I think this needs to be checked out."

"Meaning you?"

"Well, of course meaning me. Look, who else is going to do it? The government is preoccupied with Thakkar's residence. You give this intel to them and they're going to flood the slum with uniforms and whistles blowing. The guy will get away for sure. The Oversight Council said that the residence assault was no longer a Taskforce issue but that we could pursue the Chinese angle. This *is* the Chinese angle."

"You know I'm going to have to take this to the Oversight Council. In fact, why are you calling me instead of George Wolffe? I'm a member of the Council, not your chain of command."

"Because you're on the ground and he's in DC. Trust me, if you tell me no, I'm going straight to him like a kid playing mommy off daddy. We don't have time to wait for the Council to deliberate. Mr. Chin told me there's a Chinese team hunting this same intel to eliminate the threat of CCP exposure, and I need to beat them to the punch. With the time zone difference between here and DC, you won't be able to get any kind of decision out of them until midnight at the earliest. By then I'll have him in the bag."

"Those are the rules we play by."

"What's the assault timeline?"

"They're looking at going in at dawn tomorrow."

"Well, there you go. Waiting on the Oversight Council for a decision is asking for no decision, because once that assault goes down, he's gone for good."

"It's not a given at this point. We're still pushing for more fidelity on the intelligence to facilitate a rescue, and the fact that they have an American hostage is the only thing holding the Black Cats back."

"I heard we had proof of life for both the women, what about him? Is he there?"

"Yes, and no. Yes, we have a video of him for proof of life, but no consensus as to whether he's in the building."

"Huh? I thought Thakkar was vetting all these videos?"

"This one was a little different. Both of the women were done live, over FaceTime, using Thakkar's Wi-Fi node and in a setting he definitely confirmed. His was sent over Thakkar's Wi-Fi, but it was a recorded video, and it was from the exercise room."

"So? Is it *his* exercise room?"

"He can't say. Apparently, he's never used it. He says it could be his, but can't positively say it is. There was nothing in the video that he could confirm."

"Veep said you had snipers ID the floor the hostages are on. Did they see Sledge at any time?"

"No. Only the two females, but they can't see the exercise room, and according to the terrorist, Sledge was sent there because he was being unruly. At this point we don't know if it's bullshit or not."

"Veep also said Nadia tried to warn us about explosives in the building?"

"Yeah, I tend to believe the RAW on this and that she was giving us a hint, but we don't know if that's bullshit or not either."

"Give me Omega authority for my intel, and maybe I can solve both problems."

"Pike, I can't give you Omega authority."

"Let me rephrase that: I have Omega authority from the Oversight Council for the Chinese option. Give me cover with the Oversight Council if I have to go apeshit to continue exploring the Chinese option."

I heard him laugh, then he said, "Okay, Pike, I'll cover your ass. But don't go apeshit if you can avoid it."

"Only if you promise not to go apeshit on an assault before I can execute."

"I can't promise that. Sledge being in that building is the only thing holding them back. If they decide that video was faked, they're going in."

CHAPTER 68

Sledge stared at the crack of light coming through the corrugated tin roof. A seam that represented freedom. The metal roof was only four and a half feet from the top of the CONEX container he now called his cell, and the light told him that the section might merely be laid on top of the concrete walls instead of screwed together, like metal palm fronds someone put up to keep out the sun and rain.

Sitting next to the electric lantern, Manjit said, "What are you looking at?"

Startled, Sledge said, "Nothing. Just thinking."

Between the two terrorists, Manjit was the kind one, if that was even possible. Sledge knew that Kamal would kill him without a moment's hesitation, but Manjit appeared to be reluctant in his position as his guard. He was definitely the only one willing to converse.

Kamal had gone out to get their dinner—another plate of barely digestible slop, Sledge was sure—leaving Manjit to provide guard duties. Sledge had begun to enjoy the brief interludes when this happened. Kamal wouldn't say a word except for commands, and had snapped at Manjit when he'd tried to answer a question. But Manjit would talk when Kamal was gone.

Sledge said, "Why are you guys doing this? What's the point?"

Manjit said, "You wouldn't understand."

"Try me. You know, I've spent a lot of time in this country. I've seen the poverty, and I've tried to help."

Manjit scoffed and said, "What have *you* ever done to help here?"

A little miffed, Sledge said, "I started a foundation called Everclear. It brings clean water to rural areas in India. I've dug more wells than anyone."

He saw recognition on Manjit's face. "*You* started Everclear?"

"Yes. You know of it?"

"I've seen the wells in my home state."

"Where is that?"

"Punjab."

"I know it well. Enjoyed my time there."

Manjit started to ask a question, then shook his head, saying, "I know what you're doing. Don't try to sway me. You know nothing about my home."

Sledge remained quiet for a moment, then asked, "So why are you doing this?"

"You said you've been to Punjab, so you know the plight of the Sikhs."

"But you're not Sikh. You don't have a turban or a beard. I thought you were Muslim."

"We're Sikh, and I don't wear a dastaar or grow a beard precisely because it would mark me. The government has hounded us for generations and now, with this government, it only gets worse. You're either Hindu, or you're dirt, just like it is for the Muslims. Unlike the Muslims, who have plenty of places to go outside of India, there is no homeland for the Sikh. We can't go to Pakistan and be welcomed. There is no government fighting for us like the Muslims have in Kashmir. We suffer in silence, only now, we're fighting for ourselves, and our voice is being heard."

"But slaughtering innocents isn't the answer. Killing me won't do anything for your cause. It'll only bring the United States down on your head."

Manjit spit on the metal floor and said, "Tell that to the Palestinians. It seems to be working for them."

Sledge heard Kamal's voice shouting in Hindi from below. Manjit said, "Be quiet. I'm going to retrieve your food."

He disappeared down the ladder and Sledge waited, listening. The luggage shop workers had left a half hour ago, the noise of the machinery quiet. He heard Kamal talking to Manjit at the front of the shop and sidled over to the crack he'd seen earlier.

He poked it with a finger, and it moved up an inch. He put both hands on it and pushed, finding the entire section was only laid on top, without any fasteners. He gathered up his courage, his brain wanting to fling it open but his muscles refusing to commit.

He heard Kamal shout and then Manjit coming back in a hurry. He immediately dropped the section back in place and sat on his thin mattress.

Then the gunfire started.

* * *

Manjit crawled down the ladder, hoping that Kamal hadn't heard him talking to the hostage. He reached the front of the shop and saw Kamal near the open door holding two plastic bags of food, a scowl on his face, which answered that question.

Kamal said, "What did I tell you about talking to the hostage?"

Chagrined, Manjit said, "I can't just sit up there staring at him in silence. I was telling him about what we were trying to do here."

Kamal glanced out the door to the alley beyond, saying, "Trust me, he doesn't care."

"I think this guy actually might. He could be on our side."

Kamal turned back to him, dropped the food, and put his hands on his shoulders, saying, "Manjit, you may have to kill this man. When the time comes, I might not be around and it'll be up to you."

Manjit said, "Wait a minute. Listen to me. You remember that new well in our hometown? The one with the Everclear logo? That's him! He did that with his own money."

"I don't give a shit if he turned the Ganges into gold, he was with Thakkar, which means he's with the state. He is *not* your friend. If you don't believe me, google Everclear. We got one well, but I'll bet the Hindu areas got a hundred. He's not saving himself by some good works, because the bad far outweigh him."

Manjit glanced away, remaining quiet. Kamal said, "If I tell you to kill him, can you? Or is it too late for that?"

Manjit said, "He's an American. He's worth more alive than dead."

"I know that, it's why he's still breathing, but I need to know you're capable."

"I'm capable. I understand. If you give the word, I can do it."

"You didn't kill the woman at the party."

"That was different."

Kamal glanced out the door again and said, "You get the food from now on. I'll watch him."

Manjit started to respond when Kamal pushed him out of the light. Manjit said, "What are you doing?"

Kamal held a finger to his lips and pointed to the door. Outside in the alley Manjit saw two uniformed policemen walking past. Manjit sank deeper into the shadows, whispering, "It's got to be a coincidence."

They kept walking and Kamal went to the side of the open doorway, peering out. Manjit came up behind him, looking as well. Both men were wearing sunglasses even as the sun had already dropped behind the buildings. They walked another thirty feet, then stopped, standing still and appearing to simply be talking to themselves.

Kamal said, "Take a hard look at them. What do you see?"

Manjit said, "A little late in the day for sunglasses."

"True, but that's not what I mean. Look at their belts."

Manjit did, and saw both had Glock pistols in a holster on one side, a baton on the other. He said, "Police equipment?"

"No, that's definitely *not* police equipment. The patrol officers are *never* armed. They don't carry guns."

Manjit said, "What are you saying?"

He pulled a pistol from his waistband. "I'm saying those guys aren't cops on a beat. They're here for us. Go back to Sledge. If I go down, or I give the word, kill him."

Manjit started to turn back to the hallway when Kamal said, "What the fuck?"

Manjit whipped back to the doorway in time to see a Caucasian man and woman attack the policemen. His mouth fell open as they struggled, then gunfire erupted from farther up the alley.

Kamal backed up, screaming, "Go to Sledge, go to Sledge!"

Manjit took off running to the narrow hallway and the ladder.

CHAPTER 69

Jennifer and I entered the outskirts of the Dharavi slum, drawing more and more stares the farther in we went. The sun was already down below the buildings, meaning any tours of the area were long over, and the denizens of the slum were wondering what the hell we were still doing in here.

I called Brett and Knuckles, saying, "We're getting the stink eye, how are you guys doing?"

Earlier, Brett and Knuckles had run a close target reconnaissance of the terrorists' location and had sent me as much information as they could, including photos of the target building and the structures up and down the alley. When they were complete, they were supposed to come back to the Rock Star bird for a debrief, but Knuckles had called and said they'd found a place to stay within sight of the terrorists' location. An NGO canteen that had a smattering of greasy hippy-like Westerners coming and going among the slew of locals.

Knuckles looked like a hippy himself, and Brett, being African American, managed to confuse everyone. He couldn't be a tourist, so he must be with the NGO. That had been a few hours ago, and I wasn't certain how long they could stay. We'd only traveled three blocks and

Jennifer had been stopped twice for a selfie with random strangers, as if they had never seen a blond Caucasian woman.

Knuckles said, "We're okay, but our heat state is rising. This place had enough turnover in the day that nobody's noticed, but now it's slowed down. People are stopping longer, and sooner or later, someone's going to ask to sit at our table."

"Hopefully it's later. We'll be at your location in about five minutes."

"What's the plan?"

"We're going to walk past the target on our way to your location to check on activity, then we're going to make a hasty plan, walk back, and slam that place. I brought bangers and breaching charges, so we should be good if they've got him locked up in a reefer or other cage."

"You really think Sledge is here?"

"I'd say it's fifty-fifty. He might be at the residence, but that watch is here, so even if it's just a terrorist, we're going to get something."

Brett said, "What if it's a room full of terrorists? There's only the four of us."

"It's not going to be a roomful. You said you saw the work crew leave, right?"

"Yeah, they're gone."

"And one guy left and came back with food, but the Garmin didn't leave?"

"Yep. Same guy left for both lunch and dinner."

"There were only five at the wedding attack. Three who came in shooting, and the two bodyguards. One of the shooters was killed that night, and one of the bodyguards was killed later, and we know Jaiden is in the residence, so that leaves two unaccounted for."

"But you know Jaiden isn't at the residence by himself. He has help, and if *he* has help, these guys might also."

"True, but the guy wasn't carrying enough food for a platoon. I'm thinking five at the max. What's the issue here? You think these amateurs are dangerous?"

I heard Knuckles laugh, then say, "Come on, as your 2IC I just felt it necessary to inform you of the danger."

"I thought Danger was your middle name."

Brett came on, saying, "I'm not worried about the locals, but what if we've read this wrong and the Chinese are in cahoots with them? That Condor team is no joke."

I hadn't considered that. What if Mr. Chin had only told us the partial truth, and the Condor team wasn't hunting the Garmin watch like we were but was with the terrorists right now? It gave me a pause on the whole assault plan. I was all about flexing under a time crunch, but maybe this was a little bit too much of a flex and Mr. Chin was walking us into a trap. For all I knew, it was a Condor team member wearing the damn thing.

I said, "Let us get by the target and we'll reassess when we link up."

"Roger all. You having any trouble navigating?"

"Not a bit. App's working like a charm."

Like a couple of explorers in the Amazon for the first time, Brett and Knuckles had used a navigation application on their Taskforce phone to leave a trail of breadcrumbs everywhere they went in the slum, including during the CTR of the target and the final stop at the NGO canteen. They'd transmitted it to us, and now all we had to do was follow the trail.

We continued on, taking lefts and rights in the maze, following the breadcrumbs, and were about to make the final turn down the alley that ran past the target when Brett came on, saying, "Pike, Koko, Pike, Koko, hold your position."

We stopped immediately, me saying, "What's up?"

"We just had two policemen walk by and they're now standing just south of the target entrance."

Policemen? In here? Taskforce intelligence said that rarely happened, and now they were outside *our* target?

Brett came on and said, "I don't think they're real police. I think the Condor team has found the Garmin."

"Why?"

"They're pale, and the uniforms look brand spanking new."

"Can't you tell if they're Chinese?"

"No. They're hiding their eyes behind sunglasses, which is also strange, since it's close to twilight."

Knuckles said, "They're armed. Pike, the police here don't carry firearms. These guys are both sporting Glocks. It's a screwup. They don't know how the police operate."

I peeked around the corner and saw them, two men in brown uniforms, each with a shock of black hair, sunglasses on their faces and pistols on their hips, both facing away from us. They were about thirty feet away, the entrance to the target another forty feet past them down the alley.

I said, "We're out of time. Those guys are the recce for the target. They're about to assault."

"What do you want to do?"

I said, "We're going to close the gap and take them down. As soon as we initiate, you head to the target. You make breach and we'll be right behind you."

Jennifer looked at me like I was crazy. Knuckles said, "I'm not sure if that's a solid plan."

I said, "You want to just assault the place while they're standing there? Or wait on them to clean out the nest and *then* go in?"

I heard nothing on the net, but off the net, Jennifer said, "What if they're real policemen?"

I said, "We won't go lethal. You take the one on the right, I'll take the one on the left."

Knuckles came back, saying, "Pike, this is Knuckles, standing by."

I said, "Roger all. Listen, we need to get in and out as fast as possible, because we're about to make a huge ruckus. We need to beat the real police if we want to get out of here without wearing handcuffs."

To Jennifer I said, "You need to get on him quickly, wrap him up and choke him out. Knuckles said these guys are no joke, so no messing around."

If I positively knew they were the bad guys, I'd have had us both use a knife to end the fight without a fuss, but I didn't know one hundred percent, so we'd have to discriminate here, bringing them to the ground and subduing them. Which sort of sucked.

Jennifer tightened the rucksack on her back, and I did the same, cinching the straps as tight as I could so my kit wouldn't flop all over the place. She nodded at me and, on the net, I said, "Executing now."

We turned the corner and began walking up the alley at a rapid pace, ignoring the odd person staring at us. They were no longer an issue, because everyone was going to be staring fairly soon.

We got within six feet when my target glanced at us. I ignored him, like I was going to walk past, and then he looked like he'd been hit with an electric current, slapping his partner and drawing his pistol. He must have been on the team in Agra, because he recognized me.

Jennifer reacted instantly, closing the distance in a split second. She had one arm around her target's neck before he could get his pistol out, using her other arm to trap his gun hand. She swept his legs out from underneath him, slamming him to the ground on his back, her arm cinched tight, pressing his neck into the crook of her elbow with the side of her head, pushing forward with her feet like she was in a rugby scrum.

My target managed to clear his holster, the weapon swinging around to my face, but he wasn't fast enough. I grabbed the wrist holding the pistol and shoved it skyward, and it discharged, scattering the crowd. My plan now gone to shit, I punched him with a hard right cross, rotated into his body, and flung him over my hip while holding on to his gun hand. He hit the ground and his pistol went off again. I kicked it away and it fired yet again, the bullet smacking the wall next to me. The spall hit my face and I realized it wasn't from his weapon.

Someone else was shooting at us. I hit the ground and looked up the alley, seeing two supposed slum dwellers wearing raggedy clothes with scarves around their heads, both with pistols out, shooting. My target stood up, a little dazed, and I grabbed him, swinging him toward the fire as I drew my pistol. He was hit twice right in the chest, and I could feel the impacts. I fired back, then saw the men rotating, firing away from me. Brett and Knuckles had finally entered the fight.

I saw one of the men in rags go down and dropped the dead weight of my target, swinging to Jennifer's fight. She was still trying to choke out her target, but he was fighting like a banshee. I shouted, "Roll off!" And she did. The man slapped his hand on his holster and I drilled him in the head, flinging it back.

I turned back up the alley to see Brett and Knuckles running flat out to the target door, the other threat eliminated. They stacked on the right, Brett in the lead, Knuckles digging into his knapsack. I said, "Jennifer, on me," and ran to the left side of the door. She stacked behind me, and I said, "Flash-bang."

She dug into my pack and pulled out a banger, showed it to me, and I nodded across at Brett. Knuckles threw his in, Jennifer followed, and the building vibrated from the explosions.

I raised my weapon and entered at the same time as Brett.

CHAPTER 70

Manjit made it to the top of the ladder, finding Sledge next to the lantern, cowering in the corner of the small space.

Sledge said, "What's going on?"

Manjit drew his pistol and said, "I don't know. Sit down and shut up."

The gunfire grew in volume, sounding like fireworks in the alley outside. Manjit shouted, "Kamal! What is happening?"

"The police are fighting with someone. Remain calm. It might not involve us."

The gunfire stopped and Manjit inched to the edge of the CONEX container, seeing Kamal in a crouch down below, hiding behind one of the machines, his own pistol out. He waited a beat, then stood up, peering out the door. Manjit saw two cylindrical objects come through the door, then felt a shock of overpressure, like he'd been slapped in the face, the light and noise throwing him back. He sat up, his ears ringing, and saw Kamal on his hands and knees, bear-crawling back to the machine he'd been hiding behind. He screamed, "Manjit! Kill him! Kill him! Kill him!" and Manjit saw four figures boil into the room. Kamal raised his pistol, his hand unsteady, and the two on the right both fired multiple times. Manjit saw Kamal's body jerk from the rounds and then collapse.

He turned to Sledge, finding him pushing open a section of the roof. He raised his pistol and Sledge dropped the tin, holding his hands out and saying, "No, no, no."

Manjit put his other hand on the pistol and aimed, almost squeezing the trigger. Then stopped. He lowered the weapon and said, "Go."

Sledge scrambled to the section of roof and threw it open with a burst of energy. In seconds, he was through the hole and gone. Manjit turned back to the men in the room, seeing them clearing all the corners. He took aim at one of them and fired, hearing the figure scream and drop to the ground. The other three oriented on his location and began shooting, the rounds causing him to lay flat on top of the CONEX, the bullets smacking all around him.

He heard one say, "Bang that fucker," and saw another cylindrical device hit the back wall and bounce next to him. He put his feet toward it and covered his head with his arms. It went off and rocked his world, punching his body with overpressure, the light blinding him and the noise shutting down his hearing.

He rolled around in agony, then saw a man reach the top of the ladder, his face a mask of molten fury.

* * *

I saw Brett get hit, and the rage flooded through me, wanting to slaughter the man who had done it. I located the shooter on the roof of a CONEX, and said, "Up high, up high." Jennifer went to Brett while Knuckles and I began suppressing the sniper on the container. He disappeared from view, and I said, "Bang that fucker."

I kept a steady stream of rounds, keeping his head down, while Knuckles removed a flash-bang from my backpack. He pulled the pin, tossed it up, and said, "Go."

He started shooting while I ran to a ladder affixed to the container and began climbing. I paused at the top, crouching down below the edge and hugging the wood of the ladder. The flash-bang went off and I clambered up, seeing a scraggly guy with glasses askew, his face dazed. I scrambled to him, kicked his weapon away, then picked him up and threw him over the side.

He hit the ground hard, and I jumped down right next to him, the rage now out of control. I jerked him to his feet, punched him in the skull, and rotated his body until his back was facing me. I wrapped my arms around his neck, but this time I wasn't trying to subdue him. I was going to snap his spine. I applied pressure, my mind's eye seeing nothing but Brett getting hit, the wrath all-consuming, and Jennifer yelled, "Pike! No!"

I looked at her, and she said, "Don't do it," and the anger broke like I'd entered the eye of a hurricane. One second it was destroying everything in its path, and the next, it was calm. She continued, saying, "Brett's okay. He's hit, but he's not dead. Let him go."

And I did, pushing the terrorist to the ground. Knuckles exhaled and said, "The point of this thing was to capture one. What is your deal?"

I said, "I was just going to choke him out." Knuckles pulled out some flex-ties and said, "Yeah, right."

He cinched his hands and said, "We need to get the hell out of here, and I'm not sure we can use the front door after this mess."

I went to the terrorist and said, "Where are the hostages?"

He said, "He's gone. I let him go."

"He? You mean the American?"

He nodded and said, "Yes. I was supposed to kill him, but I didn't."

"Where did he go? Was he in here?"

The terrorist said, "Where you caught me. He left from there."

Knuckles went up the ladder, then leaned over, saying, "There's a hole in the roof. He went across the rooftops."

I looked at Jennifer bandaging up Brett's right bicep and said, "Brett, can you walk?"

"Yeah. I'm no good for a fight, but I can walk."

I said, "Jennifer, help Brett up the ladder." She did, him using his left hand to try to climb. Jennifer got him far enough up until Knuckles could pull him the rest of the way.

I turned to the terrorist and said, "I'm going to cut you free and you're going to climb that ladder." I pointed to the bleeding carcass of his friend lying in the offal of the factory. "We're out of time, so if you try anything, I'll leave you here just like him, understand?"

He nodded, and in short order we were climbing through the hole on the roof one by one. We began walking down the edge of the roof in the direction of the train station, hearing sirens in the distance.

Knuckles said, "So the American was here."

I said, "Yeah, and that dumb-ass is probably going to run straight into the arms of the police response here."

Jennifer said, "That's okay, isn't it? I mean, technically, we *did* rescue him."

I said, "No, it's not okay. As soon as that happens, the Black Cats are going to know he's not in the residence, and they're going to slam that place."

CHAPTER 71

Nadia realized that Jaiden was beginning to deteriorate even as he co-opted the rest of the security staff. He had grown prone to striking her whenever he caught her looking at him, but only when the in-house security wasn't around, and had actually slapped Annaka for the first time earlier in the day. He was losing control even if the other security men couldn't see it.

As the head of Riva Thakkar's protective detail, he'd somehow managed to convince the rank-and-file security guards for the residence that there was some grand conspiracy occurring, and that the government was possibly the enemy. He'd told them that protecting the life of Annaka Thakkar was their prime directive, and that they'd made a gorgeous salary for years, but now they were going to have to earn it.

She had to admit, he was good. An imposing presence with impeccable credentials, he commanded any room he was in, the scar tracing a path through his beard evidence that he was willing to fight. With no contacts to the outside world, and Jaiden having been their direct commander for years, the guards took what he said at face value, eager to please him.

While Jaiden originally had just the two red-suited guards from the pre-wedding celebration, Nadia and Annaka now had to contend with five in the room, and she'd heard him telling eight more to position themselves on the rooftop. She knew why.

Riva had built a helicopter pad on the roof big enough for three helicopters, but the Mumbai government had forbidden him from using it over an esoteric debate about noise, or air clearance, or some other excuse, forcing him to land his chopper a quarter mile away. Whatever the reasoning had been, if a helicopter came to the roof, it wasn't Riva coming home. It was the enemy—and the security men bought it.

Nadia was beginning to see the outlines of Jaiden's plan. She'd only had rudimentary explosives training in the RAW, but even she could see that they had placed the charges on support members throughout the den—and probably farther inward, toward the elevators. Jaiden was going to cause an enormous fight, which would play into the world press, and then he was going to detonate the explosives in this room, hoping to bring down the top of the building, killing as many government men as possible—along with Nadia and Annaka.

Jaiden was pacing around the space shouting orders, the wireless detonator in his left hand, his men stashing ammo caches at strategic points and rearranging the statues to build cover locations inside the room, having no idea he planned on killing them as well as everyone else. The only question she had was whether he had the guts to be a martyr, or whether he had some other escape plan.

The television flipped to a breaking news story, and he went to it, his jaw dropping open. She couldn't hear the words, but she saw a picture of the American in the hands of police officials, flashing lights and rushing men behind him.

So he's rescued. How did that happen?

Jaiden turned from the television and began barking more orders, waving his hands about. He stomped over to Annaka and her and said,

406 / BRAD TAYLOR

"The American is free, which is good news for you. It means you're much more valuable to me now."

Nadia said, "What do you intend to do with us? Did they meet your demands to set him free?"

"No, they haven't done anything I've asked for yet. Somehow he escaped captivity and ran to the police."

His cell phone rang and he looked at the screen, then answered, saying, "Manjit, what the hell is going on?"

He listened for a few seconds, then said, "What about Kamal?"

He nodded his head and said, "Are you sure he's dead? You saw his body?"

He sagged in resignation and said, "So I'm in charge now. Yes, you can come here, but understand, once you're in, you're in for the end-game."

He listened again, then said, "No, nobody will stop you from trying to enter. The government hasn't released anything to the press. How long until you arrive?"

He ended with, "Call when you're at the gate."

He hung up and held out the detonator in his hand, saying, "It's coming to a close. You two won't have to worry much longer."

Nadia saw the detonator and thought, *Get that first. No matter what happens, get that first.*

* * *

Veep saw the JSOC guys go to their kit locker, all three of them throwing on body armor and jamming magazines in pouches. He hollered, "Hey, what's going on?"

They continued wrapping themselves in the equipment of the

modern-day Samurai, with one saying, "Don't really know, but these guys are getting ready for war, so we figured we'd better do the same."

"Don't you have a liaison telling you what's happening?"

"Yeah, but he's also a team leader. He's a little busy, and honestly, I'm not sure he's not trying to leave us behind. He's been told to placate the Americans, but he's made it plain that he doesn't agree with us being on the assault. We figured we'd kit up in case he said something like 'Leaving in two minutes . . . oh, sorry, forgot to tell you. Guess you guys need to stay here.'"

They left the room and Veep thought about tracking down Kerry Bostwick. He hadn't seen the man in over two hours. Something was happening, and he knew Pike would want the latest intel before he hit the Garmin watch location.

He stood up and his phone rang. He saw it was Pike and thought, *Shit. Here comes an ass chewing.*

He answered, saying, "How'd the recce go? Are you going to hit that place?"

"We already did, and we need some damage control. Get Kerry Bostwick."

"You did what?"

"Veep, I don't have time for chitchat. Get me Kerry, now."

"Stand by. We'll call back via video."

He ran out of the room, went down the hallway to the double doors of the Black Cat tactical operations center. A guard out front stopped him, and he said, "I need the American, Kerry Bostwick. He has an important call."

The man sent a runner, who came back in twenty seconds, saying, "He's busy right now. He said come back in twenty minutes."

Veep said, "Tell him Pike went apeshit."

The man left again, and twenty seconds later had Kerry Bostwick in tow. Kerry said, "What's going on?"

Veep started walking, saying, "I don't know. Pike did the hit on the Garmin watch and said he needs backup. He's waiting on a video call."

Kerry fell in next to him, saying, "I *told* that asshole not to go ape-shit."

They entered the room the Black Cats had started calling the "American Stable" and Veep turned on the laptop, dialing a number. While waiting for it to connect, he said, "The JSOC boys were just in here kitting up. What's going on?"

"I don't know. That's what I was trying to find out when you pulled me. Something big has happened, but I can't get anyone to talk to me. It's like they don't want me to know because I'll disagree."

The screen cleared and they saw Brett Thorpe in the passenger seat of a car. He said, "Pike's driving. You guys got me in the green?" Meaning encrypted.

Veep said, "Yeah, you're in the green. What's up?"

From off-screen, Pike said, "We hit the Garmin watch place but had a little trouble. We met the Chinese on the way in and had to eliminate them. It was a gunfight and it's generated a little interest."

"How much interest?"

"A *lot* of interest. Look, we have one of the terrorists in custody, but we have a problem."

"What do you need from me? A safe house?"

"No, no. What I need is the intelligence you have on Riva Thak-kar's residence. I need to know where the hostages are, what the outside security is like, where the elevators are located, I need everything."

"Why?"

"Because they were holding Sledge, and—"

"Wait, you rescued Sledge? You have him?"

Veep saw Brett grimace at the interruption. He said, "No, we don't. Can you let Pike finish?"

Kerry pursed his lips and said, "Continue."

Off-screen again, Pike said, "One of the terrorists was supposed to kill him, but he couldn't go through with it. He let Sledge escape. Sledge went out on the roof and is now on the run. If he ends up in police hands the Black Cats are going to hear about it, and they're going to assault the residence with no hesitation about an American hostage. They'll burn it down."

"Pike, if what you're saying is true, there's nothing I can do to stop it."

Veep heard the door open and saw the JSOC assaulters come back in, taking off their kit and stowing it in a locker. He said, "False alarm?"

The team leader said, "Nope. Well, false for us, but they're going in."

Pike said, "What was that? What did he say?"

Kerry turned away from the computer and said, "What are you talking about?"

The team leader said, "They found Sledge. He ran into a police roadblock outside the Dharavi slum screaming about being kidnapped. He's safe, and U.S. interests no longer apply. They don't need us anymore, which is why they didn't say anything about us joining them."

Kerry said, "When are they going in? How long?"

"I'd say about an hour, give or take."

Pike said, "Kerry, get me that intel, right now."

Veep started working the computer, sending files, and Kerry said, "It's coming now, but why?"

"I'm going to hit that place first, before they go in and kill everyone."

"Pike, that's crazy. The snipers have reported upwards of twenty to thirty security men."

"They won't matter. Just get me the intelligence."

"How are you going to get in? You have a helicopter I don't know about?"

"I'm getting in the same way they did. I'm going to become a Trojan horse."

CHAPTER 72

Driving our vehicle, I had Brett in the passenger seat download all the data on Riva Thakkar's residence. Knuckles was behind the wheel of the follow vehicle, getting the same download, with Jennifer guarding the terrorist and working the tablet.

Brett started swiping through the data, saying, "Pike, this place is huge. Nine elevators, twenty-seven floors, bedrooms out the ass. No way are we going to be able to clear it all."

"We don't have to. Find the sniper reports. Nadia and Thakkar's daughter are on a specific floor. That's where we're going."

He continued flipping through the reports and diagrams, then stopped, saying, "Our analysts think Nadia was right, and Jaiden's rigged the place with explosives. This just gets better and better."

I said, "What do you care? You're not going in. You're the exfil."

He chuckled and said, "Nothing like getting shot to save my ass. What are you going to do about the possible IEDs?"

"I'm thinking of sending Jennifer up the outside to the balcony. Let her get eyes on and see what's what. Do you think she can do it?"

He flipped through various documents until he had a three-dimensional image of the outside of the residence. He said, "Yeah, I think she can. This structure is built like a kid's LEGO set."

He turned the picture to me and I saw a tall skyscraper, but, outside of the lower six floors, most of it was some artsy-fartsy construct, with various ledges, balconies, and outside fixtures all the way up. It did look like something a kid built with a LEGO set.

I said, "What's that on the lower six floor walls?"

"Those floors are apparently a parking garage for his car collection."

"Great, so we won't have to clear that. What I meant was what's on the outside walls? Can Jennifer get up that?"

He zoomed in and said, "Believe it or not, it's foliage. The lower six floors have threaded vines all the way up."

Perfect. Well, maybe not for Jennifer.

Brett said, "What was that about a Trojan horse?"

"Well, we sure as shit can't fight our way in. Not with those odds. I'm going to put Knuckles and me in the back of the Rover and have Manjit call Jaiden, giving him a song and dance about how the Chinese found them and he escaped. When they let us in, I'm going to start slaying."

"The hostages are on the twenty-second floor. You think you and Knuckles can fight your way up twenty-two floors?"

"No. I think we can fight our way to an elevator, then ride up twenty-two floors."

"You don't think you'll be stopped by the police on the way in? At a checkpoint or something?"

"No. Veep says this entire residence thing is close hold. The Black Cat spotters might report us arriving, but they won't stop us."

We were driving down the shore, a smattering of beaches to our right, and I looked at our GPS, seeing we were about ten minutes away from the famous Altamount Billionaires' Row. The road left the shore, cutting into the peninsula, and I pulled into a parking lot full of rickshaws, Knuckles right behind me.

I had Brett set the tablet on the hood and they gathered around. I told them my assault plan, and they were suitably unimpressed. Jennifer said, "What if we get into the garage with your Trojan horse and we find thirty security men with their guns aimed at us?"

I said, "Then Knuckles and I will have to go out in a blaze of glory, but that's not going to happen. They'll have security on the gate that we'll pass through, and security up on the roof looking for helicopters, with more security on the floor with the hostages, but they aren't going to swarm the parking garage just because Manjit calls Jaiden. At most, there will be four or five guns—hopefully with Jaiden himself—and they'll relax when they see it's only Manjit."

She missed the "Knuckles and I" part of the statement. She said, "That's a big wish instead of a plan, and it's going to be hard for all three of us to get out of that vehicle synchronized."

I said, "Two. Two of us can do it. Just Knuckles and me."

She gave me a puzzled look, and I said, "Taskforce intelligence thinks they've wired the living space the hostages are in with explosives. We need to know if that's true before we assault. If it is, we need someone focused on that while we're killing bad guys."

She said, "I don't understand. While you're assaulting, you want me to run past you to see if there are IEDs all over the room?"

"No, I mean *before* we assault."

"How?"

I flipped to a three-dimensional picture of the residence and pointed at the large balcony jutting out over the Mumbai skyline on the twenty-second floor. "This is where the hostages are. I need you to take a look from the balcony."

I rotated the picture until the northeast corner was facing us and said, "The snipers have a view of the building exterior from this angle."

I rotated it the other way, until the southeast corner was showing, and said, "But they can't see anybody going up this side. The vehicle entrance is also covered by a sniper team, but you won't have to worry about them. That's our problem."

It took a minute for that to settle, and then she understood. Her eyes flew open and she said, "Pike, no way. I can't climb up twenty-two stories. That's not possible."

I said, "Wait a minute, hang on, I'm not talking about scaling plate glass. Take a look at the picture. This thing is like a Lincoln Log climbing wall. Once you're past the first six floors, it has approaches that are almost walking. You just need to be sure you're out of view of the Black Cat snipers."

She said, "Pike, forget about the snipers, six floors is a fucking lot."

Jennifer never cursed unless she was under extreme duress, so I knew she was really uncomfortable with what I was asking. I wasn't sure if it was the risk of the climb, or the weight of the mission I was placing on her shoulders.

I said again, "Take a look at the picture. They laced the first six floors with greenery. It's like they built a ladder to the first residential section. From there, it's an easy climb. Yeah, it's high, but it's easy."

She locked eyes with me, and I could see the hesitation. I said, "Just look at it. Study the pictures. If you can't do it, you can't do it, but at least look."

She took the tablet with the pictures and I went back to Knuckles and Brett, studying the street entrance of the compound on his tablet. I said, "There are guard towers on the wall surrounding the place, but there's an alley that goes up the north side of the compound. It's open to the public. Brett, if Jennifer agrees, you'll take the sedan and drop her there, then position yourself where you can see activity coming from the ground."

He nodded, and I said, "Knuckles, we'll take the Range Rover.

We'll wait for Jennifer's call, then go in right through the front gate. They'll obviously have cameras on the vehicle when Manjit makes the call, so that should help our cover. Once we're past that security gate, we'll be inside the garage."

Knuckles said, "What if Manjit does something crazy once we're in, while we're still hiding in the back like a couple of kids sneaking into a concert?"

"He won't. I'll make sure he knows his life is on the line if he does."

Jennifer came back to the vehicle. We all waited expectantly, and she said, "Can I speak to you a second?"

I said, "Sure," following her away from the vehicle. I thought she wanted to tell me in private she couldn't make the climb, but that wasn't it at all.

"I don't think you're on an even keel for this one."

"What? What are you talking about?"

"You were going to kill that guy Manjit in the slum. I know it, and you know it. You lose your judgment when the beast is out running amok, and he's out tonight. I need to know you're not letting your bloodlust overwhelm your critical thinking here."

Questioning my leadership abilities was a sure way to set me off, but I knew she was at least partially right, but not in the way she thought. I understood what had happened in the slum, and it embarrassed me. I also realized—in that moment—that I didn't need to succumb to it. Jennifer had broken the rage, and I could do the same, internally. I just needed to learn how, and this assault might show me that. It wasn't bloodlust that was driving me toward the residence, it was the opposite.

I said, "Jennifer, I stopped when you told me to. I didn't kill him. I can control the beast."

"You stopped *because* I told you to, but I'm not going to be with you, and Knuckles doesn't understand the beast."

"I can control it. I have to, because this isn't about me. It's about Nadia and Annaka. I can't allow anything to cause me to lose focus on that, and I won't. We're all they have at this point."

She locked eyes with me, judging whether I was speaking the truth or just trying to placate her. She said, "This plan isn't what I would call a well-oiled machine. It's verging on insane. The team will follow you into hell if you order them to, but maybe you should ask this time."

I had won the battle about my psyche, but she was right about the mission. I said, "Okay, I'll ask, but I'll start with you, because if you can't get to the balcony, it's all off anyway."

She pursed her lips, considering what I'd said, still judging me. Finally, she said, "I can climb it."

"You sure?"

She said, "No, but it'll be safer than what you idiots are planning."

I smiled and walked back to the vehicle, Brett and Knuckles waiting expectantly. I said, "Jennifer's good to go, but she's informed me that my plan is a little loonier than normal."

I looked each of them in the eye and said, "So if you have any hesitation—if you think we should leave this to the Black Cats—say so now."

Brett said, "I'm just an infil platform. All I'm doing is dropping off Jennifer and then parking for early warning. Not my call."

I turned to Knuckles, and as expected, he said, "This isn't any stupider than sliding three stories down a rope that was probably last used in the sixteenth century. If you're having second thoughts, just say so. I'm not leaving Nadia's fate to the Black Cats. I'll take Manjit and go by myself if you're that concerned."

I turned to Jennifer and said, "Apparently, it's not that stupid a plan after all. After hearing they want to continue, do you stlll think you can climb?"

She said, "Yeah, I can climb it."

"Perfect." I looked at my watch, saying, "We've got about an hour before the Black Cats hit the place, forty minutes worst case. Brett, you and Jennifer in our car. Knuckles and I will take the Rover."

I turned off the tablet, then said, "I know this sounds like a dumb-ass plan, but it's all that's standing between Nadia's and Annaka's death."

Brett said, "That's it? That's your inspirational war speech? Man, I feel pumped."

I shook my head and said, "Get Manjit. It's time for him to make a call."

CHAPTER 73

Jennifer rolled over the railing on the balcony of the lowest residential level and lay on her back, breathing hard. She felt lucky the lights were out in the attached room, letting her rest in the darkness, because she didn't know if she would have had the strength to climb parallel to a different balcony.

The climb up the foliage of the lower six floors hadn't been technically hard, but the work had been physically demanding. She'd basically had to muscle her way up all six stories, testing each new handhold in the foliage before trusting her weight with it while holding that very same weight with her other hand and a meager toehold. Her lack of equipment hadn't helped.

There hadn't been time to return to the Rock Star bird to change clothes or retrieve any safety assistance, so she was free climbing in the clothes she'd been wearing in the slum. She'd taken off her loose cotton shirt and tied it around her waist, leaving her with a sports bra, and her Solomon hikers were lashed together with the laces draped around her neck. She'd decided the soles were too thick for adequate purchase, preferring her bare feet for the work. For weapons, she'd opted only for a Staccato pistol holstered in the small of her back, leaving her rifle for Pike to bring up.

She keyed her radio and said, "Pike, Pike, I'm through the parking garage. At the first residential level."

She heard, "Atta girl! Hey, not to bring any pressure, but that took over twenty minutes. You're going to have to do the next sixteen floors faster than that."

She sat up, feeling the hum of fatigue in her hands and shoulders. She said, "I think I've found a way to make that timeline, but I can't promise anything if I'm wrong."

He said, "Just do your best. If you can't get up to the veranda and we have to assault without you, break into the building at whatever level you're on and use the stairs to meet us. We'll wing it."

This plan is getting better and better.

She went to the edge of the balcony and looked up the side of the building, spotting the large veranda jutting out into the night sixteen stories up. She studied the walls and found the potential climbing route she'd seen earlier on the tablet, a zigzag of concrete going back and forth down the side of the building, making a design that could only be perceived from the ground. On the tablet it had looked about an inch thick and solely for aesthetic purposes, but she suspected it was more. The design extended down to the balcony of the first residential level—the one she was on—and she was relieved to see it was at least a foot in width.

Rising at about a fifty-degree angle, it would allow her legs to do the work, with the only tricky part being climbing over to the top when the concrete conducted a switchback in the other direction.

She crossed the balcony rail and put her left foot on the ledge, the concrete cool to the touch. She followed with her right, then let go of the railing, crouching down and grabbing the edge with her right hand, her left flat against the glass of the building.

She hesitantly scooted forward, then began gaining confidence. In short order she was scrambling up the side of the building like one of the baboons she'd seen in Delhi. She reached the first switchback and stood up, pressing her hands against the higher shelf. She glanced below and immediately focused back on the shelf, the earth so far away it was dizzying.

She cinched her hands on the edge of the higher shelf and shinnied herself up, sliding her legs over like she was mounting a gymnastics beam. She took a breath, calming herself, and pulled her knees up underneath her, then began scampering again.

She made it to Thakkar's residential rooms on the twenty-first floor in fourteen minutes, the large veranda stretching out one floor above her. Unfortunately, she was at the end of her concrete highway, the shelf's final turn going to ninety degrees and running under the large plate glass windows of a bedroom.

She looked up again, seeing the veranda tantalizingly close, but far enough away that it might as well have been on the moon.

She studied the windows, seeing that the metal ribs holding panes in place were a little farther apart than a large doorway, maybe four feet total. She stood up on the shelf and put her hands out until her palms rested on the metal, pressing against the ribs. They held. She placed her bare feet against the metal and tested the ribs with her full weight, hanging in space like a giant spider in a web.

She slid her hands up, then her feet, moving inches at a time, chimneying her way to the top. She came level to the lower shelf of the veranda and saw she was going to have to make a dynamic move to reach it, leaving the safety of the window to launch herself in the air. If she missed, it was a long way to the ground.

She grasped the outside rib with her right hand and turned her body until her left foot was straight up and down on the left rib. She bent her leg like she was cocking a spring, then pushed off with all her might, sailing through the air and catching the floor of the veranda.

The momentum swung her body underneath, but she held on. When she swung back, she chinned herself up until she was at waist level. She grabbed the top of the glass railing with her right hand, then her left, and pulled herself over.

She scuttled to the side to get out of the light spilling onto the veranda from the cathedral-like den. She crept forward, seeing Nadia and Annaka sitting on a couch, several security men in black uniforms in the room. On the far side she saw Jaiden talking to another man, this one in a red uniform.

She keyed her radio and said, "Pike, I'm up. I have both hostages in sight. Approximately five security."

Pike said, "Holy shit, Koko, you made it! That's a record."

"You didn't think I could?"

"Well, let's just say I thought it was iffy. So it *is* the twenty-second floor. What about the suspected IEDs?"

She scanned the room, going from left to right, but saw nothing. She started back the other way and spotted something black taped to a pillar, a cord coming out of it. She followed the cord to another fixture, this one also on a pillar. She kept tracing, finding one black blob after another, ending up at a final package near a doorway, this one having a square top. She saw it had some sort of box affixed to it, a blinking red light flashing intermittently and what looked like a small spiral antenna sprouting from the center.

She said, "Pike, Nadia *was* trying to warn us. The room's rigged to blow, but I don't think the IEDs are anti-personnel. They look like they're positioned on support structures, like they want to drop the roof."

"How are they initiated? Trip wires?"

"No. It looks like it's command detonated. The last in the daisy chain has an antenna."

"Figure out who's got the detonator. We're out of time."

"How the hell am I going to do that?"

"I don't know, but we're coming in now. I can't wait anymore."

CHAPTER 74

N adia saw the house security men starting to fidget nervously, pacing about with their weapons, but didn't understand why. She assumed they were taking their cues from Jaiden, who was becoming more agitated by the minute. The American's escape had seemed to break something within him, as if it had taken a leg out of whatever he had planned.

He began speaking into his radio, waving his hands in the air while he walked in a circle. She couldn't completely hear what he was saying, but it had something to do with the defenses on the roof. He turned to one of the red-uniformed men who had been with them since the kidnapping and handed him the detonator, pointing at the ceiling with his hand.

He spun on his heel to leave the room, and his cell phone rang. He put it to his ear and talked for a good three minutes, then went to a security monitor on the wall. She stared at it and saw a vehicle outside the gate. He said something on the phone, and Nadia saw a hand come out of the driver-side window.

Satisfied of the identity of the vehicle, he clicked his radio, talking to the guards at the gate. Nadia saw the gate begin to slide open, wondering who was joining them.

Jaiden gave instructions to the other red suit, and the man left in the elevator. Jaiden went to the stairs leading up to the mezzanine, presumably checking on whatever the people on the roof had told him, leaving the single red uniform holding the detonator.

Nadia felt the adrenaline rise, knowing this might be her only chance. If she attacked the man and got the detonator, she could use it as a threat to get the black-uniformed guards to drop their weapons. She was sure they wouldn't shoot her immediately, because they assumed they were there to protect her.

Maybe she could talk some sense into them. Show them that Jaiden was evil and planned on having them killed. She casually glanced around the room, trying to pinpoint the location of each of the house security. She counted four and knew she was missing one. She turned around, looking behind her, and felt a shock almost as bad as when she'd been kidnapped.

Jennifer Cahill was on the balcony outside, hiding just out of the light and holding her hand forward, beckoning Nadia to come to the balcony with a finger. She disappeared back into the shadow, and Nadia wondered if she was hallucinating. She turned around and whispered to Annaka, "I'm going to the balcony. Stay here. Do not look at me, and do not follow."

"What?"

She stood up, hissing, "Do as I say."

The red-uniformed guard saw the movement and said, "What do you want? You've already had dinner."

Nadia knew she had to get this underling to agree before Jaiden came back. If that happened, she'd never be allowed to leave.

"I just wanted some air on the balcony. Is that okay? I haven't been outside in two days."

The guard considered, and she said, "Where am I going to go? Jump down twenty-two stories?"

The guard nodded, saying, "Two minutes. No more."

Nadia said, "Thank you," and hurried to the door. She slid open the glass and stepped outside, moving past Jennifer to the far rail. She stared out at the Mumbai skyline for a moment, then went to the right, circling around the hanging plants and statues until she was at the railing next to Jennifer. She glanced back at the room and saw the red-uniformed guard next to the couch, watching her every move.

She kept her face forward but said, "How on earth did you get here?"

Jennifer said, "I climbed up. We don't have a lot of time. Do you know who's holding the detonator for the explosives?"

"Yes. It's the man in the red uniform, but he'll only have it until Jaiden comes back. I don't know how long that will be."

"Okay, okay, listen, Pike is on the way. When he begins his assault, my mission is to eliminate whoever is holding that thing. I'll do the killing, but you could help with a distraction."

The words were a little overwhelming. Nadia said, "Pike's coming? Is he climbing too? How will he get in?"

"He has a plan, but we have very little time. Your government is gearing up to hit this building with overwhelming force, and when they do, they aren't going to care about dead hostages after the smoke clears."

Nadia said, "Let me guess: Riva Thakkar would rather protect his pride than his daughter."

Jennifer said, "Yeah, that's about it," then she touched her ear, saying, "Roger all. I have the detonator target. Clear to breach."

She came back to Nadia and said, "It's showtime. Get back inside, but leave the door open."

CHAPTER 75

I told Jennifer we were at breach and heard the most beautiful words on earth. I leaned into Knuckles under a blanket in the trunk of the Rover and said, "Jenn's got the detonator target. He'll be out of play."

Knuckles exhaled and said, "Man, we really owe her a few cases of beer. Now let's just hope this fucker doesn't say something to give us away on the phone."

I said, "That won't happen. He thinks I speak Hindi."

Knuckles rolled his head to me, both of us crammed in the back of the Rover, and said, "You telling him 'no funny stuff . . . I speak Hindi' while talking in English isn't really giving me confidence."

We felt the car slow, heard Manjit saying something to a guard, then heard him talking on the phone. He passed the phone to the guard, and we heard more talking, none of which we could understand. I was starting to grow a little tense until the groaning of the giant metal gate opening split the air. I nudged Knuckles and whispered, "Oh ye of little faith."

I felt the Range Rover start rolling forward and waited, the adrenaline beginning to course through my body like an electric current.

Knuckles said, "It's going to be a little embarrassing if we get inside, then they open the rear hatch with thirty guns pointed at us."

"Not going to happen. If it does, I'll have Jennifer come rescue us."

He said, "Jesus, after what you made her do, she'll just let us get killed."

We felt the vehicle stop, then heard a sliding door close. We were in the garage. Manjit said something in Hindi, but I didn't hear his door open. Someone answered back through an open window, and Manjit started arguing with him.

What the hell?

I wanted to separate Manjit from any suspicion of treachery, so I'd given him instructions to tell Jaiden that the Chinese had found them and tried to kill everyone, knowing that the bodies they'd found would be on the news, so it was plausible. His cover story was that he was the only one who'd escaped alive. Which was sort of true.

Manjit seemed to be a bit of a sensitive sort, more a bespectacled student than someone who would enjoy cutting a head off solely for the thrill, like I'd seen with Al Qaida, Hamas, or ISIS. I believed he'd been wrapped up in something that had gone out of his control—much like what had happened to the Chinese—and I had tried to use that against him. I'd told him what the government had planned for Thakkar's residence, and that everyone inside—Hindu, Sikh, and Muslim—was going to be slaughtered because of his actions, so helping us wasn't going against his brethren but alleviating unnecessary bloodshed.

That was the carrot. For the stick I'd told him he would be the first one I shot if he gave away that we were in the vehicle.

I hoped I'd at least convinced him enough to waver on screwing us over, but maybe I'd gone too far, since arguing with whomever was outside this vehicle wasn't what I wanted.

After a few seconds of raised voices the argument stopped, and I heard the car door open. I said, "Remember, we need Manjit and one security guy alive."

When it shut, I reached over and pulled the latch opening the tail-gate. It popped about an inch and I said, "Ready?"

"Yeah. Do it."

I pushed it up and rolled out, bringing my Staccato to eye level and moving to the driver's side, Knuckles right behind me. I saw Manjit talking to a man in a red uniform, two others with black uniforms behind him, all of them holding rifles. None of them Jaiden.

I really didn't want to start blasting bullets this early in the assault, alerting anyone who could hear the gunshots, so I went into rapid domination mode, shouting, "Down, down! Everyone get on your belly!"

One of the guards started to raise his weapon, but Knuckles reached him before he could aim. Knuckles slapped the barrel down and pistol-whipped him in the head, dropping him to the concrete. I trained my weapon on the others and said, "Get the fuck down." They immediately complied.

I kept my pistol on them while Knuckles stripped them of their weapons and flex-tied their wrists and ankles, leaving Redcoat and Manjit free. I said, "Go get our long guns."

He returned to the vehicle and my radio came alive: "Pike, Pike, this is Blood. I've got movement down the street. Police cars with sirens and some type of armored personnel carrier coming your way."

I shouted, "Knuckles, it's on. We have to move."

He tossed me a SIG Sauer MCX chambered in 300 Blackout, and I holstered the Staccato, putting the AR sling around my neck. He waited until Jennifer's weapon was over my back and then tossed me another. I checked to make sure a round was in the chamber, flipped open the folded buttstock, then said, "Get them up."

Knuckles did so. I went to Redcoat and said, "Take us to the elevator that leads to Jaiden."

He sneered at me, and I felt the beast stir. I immediately tamped down the emotion, shoving it back into its cave—and it worked. Satisfied, I punched Redcoat in the gut, leaving him bending over and hacking, gasping for air. I put my barrel in his ear and said, "You want to try again?"

He nodded and pointed. I felt my cell phone vibrate in my pocket and said, "Knuckles, take 'em to the elevator."

He started marching them at a fast walk, me falling in behind with the cell to my ear. I heard Veep say, "Pike, the Black Cats have launched. Don't go for the Trojan horse. They're on the way, and you'll get annihilated in the crossfire."

I said, "Too late for that. We're inside. What's the ETA?"

"Maybe ten minutes. Maybe less."

"Do we have any radio contact with them?"

"I don't know. Maybe, why?"

"Tell them the twenty-second floor is wired to blow and they have some Americans on the inside."

"I'll try, Pike, but I'd suggest just getting out."

"Can't. They're doing a ground assault too. We can't get out now."

He started to reply and I said, "Get someone to tell them what I told you," and hung up. The elevator door opened and Knuckles said, "Good news?"

"Only if you're a Black Cat."

The doors closed and I poked Manjit in the back, saying, "Just walk out like you expect to be here. Understand?"

He nodded, and Knuckles punched the twenty-second floor. I called Jennifer on the net and said, "We're on the way. Get ready to execute. Black Cats are about to land, so we need to eliminate the explosive threat and secure the hostages."

All I heard was a short, "Roger all. Standing by."

We started going up, piped-in Muzak floating down around us. It was surreal. I said, "Hey, have you ever seen *The Matrix*?"

Knuckles smiled and said, "I was thinking the same thing. The courthouse scene?"

"Yep. When these doors open, it's going to be just like that."

CHAPTER 76

J ennifer heard Pike's call and scooted closer to the door. She could see the elevator at the back of the sunken den, at the rear of its own anteroom. She waited for it to open, knowing the blood that was coming when it did. She heard the distinct whopping of helicopter blades splitting the air, then felt a boom that shook the building. Raging gunfire split the air above her on the roof of the building, sounding like a fireworks display that had gone awry.

The Black Cats.

She saw the men in the room stiffen, their weapons raised for an enemy that hadn't appeared, the men swinging their barrels left and right. The man with the detonator started shouting orders, and the elevator door opened. She saw another red-uniformed guard step out, then the terrorist from the slum.

Detonator Man screamed something, and his men opened up. Both of the men exiting the elevator were cut down by the jittery black-clad guards, their weapons firing on full automatic even after the bodies had fallen. Pike and Knuckles came out right behind them, weapons up and firing, ripping rounds into the men shooting at the elevator. She ran to the open sliding-glass door and raised her pistol, seeing the man with the detonator throw a hand grenade toward the elevator and take off running.

She took a knee and started shooting. She got off one shot before one of the other guards turned to her, forcing her to defend herself instead of killing the man with the detonator. She put two rounds into him and the grenade went off, shattering the elevator.

She looked for another target and saw Nadia leap up, giving chase to Detonator Man. He reached the stairwell leading to the mezzanine with Nadia right behind him. Jennifer gave chase, passing Annaka and shouting, "Get on the balcony, get on the balcony!"

Annaka started to run and Jennifer raced to the stairwell, taking the steps two at a time to the mezzanine level. She reached the top and saw Nadia fighting the man for the detonator, both of them rolling on the ground, the man's rifle flopping around between them.

She sprinted to the fight, putting her pistol an inch from the man's head. He screamed and she pulled the trigger, blowing out the back of his skull, the bullet spraying the wall with brain matter and blood.

Nadia rolled off him, the detonator in her hands. She leaned against the wall and said, "That was close."

Jennifer said, "No time for relaxing. We have about two minutes to live. We need to find Annaka and get somewhere safe."

CHAPTER 77

The elevator doors opened and I pushed out Redcoat and Manjit, hoping they'd be recognized and cause everyone to relax. Instead, I heard a raging firefight happening a few floors above us, sounding like an unruly guest was pounding drums in a hotel room. I raised my weapon, and all of a sudden the interior of the elevator began to echo like someone was throwing rocks against the metal, bullets flying into it on full automatic.

I saw both Redcoat and Manjit shredded right in front of my eyes and hit the floor, Knuckles right next to me. There was a lull in the fire, the guards realizing they'd killed their own, and we started returning fire before they could recover.

I hit one, heard Knuckles on my right shooting, then I saw something floating in the air. It clanged off the back of the elevator and I shouted, "Grenade!"

We both dove out, rolling left and right, using the wall as cover, and the grenade went off, destroying the elevator.

My first thought was, *Need another exfil plan,* but it was banished a moment later by fire coming at us from two directions, the room and a stairwell leading to a balcony on my left.

I started suppressing the stairwell while Knuckles dealt with the few remaining guards in the room. He shouted, "Moving!" and I covered him. He took up a position in the sunken den and began firing at the stairwell, the men now retreating up it, which I thought was a good thing until I saw them fanning out on the mezzanine that looked down into the den.

Shit. That was the worst. They'd line up and start shooting us like fish in a barrel. I ran to Knuckles' position, calling on the radio, "Koko, Koko, what's your status? Where are the hostages?"

She said, "I'm up one level. We've got the detonator, I'm with Nadia. Annaka is on the balcony outside."

The rounds started coming in and I rolled behind a pillar, Knuckles doing the same, both of us trying to squeeze behind a space that was too small.

I said, "Stay up there. Get to the mezzanine overlooking the den and start suppressing the guys shooting at us. We're pinned down."

Bullets were pinging off the marble and I tried to scootch farther in, hitting something with my hip. I looked down and saw a package of explosives taped to the pillar.

Jesus Christ. If they hit that we're all going to die.

I said, "Koko, Koko, need some suppression."

She said, "I'm here, but I've only got a pistol. I'm shooting but they don't even seem to know."

I realized her long gun was still on my back. I said, "Are you fucking hitting anything?"

"Pike, it's a seventy-meter shot."

Knuckles said, "Fuck this shit. I'm moving."

He rolled out and took off running to the balcony. The shooting shifted from me to his moving figure, and I rotated around. I started squeezing the trigger like I was at a carnival midway shooting at rotating ducks, hitting man after man until someone recognized I was a threat.

I saw Jaiden for the first time, standing one row back and screaming. He looked behind him, then at the stairs, and I realized that the Black Cats were coming down, but I was preventing him from fleeing.

Knuckles took a knee outside on the veranda and started suppressing the mezzanine, shouting, "Move!"

I ran to him, threading the needle of fire and making it outside without getting hit. I took a knee next to him and he said, "I found Annaka."

I saw her behind him cowering in fear. I said, "Don't worry, we're going to get you out of here."

She didn't look like she believed it.

Knuckles said, "How the fuck are we going to do that? The Black Cats are clearing each floor, and from the gunfire, they're one floor above us. It sounds like their clearing technique involves hand grenades and plenty of firepower. They aren't discriminating."

I looked into the den, seeing the explosives still daisy chained together, and said, "If they do that down here, they're going to bring the entire floor down."

Knuckles said, "We need to get down, now."

I called Brett, saying, "Blood, Blood, what is the ground force doing?"

"About a platoon went in. I assume they're clearing from the bottom to the top."

So trying to get to the bottom using stairs isn't going to work. I called Veep on my cell and said, "Did you get the Black Cats? Can you tell them I have the hostages? Tell them to back off?"

"We got through, but I don't know what good it will do. They aren't that good at flexing. They have their plan, and they're executing."

I hung up and said, "I guess our best bet is to stay out here on the balcony."

Knuckles said, "If they hit those explosives with a grenade, it won't matter. We're all going down."

I muttered, "What I wouldn't give for a good holocaust cloak."

Knuckles chuckled at the *Princess Bride* reference and said, "I'd rather have an armored room at this point."

The shoot-out on the mezzanine was growing more intense, Jaiden's men now firing at oncoming Black Cats, grenades going off and men screaming.

Annaka said, "I have an armored room. A safe room."

I looked at her in amazement and said, "Where? Where is it?"

"One level up, down a hallway from the mezzanine."

Deflated, I said, "Where everyone's shooting?"

"No. The other side."

I saw Jaiden crawl over the mezzanine railing and hang, dropping to the floor. He hit awkwardly and began limping to the elevator. He saw it and just stood for a moment, shocked. He turned to the left and hobbled out of sight.

I called Jennifer, saying, "Koko, Koko, you still on the second-floor mezzanine off the den?"

"Yeah, but we backed off down a hallway. What's the plan?"

"We're coming to you. Hold what you have."

I turned to Knuckles and said, "Put her between us."

He did, and I said to Jennifer, "Koko, we're coming up your stairwell. Don't shoot us."

"Roger all. Standing by."

I turned to Annaka and said, "Get between us and put your hand on my shoulder."

She did and I said to Knuckles, "Ready?"

"Yeah."

I entered the den at a run, seeing the security guards backing down the stairs on the other side of the room, firing up. I ignored them, running to the left stairwell. A grenade went off on the other side, the concussion slapping into me, and I felt the hand leave my shoulder. I turned around, saw Knuckles hoisting Annaka to her feet, and we began running again. I reached the stairwell and made it to the top, finding Jennifer and Nadia crouched in a hallway.

I said, "Annaka, where do we go?"

She took the lead, running down the hallway until she reached the end, the skyline of Mumbai spilling out from a plate glass window. I turned a circle, seeing nothing but an alcove with art, no other hallways or doors. I said, "Where is it?"

She ran to a vase on a pedestal and picked it up, revealing a keypad. She punched in a sequence of numbers and a section of the wall separated, moving back seven inches and then sliding to the right. Behind it was what looked like a single-room apartment.

We ran inside and she punched another sequence on a wall keypad, and the door slid shut. I exhaled and said, "How safe is this place?"

"That door is armored, and we have our own power generator, water, and food. We can stay in here for days."

She ran to a bank of monitors and began turning them on, then typed on a keyboard until she had the cameras in the den. The battle was still raging, but it appeared that the Black Cats were simply using firepower because they could.

Knuckles said, "I hope they see those explosives before someone tosses a grenade in the living room."

Jennifer pointed at the upper-left monitor and said, "There's Jaiden."

Knuckles pointed to a lower monitor and said, "The Black Cats are chasing him."

Annaka ran to the keypad and hit some buttons, saying, "I'm locking out the other keypad."

We watched Jaiden run down our hallway, jumping from monitor to monitor, until he was in the alcove. He ripped up the pedestal and punched the buttons, but nothing happened. He ran to the wall and pushed, staring into the camera he knew was there, shouting in a frenzy we couldn't hear. Four men appeared in the hallway, each dressed head to toe in combat gear. He went to his knees, his hands in the air. The lead man put his barrel between Jaiden's eyes and squeezed the trigger.

Nobody said anything for a moment, watching the Black Cats mill about. Eventually, they left, leaving behind Jaiden's broken body.

Knuckles said, "Should we let them know we're in here?"

I sat on the bed, running my hands through my hair, the adrenaline seeping out and the exhaustion starting to set in. I said, "No. Let them finish clearing. Let them calm down a bit."

He said, "That could take a while." He turned to Annaka and said, "I don't suppose you stocked this place with any beer, did you?"

CHAPTER 78

The Rock Star bird took off from Mumbai, the interior of the aircraft maxed out with people. We had Mr. Chin bolted to a chair in the back, blindfolded, with noise-canceling earmuffs over his head— and apparently I now owed the pilots about seven cases of beer because I'd made them watch him the entire time we'd been gone.

The rest of the space was occupied by my team and Kerry Bostwick, all headed to New Delhi. Kerry wanted to get us out of the country as soon as possible, before too many questions could be asked. He didn't even want to delay long enough for Brett and Veep to get proper medical attention in a civilian hospital, saying that the quickie patchwork they'd received from the embassy doctor would do until they were under proper Taskforce care, and that requirement was even more reason to get out sooner rather than later—but first, he had to get Mr. Chin off the plane.

I knew that wasn't the real reason, but I let it ride because both Brett and Veep were doing fine. No, Kerry was afraid that the longer we waited, the more chances there were that we'd be prevented from leaving the country, with some opposition government types trying to get to the bottom of what had happened in Riva Thakkar's residence.

We'd stayed inside the safe room for twelve hours, only coming out after the frenzy of the assault had died down. I couldn't get a cell signal inside the room because of the thickness of the walls—which was a glaring deficiency in my mind—and tried the landline next to the bed, but it was dead, somehow cut by the fighting outside. I managed to use the Wi-Fi to contact Kerry Bostwick through FaceTime.

He'd been pulling his hair out for the duration of the assault and at first, when he saw my background, he thought I was calling him from a hotel room, hostages secured and everything hunky-dory. I could see he was about to jump for joy and I brought him down to earth, telling him where we were and what the situation was.

I told him we were good for a few days, but he needed to find a way to get us out of there. He contacted the RAW, and when things had calmed down enough, they entered the building—ostensibly looking for intelligence in the aftermath. Kerry and a couple of Caucasian analysts came with them, the RAW letting them in as "CIA partners."

The RAW spread out, taking a look at the damage and collecting "evidence," and Kerry and his crew came specifically to our hallway. Once I saw him outside, I opened the door, and we blended in with the other analysts, exiting the building with a larger group than the CIA had entered with, but who was counting?

I'd asked Annaka and Nadia to stay inside, making them promise to say they'd simply escaped the carnage and made it to the safe room on their own. Four hours after we'd left, Annaka opened the door and was "discovered" by the RAW.

It was a complete success for the government and the Black Cats. As far as the world knew, they'd not only rescued the American, Sledge, but had surgically assaulted a twenty-seven-story building, eliminating all the terrorists and saving the two hostages they held. They were national heroes, and I knew they wouldn't look too hard to find out if they'd had any help.

If Annaka stuck to her story, we were good.

Nobody on the news talked about the massive carnage the Black Cats had engendered, but I didn't blame them for what they did. It turned out that Jaiden had set a trap on the helipad, actually knocking one helicopter out of commission and causing it to hard-land on the pad. That had fouled up the insertion of the other two, forcing them to fast-rope to the deck while they were being shot at.

The Black Cats had nine casualties on infil and decided that it was a fight to the death, and then executed. I like to think I'd have kept my goal of hostage rescue at the front of my mind, but I don't know if I would have handled the situation any differently. It would be like landing on Normandy Beach for a hostage rescue and then running into the German buzz saw. Eliminating the enemy would have been the first thing on my mind too. On the other hand, I was pretty sure that the whole hostage rescue thing had taken a back seat for the Black Cats from the very beginning.

The true miracle was that those guys had had the presence of mind not to drop grenades next to the explosive charges Jaiden had placed. In the end, the Black Cats had been trained well enough to recognize the threat and had executed accordingly.

Jaiden had four different key fobs on his body, each to a car in Riva Thakkar's giant collection, so the bet was that he planned on taking the elevator to the garage and driving out of the building, but he'd pushed it too long, not leaving before the Black Cats assaulted. Some thought he intended to be a martyr the entire time, but I figured he had an escape scenario involving Sledge and the other terrorists in the slum. Our assault there probably short-circuited the overarching plan, but nobody could prove his endstate one way or the other.

We still had one big problem that extended beyond Sikh nationalism, and he was handcuffed in the back of our aircraft.

Sitting across from Kerry, I said, "Are you going to jam Mr. Chin up China's ass?"

"Believe it or not, no. China gets a pass on this one."

Knuckles said, "What? Are you serious? That fucker tried to kill us, and he did it on behalf of the CCP. They tried to assassinate Riva Thakkar—a CIA asset working for you on an international covert operation."

"Yeah, but that operation is still in play. Riva is pleased with how this went down, and has doubled down on how much he wants to invest in the mine. We'll get what we want out of it, even if that guy is a complete asshole."

We'd heard he was satisfied that the Black Cats had killed all the terrorists, but Nadia had told us he didn't even seem to care that his daughter was alive. I would have really liked to meet him face-to-face, if only to punch it, but that wasn't to be.

I said, "But you'd really get what you want if you laid your cards out to India. It would be more than just a rare earth element mine. We're always worried about them cozying up to China, since India is in their backyard. This would be one way to ensure they told China to screw off for years, if not decades."

Kerry said, "True, but if we did that, we'd have to explain how we caught ol' Mr. Chin, and that would then involve us explaining how we were doing our own operations on their soil."

"So what? We have definite proof they tried to assassinate a Sikh separatist on U.S. soil, and we let that slide in the interests of being good allies. They'll do the same. What the hell is POTUS thinking on this one?"

Kerry said, "The president wanted to do what you say. I'm the one who talked him out of it. This is my idea."

Knuckles said, "Why? It's like we scored a victory, but you don't want to use it."

"No, I do. Mr. Chin is a wealth of knowledge on all MSS operations, including their use of supposed civilian companies to steal intellectual property and conduct intelligence operations all over the world. Right now, the Chinese don't know we have him. As far as they know, he's running from them, and I want to keep it that way. If they find out we have him, they'll try to kill him, but they'll also start shutting down every cover organization he knows about, shifting tactics. This way, it's like having the Enigma machine. We can crack the codes, but they don't know we can do it."

He went from Knuckles to me, then said, "Trust me, it's for the best. This time we're winning the battle in the gray zone."

Knuckles said, "That's all above my pay grade. You want to play games with that guy, have at it. Just don't set him up as a manager of a Holiday Inn somewhere. If he has to have a job, make sure it sucks."

Kerry laughed and glanced out the window, saying, "New Delhi coming up. You guys don't have to worry about it. Your job is done. I'll get off with Mr. Chin, and you just fly on back to the United States for some R and R."

I said, "We were thinking about taking a little vacation here. You know, since we didn't get to really see any of the sites. Annaka Thakkar said she'd make it all first class, and there's no way we're turning that down."

Kerry said, "Uh, no. You're not leaving the aircraft. Sorry. That's straight from the Oversight Council, and George Wolffe concurred. He wants your ass home, since you do nothing but get in trouble when he's not involved."

The Oversight Council was a little miffed that I'd stretched their Omega authority for Mr. Chin as far as I had, but luckily, I looked like a damn hero, so there wasn't much they could say. Wolffe, on the other hand, as my direct boss, could say a lot, and he was extremely pissed

I'd kept him out of the loop. I knew I was in for an ass-chewing when I got back, but I also knew he'd get over it. He always did.

I said, "But Annaka is going to pay for it all. It won't be on the Taskforce dime. We're going to get treated like Sledge, the rock star."

Since he'd been freed, Sledge had been making the rounds all over India, being treated like a hero for doing nothing more than running away. I will say it was helping his Everclear Foundation, so I guess it was for a good cause.

The aircraft touched down and began taxiing to a special hardstand that the RAW used, now detailed to the CIA.

Kerry said, "Sorry, Pike. Orders are orders."

I saw four SUVs and a cluster of men in suits waiting for us to stop. We did, and they raced on board, slapping a hood over Mr. Chin, unhooking him from the chair, and then bundling him straight out the door. They put him in the back of a tinted-windowed SUV, then departed. The entire episode took about four minutes.

I said, "Well, that was quick."

I turned to Kerry and said, "Now that Mr. Chin is taken care of, are you sure you can't sweet talk the Oversight Council for a little Indian R and R?"

He stood up, pulling a briefcase out of the overhead bin and saying, "No chance on that. Enjoy the flight home."

I saw another vehicle arrive, thinking it was for Kerry, but was surprised when Nadia exited.

I said, "Knuckles, Nadia is here. At least somebody wants to say goodbye properly."

Kerry looked at me quizzically. "She's not saying goodbye today."

I laughed and said, "What, are we supposed to evacuate her with us?"

Kerry scrunched his brow and said, "Well, yeah. Knuckles had me walk through a visa for her."

Now *I* was confused. I looked at Knuckles and he held out his hands, saying, "I didn't figure they'd let us stay. And she wants a vacation too. She says she can get Annaka to pay for everything, for the whole team, wherever we want to go."

I glanced at Jennifer, saying, "Did you know about this?"

I saw from her innocent expression that she most certainly did.

Nadia said, "Don't worry, Pike. I won't ask for you to break into any hotel rooms this time. Unless I find one with Jennifer in it."

ACKNOWLEDGMENTS

In the modern era, arguably, hybrid warfare began in earnest after the 1991 Gulf War. Every country on earth saw the awesome might and power of the United States crushing Saddam Hussein's army—at the time the fourth largest in the world—like a child stomping an ant. All our foes took a step back and said, "We need to find a different way to achieve our goals. One that doesn't involve a direct confrontation with the U.S.," and competing nation states began operating in the Gray Zone between peace and war. For the most part, we just kept building better and smarter weapon systems.

Shia militias flying explosive drones into bases of U.S. soldiers in Iraq? Hybrid warfare on behalf of Iran. Belt and Road initiatives loan-sharking most of the African continent? Hybrid warfare on behalf of China. "Little green men" springing up in Crimea in 2014? Hybrid warfare on behalf of Russia. Sony Pictures getting hacked, revealing multiple embarrassing details about the company? Hybrid warfare on behalf of North Korea.

Of course, Putin and Hamas have shown that plain old-fashioned bloody conflict is still a thing in this world, but in great power competitions, fighting in the Gray Zone has become a prominent component, and in our competition with China, India is now ground zero, being pulled in different directions by both countries and making it fertile ground for a Pike Logan adventure.

I have my wife to thank for coming up with the idea of using rare earth elements as a point of leverage. China really does have a monopoly on extraction and refinement of them, which is a little ironic, since we don't extract or refine them in the United States due to the incredible harm to the environment mining of such elements engenders—yet lithium and rare earth elements are precisely what allows EVs to exist. China has no such concerns about the environment, and because of it, they have developed a monopoly. We drive around in our electric cars, proud to stop harmful emissions while being blissfully ignorant of the harm done to produce those very vehicles—or the harm to our own national security that has been created by allowing such a monopoly to exist.

I started researching India and as fate would have it, three months before I began writing, India found a huge reservoir of lithium and rare earth elements in its country. And so a story was born.

India is a country of extremes, with bone-crushing poverty juxtaposed against incredible wealth, and I'm indebted to various anonymous guides for helping me understand both. One led us through the Dharavi slum. Having grown up within its confines, she was well-versed on its history and machinations. The extreme poverty was heartbreaking, but the people living there were incredibly industrious. We saw a multitude of little factories producing everything from soap to clothing—and yes, taking reclaimed bumpers to create luggage. The working conditions were beyond harsh, but the workers seemed to stoically survive the environment. One "factory" did nothing but manufacture pants for an expensive brand that can be purchased at many high-end stores here in the United States, and I found it appalling that those same pants probably cost a thousand percent more than the workers earned for making them.

On the other end of the scale was the extreme wealth on display. Thakkar's twenty-seven-story residence in the book is real. Owned by an Indian billionaire, it actually has six floors for his car collection, a snow room, and is the most expensive personal residence in the world. Complementing the ostentatious wealth on Mumbai's Billionaires' Row were the outrageously over-the-top wedding celebrations for the families who could afford the luxury. Weddings for such wealth take over a year to accomplish, with multiple pre-wedding parties attended by luminaries as varied as Mark Zuckerberg and Rihanna. I obviously didn't get a tour of the residence, or invited to hobnob with Tom Brady at a wedding party—as much as I would have liked—but luckily, the building and associated celebrations are such a draw that there are a plethora of news articles and videos detailing both.

Getting on the ground for research usually ends up being critical for atmospherics that I can't find in travel guides or YouTube videos, and India proved no different. I've been stationed in Japan, where the homogenous nature of the population is stark, but if anything, India is worse. Within about six hours of setting foot in Mumbai, I realized that the Taskforce conducting any sort of dismounted surveillance inside India would never work. There were very few Westerners around— even in so-called diverse cities such as Mumbai or New Delhi, forget about towns such as Jaipur or any village in Goa. No matter where we went, we drew stares as surely as a person wearing a Bozo costume in church would, with families wanting to introduce their children to us and full-grown men wanting selfies with my wife. Everyone was extremely nice and friendly, but the fact remained that Pike Logan or Jennifer Cahill trying to follow someone on foot and remain undetected in an Indian city would be a non-starter.

Another aspect I wouldn't have known was the security at every location that had a sizable visiting population. After the horrific Mumbai terrorist attacks in 2008, India has gone on lockdown. Metros, malls, museums, archeological sites, ferry terminals, hotel entrances—all of them had metal detectors in use, but 2008 was a long time ago, and now only about a third of them were actually monitored. For instance, the main train station in Mumbai had about eight metal detectors across the main entrance, all of them blaring every time someone went through, but nobody stopped the offender to check to see why it had gone off. Something Pike Logan would definitely need to know as he moved about the country.

While 99 percent of the population was friendly, not everyone wanted just a selfie. Mr. Chin's experiences on Elephanta Island mirrored our own. While I didn't smoke the man who wouldn't leave us alone, I was fairly sure he was looking to fleece us of our valuables and forced him to leave us without using lethal means.

One aspect that was wildly better than I expected was the service at every hotel where we stayed. The worst was a convention hotel near the Taj Mahal, where the roof caved in from a leaking pipe—but even there the service was impeccable, with the staff taking care of us immediately and providing extras for the trouble. The best was the Oberoi Rajvilas in Jaipur, where the terrorist attack against the party occurs in the novel. That place was beyond anything I had ever experienced before—and I've been to a hotel or two in my time. We picked it simply because we wanted a nice place after a five-hour drive, and it exceeded all our expectations—so much so, I felt a little guilty attacking it in the novel. You'd wake up to the words "Good Morning" spelled out in rose petals on the doorstep of your villa, and go to bed with "Good Night" replacing the petals from the morning. With peacocks roaming the grounds, a bar straight out of a Bogart movie, a full fitness center and spa, and an almost one-for-one of staff to guests, I could have stayed there for a month. After we returned to the states, *Travel + Leisure* magazine rated every hotel on the planet and listed the top 100 worldwide. The Jaipur Oberoi was listed as the number one hotel on earth, and I believe it. I apologize to them for using the property in such a heinous manner in the book, but it certainly fit what a billionaire would use for a pre-wedding celebration.

We had the usual help from unnamed taxi drivers and rickshaw operators, all of whom were more than willing to show us something they considered important—the funniest being a rickshaw driver who raced through the rat-maze of alleys in the spice market of Old Delhi like he was preparing to start competing in NASCAR. If anyone was unlucky enough to not leap out of the way, they were getting run over while Elaine and I white-knuckled it in the back, praying we'd survive. Of course, he expected a healthy tip for all the extra effort, and I obliged. We also learned of the "Gringo Tax" that Westerners paid all over India without knowing it. In the "foreigners only" line, we had a choice of a first-class ticket for the ferry to Elephanta Island, and paid it, thinking it would be better than taking one of the rickety boats that looked like something migrants used to go across the Mediterranean from Africa. Once we arrived at the dock, we realized there was no such thing as "first class," and every ferry was a belching, rickety rustbucket crammed with people just like a boat leaving Libya for Europe. This was only after Elaine told the dock worker, "There must be some mistake. We have first-class tickets." The man only laughed and said, "That's a first-class boat."

Writing is a solitary business about 85 percent of the time, but the last 15 percent is a definite team effort. I'm grateful to my agent, John Talbot, for all of his assistance and to Morrow for giving me one of the best teams in publishing. Danielle is my new editor, and I had a little trepidation about how she would go about editing Pike Logan, as everyone sees things a little differently on the page. As it turned out,

I had nothing to fear, as every one of her suggestions was spot-on, hitting both big-picture items and little details that honed the manuscript to a razor's edge. My marketing and publicity team remained the same stellar dynamic duo as before, and as usual Danielle (in Dallas) tries to kill me with in-person events, while Tavia tries to bleed out the last ounce of marketing from every platform on earth. There is no doubt that Pike Logan's success is a direct reflection of these efforts, and I greatly appreciate it.

ABOUT THE AUTHOR

Brad Taylor, Lieutenant Colonel (Ret.), is a twenty-one-year veteran of the U.S. Army Infantry and Special Forces, including eight years with the 1st Special Forces Operational Detachment—Delta, popularly known as Delta Force. Taylor retired after serving more than two decades and participating in Operation Enduring Freedom and Operation Iraqi Freedom, as well as classified operations around the globe. His final military post was as assistant professor of military science at The Citadel. He is the *New York Times* bestselling author of eighteen Pike Logan thrillers and is a security consultant on asymmetric threats for various agencies. He lives in Charleston, South Carolina, with his wife and two daughters.